NEW YORK TIMES
BESTSELLING
AUTHOR

JULIA LONDON

"Dangerous intrigue and
deliciously sexy romance."
—*Booklist* on *The Year of
Living Scandalously*

Will the woman he seeks
to ruin become the lover
he can't live without?

THE REVENGE of LORD EBERLIN

WHAT OTHER SECRETS DOES HADLEY GREEN HIDE?

Be sure to look for

THE YEAR OF LIVING SCANDALOUSLY
THE SEDUCTION OF LADY X

and the novella available exclusively as an eBook
THE CHRISTMAS GIFT

And catch all the novels in the
delightfully sexy Scandalous series by

JULIA LONDON

THE BOOK OF SCANDAL

HIGHLAND SCANDAL

A COURTESAN'S SCANDAL

Available from Pocket Books

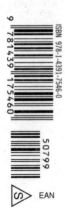

ISBN 978-1-4391-7546-0

50799

Also by Julia London

The Year of Living Scandalously
One Season of Sunshine
Summer of Two Wishes
A Courtesan's Scandal
Highland Scandal
The Book of Scandal
The Dangers of Deceiving a Viscount
The Perils of Pursuing a Prince
The Hazards of Hunting a Duke

Guiding Light: Jonathan's Story

JULIA LONDON

The REVENGE of LORD EBERLIN

Pocket Books

New York   London   Toronto   Sydney   New Delhi

Pocket Books
A Division of Simon & Schuster, Inc.
1230 Avenue of the Americas
New York, NY 10020

This book is a work of fiction. Names, characters, places, and incidents either are products of the author's imagination or are used fictitiously. Any resemblance to actual events or locales or persons, living or dead, is entirely coincidental.

First Pocket Books paperback edition March 2012

POCKET and colophon are registered trademarks of Simon & Schuster, Inc.

For information about special discounts for bulk purchases, please contact Simon & Schuster Special Sales at 1-866-506-1949 or business@simonandschuster.com.

The Simon & Schuster Speakers Bureau can bring authors to your live event. For more information or to book an event contact the Simon & Schuster Speakers Bureau at 1-866-248-3049 or visit our website at www.simonspeakers.com.

Designed by Julie Schroeder

Manufactured in the United States of America

10 9 8 7 6 5 4 3 2 1

ISBN 978-1-4391-7546-0
ISBN 978-1-4391-7550-7 (eBook)

The
REVENGE
of LORD EBERLIN

ONE

Summer 1808
Hadley Green, West Sussex

Count Eberlin left London like a man with the world firmly in his grasp. His town home was in the fashionable Mayfair district and his horse was a sturdy gray Arabian he'd had delivered from Spain. He wore a coat of the finest Belgian wool, a silk shirt and neckcloth made by a renowned Italian tailor, Scottish buckskins, and Hessian boots fashioned in soft French leather. Confident and wealthy, he sat his horse like a king commanding an army.

Five hours later, he crested the hill on the main road through West Sussex. The village of Hadley Green nestled prettily in the valley below, with her thatched roof cottages, vibrantly colorful gardens, and a High Street bustling with commerce. And, very clearly, a village green.

His chest tightened painfully. He suddenly felt clammy, his skin flushed and damp, and he was strangely light-headed. Fearing he would topple right off his horse, he reigned up hard.

He'd believed the memory of what had happened there to be dead to him, but now he struggled to catch his breath as he watched children play on the green where his father had been hanged for thievery fifteen years ago.

Count Eberlin—or Tobin Scott as he'd been known then, son of Joseph Scott, the wood-carver—hadn't traveled this road since his father's death. He'd forgotten the lay of it and had not expected to see the green like this. He certainly hadn't expected such a visceral reaction. He could feel the crank of rusted and disintegrated feelings awakening, though he'd believed himself to be dead inside, incapable of any sort of passion, dark or light.

As he stared at the green he was amazed that his head and his heart could trick him so. He could almost see the scaffold, could nearly smell the mutton and ale that had been sold the morning his father was executed. It was as if the carts still lined the streets beside the gallows.

A child raced across the green into the arms of a man who lifted her up and swung her high overhead.

There had been children at his father's execution, too, playing around the edges of the green. The adults had been the spectators, come early to drink their ale and eat their mutton. Only thirteen years old at the time, Tobin hadn't known how absurdly festive an execution could be. When his father was led across the green, the crowd, warmed by their ale, had cheerfully shouted, *"Thief, bloody thief!"* before taking another swig from their tankards.

He thought he'd buried the image of his father standing on that scaffold with his gaze turned toward the heavens and resigned to his fate; buried it deep in the black mud inside him, from which nothing could grow. But he saw the image again this summer day with vivid clarity. He pulled at his neckcloth, seeking relief from his sudden breathlessness.

He wasn't supposed to have seen his father hang, naturally, for who would subject a man's son to such horror? But precisely because he'd been thirteen, he'd disguised himself and gone to see it. Nothing could have kept him from his father's last moments on this earth—not his grieving mother, not his despondent younger siblings. Not the reverend, who'd sought in vain to assure him that Joseph Scott would receive his forgiveness and comfort in heaven. A boy standing on the cusp of manhood, impotent in his rage, Tobin had been propelled by a primal need to be there, to witness the injustice, to have it scored into his mind's eye and into his soul so that he would never forget, never forgive.

But until this moment, he'd thought he was irrevocably numb to it.

He dismounted and crouched down, and concentrated on finding the breath that had been snatched from his lungs. He closed his eyes and tried desperately not to replay the events of that horrific day, or to envision his father twisting all over again . . .

Yet the images came at him hard and fast. The day had been bright, warm, and cloudless, much like this day. Tobin had stood on a horse trough so that he could see over the heads of the onlookers, his hat pulled low over his eyes. His heart had beat out of his chest as the clergyman had offered his father a last word. His father had declined, and Tobin had been furious with him. Furious! That was his moment to shout that he'd *not* stolen the countess's jewels, that he'd been unjustly accused and convicted! It was the moment he should have condemned them all for their stupidity and prejudice! But his father had remained intolerably silent.

With the crowd jeering, the clergyman had recited the Lord's Prayer while the hangman had covered his father's face with a black hood, then fitted the noose around his neck. He'd helped his father, as if he'd been infirm, onto the block. And then he'd kicked the block out from under his feet at the same moment that two men had hauled his father up by his neck. His father had twisted at the end of that rope, his legs kicking madly, desperately seeking purchase and finding nothing there to save him.

Thankfully, Tobin had been spared the actual end of his father because he'd fainted, and when he'd come to, the crowds had dispersed and his father had been cut down. Tobin had found himself lying on the walk, his nose bloodied from his fall, collapsed under the weight of horrific grief.

The unconscionable crime that had been committed against his family had indelibly marked his soul. He'd lost all his innocence and hopefulness. He'd been made completely immovable, blind to common emotion, incapable of sentimental feelings. If someone were to open him up, they'd see nothing but black rot oozing inside of him.

The only emotion Tobin felt anymore was revenge. And it was the reason why he'd finally returned to Hadley Green.

Tobin mounted his horse and turned onto an old, rutted road that, if memory served, skirted the village and avoided the green. As he rode along the seldom-used road beneath gnarled tree limbs and past weedy undergrowth, he recalled how the trial and his father's execution had ruined the Scott family. Tobin, his mother, his sister, Charity, and his brother, Ruben, had become pariahs. They were the offspring of the man who'd been was accused of stealing priceless jewels from the beloved, alluring countess of Ashwood— jewels that had never been recovered, of course, because Tobin's father had not taken them and had not been able to say where they'd gone.

Joseph Scott was a good, honest man. He'd been a master wood-carver, and with his death, his family had been left with no income. They'd become wards of the church, living on the charity of the parishioners. A proud woman, Tobin's mother had not been able to abide the censure of a society in which she'd once been a respected member. Nor could she abide charity. So she'd decided to move her family to London a few weeks after her husband's death.

On the day they'd carried their bags to the center of town and awaited the London coach, the Ashwood coach, with its red plumes and gold scrolls, had rolled down High Street and come to a stop outside a cluster of shops. As the Scotts had watched, a liveried coachman had opened the door, and out hopped Miss Lily Boudine in a pale blue frock. Her black shoes were polished to a sheen, and her hair was held up with the sort of velvet ribbons that Charity had coveted through the window of Mrs. Langley's Dress Shop. Lily Boudine had waited for the coachman to hand down a woman who Tobin knew to be her governess, then she eagerly took the woman's hand, bouncing a little as she'd tugged her along, smiling and pointing at the confectioner's shop.

His heart had beat painfully at the sight of the girl, fueled by his rage and hatred. She was the ward of the countess, the lone witness who'd claimed to see his father at Ashwood the night the jewels went missing. *Liar.* To think of all the days he'd spent in that girl's company while his father had built a staircase at Ashwood so grand that people came from miles about to see it. Tobin had been his father's assistant, but there were days when his father had sent him out with the girl with strict instructions for Tobin to occupy her. Lily was five years younger than he, younger than even Charity, and Tobin had chafed at being made to play games with her. But he'd done it, had been her play-mate, her companion, her servant.

In return, she'd told the magistrate she'd seen his father riding away from Ashwood the night of the theft—in the dark, in the rain, but she was certain it was Joseph Scott because of the horse. The moment she'd uttered the words, there'd been no hope for his father.

And then Lily Boudine had come to the village for a sweetmeat while he and his family had waited for the public coach that would take them from the only home they'd ever known.

She'd lived in luxury while his family had lived in two rooms near the notorious crime-ridden area of St. Giles. His mother had taken in sewing, squinting through the smoky haze of burning peat to see her tiny stitches. It was a mean existence for a family that had once enjoyed a good standard of living, and the change in their circumstance had soon taken its toll. Tobin's young brother Ruben had died their first spring in London, when the filth of the rookery had spread through the streets in the form of a wasting fever. His mother had followed soon after.

Tobin was just fourteen and his sister eleven when their mother had died. Even now, he could recall the panic he'd felt at what would become of them. The worry had made him ill; he'd been unable to keep what little food they'd had in his belly. "You cannot die!" Charity had shrieked as she'd clung to his arm. "If you die, what will happen to me, Tobin? If you die, I shall die, too!"

Her frantic plea had given him the strength he'd needed to rise up, to press on. He'd thought of everyone in Hadley Green, warm in their beds with enough food to eat, with fuel for their hearths and candles to light their way, and he'd decided then that one day, he would avenge his family.

With only a few coins to his name, Tobin had taken Charity to a dress shop and bought her a good, serviceable gown. He'd then taken her to church. The rector, a wizened old man with tufts of silver hair in his ears, had squeezed Tobin's shoulder with his liver-spotted hand. "We'll find a place for her as a chambermaid, have no doubt," he'd said. "The Ladies Beneficent Society is quite taken with orphans."

Tobin hadn't known what that meant, precisely, and his fists had curled as the vicar led Charity away. She'd looked over her shoulder at him, her eyes wide with fear. He'd promised his sister he would return for her as soon as he could, but that day, standing in the narthex, he'd had no idea how or when he would come for her.

As thin as a beanstalk, as dumb as a blade of grass,

he'd risen up and pressed on, striking out on his own and surviving by sheer luck.

Naturally, he'd made his way to the docks, for what would a boy with no prospects do but dream of a different life in a different land? He'd had his size—tall with broad shoulders—and the fact that he could read and write and figure sums to recommend him. He'd planned to hire onto one of the three-masted merchant ships, but he'd been robbed and beaten almost senseless by some sailors who'd spotted an easy target. He'd come to when someone had hauled him up by the scruff of his collar, and a florid, fleshy face had danced before him. Tobin had swung out, connecting with nothing, and the man had chuckled. He'd examined Tobin with small, dark eyes. "Calm yourself, lad. You've been soundly beaten, but not by me."

That had been painfully obvious to Tobin. His hat was gone, his jaw ached, and his pockets turned inside out.

"Can you cook?" the man had asked.

"No," Tobin had said, his voice breaking.

"Say aye."

Tobin had been confused. Why would he say aye when it wasn't true?

"Come now, say aye," the man had said again, giving Tobin a good shake.

"Aye," Tobin had said, bewildered.

"Very good. You'll be my helper in exchange for

a berth and food and five pounds at the end of the voyage."

Only then had Tobin realized he was in a ship's galley.

"Ethan Bolger's me name," the man had said. "I'm the cook on this ship. Most calls me Bolge. And what be your name, young man?"

"Tobin. Tobin Scott."

"Ah, Scottie, you'll make a fine apprentice, you will," Bolge had declared as he'd dropped Tobin to the floor. "You can start with chopping the carrots."

That was how Tobin had begun his life at sea. For two years he'd sailed the seas with Ethan Bolger, chopping carrots and stirring big vats of ship's stew. For two years, he'd stood by the tables of officers and poured their wine, absorbing everything he could about the English merchant trade.

He'd seen dozens of ports. He'd walked through crowded markets, past snake charmers and silk merchants, spice traders and hashish pipes. He'd seen people unlike any he'd ever seen before, people whose skin was as black as night, whose eyes were round or angled, who dressed in clothing as colorful as rainbows, and spoke in languages that had sometimes sounded lyrical and other times harsh.

He'd seen women, beautiful women! Redheads, brunettes, and golden-haired. Women with big bosoms, small bosoms, and generous bottoms, thin and tall, women with blue eyes, green eyes, brown eyes, black eyes. All of them intriguing, all of them enticing, all of them beckoning a young man.

Tobin had learned that men valued power above all else, and he'd learned about muskets in Cairo. A small melee had broken out when French sailors had come running to the aid of their countryman in the souk one day. The Frenchman had been trying to trade two crates of guns. A thought had occurred to Tobin: there had been war on the Continent for as long as he could recall. He'd never thought of the armaments that must be needed to wage war, and it had seemed to him a brilliant sort of trade. There'd always be a need for it.

He'd purchased his first crate of guns there in Cairo with the money he'd saved from his meager wages. He'd sold the crate to a French mercenary a month later and had agreed to bring more.

That was ten years ago, yet it seemed an entire lifetime now. He'd survived seasickness, survived men who'd wanted his purse. He'd survived being chased by pirates, being fired upon by the French navy, and weather that had been stirred up by Satan himself. He'd survived, and he'd learned how to trade.

He'd also learned that men who made their living from war were seldom loyal to country or women, but they were loyal to conflict and guns. He'd made a bloody fortune and now owned five frigates that ran guns between Europe and North Africa. He'd led an exciting life full of danger and intrigue, beautiful women, and fine living.

Yet it was not enough. Nothing seemed to fill the hole that his father's hanging had burned in his heart. Nothing could redress the suffering of his family from that false accusation.

In the spring of 1802, Tobin had rescued Charity from a life of cleaning the piss from rich people's pots. She was now mistress of his grand Mayfair town home. He lavished her with gowns and jewels, and while Charity appreciated his efforts, they'd come too late for her. She'd borne a daughter out of wedlock, and society discounted her because of her humble beginnings, her mean occupation, and her bastard child. There was no amount of money that could remove the censure society heaped on women like Charity.

The only thing that might have redeemed his sister had been to lend her some legitimacy. If Tobin had had a title, he'd believed it would have given her entry into at least some quarter of society. Obtaining a title might have seemed impossible to any other man, but he'd been determined that society would never dictate the course of their future again.

So he'd gone out and bought a title.

In truth, it had fallen into his lap. A minor Danish count, Lord Eberlin, had arranged for Tobin to bring him enough guns to equip a small army but had not been able to pay. Tobin had been infuriated. He'd delivered the arms at considerable risk to himself and his company, and he would not be hoodwinked.

As it had happened, the people of Denmark had

been in the throes of internal turmoil. Old acts of enti-tlement had been giving way to the popular will of the people and a desire for serfs to be landowners in their own right—just like the French had done a generation before. Tobin had seized on that knowledge and had assured Eberlin he could make his life quite difficult. And then he'd made him an offer he hadn't possibly been able to refuse—a generous payment for his estate and his title.

The former Count Eberlin had taken what money he'd had and decamped to Barbados. It had taken only a generous endowment to the courts in Copenhagen to turn a blind eye to the deal and transfer Count Eberlin's small estate and title to Tobin. He'd kept dis-sension among the tenants to a minimum by giving arable parcels outright to the serfs who had tilled the count's land for decades. As a result, the estate was now little more than forest and manor.

Tobin didn't care about the estate; what mattered to him was England. He was now a count in an En-glish society that was rather sensitive to titles and entitlements. He'd accomplished the impossible—he'd become one of them.

In the winter of 1807, the newly minted Count Eberlin had returned to London to spend Christmas with his sister. Over dinner one evening, she'd told him that the old earl of Ashwood had died.

"Good riddance," Tobin had scoffed, and gestured for a liveried footman to fill his wineglass.

"He left no heir, you know," Charity had said.

Tobin had shrugged.

"Miss Lily Boudine is now his closest kin, so she has been named countess and inherits the whole of Ashwood."

That had gained Tobin's undivided attention. He'd looked up from the goose that graced the Limoges china plates.

"Imagine," Charity had said as she'd picked up her wineglass, "that she, of all people, should find herself a countess after all these years."

The news had made Tobin's blood run cold. He'd thought of the injustices she'd heaped on him with her lie, a lie that still festered in him like a septic wound. And he'd come back to Hadley Green to right that wrong, once and for all.

The memories kept Tobin so lost in thought that he didn't realize where he was until Tiber Park rose up majestically before him. He reined up for a long look at the place. It was as he recalled it—a monolith, too big for anyone but a king to maintain, abandoned for the want of cash.

Sometimes it seemed to Tobin that God had all but divined him here. It was a fluke that he should have remembered this place at all, but quite by coincidence, Tobin had hired an Irishman to breed a premier racehorse for him. When his agent had told him that the Irishman would breed the mare at Kitridge Lodge in West Sussex, it had almost been as if the heavens had set the stage for him. Of course Tobin knew of Kitridge Lodge; his father had worked there when Tobin was a boy. It had reminded Tobin that there were several mansions in West Sussex, and he'd wondered . . .

As soon as he'd completed the purchase of Tiber Park, work had begun on the estate. He was pleased to see the progress thus far. The white stone had been cleaned of grime and soot, and construction was under way on two new wings that, appended to the existing house, would form a square around the lush gardens. He'd ordered European rugs and furnishings for it, had bought generations of art collections from estate auctions. He'd bartered for Sèvres porcelain fixtures and Gobelins tapestries, and even eighteenth-century French furnishings from a displaced member of the French aristocracy trying desperately to maintain his life of privilege in England. Tobin had ordered orange trees from Spain to fill the orangery, and had retained a head gardener who subscribed to the philosophy and techniques of the late but notable Capability Brown. No expense would be spared in building Tiber Park into the jewel of West Sussex.

As the power of the Ashwood wealth and name had destroyed his family fifteen years ago, Tobin would use the power of his wealth and name to destroy Ashwood and its new countess, Lily Boudine.

TWO

Autumn 1808

A gust of wind rattled the windows of Ashwood. Lily glanced up from the mess she'd made of the wall in the salon to see autumn leaves scudding past the window in small clusters of red and gold. Dark clouds were accumulating on the horizon, seeping in over the golden landscape. Lily could hear Linford, the old Ashwood butler, shouting at the chambermaids to close the windows ahead of the rain that would surely fall.

He might shut the windows, but he couldn't stop the leaks around the old window frames. Or patch this hole she'd made. In a moment of mad frustration, Lily had taken it upon herself to remove the wallpapering. It had begun with a frayed corner, and she'd seen paneling beneath it and she'd thought, how difficult can it be to remove the paper? She'd ripped off a strip. And then another. And several more with varying degrees of success. It seemed that the paste held quite well in some places, and not in others.

Her inability to do something as simple as remove the papering made her anger soar. She wished the rain would fall so hard that it washed away Tiber Park. She pictured it; the grand Georgian estate sweeping down the river, colliding with the construction of Tiber Park's new mill, and both being churned to pieces.

"Have a care in your wishing, lass," she muttered, and gave the paper a hearty tug. Two small pieces came off in her hands. "Blasted wall!" Given her luck of late, it was far more likely that Ashwood would wash away. In fact, she was rather surprised that Tobin Scott hadn't ordered it up. Oh, what delight he'd take in seeing Ashwood wash away and Lily Boudine turning head over heels down the river with it!

With a sigh, she let the torn paper flutter onto the pile she'd made as Linford hobbled in.

"Oh dear, does your knee pain you, Linford?" Lily asked.

"A bit," the old man agreed with a slight grimace. "Foul weather is coming. Mr. Fish has come, mu'um. I took the liberty of ringing for tea."

They might be poor, but they were quite rich when it came to decorum. "Thank you. Please ask Mr. Fish to come in."

A moment later, a stern-looking Mr. Fish, who stood two inches shorter than Lily in his boots, entered. He slowed his efficient step when he saw the mess Lily had made and gave her a questioning look.

With the back of her hand, Lily pushed a dark lock of hair from her brow. "You look rather glum, sir."

His frown deepened. "Five tenants have notified the estate that they intend to farm greener pastures."

Lily's pulse ratcheted. She folded her arms. "I suppose you mean Tiber Park."

"Naturally."

There was no end to it! Since she'd come back to Hadley Green, Lily had suffered through a slew of letters, all from Mr. Sibley on behalf of Tiber Park, all demanding one thing or another. One letter informed her that Tobin had offered her tenants a lucrative share of the harvested crop at Tiber Park in exchange for their tenancy. Another letter reported that he'd lured men away from the mill she was building at Ashwood in the hopes of generating some income, to build his bigger and better mill upstream. She'd lost three footmen to Tiber Park, as well as a groom.

And of course, there was the one hundred of her most profitable acres, against which he'd filed a suit, claiming they rightfully belonged to Tiber Park. Mr. Fish and Mr. Goodwin, Ashwood's solicitor, had assured Lily that he would be successful in his suit, and that at a hearing on the morrow, Eberlin—*Eberlin!* Honestly, not Tobin Scott, but *Count Eberlin* of *Denmark,* of all things!—would receive the acreage, all because of some arcane, ridiculous glitch in the laws of inheritance and entailments.

Lily had argued that her standing as the new, *rightful* countess of Ashwood might work in her favor. The estate and titles had been ordained by none other than King Henry VIII himself, when, in giving the gift of Ashwood to the first earl, had set out the permissions of inheritance: to wit, any heir, male or female, had title to the land that was Ashwood, and claim to the title! Any *blood* heir, any *adopted* heir, any heir at all!

But Tobin had found some tiny keyhole in the law that allowed him to take her acreage. "It would take a miracle of biblical proportions for the ruling to go in your favor, I fear," Mr. Goodwin had said apologetically.

And now five tenants were leaving.

"What did he offer?" Lily asked.

"I cannot say precisely," Mr. Fish said. "But apparently, new cottages have been constructed and fields that have lain fallow for years have been harrowed. They will sow them in the spring."

Honestly, if Lily had had a cannon, she'd have pointed the thing at Tiber Park and lit it herself. "Which tenants?"

"The Peterman family. There are five crofters with that name, all related by marriage, all farming on the east end, and all convinced of the prosperity at Tiber Park," Mr. Fish said.

The east end was the opposite end of the one hundred acres and, naturally, the next most productive, profitable bit of land at Ashwood. "He is awfully determined, is he not?" she snapped as Linford hobbled lopsidedly into the room carrying a tea service. "As if destroying Ashwood will bring his father back," she added angrily. She whirled around to the window.

"As we have discussed, you are suffering from years of poor fiscal management here at Ashwood, and he is a master at preying on estates such as this. And yet, there is more," Mr. Fish said.

"More!" she exclaimed and turned around.

Mr. Fish looked thoughtfully at his hand. He squared his shoulders.

"What is it, Mr. Fish?" Lily prodded him. "Please speak plainly, as I find myself desperately short on patience today."

Mr. Fish cleared his throat. "I have been studying our ledgers. My fear is that if we do not stabilize the income of Ashwood over the winter, we stand to be bankrupt by summer."

Lily could feel her blood rush from her face. "You must explain what that means."

"That we'd go the way of some other estates. That is to say, sold in parcels to satisfy creditors. The house turned into a museum. Your title . . ." He glanced at Lily. "The title stays with the estate, of course."

Lily couldn't bring herself to speak for a moment. Her mind was full of conflicting, jumbled thoughts.

"That is his plan, isn't it? He intends to see us parceled out." She began to pace, her mind racing, trying to think of something, anything, they might do. "We must do whatever it takes to avoid it," she said to Mr. Fish. "Have you any idea how we might do that?"

"A few," he said. "First, we must conserve cash. We will look for any way that we might profit as we sow our winter crops. But Lady Ashwood, we cannot sow without crofters."

"Perhaps we might reduce the rents to attract them," she suggested. "Or sell things. Furnishings. Anything that isn't absolutely necessary."

"I daresay it will take more than a few furnishings to save the estate."

There was something else that might save them: the missing jewels, wherever they were, but no one had managed to find them in fifteen years.

"I have one suggestion," Mr. Fish said, and surprisingly, his cheeks colored.

Lily paused in her pacing and looked at him curiously. "What suggestion?"

"You might actively seek a husband."

Lily's brows shot up.

"Madam, forgive me," he said quickly, "but the original decree states that any female heir must marry a titled man or forfeit the estate and title upon her death." At Lily's look of surprise, he explained, "It was a way of protecting the property. No . . . ruffian could seduce his way into this holding. Your estate is your dower. You simply choose a titled man who is not entailed to his neck and has cash."

"That is not precisely the way I intend to go about gaining a husband, Mr. Fish. And I daresay it is not as easy as that. To begin, after Keira's disastrous turn here, I am hardly in high demand in society."

Mr. Fish looked at his hands again. He cleared his throat once more. His cheeks were quite dark now. "Madam, forgive me for being forward, but I rather think any man worth his salt would fall in love with you given the slightest encouragement."

Lily blinked.

"And the ladies in Hadley Green are very fond of matchmaking. Lady Horncastle in particular has connections in London. I am certain she would very much enjoy helping you." He glanced up.

Lily gaped at him. Mr. Fish was a very clever man indeed. He'd devised a way she might kill two birds with one stone.

"At the very least, you might think on it," he said.

"Yes," Lily said, eyeing him closely. "I will think on it. However, I have a different suggestion."

"Oh?" Mr. Fish asked, looking quite hopeful.

"We find ourselves in hemorrhaging cash because of *him,* do we not?"

"Yes, in part."

Lily smiled a little crookedly. "Then if we knew what he intended to do before he did it, we might be able to take steps to prevent it."

Mr. Fish looked confused. "Pardon?"

"Think of it, Mr. Fish," she said, moving closer. "If we'd known of his offer to the Peterman family before he'd made it, we might have offered them something more attractive. Perhaps a larger share in the yields, for example."

Mr. Fish's look of surprise slowly melted into an indulging smile. "But madam . . . how could we possibly know what he intends to do before he does it?"

This part of her plan was a bit tricky. But Lily smiled right back, as if she had it all charted out. "It so happens that on Wednesday, I went into the village, and Louis—the footman, you know him, do you not?"

Mr. Fish nodded.

"Louis accompanied me. As we were walking across the green, I noticed a young man who looked oddly familiar to me. I said as much, and Louis informed me that the young man was Agatha's brother." Her smile widened. "Agatha is a chambermaid here."

Mr. Fish looked puzzled. "And?"

"And," she said, trying not to sound too terribly eager, "Agatha's brother serves Lord Eberlin, and he might be persuaded to relay information to us—"

"Lady Ashwood!"

"We would pay him, of course," she said quickly.

Mr. Fish gaped at her. "Madam . . . are you suggesting that we *spy* on Lord Eberlin?"

"Yes!" Lily cried. "Indeed I am! We must do something before he ruins us!"

"But if you were caught—"

"*If*," Lily said.

Mr. Fish blinked once. And then again. "I cannot advise it," he said sternly, shaking his head and looking quite appalled.

Lily shrugged. "Unfortunately . . . it might be too late." She smiled sheepishly. "I may have suggested to Louis . . ."

"Ah, for the love of heaven," Mr. Fish muttered, and in an uncharacteristic lapse of decorum, he sank onto a chair.

"Now, now, Mr. Fish. It is not as dire as you think," Lily assured him, taking a seat across from him to tell him what she'd done.

And when Mr. Fish left for the day—not the least bit pleased with her plan, and really, with his head hanging a bit—Lily reasoned that he was not entirely wrong in his objections. She would never have believed herself capable of such machinations and trickery.

But then, she had never run across the likes of Tobin Scott before.

Tobin Scott. She remembered a fair-haired, serious boy who had not been quick to smile, but when he had, it had been warm and easy. Nothing that she could recall indicated that boy would have grown into this man. Tobin Scott *despised* her. Perhaps even wished her dead. He hated her so much that he'd come back here to see her and Ashwood destroyed.

That was where Lily differed from him—she would never have come back here if she'd not been forced to.

She abruptly stood and walked to the windows. She folded her arms tightly across her against the chill she could feel through the panes and watched the trees in the park behind the mansion dance in the wind. She could see Mr. Bevers, her gamekeeper, at the lake, struggling to cast his line for fish. She could feel his struggle; she felt as if she was struggling every day, trying to cast her line, to find where or what she was supposed to be in this new life of hers.

When she thought of all that had happened in the last year, it made her head ache. This—what, adventure? . . . punishment? . . . dream?—had all begun several months ago, as Lily had been preparing for a long-awaited trip to Italy. She'd been in Ireland, at the home of the Hannigans, on whose charity Lily had lived since she was eight years old. She'd arranged to be the paid companion of Mrs. Canavan, who'd been traveling to Italy in the company of her very handsome son, Conor Canavan. Lily had had precious little else on her mind than a prolonged flirtation with Conor and perhaps some Italian gentlemen, and seeing the art and architecture of Italy.

Then the bloody letter had come to Ireland, announcing that she was the only surviving heir of Lord and Lady Ashwood, and as such, she'd inherited the estate of Ashwood, as well as the title of countess.

Lily had been stunned. Astounded! To think that she, of all people, was a countess! She wasn't even blood kin to the old earl. Eighteen years ago, when she'd been all of five years old, her parents had died of a fever and someone had shipped her—an unwanted orphan—to one of her mother's sisters, Althea Kent, the Countess of Ashwood. Aunt Althea had legally adopted Lily at some point, but Lily had been at Ashwood only three years before she'd been shipped off to Ireland and her aunt Lenore, all because she'd had the misfortune to see Joseph Scott riding away from Ashwood late one rainy night.

"Would that I'd gone to bed that night as I ought to have done," she muttered morosely. She turned from the window and walked to the settee, sitting heavily, her head resting against the back, one arm draped across her middle. She stared up at the cherubs painted on the ceiling. They were looking at her, their fat little arms outstretched, their little sausages of fingers pointing at her.

Lily had such wretched memories of what had followed after that rainy night—the accusations, the trial. The hanging. She'd been sent away from her beloved aunt Althea, who had drowned accidentally in the lake shortly thereafter.

To find out fifteen years later that this estate, and all the awful memories of that summer, were now hers had been almost more than Lily could absorb. So she had begged her cousin Keira—bold, unpredictable Keira, who was more of a sister than a cousin—to come to Ashwood and tend to whatever needed tending, while Lily went to Italy as she'd planned and tried to prepare herself to return to a place of dark memories.

It had seemed so easy! But Ashwood had been a distant clap of thunder in her mind, slowly moving closer until she'd no longer been able to ignore the storm.

Her journey back to England and Ashwood had been quite hard. They'd sailed through weather so foul that Lily had been certain she would die. Omens, surely, for when she'd arrived, she'd walked into disaster. She'd discovered that Keira had not merely tended to Ashwood's affairs as Lily had asked but had actually *become* her. Lily and Keira resembled each other enough that when Keira had come to Ashwood, everyone had believed her to be Lily, and Keira had not taken steps to correct their misunderstanding. The foolish girl had assumed Lily's identity, had signed her name, had been feted around Hadley Green! As if that hadn't been enough, Keira, who had a good heart beneath all her impetuosity, had taken in the orphan Lucy Taft and tucked her firmly under her wing.

A maelstrom of scandal had followed, for when Lily had arrived, those who had known her as a child had been able to see that they'd made a mistake and had realized they'd been duped. Because of Tobin Scott, authorities had been summoned and Keira had had to flee.

Lily had been left alone to deal with the consequences. She'd walked the halls of Ashwood to see for herself the disrepair, trying to piece together memories as she'd gone. The mansion had once seemed like a palace to her: the fine woodworking of the moldings and wainscoting, the soaring, painted ceilings, the deep windows and brocade draperies, fine English furnishings, Aubusson rugs, Sevres china. Every corridor of the three-story home had been a different adventure, every one of them uniquely furnished with paintings and hothouse flowers and thick carpets.

It was no longer a place of opulence; one had only to look closely to see the ravages of time. The salon, for example, painted green with gold trim, boasted a ceiling with an elaborate scene from heaven. But there was a crack in the wall above one of the deep windows, and the spots where the carpet had been worn down were covered with small tables. Her writing table was propped up with a book beneath one leg.

Yet in every room, fragments of memory came floating back like little snowflakes, landing softly in her, waking sights and smells and sighs that had been buried for many years. Her aunt, whispering to Mr. Scott, the two of them chuckling together. She remembered Aunt Althea's smile for Mr. Scott, the way she would touch his arm, her fingers touching his. Little things an eight-year-old girl would have never paid much heed but a grown woman saw differently.

And in those early, confusing days after her return to Ashwood, as Lily had tried to sort through her memories and the reality of her new station in life, she'd met the mysterious Count Eberlin.

She'd felt trepidation and anger when Linford had presented her with Eberlin's calling card. He'd been completely wretched to Keira with the one hundred acres and the mill, and it was he who had summoned the authorities when he'd guessed that Keira was not who she'd claimed to be. Lily could recall thinking tempestuously that afternoon that she would demand to know why he seemed so determined to harm Ashwood and her cousin.

She had expected an older man. Someone small in stature, rotund, with an ugly countenance—in short, someone like the old earl of Ashwood. She'd been completely taken aback by the tall, proud man who'd stridden into the salon. He was handsome, quite strikingly so. He had piercing brown eyes the color of molasses, and wavy, honey-colored hair, with streaks of wheat. Solidly built, with square shoulders and a strong jaw, he was impeccably dressed and carried an aura of power about him, as if he could scoop Ashwood and take it if he so desired.

There also had been something vaguely familiar about him, something that Lily hadn't quite been able to grasp as he'd come forward to greet her. His voice had been quiet and smooth, and he'd spoken with a slight accent that had sounded neither English nor European. When she'd inquired as to the nature of his call, he'd looked at her intently, and Lily had been able to feel the heat of his recrimination down to the tips of her toes. "I thought it was time," he'd said.

"Time?" She'd wondered if he was mad. "Time for what?"

One of his dark brows had risen. "Is it not obvious?"

She'd thought he was toying with her. "On the contrary, my lord, there is nothing obvious about your call or the ill will you hold for Ashwood." She'd meant to put the man on notice that he spoke to a countess.

But Eberlin had disregarded her regal bearing. He'd disregarded protocol and propriety, too, and had moved closer, studying her face so intently that Lily's pulse had fluttered.

"You are as beautiful as I knew you would be," he'd said, shocking her again. Lily's pulse had quickly gone from fluttering to racing. She'd been able to feel the raw power of seduction in him as his gaze had lingered on her décolletage, on her mouth. "Perhaps even more so."

Men had flirted with Lily all her adult life, but she'd never felt so . . . exposed, or quite so vulnerable. "I beg your pardon," she'd said stiffly.

Something had flickered in his eyes, but they'd quickly shuttered. "Do you truly not know who I am?"

A tiny spasm of trepidation had slithered through her.

"Perhaps this will stir your memory. My name is Tobin. Do you recall me now?"

Lily had seen it then, that vaguely familiar thing. It was the face of the boy who had been her companion. She'd not seen him since the day of his father's trial, when he'd stared daggers at her as she'd testified about what she'd seen. "*Tobin,*" she'd whispered as her brain accepted that the boy was now this handsome, strangely alluring man. "I can scarcely believe it is you."

"Surprised, are you?" His gaze had turned hard and cold.

"Yes," she'd answered honestly. "I never knew . . . I never knew where you'd gone. And your name, Eberlin—"

"A title that derives from an estate I own in Denmark."

"Denmark? But how—"

"I have returned to Hadley Green and Tiber Park with but one goal in mind," he'd said, interrupting her. "Would you like to know what that is?" With a cold smile, Tobin had carelessly, boldly, caressed her cheek with his knuckle, tracing a line to her mouth. "To destroy Ashwood." He'd said it low, almost as if he were speaking to a lover.

Lily had gasped and jerked away from his hand.

"I'll not rest until I have." With that, he'd walked out of her salon, leaving Lily to stand there, her heart beating with the strength of a thousand wings.

Every time she thought of that afternoon, she felt a strange flutter. He clearly held her responsible in some part for his father's demise, but she was not going to accept that from him. She had her own demons—she did not intend to adopt his as well.

Nor did she intend to let him win.

THREE

Benedict Sibley was in fine spirits, having convinced himself that his mastery of the law had helped earn Count Eberlin a favorable ruling. However, Benedict Sibley was a middling solicitor and a fool: the judge had been bought, just like everything else in Tobin's life. The victory was expected.

But Tobin was denied the small victory of seeing Lily Boudine's face when the ruling was delivered; she was not in attendance.

Mr. Goodwin, Ashwood's solicitor and a formidable opponent, had known he'd lost before the magistrate had even been seated. Still, he'd given a good fight, and when the inevitable had come, and the one hundred acres had been ruled as belonging to Tiber Park, Mr. Goodwin had sought at the very least to shame Tobin. He'd accused him of preying on an innocent woman and stealing the land from beneath her feet.

Tobin was beyond shame and had been for many years.

It was Sibley's idea that they have a celebratory pint of ale at the Grousefeather, and Tobin obliged him. As they walked out of the common rooms where the hearing had been held, Tobin spotted the Ashwood coach, with its showy plumes and crest. He imagined Mr. Fish and Mr. Goodwin giving Lily the news, of how she would blink her big green eyes and her bottom lip would quiver. Good.

At the Grousefeather, Tobin nursed his pint along, saying little as Sibley talked about his lofty ambitions. A full-bosomed serving girl caught Tobin's eye; she smiled at him and walked by their table with an exaggerated swing of her wide hips. Tobin supposed she'd had her fair share of gentlemen abovestairs; however, he would not be among them. He'd give Hadley Green nothing untoward to say of him. They would see that they could not destroy the Scotts, that he'd come back stronger than ever.

When Sibley turned his attention to two gentlemen who had overheard his bragging, Tobin left the tavern. He was untying his horse's lead when he happened to see Mr. and Mrs. Morton. They saw him, too—then turned the other way and pretended they had not.

Tobin yanked the rein free.

He'd dined at their home, for God's sake. Once word had circulated that Count Eberlin was at Tiber Park, the invitations had begun to flow. It had seemed that everyone had wanted to get a look at him, to put themselves in his circle of acquaintances, and the Mortons—an influential family—had been among the first. He'd accepted their invitation, for he remembered they'd been in Hadley Green at the time of his father's demise.

Tobin hadn't known that his father had been all but forgotten until he'd arrived at the Mortons' home in a brand-new barouche coach just delivered from London, expecting to see a house that, in his memory, was quite grand. He'd been disappointed to find it much smaller than that. He'd been shown into the house by a hired butler and invited to sit on furnishings he'd found quite pedestrian.

He remained standing.

The company was likewise pedestrian. There were no sea captains, no mercenaries, no wealthy traders. Just country folk who believed their pastoral lives were somehow interesting.

At some point during the main course, a guest had asked Tobin about his title. He'd said that it was a Danish title. The look on the guest's face—Freestone or Firestone, something like that—had been quite puzzled. "I suppose it is inherited from your mother?"

Tobin had chuckled. "If I had inherited even a few farthings, I doubt I would have risked running the naval blockade. No, sir, I bought the title and the estate from a displaced Danish count. That is the only manner in which Tobin Scott could ever possess a title." He'd chuckled again and drunk his wine.

The room had grown so quiet that he'd heard some-one's belly rumble. There was quite a lot of nervous shifting and looking about. Mr. Morton had peered closely at him. "Might I inquire, my lord . . . who was your father?"

"Joseph Scott, the wood-carver," Tobin had said casually, as if it was common knowledge, as if they ought to have known—which, to his thinking, they should have.

Tobin didn't know precisely what he'd expected, but as he looked around the dinner table, he was a bit nonplussed. Could they not see how he'd persevered? Did they not hold at least a bit of respect for his having pulled himself up and out of the abyss?

Apparently not. The dinner had grown increasingly uncomfortable. The people around him had made stilted conversation. He'd understood then that not one of them understood that he was, in fact, the oldest son of that condemned wood-carver.

Tobin had found that rather curious. He had a per-sonal portrait of his father, done when his father had been a young man, and he thought that the resem-blance between them was quite marked. Had the resi-dents of Hadley Green completely forgotten Joseph Scott? Was he nothing but a footnote in the history of this village, the man who had carved a magnificent staircase at Ashwood that had cost him his life?

Tobin did not seek to hide his identity. If anyone cared to look, they'd find his given name was on any

legal document having to do with Tiber Park. If anyone had asked him if he was, in fact, the son of Joseph
Scott, as had Mr. Greenhaven, the man he'd employed
to be his groundskeeper, he would have told them that
he was.

From that point in that interminable supper, Tobin
had been counting the moments until he might leave,
but in the course of the meal he'd had one of his spells.

These bloody spells—he'd never had one until that
moment on the road to Hadley Green, but now they
seemed to come on him with alarming regularity. That
worried him greatly, particularly as they seemed to
occur when there were people about and he was away
from the comfort of his private estate. He feared some
sort of fatal malady. Or worse, something so debilitating, so emasculating, that he would be nothing but a
shell of a man, capable of lifting nothing heavier than
a goblet . . . not unlike the men seated around that dinner table that night.

Tobin hadn't mentioned the spells to anyone, not
even to Charity, for fear that he would be perceived as
weak. Or *sickly*—if that were the case, he'd just as soon
be dead. But the spells came over him without warning, triggered by things that seemed so innocuous that
he couldn't help believing he'd been invaded by some
demonic fever.

That evening, at the Mortons' dinner table, he'd felt
a growing discomfort. Someone made a jest that had
prompted several people to laugh, and that was it. The

sound of adults laughing made Tobin suddenly flush, and his neckcloth felt as if it were tightening around his throat. His chest had tightened painfully; his hands had trembled so badly that he'd dropped his spoon into his soup bowl with a clatter.

It had horrified him. He'd had to excuse himself for a few moments, walking almost blindly outside onto the walk, gripping his fists so tightly against whatever invisible thing had him by the throat that his fingers still ached the next morning. He'd recovered within a few moments, thankfully, and explained it away by saying he'd swallowed wrong. But he'd spent the rest of the evening in mortal fear that it would happen again.

The Mortons had blamed his attack on the tepid soup, apparently believing he was the sort to lose his composure over an unsatisfactory meal. They'd exclaimed over him, threatened to dismiss the cook and, for all Tobin knew, spiked the poor woman's head on the fence. They believed they'd all but poisoned Lord Eberlin, or poor Tobin Scott, the improbable new owner of the newly grand Tiber Park.

The son of a condemned thief.

Seeing the Mortons turn from him now—even after he'd extended the invitation to the winter ball he would host at Tiber Park—redoubled Tobin's determination for revenge.

He'd extended the invitation to the ball to all of Hadley Green's meager *bon ton*. He intended to give them a fireworks display the likes of which they'd never seen, wanted them to see the palace he was making of Tiber Park; wanted them to know who was the son of Joseph Scott.

Mr. Morton turned and glanced back at Tobin. It appeared as if he was having second thoughts for his retreat, for he touched the brim of his hat with a nod. Tobin lifted a pair of fingers, acknowledging him. But the last-minute gesture did not appease him.

He moved around his horse to mount him, and in doing so, his gaze caught a flash of blue. He paused; that was Lily standing on the walk with her two agents. She saw him, too, and fixed him with a look so glowering that he nearly laughed. She was wearing a dark blue gown and spencer that hugged her tightly, and a hat set at a slight angle and with as much plumage as the bloody coach. Just looking at her, Tobin felt a tug of something in his chest. A tic of . . . lust? Or a spell? Whatever it was, he clenched his hand in a fist, nodded at her, and swung up on his horse.

Lily turned away from him and walked down the street, the two men casting dark gazes at him as they followed her.

Tobin touched his horse's mane. It was black, as black as Lily's hair. He thought of her skin, like cream, with rosy patches of anger in her cheeks. He thought of her blistering green eyes with long, dark lashes. He thought of her hair undone, flowing down her back, and the curve of her waist into her hip. He thought of the pleasure he would feel if he had her in his bed—exquisite, wet, warm pleasure.

A swell of physical discomfort reminded Tobin of just how long it had been since he'd lain with a woman. But he wanted to keep his need boiling just beneath the surface—that gave him the power to do what he needed here.

Then discomfort extended up to his chest, tightening oddly and shooting painfully down his spine. These bloody thoughts of Lily Boudine were giving him one of his spells. His scalp was perspiring. He resisted the urge to take out his handkerchief and dab at his face, lest anyone notice. He grappled blindly for the reins of his horse and surreptitiously glanced about him to see if anyone saw him there, practically choking on his own innards, and his gaze landed on the village green. In a blinding flash of memory, Tobin could see his father hanging there, twisting helplessly at the end of a rope.

He quickly dropped his gaze and focused on the reins, wrapping them tightly around his hand. He remembered the night before his father hanged, the last time Tobin ever spoke to him. Tobin had sobbed with grief, had railed against the people of Ashwood, and most especially against Lily Boudine. His father had embraced him, had held him tight. "She is a mere girl, Tobin. You cannot lay my fate at her feet. Look to God, son. There is no satisfaction in hate or anger. This is God's will, for whatever reason, and you must accept it."

"Why aren't you angry?" Tobin had demanded. "Why do you not speak out against them, against the lies?"

His father had smiled sadly and had run his hand over Tobin's head. "It would serve no purpose. It would change nothing. The die has been cast and it is no one's fault but my own."

Tobin's heart was pounding now, and he wheeled his horse about and galloped down High Street. He rode blindly, pushing the horse, heedless of the clouds darkening in a pale gray sky, heedless of anything but the need to be away from the village of Hadley Green and this bloody spell.

When he felt the constriction in his chest easing, he was in a clearing along that seldom-used road he'd adopted as his own. He reined his horse to a stop, flung himself off its back and marched forward, his stride long and determined, drawing deep breaths. He strode to a rock and sat heavily, his elbows on his knees, pushing his hands through his hair. *What was wrong with him?* Was it madness? Was it a malicious cancer of his brain or his heart? He'd never felt anything like it; it was as if he were crawling out of his skin, as if his veins were constricting, drawing up, and restricting the flow of blood through him.

He loosened the knot on his neckcloth, then straightened up to draw a deep breath—and looked right into the face of a little girl with blonde hair and blue eyes.

She cocked her head curiously to one side, like a little sparrow. "Pardon, sir. Are you weeping?"

"Weeping!" he scoffed. "Do I look as if I am weeping?"

She studied him a moment, then shrugged.

Tobin drew a breath, released it slowly as he took her in. She looked to be about eight years old. She was wearing a pink and white frock, but the sash had come undone. Her hair had been put up at some point, but it was mussed and a portion of it had come down and hung carelessly over her shoulder. He recognized her as the ward of Lily Boudine's cousin, Keira Hannigan.

"You look unwell," she remarked. "Perhaps you should go to bed. That's what I'm always made to do when I feel ill."

"I am perfectly all right," he said. "Why are you here? Are you alone?"

She nodded, but her gaze was fixed below his chin. "Your neckcloth has come undone."

"So has your sash," he pointed out, and the girl glanced down, looking surprised by the discovery.

"Look here, where do you live? It will be raining soon, and you have no coat."

The weather seemed to have gone unnoticed by her; she looked up to the sky with a frown.

"Run along home," he said, gesturing toward the woods. "Where is your house?"

"Ashwood," she said. "I live with the countess. The

second countess. The first countess was only a pretend one, but this one is a *real* countess, and she's quite pretty and very kind. She hasn't a *lot* of friends, not like the pretend countess. *She* had squads and squads of friends. I am going to live with her in Ireland. Lord Donnelly is coming for the horses and for me and he is going to take me all the way to Ireland. They mean to adopt me, you know."

"That is happy news, indeed, but you'll be no use to them if you are struck dead by cold. Run along home," he repeated.

"Where do *you* live?" she asked, ignoring his advice.

"Tiber Park." He looked up at the sky—the clouds were thickening and the girl was at least twenty minutes by foot from Ashwood. If she could be depended upon to walk a straight line. As much as Tobin despised the residents of Hadley Green, those feelings did not extend to children. That was the one part of him that hadn't been entirely corrupted by the life he'd led thus far.

"Come along. I'll take you home."

"Why?"

"I told you. It will rain soon and you have no cloak from the look of it, and I'll not have your death on my conscience."

"People don't die from *rain*," she said stubbornly.

"Are you quite certain of that?"

She frowned, as if she was privately debating that,

then looked at his horse. "Do you mean to take me on *that*?" she asked. "I don't like horses. Once, a horse bit me."

"Indeed," he said and stood.

"Like this," she said and snapped at him, her teeth bared.

"I have never, in all my years, seen a horse bite like that," he said skeptically. "Nevertheless, I assure you I am a competent horseman. You will not fall, and he will not bite you. Come." He held out his hand to her.

The girl eyed him warily before slipping her hand into his. "My name is Miss Lucy Taft. What is your name?"

"Eberlin," he said.

"Oh! I know very well who *you* are," she said breezily as they walked to where his horse was grazing. "I've heard quite a lot about you."

"Have you," he said wryly and lifted her up to sit before the saddle. "Hold onto his mane," he instructed. She gripped the horse's mane as he lifted himself up behind her.

"The countess does not care for you, you know," she continued.

"Doesn't she?"

"Oh, no. She once liked you quite a lot, when you were a boy, but she said you became a horrible man when you grew up. You're not really a lord, are you? Lady Ashwood says you are not *really* a lord, for you don't have an *English* title. Perhaps you didn't know you were to have an English title."

Tobin glanced heavenward and put his arm around her small middle, anchoring her to him. As he started his horse forward, Lucy Taft gasped and grabbed his arm that held the reins.

"Miss Taft, you make it impossible for me to guide the horse. Let go of my arm."

"I *told* you I don't like to ride."

"Let go," he said again. "I have a very firm grasp of you."

She reluctantly let go and shrank back into his chest. "I don't like riding in the least. I don't know why everyone does, really. The pretend countess, she liked it very much. She raced about on horses, and she wanted me to do the same. I fear she'll expect me to ride about all of Ireland. I rather like carriages, don't you? I like the very big ones, for the smaller ones are quite close. Once, I went into the village with Mrs. Thorpe and Peter, the kitchen boy, in the old carriage, and it was *quite* close, and Peter didn't smell very nice, and I had to hold my breath the *whole way.*"

Lucy Taft continued to natter on and, much like his niece, Catherine, was either oblivious or uncaring that Tobin didn't answer. When they reached the road to Ashwood, he sent the horse to a trot, and Miss Taft shrieked loud enough to wake the dead. But Tobin was anxious to hand her off to a servant and return to Tiber Park before the rains began in earnest.

Ashwood looked almost foreboding in the gloomy light. Tobin thought he saw a movement of light in one of the windows of the upper floor, and he imagined Lily looking out that window fifteen years ago.

Whatever had happened that night, he could scarcely bear to think of it without fearing another attack.

"Why do you suppose it rains in summer? It rains *all* the time in winter, and I think that should be *enough* rain for the year, wouldn't you?" Lucy Taft asked.

They had reached the drive, and Tobin reined his horse to a halt. "Here we are." He swung off his horse, then lifted her down, and as he was putting her on the ground, the Ashwood coach barreled into the drive.

Tobin looked down at the girl. "Mind you go straight inside."

"Will you come in for tea?" she asked. "The countesses always serve tea when someone comes to call."

"I would hardly term this a call," he said, watching the coach door swing open and Lily fairly leap out of it. She rushed toward them, Mr. Fish close behind. "Lucy! Lucy, come here at once!" she called.

Lucy smiled up at Tobin. "Thank you," she said and scampered forward to meet her guardian.

Lily looked the girl up and down before handing her off to Mr. Fish, then came striding toward Tobin, her expression furious, and apparently heedless of the rain that was beginning to fall.

"Well, Lady Ashwood, it would seem we meet yet again," Tobin said.

"What do you think you are doing?" she demanded.

"Obviously, I am delivering your ward. She was wandering about the woods without a cloak."

"Please!" she scoffed. "Do not take me for a fool!"

"What, then? Do you think I was spying? Preying on children?"

"What do you expect, *Count* Eberlin? You have stolen land and tenants from me—why should I think you above spying and kidnapping?"

"My, my," Tobin said, trying as best he might to keep his voice even. "You are accusing me of any number of things today—stealing, spying, abduction. I sound quite vile even to my own ears." He stepped forward, so close that she had to tilt her head back to look him in the eyes. "Let me assure you, Lady Ashwood, that I am merely righting a very deep wrong. I do not need to *spy*."

The color in Lily's cheeks deepened, and her dark brows dipped in a deep V of displeasure. "Is that so? Then tell me, how else would you know which tenants are ripe for the picking? Be forewarned—I will fight you at every turn."

Tobin arched a brow with amusement. "*Fight* me? If you want to fight, I will not stop you. If anything, it ought to make things interesting."

"Go on, then," she seethed. "Underestimate me. I will find a way to stop you, and I will show you *no* mercy."

He didn't know the meaning of the word. Tobin

could feel the band tightening around his chest, and he knew he should leave her to stew in her juices, but he could not help letting his gaze casually wander her lush form. She surprised him. He'd expected her to topple into a crying heap of crinoline, but she had responded with determination. In another place or time, he might have appreciated it more than he did at present.

"I do not wish for mercy, Lily. That will make it all the sweeter when I bring you to heel." His gaze met her pale green eyes. "And let me be perfectly clear." His gaze fell to her lips. "I *will* bring you to heel."

He expected a maidenly gasp, but Lily brazenly stepped closer to him, her eyes glittering with undiluted ire. "Do you honestly think you will intimidate me with innuendo? Let *me* be perfectly clear, sir. Do not step foot on Ashwood soil again. And stay away from me and mine!" She whirled around, marching toward her house.

Tobin watched her go in, ushering Miss Taft before her. The butler wasted no time in shutting the door at her back. The rain was falling harder, but Tobin scarcely noticed it. His body was hard from tension and desire. His fist was clenched, and his breathing labored. He made himself turn away and mount his horse, then spurred it to a run, pulling his hat low over his eyes to keep the rain from them.

Lily Boudine was bloody beautiful.

More was the pity.

FOUR

Lily was still outraged as she marched Lucy into the library to find out how the girl had come to be in that man's presence. "Foolish girl!" Lily scolded her and wrapped her arms tightly around her. "Where did you go? Where have you been?"

"I didn't want my music lesson. I went for a walk-about in the woods," Lucy said into her chest.

Lily let Lucy go, leaning back to have a look at her. "A *walkabout*? And why didn't you tell anyone?"

The girl looked contrite. "I wanted to tell you, mu'um, but there was no one about and Linford said you'd gone into the village. I didn't think there was any harm."

"Well, there was," Lily said. "Look at the rain! You might have caught your death."

"That's what Count Eberlin said as well when he made me come home," Lucy said morosely.

Lily exchanged a look with Mr. Fish, who stood

quietly across the room. Lily waited for Lucy to say more, but she merely fidgeted with her sash. Lily put her arm around Lucy's slender shoulders, then smoothed her mussed blonde hair from her face. "Darling, you *must* have a care. Not everyone you may meet is kind, and Eberlin especially not! Have I not warned you about him?"

"But he was kind to me."

Dear God. Lily led Lucy to a divan and sat her down. "Where did you happen upon him? In the park?"

Lucy shook her head. "In the woods."

"The woods! What on earth were you doing in the woods?"

"I only went to the cottage!" Lucy cried. "I've been there lots before—"

"What cottage?"

"The one by the river. By the church that's falling down. It's boarded up, and part of the roof has come down. But there are two chairs and a cat that lives inside, and sometimes I go round to see that he's fed. He likes rotten potatoes, can you imagine?"

Uppington Church. Lily knew it well. There was hardly anything left of the church. The cottage on its grounds had been abandoned many years ago, and Lily had played there as a child, pretending it was a castle, and she its chatelaine. The memory gave her a curious twist in her belly; she suddenly recalled her aunt Althea standing in the foyer of Ashwood, smiling brightly, telling Lily to go on with Tobin and play.

Behind her, Mr. Scott, looking so admiringly at her aunt . . .

Lily closed her eyes a moment to banish the image. "Was Eberlin in the cottage, Lucy?" She wondered if he remembered their excursions to Uppington Church. She did. She remembered him vividly.

Lucy shook her head again. "No, mu'um. He hadn't gone as far as that. He was sitting on a rock. I think he was weeping."

Weeping?

"He was sitting on a rock thus," Lucy said, perching on the edge of the divan and propping her elbows on her knees. "And his head was down just so," she said, and put her hands on either side of her head. "I saw him, but he didn't see me. He took great gulps of air and I thought perhaps he was sad, and I said, are you weeping? And he looked at me strangely and said he was not, that he was quite all right, and that I would catch my death and I was to go home at once, and then he asked where I lived, and I told him I lived here with you, but that I would leave for Ireland soon, for the first countess wishes to adopt me and make me Irish, just like her, and he said he should take me because it was too far to walk before it rained. I didn't want to go, because I do not care for horses, really—that is, I do not care to *ride* them. I do like to pet them. Mr. Bechtel lets me feed apples—"

"Darling, what happened then?" Lily asked, bringing her back to the point.

"What? Oh yes, he brought me home. I invited him for tea. I should have, should I not? But he said no."

"That's all there is?" Lily prodded.

Lucy shrugged. "I wonder why he should be weeping. Perhaps he lost his dog."

"I hardly think he was weeping," Lily said with a wry smile. Plotting his next act of malice was more likely. "Now see here, young miss, you are not to wander off without telling someone where you are going. And if you think to wander all the way to Uppington Church, you must have someone with you. That's very far!"

"It's not so far," Lucy protested, but Lily touched her finger to her lips to keep her from saying more.

"An escort," she said again.

Lucy slouched against the back of the divan. "Very well," she said, resigned.

"Go and ask Mrs. Thorpe to draw you a bath, and tell Ann she must wash your hair," she added at the sight of Lucy's tangled locks.

With a great sigh, Lucy stood up. "I don't *like* baths," she muttered as she went.

When Lucy had gone, Lily looked at Mr. Fish. "What was he doing in the woods, with his head between his hands? He looked rather triumphant this morning, did he not?" she demanded. "I do not trust him at all."

"I think he now has what he wants," Mr. Fish said calmly.

"The acreage?" Lily thought of what Tobin had said to her weeks ago, that he intended to ruin her. And what he'd said on the drive today—that he would bring her to heel. She suddenly hugged herself against the small, not unpleasant tremor that shot through her. Tobin was a vile, evil man . . . but he also had the sort of bold virility that made parents want to lock their daughters' doors and daughters want to climb out windows.

"I think he wants more," she said, trying to erase the image of his mouth.

"What more?" Mr. Fish asked.

"I scarcely know, but—oh!" she said suddenly. "With the events of the day, I have forgotten that our little maid has brought news from Tiber Park." Lily hurried to the door and opened it, sending the footman outside it for Louis and the chambermaid.

"Madam, I cannot advise this course of action," Mr. Fish said disapprovingly.

Lily ignored him.

When Louis reappeared he had Agatha in tow, a tiny little thing whose cap was almost too big for her head. She stood at the threshold anxiously rubbing one thumb with the other.

"Come in, come in," Lily said, smiling, and took the young woman by the elbow to draw her inside. "I understand you have something you wish to tell us?"

"No mu'um, not me. It's my brother, he's the one." She looked pleadingly at Louis, clearly distressed.

"Go on. Tell them," Louis said and put his hand on Agatha's back, forcing her to step forward.

"I fear my brother will lose his position, mu'um," Agatha said, a little frantically. "He's just earned it, and he's two babies to feed."

"He won't lose his position," Lily assured her. "Whatever news he sends will remain our secret." She gestured for Agatha to sit, and the maid perched reluctantly on the very edge of the settee.

Lily smiled kindly in spite of her racing heart. "What position does your brother occupy at Tiber Park?"

"Footman. That is, he's learning to be one."

"What is his name?" Lily continued pleasantly.

"Ranulf." She glanced at Louis; he nodded his encouragement. "He...he was to pour whiskey for the gents that had come for the weekend. So he pours the whiskeys, and he stands back as he ought to have done, and the count, he says to the gent down from London that Lady Ashwood was to sell her cattle, and that he should let it be known the cattle were diseased. And I says to Ranulf, I say, why would he say such a thing? And Ranulf, he says to me, Agatha, don't you see? So's she won't get naught for them. And then, Ranulf says the count gives the gent the name of someone who would say the cattle were ill."

Lily heard a grunt from Mr. Fish. She drew a steadying breath but kept smiling. "There, you see? You and Ranulf have done the right thing to tell me, Agatha. Thank you. I'll not breathe a word of this to the count. No one will speak of it outside this room. And as promised, you and Ranulf will be rewarded for doing such a great service for Ashwood."

"Agatha," Mr. Fish said, "you must do as the countess bids you. Whatever Ranulf tells you, you must keep quite to yourself. Do you understand? You and Ranulf must not say a word of this to anyone."

"Aye," Agatha said, nodding vigorously. "Not a word will pass these lips."

Mr. Fish looked dubious, but he gestured to the door. "Meet me in the butler's pantry and I shall reward you for your courage."

"Thank you, Agatha," Lily said, rising up from the settee.

As Louis and Agatha went out, Lily looked at Mr. Fish.

"I had hoped that we might bring in some money with the sale of those cattle," he started.

"But I think we cannot rely on any of our plans at present, Mr. Fish. We must rethink things and try to stop him."

Mr. Fish sighed. "I agree," he conceded. "However, I still cannot recommend putting this man, Ranulf, into such a precarious position. As his sister said, he has two children to provide for."

"We will take great care," Lily assured him. "But I cannot see another option available to us. Can you?"

"I must say that I do, madam," Mr. Fish said tightly. "As I have previously advised you, I think you might use your position to its fullest advantage."

"And how shall I do that?"

"By building the bridges your cousin damaged," he said flatly.

Lily sighed and glanced longingly at the window. How she would like to be out there, in the world, and away from the problems of Ashwood. "I understand you, Mr. Fish . . . but no one is rushing to befriend me, are they? I have tried very hard to atone for Keira's betrayal, but it is rather difficult after the fiasco of our summer gala."

The ladies of the St. Bartholomew's Charity Society, otherwise known as The Society, had been very helpful in staging the summer gala, the festival held at Ashwood each year to celebrate the summer harvest and benefit the orphanage. The gala had not been held in several years, but with the ladies' considerable aid, Keira had put it on this summer to great success. Unfortunately, and quite by coincidence, it had been during the gala that Lily had arrived at Ashwood. Everyone, including Lily, had discovered Keira's fraud that evening. Keira had been forced to announce to the assembled guests that she was not, in fact, the Countess of Ashwood but the cousin of the true and rightful countess, Lily.

And then she'd introduced Lily.

Oh, what a long summer it had been.

"I am aware of the obstacles," Mr. Fish said. "But if I may, there are three ladies who hold particular sway in our little community. Lady Horncastle, Mrs. Morton, and Mrs. Ogle. Any one of them would be a valuable asset to you."

"You know very well that Mrs. Ogle has refused my invitations to dine. Mrs. Morton came to tea with her friend, Miss Babcock, but they have been slow to warm to me. And though Lady Horncastle was kind enough to invite me to tea early on, I think you will agree that it was to have a good look at the latest Countess of Ashwood rather than an effort to extend an olive branch."

"I grant you, it is not an easy task," Mr. Fish said. "There are still many hurt feelings for your cousin's deception. And frankly, madam, there are some who believe you were somehow complicit in the fraud."

Lily sighed. "I know very well you mean Mrs. Ogle."

"*You mustn't pay her the slightest mind,*" Mrs. Morton had advised Lily at tea. "*Her nose is pushed out of joint rather easily. You may trust me; I have known her for nigh on thirty years.*"

Aunt Althea had been particularly adept at bringing the county together in charity for the good of the whole, and Lily wished that she could do the same. She *wanted* to belong. She wanted to marry, to have a family she might call her own. But it seemed hers would be a slow ascent.

"Nevertheless, Lady Ashwood, these are the women that might help you to make an advantageous match. I can think of no better way to save Ashwood at present. Might I suggest a soiree of some sort?"

"A proper soiree will require funds, Mr. Fish."

"In my opinion, the gains will justify the expense. It might be just the thing to bring Hadley Green around to you. I ask that you at least consider it." Mr. Fish glanced at his pocket watch. "I beg your pardon, but I must go and see to the chambermaid."

Lily slouched in her seat, feeling exhausted by the day's events. She could not bear the thought of begging these women to come to her . . . but she had to agree that an evening soiree for society might be just the thing.

She thought of Tobin and the dreadful feeling that she would be forced to beg someone for a match to save Ashwood from him. No matter how she looked at it, she could see that Mr. Fish was right.

Yet she could not help thinking of the way Tobin had looked at her on the drive, as if he despised her and wanted her both. And that curious moment when Lily believed she had seen a flash of something vulnerable in his expression, almost as if she'd been seeing the edge of a wound, a glimpse that she found oddly intriguing. Not that it changed her opinion of him, not in the least. He was a ruthless, angry man who had pushed her into a corner with alarming ease. And Lily was determined to get out of the corner before he forced her into marrying some man she scarcely knew.

She was still brooding about it when she went up to change for tea. Her fingers trailed down the curved dual mahogany staircase railing, and she could feel the curve of the vine Mr. Scott had carved into the railing.

It meandered up to the first floor, with leaves and an occasional flower to adorn it. She wondered idly how long such craftsmanship took. A year? More? Less?

And she thought of the little stool for the pianoforte in the music room. That curious stool, made to accompany a pianoforte brought all the way from Italy, its color so close to the pianoforte's that only a keen eye would discern a difference.

Lily abruptly turned toward the music room. Inside, she lit a small candelabrum and stared down at the stool.

Was it possible she'd been wrong about all that had happened here?

The day she'd come back to Ashwood Keira had dragged her in here to show her the stool and had sparked a memory that had been lurking at the edge of Lily's mind. But a memory of what? Had there been an affair between them? There was no evidence of it, really, nothing but this stool.

Lily knelt down and turned the stool over and read the inscription: *You are the song that plays on in my heart; for A, my love, my life, my heart's only note. Yours for eternity, JS.*

Lily could remember her aunt sitting here, playing. Had she known the inscription had been there? Had she thought that Mr. Scott had been sadly misguided, or had she welcomed his sentiment? Either was entirely possible—Lily and Keira both had received gifts from gentlemen whom they had not encouraged.

Still, if Keira's theory was true, and Lily's aunt and Mr. Scott had been lovers, the possibilities of what that meant were too disconcerting for Lily to contemplate.

It upset her now; she righted the stool, blew out the candelabra, and quit the room. She made her way to her suite, questioning everything she thought she knew. *Where were the jewels?* If Mr. Scott had stolen them, what had become of them? If he hadn't stolen them, where were they? Why had they never surfaced?

And when she made her way downstairs for tea, her mind was buzzing with memories and thoughts. When Lily was a girl, Ashwood had been the premiere property in all of West Sussex. The Quality would come from London to take the air here. Wine and ale had flowed freely, and the staff of more than twenty had kept the house and grounds in pristine condition. Now, Lily was lucky to employ a dozen staff, and she fretted over her ability to keep them every day.

What had happened to all the money? Mr. Fish said it was poor management, but Lily found it difficult to believe that a man as fiercely in control of his surroundings as the earl had been would be a poor steward of his inheritance. Nothing made sense to her anymore. It was terribly frustrating to think that the answers to her questions had died with Aunt Althea and Mr. Scott. There was no one left who could help her make sense of it; the only person who might possibly be able to help her piece it together was Tobin.

If that was the case, then she would go to her grave wondering.

At tea, as Lucy recounted her day in the flowing details of a child, Lily continued to brood on her predicament. She watched Lucy swirl her spoon in her teacup as she talked and thought that perhaps she could live an austere life—no new gowns, no beeswax candles. No soiree, certainly. No more charity. *No charity!* Which meant the orphans at St. Bartholomew would now suffer because of Tobin Scott's twisted desire to ruin Ashwood. Did the man have no conscience? Was he incapable of understanding how many people he hurt?

Lily's mood was as black as the gloomy sky. She had foolishly believed that a title and inheritance might give her freedom, but it was beginning to seem quite the opposite. She felt trapped until a match came along, and no match would come if she had no purse.

Lily smiled blankly at Lucy's chatter, her fingers drumming mindlessly against her teacup as Linford served a bit of bread and some kippers. When she saw them, something inside Lily burst. They'd had kippers for lunch, and kippers yesterday as well—and now they'd have kippers in place of salmon?

"Will you please explain to me, Linford," she demanded of her butler at the sideboard, "why, at an estate as grand as Ashwood, we must be made to eat *kippers* at every meal?"

"I beg your pardon, madam," Linford said with a crooked bow, "but the fish are being harvested upstream to support Tiber Park. And the hunting is not as good as it has been in years past."

"Let me guess." She angrily tossed her linen napkin aside. "Is Tiber Park hunting our forests?"

"I cannot say, madam," Linford said calmly. "Shall I have Mr. Fielding come round on the morrow?"

"That will not be necessary." Lily abruptly stood, waving off the footman who hurried to remove her chair. "Please have a carriage brought round." She turned toward the door.

"But where are you going?" Lucy asked plaintively.

"I beg your pardon, darling," Lily said, pausing briefly to cup Lucy's face. "But there is a man who needs strangling." She marched out, calling out to a startled Louis for her cloak.

FIVE
❧

Tobin's butler, Carlson, announced that Bolge was waiting for Tobin in the small study. Tiber Park was so grand that there was a small study, a larger library, private and public dining rooms, two drawing rooms, two salons, and a ballroom. Sometimes Tobin was amazed that he was the master of Tiber Park. He liked to imagine what his father might have thought of him.

"Tell him I shall join him shortly," Tobin said to Carlson. "And the others?" he asked, referring to Lord Horncastle, Mr. Sibley, and Captain MacKenzie.

"The gentlemen Horncastle and Sibley await you in the gaming room," Carlson said.

Tobin added the plush red gaming room to his mental inventory of the rooms at his estate.

"Captain MacKenzie sent word that he has been pleasurably detained in Hadley Green," Carlson continued. "He asks that he might join you later."

At the Grousefeather Tavern, Tobin surmised. "Thank you," he said and heard Carlson go out.

Carlson was another product of the piece of Denmark now owned by Tobin. Carlson never called Tobin lord. Tobin wasn't certain if it was a misunderstanding of the English language—although Carlson spoke it fluently—or if the man refused to do so on principle. Carlson had made it quite plain that he did not approve of how Tobin had obtained his Danish title, but Tobin hardly cared about Carlson's principles. It was his impeccable service Tobin wanted, and he'd paid Carlson handsomely to put aside any scruples and come to England and serve him as any man of importance ought to be served.

Tobin straightened his neckcloth. As it was wet outside, he'd planned billiards for his acquaintances before supper. He supposed Bolge and MacKenzie were the closest he had to friends, but in his years of high-stakes trading, one merely had acquaintances whom one could trust better than others.

Bolge had graduated from ship galleys and now was a wealthy man in his own right, having made a career of helping men like Tobin get what they wanted. As large as he'd ever been, Bolge was standing in the middle of the study wearing a superfine coat of navy wool and gray trousers, his hair combed in the latest style. That was new—Bolge had never been one to court fashion.

"Good to see you, Bolge," Tobin said, extending his hand.

"Always a pleasure, Scotty. Aye, but you look grander each time I see you."

Tobin smiled. "Whiskey?"

"You know me well."

Tobin gestured to a footman.

"I must thank you for your considerable help in this little matter," Tobin said. Bolge was the one who had made the "offer" to the magistrate. Tobin removed a small vellum from his coat pocket; folded within it was a very generous banknote.

"It was my pleasure," Bolge said, slipping the vellum into his pocket before accepting the whiskey from the footman.

That was what Tobin admired most about Bolge. He never questioned. He just did. He clapped his hand onto Bolge's thick shoulder. "Still unsettled on horseback?"

"Ach, I am a seaman—not a horseman," Bolge said, then began to complain about his last mount as they made their way to the gaming room.

They walked down a carpeted corridor, past consoles with fine porcelain, hand-painted Oriental vases Tobin had stumbled across in a Marrakech souk, filled with flowers from the recently refurbished hothouse. They walked past wainscoting that had been gilded, silk wall coverings woven in India, and paintings bought from failing estates around the world.

In the gaming room, where rich leather met deep red velvet trimmings, Sibley and Horncastle were playing billiards and drinking the Scotch whiskey MacKenzie had shipped here. Tobin had known MacKenzie for quite some time now. They'd met on the high seas, naturally—MacKenzie was a Scotsman with a hazy past who defied God and pure luck to sail any ship in any weather and through any blockade. Tobin considered him a kindred spirit, a fine captain, and as fine a gambler as they came.

The gentlemen greeted one another. Horncastle, who hailed from Hadley Green, held out a tot of whiskey to Tobin. "You arrived just in time for a toast."

Horncastle was a brash young man with no ambitions that Tobin could see other than to drink, gamble, and whore. He was several years younger than Tobin and had grown into an effeminate, aimless man.

"To a day of good luck and better fortune," Horncastle said.

"To luck and fortune!" the men all avowed.

The four men talked about the prospects for hunting on the morrow in the vast forests around Tiber Park. A footman—Rupert, Richard, Tobin could scarcely remember them all—brought in a platter and set it on a sideboard. He removed the dome to reveal small cuts of ham and cheeses.

The men were helping themselves to the repast when Carlson appeared and bowed. "Pardon, sir, but you have a visitor."

Tobin glanced over his shoulder at Carlson. "Is it MacKenzie? Send him in."

"It is Lady Ashwood."

Tobin stilled.

Lord Horncastle whistled low. "Lady Ashwood," he said, grinning, "is as fine a specimen of feminine beauty as I have been blessed to see. There are some who think her charlatan of a cousin is the fairer of the two, but my vote is with Lady Ashwood."

"Lady Ashwood, here?" Sibley said, frowning. "There's daring for you."

Tobin hardly knew what he would name it. He told Carlson, "You may inform Lady Ashwood that I am indisposed at present."

Bolge laughed heartily. "I should rejoice in the day that I might have the luxury of sending a comely woman away."

"What news from Charity?" Tobin asked Bolge, changing the subject. He took a seat as Bolge filled him in on his visit with Tobin's sister.

But a moment later, Carlson returned.

"What now?" Tobin asked impatiently.

"I beg your pardon sir, but the lady refuses to leave."

Bolge howled with delight at that; Horncastle and Sibley looked shocked. It was scandalous enough for a lady to call on a gentleman, but it was unheard of that she would refuse to leave.

"How can she refuse?" Tobin asked, chuckling at Bolge's reaction. "I do not wish to receive her."

"She asks that I tell you she will reside in the main

foyer if she must, but she will not leave until you face her like a gentleman ought to face a lady."

Bolge clapped Horncastle on the back. "*That's* cheek for you!" he crowed.

"Irish women!" Horncastle blustered. "They could learn a thing or two about proper feminine behavior, eh?"

Tobin thought rather that the Irish women could teach Horncastle a thing or two about daring. He sighed. He really had no patience for this—he was in a good mood, ready for a bit of gaming and a good supper. "Excuse me, gentlemen. This should take but a moment."

They laughed. "God in heaven, I'll go in your stead if you find it so painful!" Bolge cheerfully called after him.

As Tobin went out, his congenial smile faded quickly. He strode down the corridor to the foyer, intent on ushering her out like a barn cat. But as the white marble foyer came into view, he saw her standing in the middle of the circle with the flourished black *T P.* She looked almost ethereal in her azure cloak and hood. It was wet still; the rain had worsened. Behind her, the door was standing open. Tobin walked to the door and shut it, then turned around to look at her.

The hood of her cloak framed her lovely face. She glanced down as if to gather herself, and dark lashes stood starkly against the pale color of her skin. A fleeting image of Lily lying nude in a bed, her eyes closed just like that, scudded across Tobin's mind.

He clasped his hands behind his back and squeezed them hard against such thoughts. "I do not wish to receive you, Lily. Why, then, are you still here?"

"Yes, your butler made it quite clear that you do not wish to receive me, but I hardly care," she said. "For I do not intend to eat kippers again."

Prepared to do battle as he was, the reference to kippers threw him. "Pardon?"

"You heard me," she said heatedly and swept her hood from her head as she advanced on him. There was no mistaking her ire or her disdain, which Tobin found ironic, given what she had done to *him*. She stopped before him, her head tilted back. "I think that in your zeal to see me brought low, you have forgotten that I do not live alone at Ashwood. There are many other souls who depend on it, and when you punish me, you punish them all. When you attempt to starve me, you starve *them*—men and women and children with no crime against you!"

Her eyes shimmered, and Tobin smiled in spite of himself. "I am not starving anyone."

"Oh, no? Then I suppose you are feeding your own gullet with all the fish," she exclaimed heatedly, gesturing wildly at him.

"Aha," he said, the light dawning. "We have constructed a temporary dam," he said with an insouciant shrug.

"*Un-dam it.*"

Tobin chuckled. She was bloody beguiling with her sparkling eyes and high color, but if she thought she could command him to anything— "When we have caught enough to stock the lake, we will release the dam. Rest assured, I do not mean to make a lake of Tiber Park."

"That is unacceptable."

"But true nonetheless. You may go now."

"You think I have no means to stop you. Yet I *do* have means."

"And what would that be?"

Her eyes narrowed. "You will see."

Tobin grinned. "Madam, I have sat around many gaming tables in my time, and I know when someone is bluffing. And you do it very badly. But you may do as you please, it is of little consequence to me. Now do be a good neighbor and go back to your side of the fence."

If looks could kill, he'd be laid out on the floor. "Oh, no," Lily said, her voice shaking with anger. "You will not turn your back on me. I marvel at the depth of your cruelty, Tobin. I've done nothing to warrant such vile treatment."

"You mean other than put a rope around my father's neck?"

Lily gasped, and the color in her cheeks suddenly faded.

"I beg your pardon, does that offend you?" He hardly cared if it did.

"By all that is holy, your father put that rope around his own neck. I did not put him at Ashwood that night—*he* did that. I merely saw him and said that I had—no matter how badly you want to believe otherwise."

Tobin had to look away from her and move to the door. He opened it, ignoring the lashing rain. "I do not intend to debate the past with you."

"Your desire to punish me is shameless revenge, nothing more. But can you not see past your hatred of me to the people of Ashwood? Can you not see that when you take Ashwood from me, you take their livelihood? You can't possibly bring them all to Tiber Park."

"Why not? My estate is rather large. There is always room for more staff."

"Is that so? Will you bring Lucy Taft to Ashwood, too? She is an orphan, and I assure you, she has no useful purpose for you. But where else will she go?"

"To Ireland," he said shortly. "She told me she was on her way. Is that not so?"

Lily made a sound of frustration. "Then what of Linford? He is as old as Father Time! What will he do, serve as underbutler to your man? What about our gamekeeper, Mr. Bevers? He was born and raised in the cottage where he still lives with his family. Do you intend to destroy their lives because of your wretched need for revenge?"

Tobin said nothing.

"That's what I suspected," she said, her voice

dripping with rancor. "You have nothing to say for yourself."

She was staring daggers now; the color had returned to her cheeks. God, but her beauty was astounding. She enticed him to carnal desire like no other woman ever had. He could imagine her gown sliding down her voluptuous figure, pooling at her feet. He could imagine breasts plump with dark nipples, her belly softly round. Dammit, but he was hardening just thinking such thoughts. What was it about this woman that had the power to do that to him? He was dead inside. He did not want, he did not need . . . yet there was something about her that made him feel as if he did.

"You are right," he said tightly. "It is not fair."

Lily looked entirely taken aback. And then absurdly pleased, as if she believed she had won, had somehow touched humanity in him. Alas, the humanity in him had been choked out of him as the air had been choked out of his father. "But I do not care," he added.

She blinked, her bright eyes clouding with confusion.

"However, in the interest of giving you a slight chance at redemption, I shall propose a deal of sorts." He casually walked forward, admiring her.

"A deal," she said dismissively. "What have I left? You've taken my land, my tenants, my mill, my *fish*— what more is there, Tobin?"

When she said his name, something warm sluiced through him. Warm and soft, sinking slowly like rain into the mud in him. He moved closer and smiled with deliberate amusement. "I did not take your fish, Lily."

"You dammed them up," she said impatiently. "What deal, then?"

He considered the beautiful and haughty woman, the gems twinkling from her earlobes, the cloak fastened at the hollow of her throat. He lazily touched one of the earrings, his finger stroking her earlobe. She bent her head away. Undaunted, Tobin walked a slow circle around her, taking her in, admiring her profile, when she turned her head to see where he was. He came to a halt before her and gazed down into her sea green eyes.

"*What deal?*" she demanded softly.

"Allow me to ruin you properly," he said, his gaze falling to her mouth.

Those lush lips parted with surprise. "I beg your pardon?"

One corner of Tobin's mouth curved up in a wry smile. "I think you understand very well what I mean. I get you, and you get . . . your precious fish."

Her lips—full, rosy, moist—now gaped. "Do you dare to propose what I *think* you are proposing?"

He responded by lifting his hand to her face, pressing his palm lightly against her cheek and running his thumb across her bottom lip. That simple touch of her skin stirred his blood to a simmer. He could feel himself warming, wanting.

"Shall I say it plainly?" he murmured. "I propose to

have your virtue . . . or I will have Ashwood. The choice is yours."

Her lovely eyes widened, but she did not faint or cry out with alarm. Once again, she surprised him by holding her ground. "Get your hands off me," she said low.

Tobin removed his hand from her face. But he put it on her waist and pulled her close. Lily's hands flew up between them, but he ignored them. The scent of flowers on this cold, wet day filled his senses; her body felt warm and lithe in his arms. Tobin could not resist her—he bent his head and touched his lips to hers, his tongue teasing the seam of them. He hardened more and would have carried on, but Lily twisted away from him and pressed her hand to her mouth, wiping his kiss from her lips in outrage.

"Then I suppose it will be Ashwood," he said.

"You sir, are no gentleman," she said, her voice shaking.

"I never claimed to be. But have you considered that might make me the most exciting lover of all?"

"I've had enough of your boorish behavior," she said and turned to leave, but Tobin suddenly caught her by the waist and pulled her back into his chest before she could stop him. He brushed his lips against the top of her ear. "Think about it, Lily," he murmured. "Think long . . . and hard," he whispered, and touched his lips to her neck.

He could feel her body tense, could feel her skin

heat beneath his mouth. But she peeled his arm from her waist and stepped away. "I do not wish to bed you, Tobin. I wish to bury you."

Tobin remained impassive, as if it meant nothing to him, belying the desire raging in his blood. "Those are my terms, Lily. The choice is yours."

She turned about, her cloak sweeping a wide circle as she walked determinedly to the door, starting when she saw MacKenzie standing just inside, looking half drowned. But she swept past him and went out into the rain.

Tobin had not heard MacKenzie enter; he walked to his friend's side and they both watched Lily run out across the paving stones to her carriage, and the carriage pull away from the house quickly. Only then did Tobin glance at MacKenzie, who was standing with one hand in the pocket of his buckskins, the queue of his long hair wet and dripping, his gray eyes hooded. "Always had a way with the lassies, did ye no' Scottie?"

Tobin smiled.

MacKenzie squinted out the door as the carriage pulled away. "But I think you play with fire there, lad."

"Yes," Tobin agreed. "I enjoy the feel of the flames licking at my body."

MacKenzie laughed heartily and clapped him on the shoulder. "Have you whiskey for me, then? I'm chilled to the bloody bone."

SIX

The storm continued to rage outside while Lily paced in front of the hearth in her suite, her long braid draped over her shoulder, her dressing gown dragging on the floor behind her.

She was appalled at Tobin, shocked by the casual way he'd proposed such a vile thing . . . but at the same time, she was entirely, imprudently, aroused by it. That was perhaps what made her the angriest—that something about him had the capacity to arouse her deepest senses. God in heaven! She'd never known another man like him, someone who just took what he wanted. He'd kissed her without invitation—no request or apology, had just *kissed* her.

She should be furious with him, irate! And she was, she *was* . . . but she kept thinking about the boy she'd known. She could see that boy in his face now, although his complexion was a bit darker from the sun, with faint white lines fanning out from the corners of his eyes. She couldn't help but be curious about his life, and how his father's death must have affected him.

A jolt of memory, another flash incongruent with what she thought she knew. She suddenly remembered a day when she and Tobin had been in the gardens playing—pirates, she thought, one of her favorite childhood games of make-believe. She'd made him be the marauding pirate, and she the heroic captain who jumped off the quarterdeck to slay him. Tobin had been very good at falling and playing dead. But on that particular day, they'd both been startled by the sound of a man and woman arguing. Had it been Aunt Althea and Mr. Scott? More likely it had been Aunt Althea and the earl, for they'd seemed to be in a constant state of battle. But Tobin had made her go down to the lake so they would not be able to hear it. He'd protected her from it.

Lily shook the memory away. He was not the same person as that boy had been. The man he had become had no right to treat her as he had today, and she wanted to hate him. But she kept thinking of his breath warm on her ear, and the feel of his body so close, so firmly against her, almost dwarfing her. She kept seeing that ruggedly handsome face above her, his mouth as arousing as it had been today on her skin—

"*Stop!*" she chided herself, covering her ears with her hands. "God forgive you, Lily Boudine, for what you are thinking!" She lowered her hands and stared into the fire. She had best think of what to do with Tobin if she wanted to save Ashwood. She could not appeal to him on the grounds of decency. Nothing moved him, nothing seemed to sway him, other than lust.

"Then what in blazes am I to do?" she murmured.

Once, when Lily had just arrived in Ireland, and the news had come that her beloved aunt Althea had drowned, Lily had been despondent. She'd taken to her bed, mourning her deep loss. But after a day of it, Aunt Lenore had sat on her bed, had picked Lily up and hugged her, and told Lily she was so very sorry that she'd lost her dearest aunt, but that now was the time she must get up and get on with life. "Althea wouldn't have it any other way," she'd said. "She would want you to get up, gather all your wits about you, and do what you must to survive without her. Think of that, Lily darling. Think of what you must do to survive—and not how very sad you are."

Survive. Lily had to do that now: think of what she must do to survive without Althea, without Lenore, without even Keira to help her. There were so many souls depending on her that she did not have the luxury or time to be sad or bewildered. But what could she *do*?

Think.

Tobin obviously enjoyed her discomfit. He seemed to believe that he could intimidate her with his brazen talk. Why did men always believe a look, or a kiss, would entice a woman to abandon her virtue? They all thought themselves grand lovers, capable of seducing the gown off any woman—

An idea suddenly came to her. An awful, impractical, ill-advised, imprudent idea. Lily suddenly paused in her pacing.

What she was thinking was so bold that she could scarcely believe she was considering it. Tobin had given her what he believed was an impossible bargain. And she would *never* give in to such an immoral demand, for she was a woman of proper morals, a countess with a reputation to uphold.

But that did not mean she couldn't use his debauchery to her advantage. Mr. Fish had said they needed six months to turn the fields to make up for the loss of the hundred acres, and that it was imperative that they keep their tenants to help sow and harvest those fields. And in six months, their mill would be operating before Tobin's was even completed. So somehow, Lily had to make Tobin believe that for six months, he'd won.

What if . . . what if she allowed him to believe she had taken his offer and was giving herself in exchange for Ashwood? But how could she do that without actually sacrificing her virtue? And more importantly, draw it out for six long months?

Lily pondered this idea. Six months seemed an awfully long time to play a dangerous game with a dangerous man, and she had no doubts that he could be quite dangerous in this regard. But she also recalled what Mr. Fish had said to her—that any man worth his salt would fall in love with her, given the slightest bit of encouragement. It was heady praise, but was it fair? If it *was* fair, then what if . . . what if Tobin fell in love with her?

Lily slowly sank down on her chaise. *Am I capable of such trickery?* She was not Keira, who enjoyed toying with men. Yet she wasn't unpracticed in the art of holding a gentleman's attention, either. She and Keira had made a sport of it in Ireland, and Lily had perfected the skill in Italy. She had the sort of physical attributes men generally admired, and it would be disingenuous to feign ignorance of her ability to draw men to her. Why, in Italy alone, in addition to Mr. Canavan, she'd had two gentlemen who had been keen to court her, and she'd juggled them all expertly across the Italian countryside. Was Tobin so different from them?

He was unlike any other man she'd ever known. Yet she knew him in a way that she did not know any other gentleman. She'd known Tobin when he'd been a guileless, thoughtful boy. Surely that boy was still present in some part of him.

And Lily had felt his desire simmering in the way he had stood so close to her, had touched his lips to her skin, had kissed her mouth. "Lord," she murmured and restlessly put her hand to her nape, recalling the tension between them.

Was she overestimating her appeal? Did she truly have the power to beguile him? Lily tried to imagine flirting with Tobin and groaned softly. "What do you think, that he will crumble at your feet?" She snorted and stared up at the painted garlands and trees and birds on the ceiling.

She was completely mad to even imagine it, but yet again, she had everything to lose if she didn't try. She had to at least *try* to avert her destruction without losing herself completely. Perhaps she could win. Perhaps, at the very least, she could rekindle their friendship. Surely that childhood attachment still existed within him. Surely all things were possible.

With a sigh, Lily closed her eyes. "Lord save me—if not from my enemies, then at least from myself," she whispered.

∞

The problem chased Lily through that night and into the following day. She was reviewing the books, looking for anything that might help them, when she heard the sound of gunfire. She glanced toward the window. "What is that?" she asked Preston, the footman who attended her.

"Hunters, I should think, mu'um."

But . . . Mr. Bevers was in Hadley Green today. There was no one who would be hunting without him. "Oh, no," she said and abruptly stood. "No, no, *no.*"

"Madam?" Preston said, looking alarmed.

"Can you shoot?"

"Shoot?" He seemed puzzled by the question, but nodded. "Aye, mu'um."

"Splendid. You and Louis shall meet me at the stables with guns and any men who can be spared," she said as she strode from the room. "We are going to put and end to some poaching!"

A quarter of an hour later she marched across the lawn to the stables, dressed in a riding habit. Preston, Louis, and a stable boy were present, busily saddling horses. It was not precisely the army Lily had hoped for, but it would have to do. She was not going to allow Tobin to poach her grouse.

She picked up a flintlock pistol from a table where the guns had been laid and held it up, giving it a look.

"Beg your pardon, mu'um, but do you know how to shoot?" Louis asked her.

"No."

"May I?" he asked, holding his hand out for the gun. Lily obliged him, and Louis emptied the gun of any lead. At Lily's look of surprise, he said, "Most times, showing is enough. Any shooting needs to be done, I'll do it, milady." He handed her the gun.

Armed with a useless gun, Lily and her little army rode west into the forest, following the sound of the shots they'd heard fired. When they reached the top of the path where the forest broke, they paused to listen. The distant sound of voices reached them. "To the right," Preston said.

They picked their way through a thick copse of

trees, and as they approached a clearing, they could see the men gathered in the center, one of them holding up a dead grouse.

And there, sitting high on a big gray horse, was Tobin.

Lily's anger soared. She took her empty pistol in hand and spurred her horse hard, sending it careening down the path into the clearing.

Hearing the commotion as Lily broke the tree line, her men behind her, the four poachers wheeled their mounts about. Lily reined up hard and leveled her pistol at Tobin's chest.

"Bloody hell," one of his friends said.

Tobin looked surprised, but almost amused. His eyes shone with what almost looked like pleasure. And just like that, all of Lily's bravado began to leak out of her. *Pick yourself up,* she heard her aunt Lenore say, and she lifted her chin, held her gun in two hands to keep from shaking, and said, "Put your hands in the air."

Tobin glanced over his shoulder at his companions, then turned back to Lily with a grin. "Is that gun primed to shoot?"

"Do you really care to find out? Please put your hands in the air."

Tobin chuckled—until Preston cocked his gun and pointed at him. "Kindly do as the lady asks, milord."

Still chuckling, Tobin lifted his hands. "Gentlemen," he said casually, his gaze unflinchingly on Lily's face, "you have before you the Lady Ashwood."

Lily recognized Mr. Sibley and the dark-headed, handsome fellow with the amused smile who had witnessed Tobin's impossible offer last night. She did not know the large, beefy gentleman, nor did she wish to.

"A pleasure to make your acquaintance," the dark-haired man said in a Scots accent and with a smile. Mr. Sibley nodded curtly but eyed her as if he were facing her in mortal combat. The other gentleman looked entirely disinterested.

"Now that we have dispensed with the niceties, perhaps you might explain why you have brought your guns," Tobin suggested.

"Well, sir, I hope you are not very disappointed with your efforts at poaching, as the grouse at Ashwood are rather thin this year."

Tobin laughed. "You may put your gun down, madam. We are not poaching your grouse."

"Then I suppose that is a fox I see your friend holding?"

Tobin's mouth spread into a grin of great amusement, the bloody rooster. "Please do put down your gun, Lady Ashwood, before you harm yourself or someone else. We will leave the grouse to you and ride on."

"I, for one, could eat a full grouse, feathers and all," the large, disinterested man said.

If Tobin thought he would dismiss her, he was entirely mistaken, for now his gall fueled her. He hunted at Ashwood because he mistakenly believed it was his all but for the taking. She half-cocked her gun;

Tobin's eyes flew to it. "If you would like permission to hunt game at Ashwood, you may come and apply to me, as do all the gentry in Sussex."

The dark-haired man laughed heartily at that as he bagged the grouse he was holding.

But Tobin lowered his hands and stacked them on the pommel of his saddle, leaning forward. "And if I do not?"

Now Louis cocked his gun, too, and when he did, the dark-haired man and the large one pulled their guns and pointed them back. Lily's heart began to pound. She believed in a moment of sheer panic that it was possible they'd all be gunned down.

But Tobin had his gaze locked on hers, and he moved his horse a few steps forward, as if oblivious to the three guns pointed at him.

"Stand back, sir!" Louis said sternly.

Tobin ignored him. "And if I do not?" he asked Lily again.

"If you do not," Lily said, her voice surprisingly clear and even, "the next time we will not hesitate to shoot you, without warning, as is our right."

Tobin's gaze was so intent that she feared he could see her heart beating in her chest. "I have dispensa-tion—"

"Not at Ashwood," she interjected.

His gaze narrowed; he nodded. "Very well."

Was that it, then? Had she stopped them from poaching? She slowly lowered her gun. "Then we shall allow you to pass." She glanced at Louis. "Will you and Preston please see them to their side of the forest?" She reined her horse around, nodded at the stable boy, and used her crop to urge the horse to go.

She rode hard, almost giddy with relief. She had no idea if she'd won this battle or not, but she'd certainly let him know he could not intimidate her.

She arrived back at Ashwood and hopped down from her mount, smiling as she handed the reins to the boy. "Quite a lot of excitement, was it not?"

"Aye, mu'um," he said, his eyes glittering.

With her crop in hand, Lily bounced up the steps to the main entrance. She heard a rider and turned around halfway up the stairs, all smiles, prepared to congratulate Preston and Louis on their show of might. But her smile faded.

It was Tobin thundering into her drive.

She watched him throw himself off his horse and come striding forward, his cloak billowing out behind him, worried that he would laugh at her, or worse, humiliate her or demand to ruin her straightaway. She'd even dreamed about it—of him, towering over her in the grand foyer of Tiber Park, demanding she remove her clothes—

Be brave. Above all, do not allow him to see your nerves. For then he would swoop in for the kill, she was certain of it.

He came to a halt at the bottom of the steps and, with hands on hips, he stared up at her.

"You wished to see me?" she asked politely.

"*See* you? What in bloody hell were you doing out there with a gun?" he demanded. "Have you no more care for your life than that?"

"I was protecting what is mine."

He blinked. "You foolish woman, you might have been killed!" he snapped.

"But I wasn't," she said calmly. "You wanted a word?"

He stared at her. "A word," he repeated, and stepped onto the first step. "It seems to me we've had our words, have we not?" He moved up another step.

"I think you left a few words lingering in your foyer, did you not?"

That certainly caught his attention. "Meaning?" He took another step up.

"I want you to stay off my land."

One corner of his mouth turned up. "And you think your empty gun will stop me?"

She drew a breath and looked him directly in the eye. This gamble would either win or lose Ashwood, but there was no going back now. "No," she said. "But I have thought about your rather rude offer and have decided to accept it."

Lily took great satisfaction in the astonishment in Tobin's maple brown eyes. He peered closely at her as if he thought she was bluffing. "And what offer would that be?" he challenged her.

Oh, but if he thought she'd crumble *now* . . . "Have

you forgotten? I am referring to your terms," she said, her gaze narrowing, "for leaving Ashwood *be*."

Tobin eyed her skeptically, his gaze raking over her. "Do my ears deceive me, madam? Is this your idea of a jest?"

"Was your offer a jest?" she returned pertly.

Tobin looked away from her a moment. He removed his hat from his head and dragged his fingers through his hair, then reseated the hat and glanced at Lily again, his expression now full of curiosity.

She was standing two steps above him, a head taller than he. She gripped her riding crop so tightly that her fingers ached. She wanted to strike him with it, to leave a mark on his face so he would be reminded of her ire every blasted day.

Tobin took the next step up. They were only inches apart now. "How could you *possibly* misconstrue my offer?" he asked, as if speaking to a child.

"What makes you believe I have misconstrued anything? You offered to leave Ashwood alone if you could have me. I accept your offer."

Tobin looked stunned. "Lily," he said with all seriousness, "do you understand what you are agreeing to? Do you understand that I mean to have your virtue? And by that, I meant to have it in the most intimate way a man might have a woman?"

She flushed. "I understand that you intend to ruin me one way or another. Am I wrong? Or are you afraid of victory?"

She saw one of his hands slowly curl into a fist and realized she had gained the upper hand. Just as she'd guessed, he'd never dreamed she would agree, and now he didn't quite know what to do with her. "You gave me an ultimatum," she pressed on, "and I have made my choice."

He took another step up so that they were now eye to eye. They stood so close that she could see the flecks of green in his rich brown eyes. His gaze roamed over her face as if it puzzled him.

"How do I ask this without offending your tender nature?" he said. "Do you understand *precisely* what you are agreeing to? Do you understand that I mean to *bed* you?"

Lily was certain her cheeks were flaming now. "Yes," she said, her voice uncontrollably breathless. "I understand completely."

One of his brows rose high. He didn't look surprised any longer; he looked intrigued. "I don't believe you. This is some attempt to fool me, but it will not work."

Don't falter now! "I am attempting to save Ashwood. Perhaps *you* are the one who is jesting."

Something flickered in his eyes. A slow smile spread his lips. "If you mean what you say, prove it."

Prove it? How was she to prove it? Lily panicked, but she forced a sweet smile. "Shall I offer you my head on a platter? Would that do?"

Tobin grinned, his gaze on her mouth. "Now that

would be a tragic waste of a lovely head. I had in mind something infinitely more pleasurable for us both. Prove that you mean what you say here and now."

That Lily managed to remain standing was nothing short of a miracle. She couldn't believe he would insist on this *now,* in front of her home. She thought frantically and, in a moment of genius inspiration, smiled coyly at him. "Now you are taking the fun from it. That hardly seems fair."

He chuckled. "Fair is not a word generally applied to war," he said and put his hand on her arm.

She tried not to tense, to keep the smile on her face. "Then we agree—we are at war."

Tobin ran his hand lightly up her arm, to her neck. "We certainly are not in love." He touched his lips to her earlobe.

The touch burned through her, and she tried to tamp it down. "If I agree to kiss you, will that appease you for now?"

"Lily, love . . . you will barter with me?" he asked low, and kissed her neck.

God help her, she could feel her body beginning to soften. "Yes," she said breathlessly. "And besides, my groomsman is just there."

Tobin lifted his head and frowned in the direction of the boy brushing her horse. "A kiss then," he said.

"Then we are agreed?"

"Yes, yes, all right," he said impatiently.

Lily smiled sweetly. He reached for her again, but she planted a hand firmly against his chest.

"What in blazes is it now?" he demanded gruffly.

"I am to kiss *you*," she reminded him, and with her gaze on his, she put her hands on his arms and slowly slid them up, to his shoulders. She rose up on her tiptoes, cupped his face in her hands, and touched her lips to his so softly that it felt almost as if she whispered against him. The touch was astonishingly exquisite, an ethereal promise of greater pleasure. Lily couldn't imagine a light kiss could burn as brightly as hers did, and she lingered there a moment, her lips against his, the tip of her tongue touching him.

But as he tried to put his arms around her, Lily returned to her heels and evaporated away from him. "That's all for now."

His gaze was blisteringly hot, but he did not argue. And in that moment, Lily realized with a surge of elation that she had won this all-important round between them.

Tobin stepped back. He nodded curtly. "Well played, madam," he conceded.

"Good day," she said and started up the steps, intending to race to the safety of her rooms once she got inside. But she hadn't made it more than two steps when Tobin caught her arm.

"You will dine with me."

The last thing she wanted was to dine with him!

She could imagine it, forced to make small talk over soup and her grouse. It would be no worse than torture. "Ah—"

"Friday evening."

Lily smiled.

Tobin looked strangely uneasy. "It is the most civilized way we might begin our arrangement," he said, his gaze lingering on her mouth.

She had done it. She'd started down the path of either her complete ruination or a very clever ruse. "Very well," she said pleasantly. "I shall dine with you Friday evening."

"I will send a coach for you."

"That won't be necessary—"

"It is entirely necessary," he said. His color was returning, but his expression looked odd. "I'll not have your man lurking about, waiting to save you."

Lily looked at *his* mouth a moment. "Do I need saving?" she asked softly.

Tobin took a full, long look at her. "I cannot say. I have not determined if this is some foolish game you are playing. But rest assured that I would show you pleasure unlike anything your maidenly mind has ever imagined. I will not take you against your will . . . unless that is what you prefer. Some enjoy being conquered completely; others prefer to do the conquering. Which, I wonder, is Lily Boudine?"

Lily did not speak. She couldn't speak. There wasn't

a thought in her head, nothing but those eyes drawing her in to a very carnal fantasy.

"Ah. You don't know, do you?" He smiled and brushed her cheek with the back of his knuckles. Tobin's eyes had softened with a look of desire she had not seen before this moment. "I will allow you to come to that knowledge on your own. But you have made an agreement here today, and if you think to deceive me, it will go much worse for you. Are we clear?"

Lily's pulse pounded so strongly she feared she might come out of her skin. It was a peculiar feeling, to be so angry and so lustful at once. "I am more than clear, sir. Are you certain *you* are so clear?" She walked past him, her shoulder brushing against his cloak.

Lily had no idea how she managed to get into her house. She only knew that she was desperate to know if he watched her go.

∽

Tobin rode away from Ashwood, his breath growing shorter. He rode until Ashwood was out of sight, then reined up, leapt off his horse, and braced himself against a tree, gasping for breath.

God in heaven, what was this evil that plagued him?

It was too warm; he suddenly grabbed at his neck-cloth, loosening it.

He could scarcely believe what had just happened. That little fool had chosen her *ruin* over Ashwood? He should have tasted victory on his lips, knowing that his desire for revenge was at hand . . . but he didn't feel that in the least. He felt out of breath and oddly unsettled, as if this plague on him had sunk its roots deeper, tangling with his guts.

How could she agree? Ridiculous woman!

He was suddenly reminded of a spring day many years ago, when he and Lily were children. He'd been charged with looking after her, and they'd gone up to the abandoned cottage at Uppington Church. Lily had been infatuated with that musty, old, one-room cottage. She'd built little fantasies around it—one day it was a castle, the next a seaside fortress, the next a hovel where a princess of magic hid her talents. She would summon faeries to help her fight the evil forces when needed.

Tobin was older and had found her games rather tedious at times. He recalled her ceaseless chatter and how he'd generally spent his time with her engaged in his own idle pursuits. Whittling, throwing rocks at various targets, reading.

On that particular afternoon, Lily had fancied herself a warrior princess and, if memory served, marauding Vikings had beset her. It was a warm spring day, and she'd discarded her cloak and bonnet so that she might dash around and jab at the invisible Vikings with the sword she'd fashioned from a stick. Tobin had positioned himself on a rock, where he'd worked on the horse he'd been carving while keeping a watchful eye on the little hellion. However, he'd managed to lose track of her and had been startled when she'd called out, her voice coming from somewhere above him. Tobin had looked up to see her straddling a tree limb high above him, her booted feet dangling and her so-called sword stuffed into the sash of her frock.

"Bloody hell," Tobin had muttered. "What are you doing up there? You could fall and break your neck!"

"I won't fall."

"Come down," he'd said sternly, pointing to the ground. "Come down at once."

"Why?" she'd demanded, as if it were perfectly reasonable to have climbed so high.

"You are too high. Come down!"

"It's not so very high," she'd argued from her perch. "I can climb much higher."

"Then your fall will be even greater, and you will break your neck and your arms and your legs, and *I* shall be punished for it! Come down at once, Miss Boudine. I command you to come down!"

She'd laughed at him. "*You* cannot command me. I am allowed to do as I please, and *you* may not tell me how high I may go."

"Then I will not help you if you are stuck," he'd said angrily.

"Then I shall rescue myself. I am a princess warrior and I could jump if I wanted to."

"God help me, don't jump," Tobin had said nervously, positioning himself beneath the tree just in case she'd tried it. But Lily had started to slowly inch her way back on the limb. He'd cringed when she'd faltered and almost lost her balance. He'd groaned beneath his breath as he'd watched her stockings catch on the tree bark and tear. And he'd felt his heart skip a beat when she'd paused with a soft cry to study what Tobin had presumed was a cut in the palm of her hand.

By the time she'd shimmied down to where he'd been able to reach her and haul her to the ground, her frock had been soiled and torn, her hair had come undone from its braids, and her hand had been bleeding.

He'd clucked at her as he'd wrapped his handkerchief around her hand. "You've gone and done it now, haven't you?"

"Done what?" she'd asked, blinking up at him with big green eyes.

"For heaven's sake, Lily, do you understand anything at all? I'm to look after you."

"Why?"

"Because girls need looking after."

She'd seemed completely baffled by that. "I don't need looking after."

He'd scoffed at that. "*You* more than anyone. Most girls are not so foolish as to climb to the highest part of the tree."

"You may not look after me, Tobin Scott! I shall look after myself!" she'd stubbornly insisted.

"Well, her ladyship and my father do not agree that you may look after yourself."

He recalled the surprise in her expression, as if it had been the first time she'd realized he'd not accompanied her merely because he'd enjoyed her company. She'd yanked her hand from his and said, "I don't *need* looking after. I'm an orphan, and orphans look after themselves!" She'd run from him then, and with a sigh of exasperation, Tobin had gone after her.

She had seemed to believe that the rules did not apply to her, and apparently she still believed it. For no woman in her sound mind would have agreed to his outrageous proposition.

Lily was sorely mistaken if she thought she could sway him, or worse, trick him somehow. She would come to rue her decision—for there was nothing that would stop him from having his revenge now.

SEVEN

Lily had a collapse of confidence that afternoon in the privacy of her rooms. She berated herself for having been so foolish as to believe she could best Tobin. With scarcely a touch from him, she had felt herself begin to weaken. If he kissed her, truly kissed her, would she swoon? Abandon all her defenses? She had to keep him at arm's length, but how would she do that?

"Flirt, muirnín."

She heard Keira's voice as clearly as if her cousin was standing beside her. She was suddenly reminded of an afternoon in Ireland several years ago, when Keira had blithely advised her about a gentleman whom Lily had found attractive. "Give him a promise," Keira had said as she'd lain on Lily's bed, her hands folded behind her head. "Gentlemen like the chase."

"And how do you know this?" Lily had asked dubiously.

Keira had shrugged. "I just do."

Perhaps Tobin enjoyed the chase. If he did, then Lily could still direct the dangerous game she was playing. She was quite accomplished at flirting, was she not? She convinced herself she was . . . until the middle of the night, when she awoke in a panic at what she'd done.

But if she needed any more convincing that she had to flirt and tease her way out of this predicament, Mr. Fish unwittingly provided the reason.

After he and Lily reviewed the sad state of the estate finances the following day, he glanced sidelong at Lily. "I hope you will forgive me, madam, but I have done a bit of inquiring on your behalf."

"Regarding?"

"Titled men," Mr. Fish said stiffly. "It occurred to me that there is a titled man in our midst, and as it turns out, he will inherit quite a lot. Lord Horncastle is—"

"Never!" Lily cried, surging to her feet. She couldn't imagine anything worse than facing that idiotic young man every day.

"All right, I understand," Mr. Fish said, sounding a bit impatient.

"Mr. Fish, how long have you been married?"

He looked confused by her question. "Nineteen years, mu'um."

"Children?"

"Five."

Lily nodded. "And how did you make Mrs. Fish's acquaintance?"

Mr. Fish blinked. "The usual way, I suppose. We were introduced by mutual friends."

"You have what I want, sir. You have a wife whom you love, who has borne you five children. I should like to find a husband in a similar fashion, with similar feelings."

Mr. Fish smiled sadly. "I beg your pardon, Lady Ashwood, but that is not your luxury. Women in your position must marry to maintain their position. It is not a love match, it is a match of fortune and standing—for the sake of your holdings."

"But I do not want to marry for the sake of my holdings."

"Many have before you. Kings and queens, and they've managed to find some happiness. And I fear that you really must be quick about it. We've not much time before Eberlin manages to do more harm."

"Sir." Lily put her hand on his arm. "I value your advice more than I can express. But in this, you must trust that I know what I am doing." That was a lie, of course.

But not entirely. She could not sit idly by while Tobin tried to spread rumors that her cattle were diseased, and God knew what else. So early on Friday evening, while Lucy played dress-up in one of Lily's older gowns and a bonnet, Lily dressed for supper at Tiber Park.

She held out two gowns to Lucy—one a forest green organdy over velvet; the other a pale gold brocade. "Which do you prefer?" she asked the girl.

Lucy stopped in her examination of Lily's jewelry box and eyed the two gowns critically. "This one," she said, pointing to the green.

"Excellent choice," Lily agreed, and with the help of her maid, Ann, she dressed. The gown was quite tight; Lily had to take a breath so that Ann could fasten the last button. Her breasts were barely contained within the low bodice.

"Quite stunning, mu'um," Ann remarked.

Lily wondered how she could think so with her décolletage so prominently displayed. "It is very tight," she complained.

"The pretend countess wore her gowns quite tight because she said gentlemen prefer to see a lady's figure at its best advantage," Lucy said. "She very much liked to present her figure."

Lily snorted. "Darling, I think you will discover that Lady Donnelly enjoys presenting herself in any number of ways."

Behind Lily, Ann giggled.

"I didn't recall this gown being quite so *tight*," Lily said again, tugging at the bodice a little as she observed herself in the mirror. But then again, the last time she'd worn it had been in Italy, and she certainly had not lacked for gentlemen's attention. "There is an emerald pendant in the box," she said, gesturing to her jewelry box. "And some tipped hairpins. Lucy, darling, will you fetch them for me?"

When she'd finished dressing, Lily wore a pearl-drop emerald that sparkled at the hollow of her throat, emeralds that dangled from her ears, and green crystal hairpins seeded throughout her hair. She ran her hands down her sides, nervous.

When the footman announced a coach had arrived for her, Lily realized there was no avoiding the wheels she'd set in motion and hoped she was not churned to bits by them. She said goodnight to Lucy and Ann, donned her cloak, and went off to wage her private war.

EIGHT

Early Friday evening, Tobin studied his reflection in the long mirror. He wore formal clothing this evening—black superfine, long tails, a white silk waistcoat and black silk neckcloth. It was the sort of garb one might wear to a foreign palace or a London ball, not to an intimate supper party with one guest.

Tobin did not care. He would have Lily know that he was a man of extraordinary means. He would draw her in, entice her with shiny things and formalities and seduce her slowly into his bed. He intended to possess her completely, and just thinking about how he might do that made his blood rush hot.

He smoothed his hair back from his forehead. It was the color of dark honey, not pale blonde, like Charity's and Catherine's. His skin had been darkened by the years spent on various ship decks. He was not quite thirty, but he looked weathered, as if he'd been reared in the Leeward Islands instead of tranquil England.

There were faint nicks and scars in his skin, small testaments to the hardship of his life. Just below his right ear was a small, thin white line from a knife during a particularly memorable brawl in Portugal. It matched a longer scar on his back. On his finger were tiny faint marks, from the nasty bite of a volatile Italian beauty a year or so ago. She had not approved of his leaving port without her and had tried to keep his finger as a souvenir of their heated affair.

Even with the nicks of his life marking his skin, Tobin supposed he was as presentable as any dandy in Paris and London—at least as presentable as the sort of bland fop Lily undoubtedly was on course to marry one day. But even bland fops would not forgive her ruination. How ironic, that Lily would be left with nothing but an empty title when he was through with her, while his title was as meaningless as the paper it was written upon.

Tobin stared coldly at his reflection. *Rise up. Press on.* That was his mantra, which he'd begun to chant to himself when he'd found himself fatherless. *Rise up, press on. Don't think overmuch. Don't feel. Rise up, press on. Harder, stronger than before.*

"My lord . . . your handkerchief," his valet said, presenting him with a freshly ironed linen.

Tobin turned away from the mirror, took it from the valet's hand, and wordlessly left his suite of rooms.

He went directly to the yellow salon, where he would receive his guest. It was small in comparison to others, and it was here he would share an intimate meal with Lily. A table for two had been set near the hearth. Thanks to Carlson's attentions, the room was in pristine condition. The flowers had been brought up from the hothouse and arranged in large bouquets that dripped blooms of red, pink, and yellow. The furnishings, recently arrived from Italy, were set upon his new, Belgian wool rug. The draperies, delivered last week, had been hung, and heavy gold rope sashes held them back so that the view of the courtyard, already ablaze with torchlights, could be viewed.

The Louis IV table was covered in Swedish linen. The place settings of fine bone china shimmered in the low candlelight, as did the silver, which was polished to such a degree that Tobin could see his reflection in the wide soupspoon.

Pleased with the setting, he signaled at a footman standing at attention near the door to pour him a tot of whiskey. He tossed that down in the way he'd learned to do as a boy on his first voyage. The sailors made a devilish concoction from stuff scraped from the bottom of barrels and brewed on the ship's deck. Tossing it quickly down one's throat reduced the burn. These days, the whiskey Tobin drank from crystal tots was the finest Scotch whiskey available. It didn't burn, but old habits died hard.

The warmth of the whiskey had just begun to seep into his veins when Carlson entered and bowed. "The Lady Ashwood has arrived."

Tobin felt a tiny twinge in his chest, and, for a moment, he feared the fever would spread into his bones and his body would betray him. But it passed as quickly as it had come. "Bring her."

He walked to the hearth where a fire blazed, then stood with his legs braced apart and his hands behind his back. He was uncommonly restless, which he found mildly surprising, since he was no stranger to women. Yet he'd never felt quite like this—

She swept in behind Carlson on a cloud of rich, forest green velvet and organza, and Tobin had to remind himself to breathe. Lily had grown into a stunning woman; the rowdy little girl she'd once been was now a woman of exceptional poise. He'd never expected to find such an alluring woman when he'd come here. Quite the opposite.

The color in her cheeks was high and her pale green eyes were glittering. She regarded him with the cool confidence of a woman who knew she was admired.

Tobin bowed. "Welcome to Tiber Park."

She said nothing.

Tobin walked forward, took her hand, and bowed over it, kissing her knuckles. "May I say that you look beautiful this evening."

The color in her cheeks deepened. She glanced sidelong at Carlson.

"You may leave us for now," Tobin said, and Carlson walked obediently from the room, leaving a single footman standing attentively near the door.

"Please do come in," Tobin said, sweeping his hand toward a pair of chairs before the hearth. "This is the yellow salon, so named because one can see yellow roses in bloom from the windows."

Still, Lily did not move or speak. Her gaze was wandering the room, taking in the furnishings. To a casual observer she looked serene, perfectly at ease, yet her gloved hands were tightly clasped before her.

"I have some very fine French wine that I brought to England before the French blockade," he said. "Perhaps you would like a taste of it to calm your nerves."

She affixed him with a prim look. "What makes you believe I need to be calmed?"

"Aha . . . so you do speak after all." He smiled and nodded at the footman. "Then a glass of wine to warm you."

"Nor do I need to be warmed. Your coachman was most attentive and your coach very nicely heated."

"I am happy to hear it," he said with an incline of his head.

The footman delivered a glass of wine to Lily on a silver tray. "Thank you," she said softly.

"Please be seated," Tobin invited her, gesturing again to the two winged-back chairs before the hearth.

Lily hesitated, then moved around one chair and perched delicately on the edge of it. She planted both feet firmly on the ground, her back as straight as a ruler. She looked positioned to dart to the door should the need arise.

But Tobin was not an animal, and he would not take his revenge by force. He much preferred to see her crawling to him, begging for his attention.

He flipped his tails and sat on the other chair, sinking back and making himself comfortable.

Lily glanced up, staring curiously at the painting above the mantel. It was a courtly scene in which a young king was the center of attention in a sea of people.

"Is that a Van Dyke?" she asked.

Tobin had no idea who the artist was—he'd bought the painting from a failing estate in England. That was the trouble with being a self-made man—he'd missed instruction in the finer aspects of life, such as the names of renowned artists. He could well imagine that Lily had studied art in some tranquil setting at an age when Charity had been emptying chamber pots. "Are you a connoisseur of art?" he asked.

"Very superficially," she said. "But my uncle has a pair of Van Dykes, and I thought I recognized the style." Her shoulders lifted and fell with a small sigh and she looked down at her glass of wine.

"Do you find the wine to your liking?" Tobin asked wryly.

She smiled. "Does it matter?"

"Pardon?"

Lily put the glass aside and shifted that smile to him. "Forgive me for being frank, but it seems to me, since you have tossed down a gauntlet and I have picked it up, that trivial talk is rather pointless."

Surprised by that, Tobin gave her a wry smile. "I would agree. What would you like to discuss that is less trivial?"

"Actually," she said, sitting a little straighter if that were even possible, "if you wouldn't mind terribly, I am brimming with questions."

Tobin cocked his head to one side. "About?"

"About . . . everything. *You*, of course," she said and leaned slightly forward.

Her demeanor reminded him of the girl she'd been, always quite earnest. *You must be the king, Tobin. Queens have kings, and you may sit there on the rock if you like. That will be your throne. Your throne is not as big as my throne, but you don't need a very big one, do you?*

"What about me?" he asked.

"Well . . . you've done very well for yourself."

He shrugged indifferently. "Did you expect less?"

She looked slightly taken aback by his question. "No. I suppose I didn't expect anything at all."

That sounded as if she'd suffered no guilt for what she'd done, that the consequences had not weighed heavily on her heart. Tobin felt a tiny tick in his heart, a warning to remain calm or risk the bloody spell. He silently cursed his body and willed himself to hold it at bay.

"No?" he asked with a smile. "Surely you do not mean to say you never wondered what became of Joseph Scott's family . . . do you?"

"No!" she said, looking appropriately horrified by the suggestion. "I have wondered a great deal about that, naturally. I meant only that you were the last person I would ever expect to see after all this time."

"Yet here I am," he said, abruptly stood, and moved to the sideboard. He waved the footman off and pretended to study the bottles there. "I've asked cook to prepare some Scottish venison for us this evening."

"Not grouse?"

He smiled. "Not grouse."

"I have wondered why you came back," she said thoughtfully.

He was feeling a bit clammy. It was too warm in here. "Why not?"

"Precisely because you *have* done so well for yourself. One might think you would prefer to be someplace else, given the events that happened here."

Tobin downed the wine in his glass and poured more. *Rise up. Press on.* "I came back because I had some unfinished business."

"Ah, yes. Ruining Ashwood."

He actually laughed at that and turned to face her. She was smiling, albeit ruefully. "I prefer to call it clearing my father's good name. You do know, do you not, that he didn't steal the jewels for which he was hanged?"

Lily's lashes fluttered; she looked down at her lap, turning her head slightly.

"It would seem that you do," he said quietly as he admired her profile.

"I don't know any such thing at all."

"Well, I do," he said. "What sort of son would I be if I did not wish to restore his good name?" Dwelling on his father's demise created that strange, feverish breathlessness in him. He could feel it churning in his gut. "Perhaps we should move on to more pleasant subjects." Lily. She was far more pleasant, if only to look at.

Tobin felt his body relax a little, and he put aside his wineglass and walked back to his chair. He sat, then reached for her hand, taking it in his. Lily flinched, and held her arm stiffly, but she did not pull her hand away.

Tobin turned her hand over so that her palm was facing up. He could see a patch of her skin through the tiny keyhole where the glove buttoned around her wrist, and he pressed this thumb against it, feeling her pulse flutter like the wings of a small bird. He lifted her hand and blew softly into that little circle of flesh.

When he lowered her hand, Lily was staring at him. "What are you doing?" she asked low.

"Admiring you."

Lily pulled her hand free. "You are so different now, Tobin."

"So are you," he said sincerely.

Lily said nothing to that and continued to study

him. "Have you been to the cottage at Uppington Church since your return?"

"I have ridden by once or twice."

One corner of her mouth curved up. "I have very fond memories of the cottage," she said softly. "Memories of a boy who indulged a silly girl and accepted any part she desired in her little fantasies. You were very kind to me then."

Here it went again, the warmth of his skin, the sign of the spell. He settled back, his gaze on the fire at the hearth. He did not intend to stroll through their shared memories.

"Do you recall? When I desired to play alone, you sat on the rock and read your books. So many books, too—I was always fascinated with your appetite for reading."

"Yes, well, I had the luxury of attending school then." *Breathe.*

"I truly adored you," she said distantly, and sighed. "Were you aware that I did?"

Adored him? "I do not recall that you adored me in the least," he said with a smile. "Perhaps you have imagined so when seeing the cottage after all these years."

"Oh, I've not seen it."

"No?"

She shook her head. "I think I would find it too painful."

Impossible. She had lived a charmed life. "What

could you possibly find painful about your time at Ashwood?"

She looked surprised. "Everything," she said. "It was a time in my life that I cherished. I loved my aunt Althea and my life with her. I loved to play at the cottage, for it was the one place on this earth that I was completely free. And then it was suddenly all gone, and . . . and in a very dreadful way."

Tobin wanted to tell her what was gone for him, and how very dreadful it had been to see his father at the end of a rope. But as the words formed in his head, his throat felt as if it might constrict if he tried, so he remained silent.

"I know it was far worse for you, Tobin," she said. "I cannot imagine how you endured—"

He suddenly sat up and caught her wrist. "Lily . . . do you really think you will dissuade me from our bargain with these memories? They only strengthen my resolve."

Her lips parted with surprise, but she did not respond, for Carlson chose that moment to announce that supper had arrived.

With supreme effort, Tobin calmly rose and offered his hand to Lily. "Shall we dine?"

She reluctantly laid her hand in his. It felt small, its weight ethereal in his palm. Small and breakable, like the rest of her. The warmth in Tobin's blood seeped into his neck and his throat as they moved to the table. He swallowed as he handed her into her chair at the table, then took his chair across from her, gripping the seat to fight down the spell.

He had a moment to collect himself as Carlson swooped in to serve soup. Tobin picked up his spoon. Lily hesitantly did the same. She kept her gaze on her meal, daintily tipping her spoonful of soup into her mouth.

Tobin kept his gaze on her.

She was clearly aware that he did—he could see the color in her swanlike neck, and she shifted in her seat. "The soup is delicious," she said politely. "Who is your cook?"

Who was his cook? He thought he'd met her once. Charity had found her, and Tobin rarely ventured into the kitchens. "She is from London. She cooked at Marlborough House."

Lily's brows rose with surprise. "You lured her away from Marlborough House?"

Tobin lifted his wineglass in a mock toast. "I suppose I have a way of luring women into any number of occupations."

"And a way of boasting about it, too, it would seem."

Tobin couldn't help but laugh.

Carlson appeared to remove the soup bowls, then served plates of venison and roasted potatoes. "I suppose you went to London after that summer?" Lily asked as Carlson busied himself at the sideboard.

Tobin was beginning to find the conversation exasperating. "You insist on this, do you?"

"I would like to know," she said with a slight shrug. "We were companions once."

"Companions!" he scoffed, and swallowed hard.

"Yes," she said, appearing confused by his reaction. "Companions."

Tobin sighed. The woman had no sense of the truth. "Carlson, leave us," he said, drumming his fingers on the table as he waited for his butler and the footman to quit the room. He took a steadying drink of his wine and put aside the goblet. "Very well, Lily. I shall oblige you and your endless questions. What happened to us is the sort of thing that happens to families that have been made pariahs. Obviously there was no work for us in Hadley Green, no income. So my mother moved us to London."

"To live with relatives?"

He laughed. "The relatives wouldn't have us either." He gestured to her plate. "Please," he said, and picked up his fork.

Lily picked hers up, too, but she was still looking at him as if he were some sort of curiosity come out of the Indian markets. "What happened then?" she asked, as if the Scott family had gone to London on holiday.

"What happened then is that my mother took in piecework, but it was a mean income. My young brother, Ruben—the baby, you will recall," he said, glancing at her, "expired from a pleurisy or something like it within the first year, and my mother died shortly thereafter."

She blanched and cast her eyes to her plate. "Oh, dear. I am so very sorry to hear it."

Tobin shrugged. "It was a long time ago," he said, and felt nothing. He'd repeated the story of his family so many times now that he could recite it without emotion.

The black mud in him oozed, shutting out all air and light.

Tobin tasted the venison, thought it was excellently prepared and quite succulent. He paused to sip his wine and noticed that Lily was not eating.

"Is the venison not to your liking?"

She looked at her meal as if she'd only just noticed it. "I am certain it is delicious," she said, and finally forked a bite. "I thought that perhaps . . . might I ask, after your mother died, who took you and your sister in?"

"There was no one to take us in."

Lily had the decency to look appalled at the thought of two children cast out into the world, but still, Tobin felt nothing at all. Nothing. "I could not keep a roof over our heads, as you might imagine," he said cavalierly, then drank more wine. "I took Charity to a church nearby. She was lucky to find work as a scullery girl in some rich man's house."

Lily's eyes widened with astonishment.

"Oh, come now, Lily, don't look so shocked. What did you think might have happened without anyone to provide for us?"

"I-I don't . . . I can't say," she stammered. "Poor Charity."

"You must not fret for her. She was quickly graduated to cleaning chamber pots."

Lily's face fell. "Is she . . . is she well?"

"She no longer cleans chamber pots, if that is your concern. She is well enough, and resides with her daughter Catherine in my Mayfair home."

"Then she is married," Lily said, looking up brightly.

Tobin sighed at Lily's ignorance. "No. She is not married."

Whatever Lily thought of that, she had the good grace to hide it behind a generous swallow of her wine.

"A toast," Tobin said. "To old acquaintances."

"Don't tease me," she murmured. "You may as well tell me what happened to you."

"Me?" He stabbed at his meat. "As I said, I could not keep a roof over my head and I had to find work. I went to the docks looking for it."

"The docks," she repeated, as if testing the word. "Loading things onto ships?"

Here again, her knowledge of the world beyond the ivy-covered walls of privilege was astoundingly thin. "Not loading things, although I would have been happy to do anything for a shilling, I suppose. I went to sea."

"You became a sailor!" She seemed almost pleased.

"Not precisely. I was brought on to assist the ship's

cook. Forced on, I should say. Lone lads on the docks are easy prey."

She frowned. "Is that true? Or do you wish to shock me?"

Tobin said, "I had every intention of getting aboard a ship one way or the other. As it happens, Bolge rescued me from the ruffians who had me."

"Who is Bolge?"

Tobin grinned at the thought of his old protector. "You saw him—the big jolly fellow with the bottomless appetite. At the time, he was a cook who was as dangerous as any man I ever met—with his hands and with his stew."

Before he realized it, Tobin was telling Lily how Bolge had taken him under his wing aboard the *Flying Saxon,* and about his first year aboard the ship. He was surprised that he was talking as much as he was; it was unlike him. But there was something in Lily's expression—interest, sympathy, he hardly knew—that compelled him to tell her more.

He hadn't thought of those years in so long. He told Lily of the awful seasickness he'd suffered as he'd worked to earn his sea legs. And of the malaria that had swept through the crew and had left him and Bolge to work beyond the kitchen, and how he'd learned to trim sails that summer. He told her about some of the ports of call, of the vast world that had opened up before an English boy.

Lily listened, spellbound.

"It's remarkable," she said quietly when he paused, "that you have survived as well as you have."

"By all rights, I should have died many years ago," he agreed. "I knew a few lads who failed to navigate the choppy waters."

Lily ate a few bites, her expression thoughtful. "It astonishes me to know all that has befallen you and to see you now." She smiled at him with an expression full of sympathy—or worse, pity. Tobin did not care for that look. It made him feel weak.

"May I ask, how did you gain all this? And your title?" she asked, gesturing to the room around them.

"I bought it."

She rolled her eyes. "I may be naïve, but I know that titles are not bought and sold."

"You are indeed naïve, madam, for this particular title was bought and sold in Denmark."

She colored slightly, making her complexion look like rose petals in this candlelight. "I see."

"I doubt that you do," he said, leaning back in his chair. "Denmark has been under constant threat of war these last few years. Everyone is desperate for money and will do most anything for it."

"Including selling a title to an Englishman," she said skeptically.

He laughed softly. "It is no man's desire, I assure you. But I made the chap an offer he could not refuse, and then paid a Danish court handsomely to see it done."

"What sort of an estate is it?"

"Of little consequence," Tobin said with a dismissive flick of his wrist. "It was not the estate I wanted but the title."

"But why?" she asked curiously. "You obviously have a great deal of wealth."

He snorted. "Is it not obvious? A title gives me entry into society that I would not otherwise enjoy. It allows me to look into the eyes of the people who condemned my father." Tobin could almost see the light dawning in Lily's eyes before she looked away. "What is it, Lily?" he asked curtly. "Do you disapprove of my methods? I was not so fortunate to have inherited as you were."

"I do not approve or disapprove," she said. "But neither do I hold society in such high regard as you."

He laughed outright at that. "I do not hold society in high regard. Quite the opposite, really."

She looked confused. "Then why would you go to so much trouble to be part of it?"

Explaining his deepest desire to her was futile—she would never understand the desire for redemption, the desire to punish those who had inflicted such hardship on his family. "I won't attempt to make you understand." He smiled. "I am doing you a great favor in that, I assure you."

"I understand that you have suffered cruelly, yet somehow you have managed to become this . . . this gentleman and lord with riches and connections. I do not understand why you would have worked so hard to gather the wealth you need to become this person if you do not desire to be this person."

"Ah," he said lightly. "You are curious as to how my wealth came into being."

Lily shook her head. "I really do not care, to be frank."

"Ask me," he insisted. "You want to know all about me? Then ask me."

Her eyes narrowed. "I do not need to know more. You only want to astonish me further."

"You are quite right, so I will tell you nonetheless. I have made a vast fortune trading arms."

Lily did not look horrified. She looked confused. "Arms," she said carefully. "Do you mean guns?"

"Guns. Muskets. Cannons. Instruments of war. I trade in death. Whatever a government may need to wage war against another government, I provide."

Now Lily was clearly stunned.

"Ah, I have offended your tender female sensibilities." Satisfied, he picked up his fork and finished off his venison.

She seemed genuinely at a loss for words.

"Honestly, love, what did you think would become of me?" he asked, enjoying the opportunity to stun her. "Did you think some Good Samaritan would take me under his wing and pay for my schooling? Did you think my mother could provide for us, that my brother would survive the conditions in London? Did you think the earl might have bestowed a title on *me*?"

Lily suddenly stood, tossing her linen napkin onto the table. "I will not remain here and allow you to treat me so poorly," she said angrily. "You want to shock me and hurt me, and I do not care for it." She whirled about and started for the door, but she hadn't taken as many as two steps before Tobin was blocking her path. "There now, do not be angry. Finish your meal. Cook has outdone herself."

"Why?" she demanded. "You despise me in every way and have no qualms about showing it. Why would you want to dine with me? I do not understand why you want anything from me at all!"

She tried to move around him, but Tobin put his hands on her arms, trapping her between him and the table. "Perhaps you have forgotten that we have an arrangement, Lady Ashwood," he said, pushing her up against the table. The wine goblets toppled over, and something slid off the table and landed with a thud on the carpet.

"Step aside, Tobin," she snapped and shoved against his chest.

Tobin would not move. "I ask you again—what did you think would happen to the Scott family once you saw my father hanged?"

Lily looked terrified and furious at once. She leaned back away from him. "I was *eight*, Tobin. I didn't know what to *think* about any of it! I didn't know what to think when I saw your father riding away in the rain that night. I didn't know what to think when the earl threatened to hang my nurse or my governess, or any servant for that matter!" she cried. "I hoped and prayed for the best for you and your family. I know that is little comfort to you. I know that you would have given your own life to hear someone say your father was not at Ashwood that night. But he was, and I saw him, and I said what I did to save the people *I* loved! If the truth leads you to want to abuse me, then for God's sake *do* it and stop taunting me!"

Tobin suddenly turned away from her, stalking to his chair and gripping the back of it. His breath was restricting, his palms going damp. "You hoped for the best for us, yet it was *your* word that sent us all skidding into Perdition." He put his hand to his throat, ready to loosen his neckcloth if necessary. "We were not afforded a life of luxury as you were."

"I suppose by that you mean my exile to Ireland," she said darkly.

He moved farther away from her, lest she see the perspiration on his forehead. "It must have been truly terrible to be so well cared for," he scoffed.

"You pretend you do not care in the least, but I see how bitter you are," Lily accused him. "Yes, I was cared for, Tobin. No one forced me into poverty, but it was the third home I had known in my eight years of life. My parents, my beloved aunt—all gone. My governess, whom I adored—*gone*. I was orphaned *twice* as a child."

He remembered his family's first night in London

in the two rooms they'd taken. There'd been a stench in the air, the signs of rodents on the floor. "Poor child, reared in privilege," he said again, and drew a deep breath. His breathing was settling. "Then given an estate and a title. What a tragic life yours has been. And then you have the gall to come here and feign interest and kindness." He turned about, his hands casually clasped behind him.

Lily's eyes were blazing with fury. "I have feigned *nothing*. It may astound you to know that I wanted nothing to do with Ashwood. I could scarcely believe that a man who never bothered to even *look* at me would leave his entire estate to me. I did not want it. I did not want to come here, for I find it perhaps as painful as you."

That notion was impossibly infuriating, but Tobin grinned as if he found it amusing. "Are you maneuvering now? Hoping to claim my sympathies? I should warn you that it is obvious."

The fingers of Lily's hand began to tap against her opposite arm. "It is *quite* clear to me that nothing I can say will dissuade you from hating me, so I shan't even try. If it allows you to justify your abominable behavior and your abhorrent need for revenge, then *hate* me. I hardly care!"

"Oh, I don't hate you. Not in the least," he said, moving slowly forward. "But perhaps there is something you might do to appease my loss."

Lily glared at him and lifted her chin, as if she were squaring off to box. It was surprisingly arousing.

"Allow me a kiss," Tobin said. "And not the chaste sort of kiss you gave me at Ashwood."

Her eyes fired. "A *kiss*? You want a kiss *now*?"

He laughed and spread his arms wide. "Revenge, love. Remember?"

He expected her to argue, but something changed in her: she suddenly softened. Her shoulders relaxed, and she dropped her arms to her sides. She lowered her head, looking up coyly at him through her lashes. "So be it," she said silkily and stepped forward, lifting her face to his.

Tobin was taken aback. He'd assumed he'd have to entice her to kiss him, yet here she was, presenting herself. He was so surprised that he didn't move.

"Now who is afraid?" she asked softly.

He could feel the corner of his mouth turn up in an appreciative smile. "Don't taunt a caged lion," he warned her and slipped his arm around her waist. He cupped her chin with his palm and splayed his fingers across her face, tilting her head back so that he could see her. She was as lovely as any woman he'd ever seen. But there was something more—there was a spirit in Lily that he was beginning to find quite irresistible. He kissed her forehead, and then her eyes before touching his mouth to hers.

The moment he touched her lips, a monstrous wave

of desire crashed through him. Her lips were a piece of heaven, and as he touched his tongue to hers, he heard her make a little sound in her throat.

The next thing he knew, he'd whirled her around, forcing her up against the table. "I never knew revenge could taste so sweet," he said and kissed her neck.

"Sweet?" she said softly. "I find that revenge tastes very bitter." She braced herself with one hand on the table, closed her eyes, and bent her head to one side, giving him better access to her perfumed skin.

Tobin moved to her mouth again. Her breath was warm on his lips; he felt her curve into him as he kissed her, his tongue tangling with hers. It was intoxicating; Tobin bent her over the table and straddled her on either side with his legs. He smoothed her hair from her face and gazed into her eyes, now the color of warm seawaters. "You are taking the bitterness out of my revenge."

"You needn't flatter me," she whispered breathlessly as he moved to her décolletage, mouthing the skin at her breast as she pushed her hands through his hair. "You've already forced me into this."

The truth of that pricked him, but Tobin could scarcely contain himself. He rose up, crushed her to him, and kissed her hard, kissed her with what felt like centuries of pent-up desire. He nipped at her bottom lip, swept his tongue inside her mouth, found her breast and filled his hand with it. Lily grabbed his wrist and held tightly as she rose up from the table to meet him. Her kiss was full of passion and need, of hunger and loneliness—as was his. He could feel the pressure building in him, filling him up, bubbling like a cauldron in his groin.

He moved his hand to the low bodice of her gown, slipped his fingers into it, and felt the hot skin of her breast, the rigid peak of it between his fingers. Lily gasped with pleasure. "You don't seem terribly forced to it now," he growled, then buried his face in the swell of her flesh above her bodice.

"You've hardly left me a choice," she murmured huskily.

Tobin was consumed with desire, his body thrumming with it, but those words registered somewhere in the mud. He'd never in his life taken a woman who hadn't been a willing partner, and the thought of it was repugnant. He fell away from Lily so abruptly that she had to catch herself against the table with both hands. She didn't speak; she was panting. Each deep breath lifted her chest.

They stood that way a moment, staring at one another. Tobin had come back here for revenge, and here he was on the verge of having it. What in blazes had happened?

Lily pushed away from the table. "I think I should go."

Tobin did not attempt to stop her as she smoothed her hair back, smoothed her skirts, and walked quickly to the door. She paused there, looking back at him.

"Good night," she said, and in the next moment, she was gone.

Tobin fell into a chair, his legs sprawled before him. He picked up a goblet from the table and poured out more wine, draining it in one long sip.

Bloody hell, what had just happened?

NINE

Lily was emotionally spent. Tobin was such a confusing, enigmatic man! On the one hand he was a glib ogre of ice—unfeeling, rude, uncaring. But then there had been those moments when something had seemed to wash over him. His fists had clenched as if against some unseen pain, and he'd tried to hide his struggle to catch his breath. What sort of malady would inflict a man who appeared to be in such robust health? A veritable model of masculinity with strong appetites for . . . everything?

Ah, but there was a weakness there. Not that it mattered, for she was in an even bigger bind now—she had been unexpectedly moved by that kiss. Her body still tingled just thinking about it. He was so wanton, so bold, and she . . . she was so imprudent as to *like* that. She, with her lustful thoughts about her enemy, a man who wanted her for nothing more than pleasure and to win his evil game. And yet Lily couldn't keep the bothersome feelings of desire from creeping into her—disastrously *strong* feelings of desire. She kept seeing those penetrating eyes brimming with unbridled desire for her, and she fell all to pieces with longing.

What did she do now? She needed Keira's counsel desperately, even knowing Keira's counsel was often ill-advised and foolhardy. But Keira always had firm opinions of what to do in any situation, and seeing that Lily had none . . .

Lord, she missed Keira! She even missed her younger cousins, the twins Molly and Mabe, and now could look back with fondness at their bothersome habits of eavesdropping and borrowing her things without permission. She missed everything about Ireland and wished for all the world she could have been there now.

But she was here, under a mountain of debt and at war with a man who wanted to ruin her. And worse, Lily feared she would enjoy it.

The weight of her troubles made her sink onto her bed.

At least she could look forward to luncheon in two days. At long last, she'd received an invitation to dine at Mrs. Morton's with some of the ladies from The Society. Last week Lily had seen Mrs. Morton in the village and had offered to help the charity in any way she might, and the invitation was a small victory.

Hopefully, it would take her mind off the man who was persistently invading her dreams of late.

∞

Mrs. Morton's house was so filled with endless knick-knacks that it felt awfully close. She seemed particularly fond of porcelain cherubs, which gazed lovingly at Lily everywhere she looked. Even the napkin rings had little angels carved into them.

The table was set with bone china and crystal. A bouquet of hothouse hydrangeas—bought at some expense, Lily guessed—graced the middle of the table. While the blooms were spectacular on that blustery late autumn day, they were so large that Lily couldn't see over them or around them to the ladies on the other side of the table. That left her conversing with Mrs. Morton on her right and Miss Daria Babcock on her left.

Lily liked Miss Babcock. She was young and congenial and chatted about everyone in Hadley Green. From her, Lily learned that Mrs. Ogle had taken possession of a new carriage, and that Lady Horncastle was quite jealous of it. She also learned that Kitridge Lodge was being made ready for the arrival of the Duke and Duchess of Darlington.

"I suppose they are beginning to make their way into society again," Mrs. Morton said.

"Pardon?" Lily asked.

"She means on account of the duchess," Miss

Babcock said. At Lily's blank look, the young woman lit up. "Do you not know, then? She was the Prince of Wales' mistress—"

"*Daria!*" Mrs. Morton hissed.

"Well, she was," Miss Babcock said, looking deceptively innocent. "Everyone knows it." She leaned in close to Lily and said low, "The duke fell in love with her and married her in spite of his family's wishes. And the prince was quite angry, and threatened to ruin him for it, but what could he do, really? He's not yet king, is he? Nevertheless, they were shunned by the Quality. Because she's not proper."

"She's proper enough for a duke," Mrs. Morton sniffed. "So I suppose she is proper enough for Hadley Green society."

"Goodness, anyone is proper enough for Hadley Green society," Miss Babcock laughed.

Miss Babcock also seemed very enamored of things, for she commented on Mrs. Morton's angels, the flowers, and even the chairs.

"I do so much like your chairs, Mrs. Morton," Miss Babcock said cheerfully. "They are new, are they not?"

"They are from Tiber Park." Mrs. Morton responded so eagerly that one had the impression she'd been waiting for someone to ask that very question so that she might announce it. "The count took delivery of new chairs and put these with Mr. Fuquay. I was lucky enough to find them first."

"You were indeed," Miss Babcock said. "I very much

like the chairs he brought to Tiber Park. They are upholstered in fine wool with little peacocks and their plumes," she added with a flutter of her fingers.

"Really?" Mrs. Morton appeared to be smiling with effort. "You saw them at Tiber Park?"

"Yes. I was invited to dine there just last evening."

"Yes, Miss Babcock. We are all aware that you were invited to Tiber Park," Mrs. Morton said, and made a show of arranging her napkin on her lap. "I should wonder that the whole country hasn't heard of it."

"Have you seen his new chairs, Lady Ashwood? I am sure you have been invited to Tiber Park."

"Oh, I am afraid that I am terribly unobservant."

Miss Babcock daintily picked up her teacup. "Then we might have a look around together at the ball."

That wretched man was hosting a ball?

"You *do* know of the Tiber Park ball?" Miss Babcock asked. "To be held the first night of winter?"

"I am certain her ladyship is very aware, Miss Babcock," Mrs. Morton said as the doors swung open and two footmen entered carrying platters of food. "The whole of Hadley Green has returned a favorable reply."

"Do you know there are to be fireworks?" Miss Babcock asked excitedly. "Lord Eberlin promises fireworks the likes of which have never been seen in Hadley Green!"

"Well, we had rather spectacular fireworks on Guy Fawkes Night, you may recall."

"Indeed we did, but—"

"It must be very satisfying to be the count's confidante," Mrs. Morton said loudly and picked up her spoon. "Ladies, please do begin. It would seem, Miss Babcock, that your social calendar has been quite full," Mrs. Morton continued, her envy unconcealed. "Might I be so bold as to ask who else dined with you at Tiber Park?"

"I was accompanied by my parents, of course," Miss Babcock said demurely, smiling slyly at Lily. "Lord Eberlin has engaged my father to take his wool to the London market." She helped herself to a stewed fig. "I think they shall be good friends. Oh, and Lady Horncastle and her son were in attendance." She glanced up at Mrs. Morton through her lashes. "That is all."

"Almost the same number that dined here when Mr. Morton and I had his lordship to supper."

Lily resisted the urge to groan with impatience as the two women attempted to establish their respective influence with that beast of a man. A man who would kiss her as if she'd been the only woman in the world and then the very next evening entertain Miss Daria Babcock.

"Did he, by chance, mention the work on his mill—the one built upstream from Ashwood? Or his recent acquisition of land that has belonged to Ashwood for decades?"

"No," Miss Babcock said thoughtfully. "He spoke only of selling so much wool. Too many sheep, he said." She giggled. "He said they've been too well fed, for they think of nothing but procreation."

"Well, I've not had the pleasure of dining with him, but I *have* heard the most interesting bit of news regarding our Count Eberlin," a woman on the other side of the hydrangeas said. Lily tried to see who was speaking, but a particularly large bloom hid the woman's face. "I thought it rather curious that he has come from *Denmark* to an English estate, but all has been explained. I inquired of Mr. Sibley."

Oh, Lily would enjoy hearing exactly how it had been explained!

"I don't know why you should find it curious," Mrs. Morton said. "And you could have asked me. His lordship was quite clear about it when he dined with us. He procured the estate as well as his title. He escaped the Continent, because Denmark is rather lawless, and what with all the wars, he thought it best."

Mrs. Morton spoke as if she had firsthand knowledge of the situation on the Continent, or the supposed lawlessness of Denmark.

"That may be, Felicity, but the interesting bit of news is not how he came by his title and estate. It is that his surname is Scott."

God in heaven, who was speaking? Lily tried desperately to see around that ridiculous arrangement, but she could see nothing but the lace cuffs of the lady speaking.

"What of it?" Mrs. Morton asked, clearly annoyed that this woman would know more about Count Eberlin than she. "It is of little consequence, is it not, as the title he owns is the name he chooses to use."

"You miss my point completely!" the woman protested. "His given name is Mr. Tobin Scott . . . the son of *Joseph* Scott."

"Who is that?" Miss Babcock asked, as she, like Lily, tried to see around the flower arrangement.

"The wood-carver," Lily said.

"Precisely," the other woman agreed. "But of course you would be aware of it, your ladyship, given your unfortunate history at Ashwood."

"What unfortunate history?" Miss Babcock demanded petulantly.

At last, someone was imparting the truth about Tobin!

Mrs. Morton's gaze riveted on Lily. She did not look surprised; she looked, unfathomably, almost pleased. "Of course she knows about it, Sarah."

Sarah Langley, the dress shop proprietress was speaking, Lily realized. Lily had expected that she would feel oddly vindicated somehow when the truth was known about Tobin, but she did not.

"I just recently learned of it myself," Mrs. Langley said.

Mrs. Morton smiled at Lily. "Is it not heartening? To think of all that poor young man has had to overcome! It would seem impossible that he could rise to such prominence with the disgrace his family suffered. What a remarkable story!"

"It is indeed," Mrs. Langley said. "I am happy that he has brought his good fortune to Hadley Green. It is my belief that he desires to atone for his father's unspeakable crime by helping us all. He's lent money to various persons in need, and they say he does so without question—if someone is in need, he is very generous in his aid."

Lily was beginning to grasp that to these women, Mr. Scott's death was too long ago and of no consequence. But his son was an entirely different matter. He was a count now, a handsome figure of a man, and, to ladies like Miss Babcock, a highly desirable match. These ladies would not allow questions of his character or past to interfere with the prospect of his wealth; they would turn a blind eye as he slowly dismantled Ashwood, as long as they were treated like local royalty at Tiber Park and he lent their husbands money.

In that moment, Lily very much desired to kick something.

∞

When luncheon was at last over and the ladies were shown to the drawing room, Lily sat beside Mrs. Langley and Mrs. Morton while Miss Babcock displayed passable talents on the pianoforte.

Lily smiled and applauded the performance; she responded as she ought to Mrs. Langley's conversation. But privately, she was stewing. Tobin Scott had ingratiated himself to the village, and when he completely ruined her, she had no doubt they would all believe she had somehow brought it on herself. They would never say an unkind word against a wealthy, unmarried, *titled* gentleman.

How on earth was she to prevent her complete ruin with no one to help her?

The situation was made all the worse when Mrs. Ogle finally deigned to speak to Lily.

Mrs. Ogle had been particularly stung by Keira's deceit and had scarcely spoken a handful of words to Lily since her arrival. For the most part, she avoided Lily beyond the obligatory greeting and inquiring after her health. After lunch, however, Mrs. Ogle seemed more at ease and began to hold court with the others.

"A gentleman such as Count Eberlin will no doubt wish to marry soon," she said. "I rather suspect that is the reason for the ball, so that he might see all that Hadley Green has to offer."

"He didn't mention that was the reason," Miss Babcock said.

"Really, Daria, do you think he would say such a thing? Of course he would not." Mrs. Ogle eyed Miss Babcock closely. "I am reminded of the demise of the late Mrs. Crawley. Mr. Crawley mourns her so. He told me that in the beginning, he hadn't much interest in her. He said, very truthfully, that he was interested in her dowry. But Mrs. Crawley was quite determined in *him,* and she wooed him to her with felicitous patience."

"I do not think it proper for a lady to woo a gentleman," Miss Babcock sniffed. "It should be the other way around."

"One day you may see things in a different light, Miss Babcock," Mrs. Langley said kindly.

"Perhaps I should say that Mrs. Crawley *endeared* herself to her husband," Mrs. Ogle continued. "She did those things that men come to adore in a wife, and he, in turn, adored her beyond compare."

"You will have to tell us all what that is, Mrs. Ogle," Mrs. Morton said laughingly, "for I have not yet endeared myself to Mr. Morton despite twenty years of marital bliss."

"I mean that she enticed him to love her," Mrs. Ogle said. "Now, Daria, if you wish the count to love *you*—"

"Her!" Mrs. Morton said. "I rather thought Lady Ashwood."

"Heavens, no, Felicity!" Mrs. Ogle said, appalled. "He will never be accepted in the society in which our Lady Ashwood moves. And besides, Lady Horncastle has told me herself that there is a rumble of interest from her son—"

Lily was so stunned by Mrs. Ogle's dismissal of Tobin that she almost missed the remark about Lord Horncastle. "No, *no,*" she said, throwing up her hand.

"Well of course not, Lady Ashwood," Mrs. Ogle

said, as if annoyed that Lily would think she'd implied anything. "There are much better opportunities coming for you."

"Oh?"

"Yes, my dear." When no one spoke, Mrs. Ogle rolled her eyes. "The *Darlingtons*. There are *two* unmarried sons."

"By all accounts, the youngest one is a bounder," Mrs. Morton said.

"But Lord Christopher is not," Mrs. Ogle retorted. "He is quite well respected, and he is very rich. And I hear that he may join his brother at Kitridge Lodge."

The ladies suddenly all cooed and fluttered about like a covey of doves and exclaimed politely at what a wonderful opportunity that would be for Lily.

There was a time in her life when Lily would have agreed. She'd heard of Lord Christopher, and certainly she knew the Darlington name—they were a powerful family in England. Lord Christopher was precisely the sort of titled man that Mr. Fish had in mind for her: the sort that could solve all her problems.

Oddly, Lily couldn't seem to summon much interest.

TEN

Tobin had taken to chopping down hedgerows.

It was the only thing that made him feel as if he had some control over his own body.

He'd needed to do something physical to prove to himself he wasn't going mad. His malady was entirely emasculating and, alarmingly, had occurred in Lily's presence. Not with the Babcocks, nor with his gentlemen guests. Only her.

And that Lily Boudine, of all people, would see him at his weakest was not to be borne.

As it happened, there was an old hedgerow of English yew that ran for a mile along the road to Tiber Park. It was six feet high and three feet deep, and Tobin disliked it immensely. He could see nothing on the other side of it, and he liked to look out at his vast property as he traveled that road. So he'd suggested to his head groundskeeper, Mr. Greenhaven, that it ought to come down.

He had not intended to do it himself, but the morning after his evening with Lily, there he'd been, chopping away at it, swinging the ax with as much force as he'd been able to muster, feeling each strike against the trunk reverberate through his body.

It was absurd that he should have done it, given the number of men he employed to do such things. And it was bloody inconvenient, for he had several far more important matters that needed his attention. Yet it had felt so rewarding that Tobin had come back the next day, and the next, clearing a few feet each day while a crew of gardeners had watched nervously from a distance, scurrying forward at intervals to clear away the debris. Mr. Greenhaven had been beside himself. He'd hovered about, assuring Tobin as he'd worked that he and his men could remove the hedge. Still, Tobin had refused to put down the ax. He'd walked out to that bloody hedgerow every day, removed his coat, his neckcloth, and his waistcoat, rolled up his sleeves, and picked up the ax.

It felt good. It made him feel alive and powerful. It was the only thing that seemed to give him some ease.

On the day MacKenzie and Bolge had ridden out to London to inspect the rerigging of one of his ships, they'd paused at the hedgerow where Tobin had been working. Bolge had laughed, but MacKenzie had calmly examined Tobin's work, then looked curiously at his old friend. "I've never seen ye out of your wits, lad," he'd said.

"I have all my wits about me," Tobin had assured

him. "Work is good for the body humors. You might try it yourself one day."

"If this is what a woman brings a man to do, I'll keep to me scalawag habits, thank you."

"This has nothing to do with a woman," Tobin had snorted, ignoring the tiny twinge of conscience that said it did.

"No, of course no," MacKenzie had said, his eyes twinkling. "We'll leave you to it, then."

Bolge had touched the brim of his hat. "May you be delivered from the grip of this madness, Scottie." He'd laughed and spurred his horse on after MacKenzie.

The madness was much deeper than those two suspected, Tobin had thought grimly, and it went far beyond a hedgerow.

Today, he'd cleared an extra six feet, having come from his daily visit to his mill.

He'd instructed his foreman, Mr. Hollis, that he wanted the mill operational by the summer harvest, and he generally rode down in the afternoons to see the progress of the construction.

When he'd gone up to the mill yesterday, he'd been surprised by the sight of Lily and her young ward on the Ashwood side of the river. A number of days had passed since he'd seen her; days in which he had forced her out of his thoughts and buried her in the black ooze in him.

But then he'd seen Lily and Miss Taft frolicking. There was no other word to describe it, really. He'd been reminded of puppies, for the two of them had had a ball, which they'd kicked and tossed back and forth to one another, running after it, then dissolving into laughter when it escaped them. Tobin hadn't known what to make of it. He hadn't been able to imagine what had brought them down to the river, directly across from his mill, other than some sort of scheme against him.

He'd stood on the edge of the platform built out over the river, his hands on his hips, watching them, waiting. Yet they'd done nothing but wave in his direction, pick up their ball, then race up the hill with their cloaks billowing behind them to where an old, swaybacked horse had been grazing.

After he had seen the day's progress on the mill, Tobin had ridden home, his head full of the image of Lily and Lucy playing in the golden grasses on the riverbank.

This afternoon when he'd arrived at the mill, he'd seen Lily and Lucy again. They'd been sitting under an old oak tree, pretty as a picture in the afternoon sun of shimmering gold, as fine as autumn weather as one could hope to see.

Mr. Hollis had been there to greet him, as always. Tobin had nodded to Lily and her charge. "How long have they been there?"

Mr. Hollis had followed his gaze. "Oh, an hour or so. Not long."

Tobin had squinted. "Why?"

"I wouldn't know, milord. A bit of harmless fun, eh?"

Nothing about Lily Boudine was harmless. She was up to mischief, and Tobin would know precisely what. He'd walked down to the river's edge and stood directly across from the two, watching them. Sitting serenely beneath the tree, they hadn't noticed him at first, the sound of their voices drifting down to him like the chatter of morning birds.

But then Miss Taft had spotted him and waved with great enthusiasm. Lily had lifted her hand and nodded politely, then looked down again to what appeared to be a book.

Before he'd known it, Tobin had stepped into the river and waded across, then climbed the hill to where they sat, a spread of tarts between them.

"We have a visitor, Lucy!" Lily had said, smiling as if it had been perfectly natural for her to be sitting under an oak tree, with tarts, across from the mill she despised.

"Good afternoon!" Lucy had hopped up to present him with a proper curtsy.

"Thank you," he'd said to Lucy, and to Lily, "What are you about?"

"Simply basking in a glorious day!" she'd sung cheerfully.

"Why are you here?"

"We are reading." She'd folded her hands delicately across the book in her lap. "Do you enjoy poetry?"

"We read about a mouse," Lucy had said. "He is a beastie and he has a panic in his breastie."

Lily had laughed, her countenance sunny. "She is referring to the Robert Burns poem 'To a Mouse.' Have you read Mr. Burns?"

Tobin hadn't read a proper book since he'd boarded the *Flying Saxon* all those years ago. "No. May I inquire—is there a reason you are reading poetry here?"

Lily and Lucy had looked at each other and giggled.

Tobin's scalp had tingled, and he'd been reminded of the way he felt in Charity's and Catherine's company. Warm. Happy. It had been disconcerting to feel that way in the company of his enemy.

"I beg your pardon," Lily had said pleasantly, "but Lucy and I are on a silly little mission."

"It's not *silly*," Lucy had protested. "When I am gone to Ireland, you will be glad we have done it."

"I will, won't I? And I shall think of you every time I see the trees."

They'd been talking nonsense. Tobin had gone down on his haunches so he could see Lily's lovely face beneath the wide brim of her sunhat. "What game are you playing? What do you think to accomplish?"

Lily's eyes had sparkled with a gaiety that had made Tobin feel strangely soft inside, and he'd wondered, was it possible for a man to look at eyes like that and not feel some softness somewhere? Was that not the purpose of eyes such as hers, in a world such as this? To soften the hard edges of men?

"I've not given a single thought to what I might accomplish today other than to read all the way to the end of this poem so that Lucy will hear every splendid word," she'd said with the cheerful insouciance of a lady of privilege. She'd leaned forward. "Why? Do you think I *ought* to accomplish something?"

Her smile, her eyes, her demeanor, had shone through Tobin. He'd unthinkingly curled his fingers into a fist lest the spell come over him, for that was the sort of malady he had—one that would descend on him when a beautiful woman smiled at him.

"Oh, yes! I remember now," she'd said, holding up a finger. "We have accomplished something, have we not, Lucy? We found the perfect rock."

"*Almost* perfect," Lucy had corrected her.

"Mmmm," Lily had said thoughtfully and settled back against the tree, crossing her feet at the ankles. "We've had such fine weather these last few days that Lucy and I were determined to find the best tree for reading poetry. When one reads poetry in nature, one better appreciates the beauty of our natural world and poems, wouldn't you agree?"

"I have never given it a moment's thought," he'd said dubiously. "Yet I wonder at you finding the best part of natural world here," he'd added, pointing at the mill.

"Oh, not *here*. We found the nearly perfect rock at the ruins."

"It is perfectly round," Miss Taft had reported.

"But its surface was not entirely smooth," Lily had added. "And then we recalled this lovely old tree." She'd patted the trunk as if it were a dog.

"It's quite old," Lucy had informed him. "Mr. Bevers told me that one might judge the age of a tree by its trunk and its arms. But *I* prefer the one the countess climbed when she was a girl. That one is far better for climbing, for its arms—"

"Limbs, darling—"

"Its *limbs* stretch out like *this*." Lucy had stood up, stretching her arms as wide as she could. "They are quite long and go almost as high as the sky. One might climb a very long time on those limbs."

Tobin had shifted his gaze to Lily again. The color in her cheeks was high, and she had turned her attention to the tarts, which she was arranging on cheesecloth. "You've been to the cottage," he'd said flatly.

"I haven't! But Lucy has been a frequent visitor to our old playground." She'd held out a tart to him. "I made them myself."

"You made them." He'd found that rather hard to believe. "Using the ingredients from your depleted larder, I suppose?"

Lily had smiled. "The one and the same."

God save him, she'd done a complete turnabout and had not glared at him or challenged him. She'd looked for all the world as if she'd simply been a beautiful woman enjoying a fine fall day. It had been the best bit of acting Tobin had seen in some time.

Tobin had taken the tart to be civil, but he had not eaten it. "And how did you find the cottage, Miss Taft?" he'd asked, his gaze on Lily.

"It is rather dirty," Lucy had reported. "I asked Lady Ashwood if Louis might be sent down to sweep it, but she said he had other things he must do." She'd walked in a tight little circle at the edge of the blanket. "There is a large hole in one wall. The countess said the wall fell down, but I think someone *blew* it down. Bad people and dragons do that, you know. They blow down entire doors and walls."

"Lucy has a vivid imagination," Lily had said. "She may only go to the cottage in the company of one our groomsmen." She had smiled and bitten into a tart, then had moaned with delight. "Oh, my, this is *delicious*! Lucy, you must have one."

Lucy had plopped down, cross-legged, and accepted a tart. She'd bitten into it, chewed with great concentration, then nodded enthusiastically. "It is good," she'd said. "I think it better than those you made yesterday."

"Do you?" Lily had asked, tilting her head thoughtfully. "Mrs. Cuthbert thought yesterday's batch was better." And to Tobin, she'd said, "Mrs. Cuthbert believes my culinary skills need a bit of improvement. I do not think her wrong."

Culinary skills? Tobin had looked at the tart in his

hand. That was when he'd known without a doubt that she was up to mischief. He'd never met a lady of privilege who could even hang a kettle over a fire.

"You mustn't fear it. I am not in need of *that* much improvement," she'd teased.

"Indeed," he'd drawled. "Are you suggesting I may trust you not to poison me?"

Lily had laughed as if he'd meant that as a jest. Which he had not. He'd felt a twinge in his chest as those sparkling eyes had shone at him. "What are you doing here, Lily?" he'd demanded once more. "I do not believe you have come to read poetry and eat tarts. How did you know I'd be here?"

She'd colored slightly and casually tied the cloth around the tarts, making a little bundle. "What are you implying, sir? What I told you is the truth. Who knows how long we will enjoy such fine weather? I thought it in Lucy's best interests to take the air." She'd come gracefully to her feet. When she'd straightened up, she'd stood very close to Tobin, her face, just below his, beaming up like a little sun. "I should like to send these tarts to your men. They work so very hard on your little mill."

"My men do not need tarts—"

"No one *needs* a tart, but surely they will enjoy them." She'd pressed the cloth into his hand, forcing him to juggle the tart he'd held, and squeezed his palm with her fingers. "I would take them myself, but it seems Lucy and I have overstayed our welcome.

And we have not concluded our search for the perfect poetry tree. Lucy, gather our things! We must be off!"

"Where shall we go next?" Lucy had asked excitedly as she'd hurried to gather up the blanket.

"Oh, I think we shall ride along until we find a tree that strikes our fancy," Lily had said, her gaze still on Tobin.

"Yes, let's!"

A smile had drifted across Lily's features.

Tobin had found himself wanting to smile, too. But he hadn't allowed it.

Lily had touched Tobin's arm, sending a tiny jolt through him. "Thank you, Tobin, for delivering the tarts to the men." She'd smiled again, a mischievous twinkle in her eye. As she'd begun to turn from him, he'd caught her hand and pulled her back around.

"I don't know what you are about, lass," he'd said softly, "but I will discover it." He'd lifted her hand to his mouth and kissed her knuckles. "Never doubt it."

Lily had laughed, then smoothed his neckcloth with a little pat. "On my honor, the tarts are not poisoned. They are actually quite good."

He'd studied her closely. Was she blushing? He believed she was.

But she'd politely extracted her hand from his. "Come along then, Miss Taft! Linford's knee hurts him today, which means our good weather likely will come to an end."

They'd walked on, neither of them looking back at

Tobin, Lucy hopping alongside Lily, and Lily with the blanket and book tucked up under her arm.

Tobin had watched them until they had mounted that old bit of glue and started off on those ancient hooves. He'd heard Lucy's stream of chatter and Lily's lilting responses as they'd ridden away.

They are charming, Tobin had thought with consternation. But charm would not deter him from revenge, no matter what she tried. He'd watched until they'd disappeared over the rise, and only then did he realize he'd eaten the tart.

As promised, it had been delicious.

ELEVEN

W*hat was she doing?*
Grasping at ghosts of ideas, that was what, anything that might help her stem the tide that Tobin was pushing toward her. Lily told herself she was following a plan, but part of her doubted it. Part of her suspected that she *wanted* to see him. Part of her knew herself very well and suspected any number of things she could not even give voice to.

Her confusion had not been helped when Mr. Fish had learned that the Darlingtons were coming to Hadley Green. He'd been quite beside himself with optimism. "You will make a fine impression, madam," he'd said eagerly. "They will wonder where you've been hiding."

But Lily was thinking of Tobin. She was compelled to keep trying, to lure him, to entice him, so that he would not destroy Ashwood. But how to entice a man as sensually potent as Tobin Scott without giving in?

And then it had occurred to her. Food! What man

was not enticed by good food? So with the help of Ranulf's information, she'd put herself in Tobin's path with her pastries, and he had responded with bafflement and a healthy dose of suspicion. She considered that a vast improvement over cold indifference.

Today, she planned for him to see her at the orphanage. Mrs. Cuthbert was not happy that Lily intended to take their eggs for the week, but Lily assured her that they could manage for a few days. "The orphans need them worse," she said with her newly acquired serenity, then picked up her basket of eggs and cheese and handed them to Louis on her way out.

The day was lightly gray; one could smell moisture in the air. Linford's knee was rarely wrong; rain would be upon them in the next day or so.

Mr. Bechtel, the stable master, helped Lily into the saddle as Louis attached the basket to the back of her mount. "Shall I send young Wills along with you, milady?" Mr. Bechtel asked.

"No, thank you. I will be quite all right. I am only going to St. Bartholomew's, and I have this," she said, pulling out the pistol she'd tucked in a saddlebag.

Mr. Bechtel instantly reared back.

"It is not loaded, sir."

"Aye," he said, but he looked very distrusting of it.

Lily set off and reached the low stone wall of the orphanage twenty minutes later. The children were outside today, playing in the grassy meadow adjacent to the facility. Lily was very happy to see that Ranulf had not been wrong: Count Eberlin's gray horse was tethered at the side of the road, and he was in the meadow standing next to Sister Rosens.

Lily reined her horse to halt beside Tobin's and hopped down, then tethered the reins to a tree limb, as Tobin had done.

Sister Rosens and Tobin had noticed her arrival and watched her stride up the hill to them. Sister Rosens was all smiles. Tobin stood with his arms crossed across his chest, regarding her stoically.

"Good afternoon!" she called to them.

"Lady Ashwood, you are most welcome here!" Sister Rosens said.

"Thank you. I see you are engaged, so I will not keep you. I've brought a basket for you and the children."

"Tarts?" Tobin drawled.

"Eggs!" Lily chirped.

"How very generous," Sister Rosens trilled. "Eggs are always needed."

"The basket is on my horse, and I fear my footman has done a very good job of lashing it on."

"Then we will need someone of good height and strength, it would seem." Sister Rosens looked pointedly at Tobin.

"At your service, madam." He shifted a suspicious gaze to Lily. "If you will allow me?"

"Would you be so kind?" she asked sweetly and watched him stride off to the horses to fetch her basket.

"I tell you it has been a gift from heaven to have the

count here," Sister Rosens said as she openly admired him. "He is the soul of generosity. Do you know that he has repaired our badly leaking roof? He did the work himself with his helpers. I've never seen a man of his stature engage in manual labor, but there he was, with hammer in hand, repairing the roof! And now he's ordered new beds for the boys' ward."

"Indeed?" Lily marveled at how he'd managed to charm every person in the shire. She watched him unlash her basket with one hand and a swift jerk of the rope. "Do you know, Sister, that he is the son of Joseph Scott?" Lily asked as casually as she might.

"Indeed, I do. Frankly, I am not the least surprised."

Lily tore her gaze from Tobin. "No? Were you not surprised he should come back here after the tragedy?"

Sister Rosens blinked. "I think he has come back here precisely *because* of that tragedy. Don't you, madam?"

That made no sense to Lily. She wanted to ask what Sister Rosens meant by that, but Tobin was already headed back to them with the basket.

"Thank you so very much, my lord," Sister Rosens said. She lifted the top and looked inside. "Oh, Lady Ashwood, how kind. Cheese, too."

Lily smiled pertly at Tobin, who seemed amused by her eggs and cheese. "I hope it is some help to your kitchen, Sister."

"Of course. When we combine these few with the many we have from our own coops, we should have quite enough. I'll just give them to our cook, shall I? Please excuse me."

Sister Rosens went off with the basket.

"Tarts, a few eggs . . . is there no end to your virtues or your culinary pursuits?"

Lily looked at the children chasing each other about in the field. Seeing them raised an old ache of longing in her chest. She could remember being so young and so desperately wanting a family to call her own. "It is very little. But if I could repair a roof, as it seems you have done, I would," she said. "I have a tender spot in my heart for orphans, seeing as how I once numbered among them." She smiled at him. "It warms my heart to know that you have a tender spot for them as well."

He arched a brow with amusement. "You are quite a mystery, madam. After such considerable disdain, you now shower me with tarts and flattery. It would lead a man to wonder if your heart has softened toward him, as surely his would soften toward you."

Lily's heart fluttered with triumph. Her instincts were right—she *could* make a man fall in love with her! She would win this epic battle with her enemy! She would prevail; she would have him eating out of her hand—

"But I feel obliged to remind you that I am not most men. It only leads me to wonder what, exactly, you are about."

Lily faltered only slightly and tilted her head demurely. "My lord, you give me far too much credit.

How could I deceive an old friend?" She looked back at the children. "Ah, look at them. Are they not sweet?"

"Quite. Perhaps you might pick out one or two to ship off to Ireland with Miss Taft. Perhaps you might populate the whole bloody island with orphans."

Lily's heart began to flutter. "Are you impugning my good intentions?"

He merely shrugged.

"Oh dear, how you have misjudged me," she said charitably and fluttered her lashes at him. "I am loathe to let Lucy go, but she is quite attached to my cousin Keira and her husband, the Earl of Donnelly, and they to her. It is also a practical matter, for as you are well aware, Ashwood is being driven to ruin and I am not able to provide for her as she deserves." She smiled.

Tobin smiled, too. "Perhaps I am mistaken," he said politely. "Then again . . . perhaps I am not. I wonder, Lady Ashwood, how you knew I would be at the orphanage this afternoon."

"Whatever do you mean? It is a happy coincidence, is it not?"

"And is it happy coincidence that you appear at the mill at the time of day that I happen to be there as well?"

She laughed. "What would I know of your mill?"

He regarded her with the calm patience of a man at a gaming table who had lost one round and now waited for the cards to be dealt again.

Lily was saved any further speculation by Sister

Rosens's effusive return. "Your ladyship, Sister Patrick is beside herself with joy. She said you've brought enough that perhaps she might make a cake. And I thank *you* for your generous patronage, Lord Eberlin. I cannot bear to imagine where we might be had you not returned to Hadley Green."

Sister Rosens was gushing like a Roman fountain.

"Please do not mention it," he said.

Lily smiled brightly at the pair. "Well then, I shall be off before the rains come."

"Good day to you, Lady Ashwood!" Sister Rosens said.

Lily had a devil of a time getting into her saddle, as the stirrup was rather high up, but once she'd managed it, she looked back. Sister Rosens was in the throes of some great tale, judging by the animated way her hands moved. But Tobin was looking at Lily.

She adjusted her skirts, checked that her pistol was tucked neatly into the little saddlebag, and left.

She rode along the river road, but when she reached the fork that branched away from the river and up to Ashwood, Lily drew up. She was no more than ten minutes from home. But further up the river road was Uppington Church. She was curious about it, wondering if it looked very different through the eyes of an adult. She could remember clearly the way the sunlight slanted across the church, and the vines that grew on the cottage walls. She remembered the leggy roses that bobbed in the spring breezes, and the old goat that was forever escaping Mr. Pritchard's fence and stealing down to eat the cottage grass.

Lily turned in that direction.

∞

The road to Uppington Church had been made narrower by an overgrowth of the forest on either side, pushing across the margins. Lily's skirt often brushed against the foliage.

She was surprised to find nothing left of the church but crumbling stone. However the cottage at the edge of the church grounds was just as Lucy had described it—one wall was missing, and what was left of the thatched roof hung down like moss into the empty room below.

The tree in front of the cottage was even bigger than Lily remembered. She slid off her horse and walked into the middle of the overgrown lawn. Big, thick limbs towered overhead. There was the rock where Tobin had sat with his books. She could see him now, a studious boy, his cap pulled low over his eyes to shield his reading from the sun.

Lily was so caught up in her memories that she did not immediately hear the approaching rider. When she did, she started and hurried to her horse for her gun. She had it in hand when Tobin appeared.

He smiled when he saw her. "You're rather fond of that old gun, it would seem."

"One never knows when one will need it," she said.

"That is so," he agreed and fluidly dismounted.

"However, it would be a bit more intimidating if it had a flint."

"What?" Lily looked curiously at the gun.

He took the gun from her hand, and showed her the locking mechanism. "See this? A flint should be here. It strikes the steel, which ignites the powder and fires the lead."

Lily frowned. "There is no lead. Louis removed it all."

He chuckled and handed the gun to her, which she deposited in her bag. "Well then," she said, turning around to him once more, her hands on her waist. "It appears you have followed me."

His grin was so disarming that Lily mentally stumbled. "I was prepared to tell you that I just happened by this way. But truthfully, I was curious to see what you were about." He looked around him, pushing his hat back a bit. "What do you think—is the tree suited for reading poetry?"

"It is," she said, gazing up at it. It meant far more to her than she'd realized. She'd spent so many afternoons in that old tree.

Tobin glanced up at the tree, too, and for a fleeting moment Lily saw the boy who had watched over her.

But then he turned and his gaze dropped to her mouth, and Lily felt something entirely different. He put his hand on her arm, his fingers closing lightly around her wrist, pulling her toward him.

"We were friends," Lily said. "Do you remember?"

Tobin considered her a moment and pushed a strand of her hair back from her face. "What an enigma you are, Lily Boudine. Do you really believe we were friends?"

"We were."

He shook his head. "No, lass, we were not. You were a princess, a young lady of privilege. I was your servant, commanded to wait on you. We were not friends."

Something rushed through her head, another shred of memory that crowded into her thoughts. *"Tell the boy to see to her . . ."* Who had said that? The earl? Mrs. Thorpe? "But we spent many afternoons here, did we not, Tobin?" she asked, looking at the tree again. "I confess my memory has so many pieces missing that I am not entirely certain of anything anymore."

"I never think of it." He stroked her cheek with his knuckles. "I think of only the present, and at present, I am reminded that we have a bargain, you and I." He reached for the clasp of her cloak and undid it with one flick of his finger. He pushed it aside, and it fell to the ground, pooling onto the rock behind her.

The wind was picking up; it lifted the hem of her gown and swirled leaves around them. "So many memories have come back to me, but I don't understand them yet. It's rather like building a puzzle."

Tobin traced a line to the top of her décolletage, his fingers warm and smooth on her skin. Lily grabbed his hand. "Do you hear me? I have these memories of Aunt Althea and Mr. Scott. And memories of *you*, Tobin," she said, desperately seeking to maintain her footing, a feat made very difficult when Tobin easily pulled his hand free and brushed his fingers across her breasts. "Do you think that perhaps—"

"We are no longer those people," he murmured and slipped one arm around her waist, drawing her to him at the same moment he dipped down, lowering his head to kiss the rise of her breast above her bodice.

Lily closed her eyes against the urge for abandon that was creeping up her spine, whispering to her to give in to her desires. "We *are* those people," she said stubbornly as his mouth moved to the base of her throat, then her neck. "Older and wiser, but we are the two children who once played here. We saw a fox here, do you recall? And you . . ." He nuzzled her neck, and a thousand little tremors shot through her. "You . . ." *What had he done? Did she care?* "You tried to lure it to us because I wanted to pet it."

His hand squeezed her breast.

Lily grasped his shoulders. "But all you had were acorns," she added breathlessly.

He drew her earlobe in between his teeth.

"I think you are willfully avoiding my conversation, sir."

"On the contrary," he murmured as his lips grazed her cheek. "I think you are willfully avoiding our agreement."

In that fog of arousal and broken memories, Lily instinctively tried to step back, but Tobin's hold of her tightened. "No, madam. You made a bargain."

He claimed her lips before she could muster a protest, and she halfheartedly attempted to turn her head. Tobin put his fingers to her cheek and held her there. His mouth was soft, moist, and plush. Lily felt herself falling into that kiss, falling into debauchery and away from the propriety that had been instilled in her since the day she took her first step. Her determination to fell him, to keep Ashwood from his hands, to keep herself chaste, was swallowed whole by his kiss.

Lily had no idea what it felt like to be wholly and unabashedly desired, and while she meant to push against him, she was curving into the hard planes of his body, feeling his strength surround her as he put his arm around her back.

Lily gripped the lapel of his riding coat; she could feel his erection pressed against her and did not shy away—her body flared with the sheer excitement of that kiss. No man had ever affected her like this, had moved her like this, and lust, and want, and a strange burst of affection bubbled up to the surface of her mind.

Her response to him frightened her on some deep level. Why should she feel so enlivened, so desirable, in the arms of her mortal enemy? He moved his attention to her shoulder, his hands cupping her breasts, kneading them, squeezing her resolve from her.

She had to stop at once, before everything was lost.

But she was suddenly falling, landing softly, anchored by his arm around her waist, onto the rock.

Tobin was immediately over her, one knee beside her, trapping her against him. He kissed her as his hands roamed her body. "I want you, Lily," he said gruffly as he kissed her shoulder, her collarbone. "I want to feel your legs around my waist, your breast in my mouth." His hand was on her leg now, and Lily realized, through that haze of her longing, that he was touching the bare flesh of her inner thigh. It was an exquisite thrumming, an anticipation of pleasure. When his fingers brushed against her sex, she almost gave way to the pleasure.

She was powerless to resist him. He began to stroke her, his fingers sinking into the folds of her sex. His stroke was gentle yet feverish, his lips soft yet insistent, all of it driving her to an exquisite state of madness. Lily felt herself falling away in pieces, bits of her floating out into the world. She gasped; he pressed his fingers into her flesh until she lost herself, falling away completely.

Tobin pulled her up, lifting her skirts.

A fat drop of rain awakened Lily to the reality of what she was doing. Her virtue was the only bargaining chip she had, and she was on the cusp of giving it to him completely. Another drop of rain hit her squarely in the forehead, and she felt herself running out of breath, desperate to reach the surface of her senses. "We came here quite a lot, Tobin," she said roughly. "I did not imagine it."

"Lily," he said, his eyes blazing with desire. "Forget that now."

Her craving for more was a shock of light through her. So many images and thoughts competed in her head. Desire burned in her, and she tried to focus, to *think*. Doubts about what she was doing, doubts about Aunt Althea, about Mr. Scott, and the events of that summer, began to crowd in between the overwhelming desire she was feeling.

She recalled the way her aunt had smiled at Mr. Scott, the way Tobin had smiled at her. She had a flash of memory of her aunt and Mr. Scott coming out of the potter's shed one day, her aunt's hair mussed, laughing. She'd told Lily she'd broken some pots. But the way Mr. Scott had looked at Aunt Althea had been the way Tobin had looked at her only moments ago—with ravenous, unapologetic desire.

Clarity hit Lily like the cold rain beginning to fall. She pushed at Tobin. "No!" she said, startled. "They *sent* us away!"

Tobin ignored her, but Lily's lust was overcome by anger, and she shoved at Tobin again. He paused, lifted his head as if it took some effort, then brushed her wet hair from her cheek. Rain was falling steadily now.

"They sent us away, didn't they?" she demanded of him. Tobin calmly returned her gaze. "Were they . . . were they *lovers*?" She was sure of it, but she needed Tobin to say it.

He did not seem surprised by her question; he obviously knew it to be true. Lily scrambled up out of his reach as the pieces of memory began to click into place.

Tobin bent down to pick up her cloak. "It is raining," he said, and put the garment around her shoulders.

"Keira discovered it," Lily said. "She told me, but I could not believe her. She showed me the stool your father made for the pianoforte."

Tobin showed no emotion as he fastened her cloak.

"There is an inscription underneath," Lily pressed. "One that was obviously inscribed for my aunt and was signed with the initials J. S. And I . . . I've been thinking, I've been trying to put together the pieces of mem—"

"I'll get the horses." He walked away.

"They were much closer than I understood them to be, but *you* understood it!" she called after him.

He paused between the horses. She saw the clench of his fist, the rise of his shoulders as he drew a deep breath. His reluctance to speak, his infuriating calm irked her.

"You are the only one who can tell me the truth now, Tobin. Do you think I haven't wondered about it all my life? Do you think I haven't lived with the thought that I am the one who *saw* him at Ashwood that night? I saw him riding away. I saw the lovers in the hall, too, but I did not realize it was *them*."

"We should go," he said flatly. He checked the cinch on his saddle, then hers.

Lily grabbed his arm, making him take a step back.

"Did you know about the stool? It reads, 'You are the song that plays on in my heart; for A, my love, my life, my heart's only note. Yours for eternity.'"

"Foolish woman," Tobin muttered. He put his hands on her waist to lift her into her saddle, but Lily pushed back. "I will not be dismissed! I did not know—how could I have known? I was only eight years old; I had no concept of such things."

Tobin grabbed her and forcibly lifted her onto the saddle. "I cannot see the relevance of it now." He slapped his crop against her horse, which started forward.

"It is *entirely* relevant now!" she argued, drawing her horse up. "If they were lovers, then why would he have stolen the jewels?"

Tobin suddenly whirled about, his eyes hard and cold. "How can you be so bloody obtuse, Lily? He did *not* steal them. Yes, God yes, they were lovers! If he was at Ashwood that night, it was for an assignation—not to steal her bloody jewels!"

Lily gasped. Tobin vaulted onto his horse. The rain was coming down much harder now, but she didn't care. "But don't you see? If he didn't steal them, if they were lovers, we can exonerate—"

"The time to exonerate him was fifteen years ago!" Tobin shouted at her. "You are fifteen bloody years too late to exonerate my father, for he hanged at the end of a bloody rope on *your* word! He is *dead*—my father is dead, his name forever slandered, and to exonerate him now does *naught.*" He spurred his horse forward, galloping away.

The bitterness in his voice shook Lily. Her memories, so much clearer now, shook her. When Keira had told Lily, she had refused to believe it. But now . . . she wondered how her aunt had allowed her lover to hang?

Her chest felt constricted. She glanced up the road. She couldn't see Tobin, and neither could she make herself move, paralyzed by the enormity of the truth and her part in it.

She recalled Althea's mad search of the house after that night and realized now that she'd been searching for the jewels. She thought of her aunt's strange death. An accident, they'd said, but Lily had always found it curious, since her aunt had been strong and had rowed that lake so many times. She saw all the events of that summer again, spinning out before her like acts in a play. *"Tell the boy to see to her."*

She leapt off her horse and stumbled toward the cottage, recalling the many times she'd been sent away so she would not see her aunt's adulterous affair, Tobin ordered along to watch over her. They had not been friends—he had been her keeper.

"For God's sake," he said. "Come here."

She whirled around; Tobin had come back.

"I'm fine," she insisted, but Tobin grabbed her and put her on his horse. He tethered her horse to his, then swung up behind her and pulled her into his chest. He spurred his horse and they moved along at a good clip.

Lily tried to resist sitting so close, but the rain was cold and hard, the wind even colder. She felt suddenly exhausted, her mind reeling, and she sank into his support and warmth. She needed it.

When they arrived at Ashwood, the storm was raging and the rain had turned to a stinging sleet. The door swung open, and the footman Preston raced down the steps, fighting with an umbrella, as a stable boy ran forward to take her horse. Tobin had Lily down before Preston could reach them.

She grabbed Tobin's hand before he could pull away. "We could find them, Tobin."

He ignored her, gesturing to the footman for the umbrella.

"We could find the jewels and then we could clear his name."

Suddenly, nothing seemed more important. She had to do it. She could never change what had happened that summer, but she could at least find those jewels for Tobin.

But he looked at her disdainfully and pulled his hand free.

"Your ladyship, this way," Preston urged her.

Lily ran with him into the house, where Linford was waiting to take her wet things. When she looked back, Tobin was gone.

TWELVE

Tobin had discarded his wet coat and waistcoat, and had pulled his shirt from his trousers. Carlson had tried in vain to direct him to a hot bath, but Tobin had stood aboard ship decks in far worse weather and did not require that sort of pampering.

What he required was a stiff drink.

He paced before the roaring hearth with a brandy snifter dangling between two fingers. He was conflicted, and he was not a man to be *conflicted*. He never cared enough about anything to be conflicted. And on those rare occasions he *did* care, as in the case of his father's unjust death, his path was exceedingly clear— very black and white without even a hint of gray.

Yet for a few highly charged, highly pleasurable moments this afternoon, his path had *not* been so clear. The mud in him had disappeared, and in its place had come a vastly different feeling—he'd been an inferno, wanting the one woman he did not *want* to want. What he wanted was to ruin her—not to desire her. Not to feel enslaved to her body and her smile. But desire her, he had. Kissing her had breathed life-blood into him, and he'd risen from the dead in those moments. The sensation had been an odd one—not the thickness in his throat, nor the tightness in his chest. But something even deeper, even more frightening than that.

Then it had all changed again in the space of a single breath. Lily had had some sort of epiphany, and it had changed. Had she really not understood until today what had happened between her aunt and his father?

Tobin had suspected it as a lad, and he'd realized it had been true when, as a young man, he'd experienced his first infatuation. Besotted with a woman, he'd mulled over the ways he might express his adoration. He'd remembered his father's stool then, the one he'd return to night after night when the family's evening meal was done, painstakingly crafting its inscription. His father had often inscribed things in his work, but even at thirteen, Tobin had understood that one inscription to be different. It wasn't until he was a man that he understood what that difference was.

Part of Tobin wanted to disdain Lily completely for suggesting, fifteen years too late, that she ought to find the goddamned jewels. Yet part of him wanted to find the bloody things for the very reason she suggested, to exonerate his father—and without her help, he'd have no hope of it. Wasn't vindication a better path than revenge? That moral high road, the thing that a decent man would seek. Or did he owe his father and his brother and his mother an eye for their eyes, and Charity for her wretched life? Wasn't a man who had failed to protect his family impelled to avenge their deaths?

Tobin tossed his brandy into the fire, watching it flare. He'd wanted his revenge for so long now that he scarcely knew how to think of it in any other way.

But his path to seeking it was becoming less clear to him.

∞

The weather did not improve, and by week's end, a lead gray sky had begun to spit a few anemic flakes across the West Sussex landscape. Mr. Joshua Howell, Tobin's secretary, appeared at Tiber Park on a morning Tobin had chopped hedgerow. Tobin idly rubbed his forearm as Mr. Howell reviewed a tedious list of engagements, commitments, and correspondence needs. When they'd finished, Mr. Howell stood to go.

"One last thing," Tobin said, his wet boots propped carelessly on the edge of the desk as he absently watched the bits of snow floating through the air. "I should like you to pen an invitation to Lady Ashwood to my winter ball." He'd deliberately not invited Lily, for reasons that now made little sense. Now, he wanted her to see firsthand the influence he wielded here.

"Yes, my lord. Perhaps that will lift her spirits."

Tobin shifted his gaze from the window to Howell. "What do you mean?"

"I have heard she is unwell, taken to her bed with an ague." He picked up his satchel. "Seems she was caught out in the rain."

Tobin's heart skipped on a small twinge of guilt. "Pen the invitation. I'll deliver it personally."

"Yes, my lord," Mr. Howell said and walked smartly out of the study, his satchel swinging at his side.

Tobin stood and walked to the window. He stared out at his holdings, recalling that sensual afternoon. Lily had been soaked to the bone. He put his hand to his abdomen. What was that he felt in his gut? Remorse? Highly unlikely. But he'd pay her a call all the same and assure himself that she would make a full recovery.

∞

Tobin's horse kicked up a powder of snow on the route to Ashwood. The snowfall was thickening. He would make a point of not staying more than a minute or two.

At the door, Lily's butler eyed him with a perplexed look, as if he didn't know whether or not Tobin was welcome. But as the snow was piling onto his shoulders, Tobin said, "If you would be so kind as to make up your mind."

Linford stood back and bowed. "Please come in, my lord."

Tobin strode into the foyer and looked at the magnificent dual curving staircase, his father's masterpiece. The few times he'd seen it since returning to Hadley Green, he'd been astounded by the craftsmanship. Every baluster was handcrafted. The twin railings had been carved with an ornamental vine and leaves. He could recall little things, such as his father's hands, the sound of his laughter. But he'd not recalled the depth of his talent until he saw this wonder of wood and physics.

"May I have your cloak?" Linford asked.

"That is not necessary," Tobin said. "I do not intend to stay long."

"I beg your pardon, my lord, but her ladyship has taken to her bed."

"So I have heard," Tobin said as he handed his hat to Linford. "Will you please inquire if she will receive me?"

Linford set Tobin's hat on the console. "If you will kindly wait here," he said and walked to the stairs. He moved slowly up, his hand on the railing, his steps deliberate.

Linford's footfall had just faded into the corridor above when Tobin heard a giggle, the unmistakable sound of a child. He glanced up. He could see Lucy Taft crouched behind the balusters, spying down at him. It was exactly the spot where Lily used to hide to spy on the adults below. "I see you," he said.

He heard Miss Taft's soft gasp and saw her shift.

"That does not help you. And as we both know that I see you, I should think you'd come down here and tell me how your mistress fares."

Miss Taft stood up, her blonde head peeking up over the railing. "She's unwell," she said and draped her arms over the railing. "She has an ague."

"And what is your prognosis, Miss Taft? Will she make a complete recovery?"

The girl mulled that over as she kicked one foot in and out of the space between the balusters. "I believe she will," she said with a sage nod. "But she must not go out in the snow, and she must eat all her soup. Mrs. Thorpe says that soup is the best thing a sick person might eat. Mrs. Thorpe does not care for beet soup. I have never tasted beet soup but I have tasted *onion* soup, and I don't care for it. I like duck soup the best. What soup do you prefer, my lord?"

"Brandy."

"There's no such thing as brandy soup! Did you come to see the countess?"

"I did."

"I can take you to her, if you'd like. I'm allowed to sit with her and read to her. But I don't read very well, and she said that she thought five readings of 'The Rabbit and the Hare' were *quite* enough," she said, and twirled around for emphasis before hopping across the landing like a hare. "You may come up if you like," she said, just as Linford shuffled back into view.

He passed Miss Taft without a word, took the steps very carefully down to the foyer, and bowed before Tobin. "Her ladyship will receive you now."

"I'll take him!" Miss Taft shouted.

"I rather think I should, miss."

"But *I* want to do it."

Linford glanced heavenward. "As you wish." He spoke in a manner that suggested this was not the first time they had vied for the introduction of a visitor. "If you please, my lord, Miss Taft will announce you," he said, and gestured grandly to the girl at the top of the stairs.

Tobin started forward. This would be the first time he'd stepped foot on those stairs in fifteen years. He put his hand on the railing, felt the deep groove of the meandering vine and the leaves of various shapes and sizes. The staircase was remarkable.

"We are to be quiet as mouses," Lucy whispered loudly when he reached the landing. "Mrs. Thorpe says her ladyship cannot rest if you run up and down the corridor."

"I have no intention of running up and down the corridor."

"Then you must have a very good mother," Miss Taft said as she began to hop down the corridor before him. "Mrs. Thorpe says I am as wild as a monkey because I have no mother, and mothers make certain that proper young ladies do not swing from the house chandeliers like monkeys. Did your mother tell you that?" She paused to look curiously at him.

"My mother is not alive."

"Are *you* an orphan?" she asked excitedly. "*I* am an orphan. The countess is an orphan, as well, although she had an aunt who very much wanted to be her mother. I think I might have a father, but I don't remember if I do or not. Do you have a father?"

Tobin shook his head.

"Count Eberlin!" she said sternly, and slipped her hand into his damp palm without invitation. "I should think *someone* might have *told* you that you are an orphan. You are, you know, if you have neither mother nor father, and someone else must take you in and feed you and teach you proper keticut—"

"Etiquette," he said.

"*Etiquette,* then you are an orphan."

"Thank you for the clarification."

"You are welcome," she said, and let go his hand and skipped ahead to a door. She grabbed the handle with both hands and pushed the door open, then skipped inside. "I brought that wretched Count Eberlin to see you," she announced loudly.

"Lucy!" Lily croaked.

Tobin strode into her bedchamber behind Miss Taft. "That wretched count at your service, madam," he said, and bowed low.

"I beg your pardon," Lily said and smiled apologetically as Lucy rushed across the room and plopped down on a window seat. "I am very surprised to see you, sir."

Generally, Tobin had no compunction about entering a woman's boudoir, but on this occasion, he felt awkward. The room was done up in soft pinks and crème-colored walls, not unlike the private rooms he had enjoyed in Europe. But the paint was peeling and the carpets were worn. It appeared as if it had once been a grand estate, where the money had gone before the house.

As for the room's mistress, Tobin was quite taken aback by how pale and drawn she looked, save the rosy spots of fever in her cheeks.

Miss Taft suddenly gasped. She climbed up onto her knees on the window seat and leaned forward into the deep window well, pressing her hands against the panes of glass. "It's snowing! May I go out, mu'um? Please?" she asked, whirling around and bouncing off the window seat.

"What do you think, Ann?" Lily asked the maid attending her.

Ann leaned forward and looked out the window. "It does not seem too deep, mu'um."

"Please?" Lucy begged.

"You must wear a proper cloak and mittens," Lily said.

"And a bonnet!" the girl exclaimed as she hurried for the door, nearly colliding with Ann.

"You mustn't stay out for very long or you'll catch your death."

"I won't!" Miss Taft sang as she ran out of the room.

Lily smiled weakly at Tobin. Her black hair had been braided and was draped over one shoulder like a stole. She was nestled against a stack of pillows, wan and bleary-eyed. "You came in the snow, my lord? Whatever for? Surely you do not care to risk contagion of the plague," she muttered morosely. "Ann does not fear it. She stays by my side, quite unconcerned about my imminent demise."

Ann laughed. "I do not think you are in much danger, mu'um."

"Tell that to Dr. Trittman."

"I heard you had taken ill," Tobin said, feeling a tremor of worry rifle through him. He'd thought he'd find her reposing in her dressing gown looking a bit tired. Not like this.

"Do my ears deceive me?" she said with a wary smile. "Did you come to inquire after my welfare?"

He smiled and glanced slyly at the maid, who was folding linens across the room. "Well obviously I cannot ruin you properly if you are ill," he said softly. "So I respectfully request that you improve."

Lily made a sound that might have been a laugh, but it quickly deteriorated into a cough. "I shall endeavor to do my best," she hoarsely assured him.

It had been a mistake to come here. Looking at Lily now—just days ago the very picture of feminine health—Tobin was reminded of his dying mother. She'd lain in her bed, her skin sallow, her hair gray and dull. Lily did not look as ill as that, but seeing her this way made him feel so uncomfortable that he could not help shifting his shoulders to try and shake off the feeling. "Are you on the mend, then?" he asked as casually as he could manage.

"Dr. Trittman would have you believe that is not a foregone conclusion. It would seem I have a rather persistent fever. Yet I do feel somewhat better, although Dr. Trittman will not believe it. He says I look too sickly."

"You look . . . remarkably fetching," he said honestly.

Lily smiled gratefully. "Oh, Tobin. On occasion, you really are rather kind."

"I am not a kind man," he said instantly, yet Lily would not stop smiling at him, so Tobin turned away and moved to the window. The snow was falling in thick, fat flakes.

The maid puttered in and out of the adjoining room, smiling nervously at Tobin.

"Tobin?"

Tobin looked over his shoulder at Lily.

"I have lain here these last few days with memories falling into place. I must know."

"You mustn't tire yourself. Do not trouble yourself with this now." He wanted nothing more from her at present than her regained health. He did not want to think about all that had happened in this house.

"I intend to look with or without you, you know," she said stubbornly and tried to sit up. "It seems to me that if we work together, we might recall more. It might lead us to the truth—"

"It makes no difference to me," he said curtly. "It is over and done, Lily. Finding the jewels will not change anything."

"It makes a difference to me," she said. "It could mean the difference between poverty and . . . oh, never mind." She sighed deeply.

Tobin wanted to ask what she meant by that, but she looked so tired. "I did not come here to distress you," he said and moved to her bedside. He held out the invitation.

Lily's dark brows rose. "What is this?"

He did not answer.

She took the vellum and opened it. Her brows sank as she read it. "An invitation to your ball? I hope you do not feel compelled to teach me some lesson you think I ought to have learned, for I confess, I am not feeling up to it."

Tobin refused to deny it, for it was true. And while he usually felt nothing about such an admission, he was annoyingly troubled by it now.

Lily dropped the invitation into her lap and sank back into the pillows once more, her gaze on the windows.

She looked so forlorn, her braid a streak of black across her heart. He wanted to speak, he wanted something to say, but the longer he stood there trying to grasp exactly what that was, he became aware of the tightness in his throat, choking off any attempt at speech.

She sighed once more, her chest rising softly and falling again. Tobin had an almost overpowering urge to press the back of his hand against her cheek and feel her fever. But he could only clasp his hands and stand there like the ogre he was beginning to feel he was.

"Shall I ring for tea?" the maid asked, appearing once more at Lily's bedside. "It's medicinal, and Mrs. Cuthbert said it would give you a bit of pluck."

"I shall leave you to your convalescence," Tobin said. "Good day." He quit her room before she could speak and swept down his father's staircase, rushing down as if he were late for an important engagement. His head felt as if it were held in a vise. His heart raced; his throat closed tighter. It wasn't until he was out on the drive, up on his horse, that he could release the breath that had been held captive in his lungs. It came out in a coarse cough, so loud that the stable boy jumped.

Tobin spurred his horse to a gallop, drawing frigid air into his lungs. But he hadn't gone far when he realized that the snow was already several inches deep. He slowed his horse, moving cautiously. But when his mount misstepped off the side of the road, Tobin realized he had to turn back. He could not risk a prize horse for the sake of his pride.

He reined his horse around and looked at Ashwood. He cursed under his breath, and like a dog with his tail between his legs, he rode back to seek refuge.

THIRTEEN

Cold awakened Lily from a deep sleep, and she sat up, blinking in the low light of the fireplace. She looked at the window and saw that night had fallen. She squinted at the clock on her mantel. It was half past five in the afternoon. She'd been asleep more than four hours.

The door opened and Ann slipped in. "You're awake!" she said.

"Have I really slept as long as this?" Lily asked sleepily.

"Aye, mu'um," Ann said, fluffing Lily's pillows. "How are you feeling?"

"Better," Lily said, and yawned. "Quite honestly, I'd like nothing more than to get out of this wretched bed."

"Dr. Trittman says you're to stay in it."

"Dr. Trittman is overly cautious. Please find me a dressing gown and some slippers. I should like to sit by the fire."

Ann helped her into a wool dressing gown and a chair at the hearth. Grateful to be upright, Lily tucked her feet up beneath her and leaned on one arm of the chair, letting the heat from the fire warm her face. "How much has it snowed?" she asked.

"At least a foot!" Ann exclaimed. "And so early in the season yet! Enough that his lordship was forced to turn round and come back."

"Pardon? Eberlin? He came back here?"

"Aye, mu'um," Ann said as she began to strip the bed of linens. "He'll have to stay the night." She paused and chuckled. "Linford, he was at sixes and sevens when his lordship returned. He said, 'What am I to do with him?'"

"What did Linford do with him?" Lily asked curiously.

"Oh, Mrs. Thorpe, she said, 'Linford, you will put him in the green suite, as far from her ladyship as he can be.'" Ann glanced sheepishly at Lily. "Beggin' your pardon," she added with a dip of a curtsy. "Louis showed him up, and when he came back to us below stairs, he said that the count instructed him you were not to be disturbed, that he didn't want to interfere with your convalescence, and he would take his supper in his rooms at seven o'clock."

"He said all that, did he?" It was just like Tobin, Lily thought as she leaned her head back against the chair. Presuming to direct her staff as if they were already his own. "And Lucy?"

"Oh, she kept his lordship company most the afternoon. Mrs. Thorpe said Miss Taft had his lordship to tea in the nursery, made him sit at the little table and chairs all folded up on to himself until Mrs. Thorpe rescued him. She said she'd take her supper in the nursery with Miss Taft." Ann smiled. "Mrs. Thorpe said that her hopping about like a mad hare would try anyone's nerves, most especially the infirm. And Miss Taft, she said, she didn't know what infirm meant, but she reckoned Mrs. Thorpe must be the most infirm of anyone she'd ever met, as she tried her nerves best of all."

Lily laughed softly. "Perhaps I should bring her here and spare Mrs. Thorpe."

"Oh, no, mu'um. Mrs. Thorpe, she talks as if she's put out, but she could have any one of us to dine with Miss Taft, couldn't she? She prefers to do it herself. I think she'll sorely miss the girl when she's off to Ireland."

Wouldn't they all? "Well then," Lily said, "it appears as if I will be hostess this evening. Tell Linford I shall dine with Count Eberlin in my sitting room here, whether the count likes it or not."

"Lady Ashwood!" Ann exclaimed. "Are you certain? You're quite ill yet, and he is . . . he is . . ."

"He is a guest in my house. And I should rather know what he's about than lie here wondering."

With Ann's help, Lily washed her face and combed her limp hair. She was too weary to have it dressed, so she let the long tresses hang free. She donned a plain day gown and wrapped herself in a wool wrap. It was hardly the most fashionable thing she owned, but tonight she hardly cared. She wanted only to have her supper and go to bed.

At a quarter 'til seven, Linford arrived with Preston in tow to ready her sitting room for supper. "Shall I help you into the sitting room?" Ann asked.

Lily smiled at her. "I am only ill, Ann, not lame. I can manage."

In the sitting room, Lily was instantly drawn to the warmth of the roaring fire Linford had built. She was leaning in to soak up the heat when Tobin arrived. "Lady Ashwood."

So formal! "Count Eberlin," she said gravely.

"I came as you asked, but I would have preferred to dine in the rooms your staff has so graciously allowed me for the night. I do not want to disturb you."

"Yes, so I've been told," she said and gestured to the chair beside her. "But I would prefer you here, where I can see you."

He arched a brow. "If one did not know better, one might assume you had grown fond of me."

"And if one did not know better, one would assume you could be trusted." She smiled. "Please sit, Tobin."

He sat, leaning back in the chair, crossing one leg over the other, his brown eyes steady on her. "You seem improved. Not as pale."

"I am feeling improved." She drew her wrap more closely about her.

"Are you cold?" He instantly moved to the hearth, going down on one knee to stoke it.

"My lord, allow me," Linford said, hurrying forward.

"I don't mind in the least," Tobin said.

He was the sort of man accustomed to doing for himself, Lily guessed. Building his own fires, sailing his own ships . . . if one were not engaged in battle with him, one might admire him very much. One might see the strength in his shoulders and hips, and the swell of muscle in his arms and legs and think, now *there* is a man who—

"Is that better?" he asked, turning to face her again.

Lily blinked. "Yes. Thank you."

"Shall I serve, madam?" Linford asked.

"Please."

Tobin was quick to help her to her feet, then into a chair at the small table. He kept his gaze on Lily as Preston served soup into their bowls.

Lily ignored Tobin's intent gaze—the smell of food stirred her, and her body reacted. She picked up her spoon and tasted the onion soup, briefly closing her eyes as the warmth trickled through her. When she opened them again, Tobin was smiling.

"Do you mind?" she asked apologetically. "I feel as if I haven't eaten in months."

"Not at all," he said, gesturing to her bowl. "I am happy to see you with an appetite. I had not given you favorable odds of survival earlier today. Now, I have hope that you will recover completely."

"You should never have doubted it," she said as she gladly took the bread that Linford offered her. "I can't possibly expire before I've won our little war."

"So we are back to war, are we?" he asked. "I rather thought we'd agreed otherwise."

Lily glanced up and Tobin gave her a subtle wink that spread more warmth through her and prickled at her scalp. "Make no mistake, sir, we are still very much at war. Unless, of course, you've had a complete change of heart?"

"Hardly." He grinned and lifted his wineglass. "To a worthy adversary whom I hold in very high regard."

Lily wished she had the strength to kick his shins. "Is it your regard for me that makes you so determined to—" She remembered Linford and Preston, who stood in silent attention, and caught herself.

"That, madam, is something altogether different."

Lily blushed.

Tobin grinned.

They spoke idly of the weather through the first course, but when the butler had served the main course, Lily said, "Linford, thank you. I think the count and I shall manage from here."

"Yes, madam," he said.

Tobin picked up his fork as Linford and Preston removed themselves from the room, leaving the door open.

"You always have so many questions for me, but tonight, I have one for you," Tobin said.

"Oh?"

"How have you remained unattached?"

Surprised, Lily asked, "I beg your pardon?"

"Surely I am not the first person to wonder. Is it not true that the most desirable women are snatched up the moment they are deemed old enough to wed?" he asked, and ate a healthy bite of ham. "I wonder why you have not been snatched up, Lily Boudine."

With a flick of her wrist, Lily said, "The answer is simple. I have never felt what one should feel for a gentleman if one is contemplating spending the rest of one's life with him."

"No?"

"I don't think it comes to me as easily as it does for others." She laughed softly. "I have two cousins who feel that way about every gentleman who pays them attention. But I've never had that feeling."

Tobin dropped his gaze and shifted uncomfortably. "I understand."

"Do you?" she asked lightly. She really doubted he understood her at all. Men had a different sort of experience after all. The freedom to choose whom they liked. To pursue and court and wed as they desired.

"I have long believed I am incapable of that sort of feeling," he said.

That admission surprised Lily. "You're not incapable."

He shrugged as if it had been a trifling matter and continued his meal.

"A pity, for I would guess you to be in great demand, with so much to recommend you."

He snorted. "Even in your state of ill health, you do not believe that."

"But I do!" she insisted. "The people of Hadley Green are quite taken with you. You are, without a doubt, the most desired and eligible bachelor for miles around."

He chuckled. "Then you must be the most eligible unmarried female in perhaps all of England."

Lily groaned playfully. "If that were the least bit true, Mr. Fish would be quite pleased to hear it. He is determined that I shall marry a titled man as the original decree demands, you know."

Tobin gave her a sly look. "Have you any prospects?"

"Not a single one," she said laughingly. "But Mr. Fish is quite happy the Darlingtons are coming to Kitridge Lodge, for apparently there remain scores of unmarried, wealthy sons in that family."

Tobin smiled, but it seemed an absent smile to her. He turned his attention to his plate.

Lily put her fork down. "And what of you?" she

asked. "Have you anyone in mind to marry? Perhaps Miss Babcock?"

Tobin shrugged. "She is handsome, I'll say that for her."

"She is very much anticipating your ball. I suppose I must find something suitable to wear." Lily sighed. Already full after only a few bites of her supper, she leaned back, contemplating her wardrobe. "What should a lamb wear to a slaughter?"

"Slaughter," Tobin scoffed. "There will be no slaughter, Lily."

"Oh, but I don't trust you in the least," she said. "You did not invite me until weeks after you'd invited everyone in Hadley Green. How can I possibly trust your motives?"

"You will have to take me at my word—have I not been true to my word thus far?"

"Yes, you have." She smiled at him. "What if I declined your invitation?"

"I would come and drag your from your rooms," he said with a wink.

Lily could feel a current running between them, a familiar current that was beginning to run quite deep. She smiled wryly. "You will cause me to believe I have misjudged you yet again."

"You always were a clever girl."

"Was I?" She was strangely pleased to hear him say it.

"Very. Obstinate and stubborn, as well," he added with the hint of a smile. "But always clever."

"You were quiet," she said. "You rarely had much to say."

"I could rarely manage to insert a word amidst all that chatter."

"What chatter!"

"It was constant," he said, grinning. "A veritable river of words flowing forth."

Lily laughed warmly. But her thoughts quickly swirled back to her aunt, and she imagined her, as she had through many grotesque dreams in Ireland, floating facedown on the lake behind the house. "Tobin?" She sat up, leaned forward. "Let's find the jewels."

He sighed. "Ah, Lily—"

"I do understand your view of it, I do," she insisted. "But I feel it is the only thing I can do to correct the many terrible things that happened that summer. It is as much for my aunt as it is for your father."

"Your *aunt*? She could have saved my father's life," he said and picked up his wine, drinking fully.

"I am painfully aware of that. I cannot fathom why she didn't, but knowing her as I did, there had to have been a reason."

Tobin looked away.

"She tried, you know," she said quietly. "In the days before your father was . . . was hanged," she said, nearly choking on the word, "she tried to find the jewels. She searched every room of this house. She took the books from the shelves, opened the drawers and emptied their contents."

Tobin made a sound of impatience.

"I remember overhearing my nurse tell one of the maids that Aunt Althea was quite mad. But she wasn't—she was desperate." Lily shook her head at the memory. Lily had been so young, so naïve! She could recall trying to reason with Aunt Althea, to tell her that if Mr. Scott had stolen the jewels, she could not possibly find them. Lily could not bear to think of how her aunt must have suffered. To see her lover hanged! To endure the marriage she must have endured!

"I don't expect you to understand me. But I must do it for Aunt Althea and your father. And for me, quite honestly."

That brought Tobin's head up. "What do you mean?"

"Is it not obvious? If I can find them, I can end Ashwood's slide into complete disrepair. And I won't be forced to pursue a husband like a hunter after a wily fox."

He stared at her as if he'd never considered it.

She smiled ruefully. "Surely you are not surprised. A rich and titled man will save us all," she said dramatically.

Tobin looked oddly disconcerted. Perhaps even a bit guilty.

Let him feel guilty. But when she looked at him again, she saw sympathy in his eyes.

She closed her eyes so she'd not see it.

When he looked at her like that, it made her soft. She couldn't allow herself to be soft with him, not even for a moment. Any weakness, and he would win their war . . . if he hadn't already.

"Lily, are you unwell?" Tobin asked quietly.

She opened her eyes. He was gazing at her with genuine concern. "I'm quite all right."

"Perhaps you should return to your bed."

"But I am feeling much improved. Perhaps you will humor me and play a round or two of cassino? I am desperate for a diversion."

His brows rose with surprise. "Lady Ashwood, are you a gambler?"

"As it happens, I do enjoy a good wager," she said pertly. "Alas, I have no coin to spare."

"Allow me," he said, withdrawing a pouch from his pocket.

"I wouldn't dream of it. I can't begin to guess what you might demand in payment if I were to lose."

He smiled at that and withdrew several coins, which he placed on the table before her. "No payment but the pleasure of your company."

"Oh, my." She smiled brightly. "It would appear I have come up in the world."

She rang a bell to signal Linford. When the table was cleared, the fire stoked, and Tobin had his port and Lily a cup of medicinal tea, he shuffled the cards and dealt them to her. They played one round, Lily winning quickly. The next hand was won by a very stoic Tobin, who helped himself to the crown she had just taken from him.

"You are very practiced at this," she said.

"One cannot sail the high seas and not be," Tobin said as he shuffled the cards. "There is little else to do when one is not working. Tell me where you learned to take a man's hard-earned money?"

"Here and there," she responded coyly.

He smiled a little lopsidedly at her. "I would rather imagine a line of gentlemen would be at your disposal to teach you the art of card-playing . . . among other things."

"A lady never speaks of such things," she teased.

"Aha," he said, and laid his first card. "I believe I have my answer. You are a temptress."

"I'm not."

"You are. You are very coy and you smile with your eyes. I can see a line of London fops toppling over with just a glance from you."

"You make them sound as if they are easily toppled, like wooden soldiers."

"I would know a thing or two about what would cause a man to topple, and I think you possess an abundance of that particular magic."

Lily smiled and trumped his card, drawing the pair to her side of the table. "I sense a thawing of your cold heart, Tobin Scott."

He grinned a little sheepishly. "It is your fault—your fair looks are quite disarming. But I have iron resolve."

She was gaining on him, she could see it. He was becoming less disposed to hurt her. "What do you think," she asked idly, "might have happened to the jewels?"

Tobin groaned to the ceiling. "That again?" He trumped the card she'd just played.

"Come now, you must be curious."

"Of course I am," he said and threw down another card. "But the jewels are gone, Lily. A servant probably took them."

She rolled her eyes. "Why does everyone assume a servant would be so eager to risk so much? I don't believe it—I think Lord Ashwood was looking for someone to blame. It was as if he wanted to point at someone instantly, without evidence, and see them hanged. Why would he not want to understand what had happened? Why was he so eager to accuse?"

Tobin shrugged and trumped her again.

A thought suddenly occurred to her. "I know! He was eager to accuse someone, anyone, because *he* knew where the jewels were." It suddenly all made sense! The earl *had* been eager to accuse and to blame, without benefit of investigation. He hadn't searched for the jewels at all that Lily could recall; he'd just assembled the servants and accused them one by one. "He knew all along where they were and who had taken them, and he wanted to find someone else to blame. And I . . . I unwittingly provided him with that person."

The memory of that awful morning, when he'd threatened to hang any of the servants, was still vivid. To think she had played into his hands! She closed her eyes against the image.

"Lily." Tobin's hand on her cheek startled her, and she opened her eyes. He was leaning across the small table.

"You are fatigued," he said. He felt her forehead. "And warm."

"I am fine—"

"Do not deny it," he said. "You should be abed now. I've kept you too long."

"Tobin, please," she said, wrapping her fingers around the wrist of the hand that caressed her face. "Help me find the jewels."

He lifted her hand to his lips, kissing her knuckles. "All right, you foolish girl," he said at last. "I will help you look."

Relief weighed down her body. "*Thank* you," she said. "Where should we begin?"

"We will begin with you in your bed, recovering from this illness. No," he said, squeezing her hand as she tried to speak. "I will not entertain any argument." He stood, and before Lily could move, he picked her up.

"Tobin!" She pushed against him. "I can walk!"

"Hush." He carried her to the adjoining bedroom,

holding her against his solid frame as if she'd weighed no more than a child, and deposited her on the bed. "Take good care of your mistress," he said to Ann, who stood with her mouth gaping open. "Get well, Lily. I cannot have you ill." He moved to the door and opened it to go out.

"Wait!" she said. "What of our search?"

"Start with the books," he said. "See if anyone was owed a great deal of money. But not a moment before Dr. Trittman says you might. And be warned, madam, if I hear that you are disregarding the doctor's advice, I shall increase your demise tenfold."

Lily smiled at that ridiculous notion.

She sank back into the pillows when he'd gone. For the first time, she felt as if she was winning the war.

∞

Tobin reached Tiber Park just before noon the next morning, having resisted an unholy desire to see Lily once more. But he'd already waded ankle deep into unfamiliar waters, which had left him feeling at odds with himself.

Rise up, press on, he'd told himself, and he'd left just as soon as the snow had begun to melt.

He found Bolge at Tiber Park, ale in one hand and a loaf of bread in the other. "Well, well," Bolge said. "I wondered when the dogs would drag you home."

"What brings you here?" Tobin asked.

"A problem with your newest ship," Bolge said. "Where the devil have you been?"

"Ashwood. I was snowed in."

"Were you, now?" Bolge said jovially and bit off a hunk of bread. "And here I made it all the way from London in the snow. I hope you kept warm between her legs—"

Tobin grabbed Bolge's collar, yanking the larger man halfway out of his seat. "Watch your tongue," he said sharply and shoved Bolge back in his chair.

The moment he let go, he felt appalled. His reaction had been so visceral, so . . . *protective*.

Bolge merely looked amused. "Well, well," he said, nodding sagely.

Tobin colored. He ran his hand over his head and moved to the hearth. He couldn't imagine what had just happened to him. Had he lost his bloody mind?

"What you need," Bolge said, pointing the bread at him, "is to clear your head, lad. Come to London and have a look at the ship. I think we must replace the masts if she's to sail."

London suddenly seemed like an excellent idea. "When do we leave?"

FOURTEEN
❧⚜❧

L ily slept deeply and dreamlessly, and didn't awake
until the bright sun was high in the sky. Ann told
her that Tobin had left.

"Good," Lily said.

She'd awakened with conflicting emotions about
their snowbound evening. He'd been so different, so
gentle—not the man he'd tried to make her believe he
was. It confirmed that there was so much more to him
than he was willing to allow anyone to see, but that was
dangerous thinking. That sort of thinking led to sen-
timentality, which led to weakness, and Lily was not
foolish enough to believe that a gentler Tobin was any
less her enemy.

In the days that followed, Lily slowly regained her
strength. Dr. Trittman finally allowed her to rise from
her bed and do more than just sit about and answer the
letters of concern that had been delivered. Mrs. Morton had written to request that she and her friends be

allowed to call and see for themselves that the countess's health was improving, so on a cold, overcast day, Lily received the ladies for tea.

Mrs. Morton and Lady Horncastle were filled with gossip about Tobin's sister, who was, apparently, coming down from London for the ball. Lily tried to remember Charity, but she could conjure nothing but a fair-haired girl who'd been close to her in age.

"She's to be his hostess," Lady Horncastle said behind her lorgnette in a voice of disapproving authority. "One cannot begin to fathom how she might handle the duties of a hostess, given that she was reared in plain circumstances."

"Well." Mrs. Morton patted a sausage-like curl back from her temple. "They *say* she has been schooled in proper etiquette in London. I rather suppose that one cannot rise to such prominence as Count Eberlin has done without bringing up the rest of the family, can one?"

"That is not at all true," Lady Horncastle said, letting her lorgnette drop. "You may recall Mr. Hutton, who found himself suddenly in possession of seven thousand pounds a year after the death of his uncle, yet he did not bring up *his* family."

"I should think not!" Mrs. Morton laughed. "I should think it impossible to bring up a family that practically swims in their handmade whiskey and considers poaching to be a sport! One cannot possibly compare the two families, madam. The Scott children were born into a good Christian family and were brought low by the incomprehensible actions of their father. Of course the count would raise his sister up."

"She has a daughter," Miss Babcock said idly.

Lady Horncastle and Mrs. Morton's heads swiveled around and their gazes fixed on the young woman.

Miss Babcock smiled prettily and held up the teapot. "Shall I refresh your tea?"

"What do you mean, she has a daughter?" Mrs. Morton demanded. "I had not heard she'd married."

"I did not say she had married," Miss Babcock said coyly.

Miss Babcock's words hung like anvils over their heads, and Lily's guests reared back, as if they feared they would be tainted by mere association.

"And how are you in possession of this knowledge, Miss Babcock?" Lady Horncastle asked. "I am certain I would have heard such news from the *many* contacts I maintain in London," she said, clearly angered she had not been the first to hear of it.

"Mr. Fuquay mentioned it in passing," Miss Babcock said, to which Mrs. Morton snorted. "He took a delivery of furnishings to Mayfair for Lord Eberlin. He happened to mention he'd made the acquaintance of both and that they are a handsome pair."

"*Well,*" Lady Horncastle said. "Well, then!"

"And *she* will serve as his hostess?" Mrs. Morton was clearly appalled.

"As I understand it," Miss Babcock said, obviously

enjoying her role as the fount of all knowledge regarding Charity Scott.

"It is not to be borne!" Lady Horncastle blustered, now quite pink. "It will only invite scandal and gossipmongering. Count Eberlin must have a care for his actions! He must be aware of how he presents himself to the world. His actions reflect on all of us—have we not suffered enough scandal and gossip of late?"

If there was any gossipmongering that would result in this shire, Lily had no doubt that it would be these three women to do it. She said, "I hardly think it is the end of the world as we know it."

"Some of us are perhaps more tolerant of bad behavior than others," Lady Horncastle sniffed, and brushed the crumbs of her teacake from her bodice.

An awkward moment passed as Keira's ghost hovered above the tea. "I am not intolerant," Lily said calmly, to which Lady Horncastle flicked her wrist dismissively and looked away. "I feel very sorry for Charity Scott."

"Why would you feel sorry for a woman who took no more care of her virtue than that?" Mrs. Morton asked.

"You are assuming she was careless, Mrs. Morton. I know only that she was scarcely older than me when her father died, and her mother soon thereafter. How would a girl without protection guard her virtue? She was quite helpless, and I cannot condemn her for that."

Lady Horncastle blinked. "Do you mean to say you knew of this, Lady Ashwood?"

"Yes." Lily glanced around at the three women. "I asked Eberlin and he told me what happened to his family after . . . after that summer."

Her three guests exchanged a look. Lily did not care to talk about that summer to these women, and suddenly, she did not care to talk to them at all. They sat in their tidy houses in Hadley Green and gossiped, judging others by some ridiculous social standard. They could not begin to imagine the trials that other people endured!

"Well *I* shall be on tenterhooks to meet her," Miss Babcock said, trying gamely to turn the conversation. "She's down from London and I am certain she will be dressed in the finest fashion. I intend to make a proper acquaintance of her."

"That is very shrewd of you, my dear," Mrs. Morton said. "A man as rich and handsome as Eberlin will certainly look for a wife among women who are not put off by the misfortunes of his sister or his questionable occupation, will he not?"

"Pardon?" Miss Babcock asked.

"*Arms,* my dear," Mrs. Morton said. "The man trades in *arms.*"

"Oh! How very disagreeable," Lady Horncastle exclaimed.

Miss Babcock faltered for only a fraction of a moment, then turned a bright smile to Lily. "Lady

Ashwood, have you heard the Darlingtons have come? The duke and duchess and their infant daughter, Lady Allison, as well as the dowager duchess. Rumor has it that Lord Christopher will join them, as well."

"Now *there* is a man for you," Lady Horncastle said. "Lady Ashwood, you should set your sights on him. He is as fine a match as you would ever hope to make, and he is a man of high morals."

"Yes, yes, it would be a perfect match of fortunes and holdings," Mrs. Morton eagerly agreed. "And what beautiful children the two of you would make!"

Lily felt hot. She tried to smile but failed.

"You will make his acquaintance, won't you?" Mrs. Morton pressed.

"Of course she will! I shall see to it myself," Lady Horncastle said. "I take great pride in my ability to match young people."

As Lady Horncastle nattered on about her incomparable ability to pair young lovers, Lily thought that at the very least, Mr. Fish would be made happy by the arrival of the Darlingtons.

∽

Neither the Tiber Park ball, nor the arrival of the Darlingtons, occupied Lily's mind over the next few days. She was preoccupied with Lucy's imminent departure, which also overtook any thoughts of how she might find the jewels.

Worse, Tobin had managed to dispel her idea that a kind human being existed beneath his hard exterior.

One morning, Louis escorted Agatha into the study, where Lily and Mr. Fish were reviewing the accounts. Agatha's news quickly deflated them.

"He's got a granary in Eldagirt," she reported nervously. "He'll carry grain to it and store it free of charge for anyone who promises to mill with him in the summer."

Mr. Fish's face darkened. He looked at Lily. "Free granary now?" he said sharply and tossed some papers he was holding onto the desk before stalking to the windows.

"Thank you, Agatha," Lily said.

"He is *vile*," Mr. Fish said after they'd gone. "I fear I will fail you, Lady Ashwood. I am not skilled in combating such a virtueless man."

"We mustn't fret," Lily said, although she sounded unconvincing to herself. "As he has not yet begun to store grain, we have a window of opportunity, do we not?"

Mr. Fish looked dubious. "I think our best opportunity is your introduction to the Darlingtons."

"That may be, but I am also determined to find the missing Ashwood jewels," Lily countered. "If I find them, our financial problems will be solved. It's at least as good a chance as wooing some gentleman to make an offer."

Mr. Fish arched a brow. "You do know that many have tried to find the jewels and have failed?"

"Yes, I know. But that means they are still out there

somewhere, Mr. Fish, and I daresay no one can possibly be more motivated than me to find them."

He shook his head, much as Tobin had done. "I hope, for your sake, that you are successful, madam. But I must caution you from putting your hopes too high—those jewels are likely in many pieces and now scattered."

Lily was not going to let that strong possibility dissuade her or discourage her. She had to find them. She remembered what Tobin had advised her the night he'd been snowed in at Ashwood, and she asked Mr. Fish for the books.

"I doubt you will find anything particularly illuminating in them," he said as he led her to the ledgers that chronicled years of expenditures and income for Ashwood. "I have reviewed them many times myself."

But he hadn't been searching for clues to the jewels' whereabouts.

It proved to be tedious work—the business of the estate went back more than two hundred years, obscure details duly recorded in those ledgers, day by day, and week by week. Mr. Fish was probably correct that she'd find nothing—she hardly even knew what she might look for—but she had to start somewhere.

She searched the ledgers for one that encompassed the year 1793. When she found it, she took it from the cabinet and opened it on the desk. Dust mites swirled out from the pages and sent her into a fit of sneezing. With her eyes watering, she opened to the frontispiece.

The recording had begun in November of 1792, just a few months before Mr. Scott's demise in June of 1793. Lily ran her finger down the entries on the page, finding nothing remarkable. What had she expected? That she might find an entry: *Sold, to a curator in London, one ruby coronet, one ruby necklace, one pair of ruby earrings, the sum being the gift of King Henry VIII to the first earl of Ashwood?* Hardly.

There was nothing in the pages of that ledger but the purchases made over the years on behalf of Ashwood: a dozen head of cattle, beeswax for candling, flour and fowl and linens and carpets and new livery uniforms. The rents also were recorded, with each tenant's name listed each month, the amount of rent due, and the amount of rent that was owed. And there was, as Mr. Fish had explained, a steady increase in expense and a decrease in revenues.

Lily slowly turned the pages until halfway through, her eye caught the name Mr. Walter Minglecroft. He had been paid a sum of five hundred pounds in the spring of 1793, a generous amount by any measure. Yet there was no mention of what Mr. Minglecroft's services had been. Lily was not surprised—there seemed to have been a lack of accurate record keeping through the years. She found two more entries for comparable sums paid again to Mr. Minglecroft in 1798 and in 1799, both without mention of the services he'd performed. How odd.

Lily wondered if Mr. Minglecroft was a vicar, or

perhaps a merchant of some sort. It was also curious that there was a gap of five years between the first payment and the last two.

She continued her search in the next ledger.

Curiously, Minglecroft appeared again. From 1800 to 1803 she found two payments, the last being for one thousand pounds. Then from 1804 onward, a full two years before the old earl went missing, the payments to Mr. Minglecroft ceased. Now curious as to when they had started, Lily pulled out earlier ledgers and discovered that the payments to Minglecroft had begun in 1791.

But that was all. The entries did not provide a hint of where the jewels might have been. It was more likely that Minglecroft was just some merchant or tradesman and nothing more. Disappointed, Lily put the ledgers away.

But what trade? Lily wondered as she made her way upstairs. She was mulling that over when Linford entered the study with a tea service. "I beg your pardon, madam, but Mrs. Thorpe had asked that you take your medicinal tea." He moved a bit crookedly to place it on a small table near the desk.

"Linford, have you ever heard the name Minglecroft?" Lily asked as he readied the tea.

"Can't say that I have," he said. "But my memory isn't as keen as it once was." He poured tea.

"I found his name in the estate records. Who might know who he was?"

"Mr. Fish, I should think. He seems a rather clever young man."

"But he was not in service at Ashwood at that time."

Linford thought for a moment. "There was Mr. Bowman. He was the estate agent for many years. Although I have heard recently that he has been afflicted by a stroke."

Lily remembered Mr. Bowman quite well. He was the one who had interrogated her the morning after the jewels had been discovered missing. He'd sat her in a chair and asked her what she had seen and precisely when she'd seen it as the earl had stood with his back to her, gazing out the window.

There was something else, too, Lily thought, trying to recapture that sliver of memory. What was it?

"Before him . . ." Linford frowned in concentration. "Mr. John Valmont, I believe. Goodness, I am pleased that I should recall that name, it's been so long ago. He was an affable fellow, really. I rather liked him."

"What became of him?" Lily asked as Linford set the cup of tea on the desk where she was sitting.

"I think the earl did not much care for him. The man was young and eager and asked quite a lot of questions. His lordship did not care to be questioned."

Lily could certainly believe that was true. "When was Mr. Valmont dismissed?"

"Not long after you came to us, as best I can recall." He clasped his hands at his back and bowed. "Please do drink your tea, if I may be so bold, mu'um. I dare say neither of us will want to face the wrath of Thorpe."

Lily picked up her tea. "For our sake, Linford," she said gravely, but when the old butler had shuffled out, Lily put the foul-smelling tea aside.

"A vision of loveliness you are, Lady Ashwood."

Startled, Lily looked up. Standing in the door was a tall, blue-eyed, dark-haired man who looked even more appealing than the last time Lily had seen him— which had been here, when he and Keira had made their escape.

"Declan!" she cried, leaping from her chair and rushing forward to throw her arms around him. "When did you come?"

"I have only just arrived." He was grinning from ear to ear and looked exceedingly happy as he held her tightly, kissing her on both cheeks. "You are a sight for Irish eyes, lass," he said.

"You were not expected for another two days! What a welcome surprise. Come, come," she said, grabbing his hand, pulling him into the study. "I must have all the news."

"What shall I tell you?" Declan said. "Keira has outgrown her gowns. You will not believe me when I tell you that she consumes twice as much food as I do. It is astonishing."

Lily laughed.

"The twins are still incorrigible," he added with a shake of his head. "I should very much like to send them off to London and see them married, but Mr. Hannigan complains that he has lost two daughters as it is and cannot bear to lose two more. I think he could bear it quite excellently if he'd only allow himself the happy thought."

Lily laughed. "Uncle grows sentimental in his old age. It wasn't so long ago that he threatened to see us all married before our eighteenth year so that he could pass one Sunday afternoon in leisure."

"Lord Donnelly!" Lucy's voice was filled with elation; she was rushing into Declan's arms before he'd even registered her arrival, throwing herself at him.

Declan wrapped her in a tight embrace. "There's my girl! Look at you, lass—you've grown a foot!"

"I've grown scarcely at all! When do we go to Ireland?"

"In a few days," Declan said and kissed the top of her head.

"Where shall I stay in Ireland?" Lucy asked excitedly, tugging at Declan's arm. "Shall I have a room?"

"A room? You will have more than a *room,* lassie. You shall have a pair of them, just like a princess."

Lucy beamed at Lily. "The new countess says that Ballynaheath is very large and I might get lost."

"There are lots of people about to guide you," he said with a wink. "We won't allow you to be lost. Ah, but that reminds me." Declan reached into his coat and removed two folded vellums, which he put in Lily's hand. "Keira has written at length."

"How long will you stay?" Lily asked.

"I'll need at least a day or two to prepare the horses, as I have brought only one man. Thursday morning should see us off. I want to get home as soon as I might."

Of course he would want to be home with his pregnant wife and Lucy. Oh, how Lily would miss the girl!

"Shall I show him to his rooms?" Lucy asked excitedly, already tugging on his arm.

"We should leave that to Linford, darling," Lily said. "He'll know where to put him."

"I know where to put him! In the green room, where he put the count!" Lucy exclaimed.

One of Declan's brows drifted up; he gave Lily a questioning look.

"A rather long and boring tale," she said, trying to sound light.

But Declan's eyes narrowed suspiciously. "Then I shall be on tenterhooks to hear it."

"Come, I want to show you!" Lucy said, pulling on Declan's hand. He cast a helpless look to Lily.

Lily laughed and gestured to the door. "I think your attention is very much desired."

When he and Lucy had gone, Lily eagerly opened the letter from Keira. It was filled with instructions, as usual, as Keira had never been one to shy away from assuming authority.

If you would be so kind, darling, do send a basket with Lucy so she does not go hungry. I fear my husband will be so determined to return to Ireland, he will not be attentive to such things as feeding his young charge. We both know he has always been more interested in horses than in humans. Kiss Lucy liberally for me and tell her that I can scarcely abide the wait to see her here at Ballynaheath.

Lily sighed. "I can scarcely bear to see her go."

Molly and Mabe send their love, as do Mamma and Pappa. Pappa is sitting very nearby at present and he wishes me to tell you that we all miss you dreadfully and he should like an invitation to Ashwood to see your lovely estate when you will have him. I caution you to think very carefully before inviting Molly and Mabe, as they might see their way to make the dreadful situation I left you in even worse. It is rather hard to imagine that could be so, but you know very well how they can be.

"Oh, I know." Lily tried briefly to imagine Molly and Mabe in the company of the women from Hadley Green and shuddered lightly.

*Oh darling, I nearly forgot! I can scarcely keep
a thought in my head in my present condition,
but I have long meant to tell you that there are
a few letters written to Aunt Althea tucked away
in a box in the window seat of her sitting room.
I thought you might find them interesting. You
must write me and tell me how Ashwood fares. I
pray that Eberlin has left you alone.*

Oh, Keira! If only she were here now.

"I beg your pardon, mu'um," Louis said, walking into the room.

Lily looked up from her letters.

"Lord Eberlin is calling."

"I wasn't expecting him." And she wasn't certain she wanted to see him, what with the news of the granary.

"He's got a box for you."

Curiosity was enough to persuade her. "Bring him in, please."

A moment later Louis returned with Tobin, who was carrying a box.

"What in heaven?" Lily asked as Tobin set the box on the settee and Louis left.

"Good afternoon." He was smiling. "You seem quite recovered, Lady Ashwood. Naturally that gladdens my heart, as it means we might resume our devil's bargain."

Lily flushed, and she looked nervously to the door,

expecting Declan to return and hear about that bargain.

"You may think me uncommonly bold, but I saw this gown in London and happened to think of a lamb who would look particularly fetching in it. I guessed that your recovery has prevented you from making a timely call to your modiste, so I offer this with salutations for your continued good health."

He removed the lid from the box and lifted up a gown. It was a soft, shimmering gold brocade trimmed in creamy satin. The hem and the sleeves were embroidered with dark gold thread and tiny crystals that sparkled in the afternoon light. The décolletage was quite low.

"I don't understand," Lily said uncertainly. The gown was gorgeous, as beautiful as any she'd ever seen. "That is far too generous." What would people think to see her wearing a gown he'd bought for her? What would they assume she'd done for such generosity? What would Tobin think he'd won for it?

"It is a gift," he said. But his buoyant look began to fade.

The gift was too extravagant, too assuming. As if she'd been his mistress! "I'm sorry," she whispered. "I cannot accept it."

Tobin looked baffled. He glanced at the gown. "I assure you, it was purchased in a Bond Street shop from a reputable dressmaker—"

"It's not that, Tobin."

"Then what?"

"Lily? Who have we here?"

Lily's heart began to flutter uncomfortably. She turned to the door. "Lord Donnelly, may I present—"

"You needn't introduce us," Declan said as he walked into the study, his gaze fixed on Tobin. "I know who he is." His gaze flicked to the box. "What is that?"

"A gift," Tobin said.

"Which I am refusing," Lily said quickly. Too quickly. Tobin looked at her now, his expression hard. She felt ashamed and guilty and angry at once. How dare he put her in this position?

"What is it, Lily?" Tobin asked, his voice dangerously low. "Are you ashamed of your bargain?"

Lily blanched. She did not dare look at Declan.

"Leave," Declan said. "You are not welcome at Ashwood."

"And you are . . . what? Her protector? Her lover?" Tobin asked coldly.

Declan picked up the box and shoved them at Tobin, forcing him to take them. "Leave now, sir, or I shall delight in removing you myself."

Tobin looked at Lily. It seemed as if he was waiting for her to speak, to offer Declan some explanation. When she did not—she *could* not, how could she?—he let the box drop and walked out.

Declan followed him to the door. "Louis," he called to her footman. When Louis appeared, Declan pointed to the box. "Return it to Tiber Park."

As Lily watched Louis pick up the box, her heart was pounding, her breath short. The beautiful gown was precisely the sort of thing a gentleman would give his mistress. She'd clearly lost the edge in this battle with Tobin and had to regain the upper hand.

When Louis had left the room, Declan folded his arms. "We need to talk, *muirnín.*"

FIFTEEN

"Look!" Lucy cried as she scudded into the salon. She was holding an enormous pinecone. "I found this by the river. I'm taking it to Ireland," she said proudly and held it up to Declan to have a look.

"A fine specimen," he said.

"Come," Lucy said, her hand in his again. "I have more to show you."

Declan looked at Lily. "I shall return for tea," he said pointedly. "You will join me, will you not?"

"Of course," Lily said, waving him away.

An hour later, Declan returned to find Lily in the salon, reading through Aunt Althea's letters which Keira had directed her to in her letter.

"My soon-to-be daughter is a wee bit precocious," he said fondly.

Lily laughed. "That is precisely what Keira deserves, if you ask me. There are times the girl seems to be a wee Keira."

"She worries about you," Declan said.

"Keira?" Lily asked, and shook her head.

"No, Lucy."

Lily laughed. "I cannot imagine why she would worry about me."

Declan smiled. "It would seem you haven't any friends because Keira rather ruined it all for you."

"She said that?" Lily asked, astounded.

"Not in so many words, but she has deduced it. She fears that the only friend you will have is Mr. Fish, whom she does not find the least bit suitable, as he is rather tiresome and does not possess the talent of conversation to suit her."

Lily laughed. "He is rather terse."

Declan sat next to Lily on the settee. "Lucy is further convinced that you should help yourself to another orphan from St. Bartholomew's," he said lightly. "Or better yet, produce your own child, although I was quite relieved that she recognized that was not something a lady of proper breeding undertook without a husband."

"Thank God for that."

"Is it true?" Declan asked. "Do you lack for companions?"

Lily shrugged. "There were some hard feelings in the beginning," she said as lightly as she could. "Keira deceived people; it is little wonder that the trust for Ashwood had eroded. But I think the citizens of Hadley Green are beginning to come round."

Declan sighed. "I tried to tell Keira as much, but she steadfastly refused to heed me. Nevertheless, I think you are surrounded by fools here, Lily. I have rarely known a finer woman than you."

She blushed at the compliment. "Declan, you are very kind, but—"

"I am not. I have known you some fifteen years, and you are *not* your cousin and you do *not* go about things as she does, God save us all," he said.

Lily couldn't help but smile at the impetuosity of her most beloved cousin. "Keira has always had her own ideas, and if you were to compare the devil to her, the devil would seem an angel," she said laughingly. "But I am not as perfect as you believe, Declan."

"Nonsense. I am an excellent judge of character," he said grandly. "I know a good woman, and you, *muirnín*, are a good woman. Now tell me, what has happened here?" he asked, gesturing to the room. "Things seem much worse for the wear since I last saw it. And how are you faring? Frankly, your appearance worries me— you are too thin, aye?"

"I've been ill," she said. "But I am much improved."

He did not look persuaded. "After all that has happened and the threats against Ashwood . . . how do you fare?"

For a moment, Lily felt herself on the verge of telling him everything. She wanted to rest her head on his strong shoulder and allow it all to come tumbling out—

the isolation, the finances, the threat to Ashwood—but she could imagine what he would say to Keira, who in turn would speak to Aunt Lenore, and then they would all fret about her. So she smiled reassuringly and squeezed Declan's hand. "Thank you, I am well. I had a bout of ague, but I feel fine and I am doing well."

He frowned. "Stubborn as any Hannigan I've ever known," he muttered. "At least allow me to give you money—"

"I would never!"

"Lily, for God's sake, you obviously need it," he said plaintively. "I am a wealthy man, I am your cousin, and I can help you."

But Lily had no way to repay him. She couldn't conceive of another debt on top of those that seemed to erupt like tiny Mt. Vesuviuses around her. So she smiled as cheerfully as she could force herself to do and said, "Declan, you are a dear. But I do not need your money. And besides, I intend to find the jewels."

Declan blinked, then groaned. "Ah, lass . . . you cannot pin your hopes on finding those jewels! They are nowhere to be found. They will *not* be found."

"You cannot know that for certain. I am now firmly convinced that Mr. Scott did not steal those jewels, and if he didn't, someone else did, and I daresay no one besides Keira has looked at who else might have had them."

Declan snorted.

"If I can find that person, and what became of the jewels, I can end the poverty on the edge of which Ashwood is teetering and satisfy Eberlin as well."

"Eberlin," Declan snapped. "What's he to do with it? And why was he here? Has he threatened you? Does he mock you somehow?"

"*Mock* me?"

"I can think of no reason a man might present a lady who is not his wife with a gown, unless he is making an overture or has corrupted her—"

"No, *no*," Lily quickly interjected.

"Then what? Tell me what it is, and I shall ride to Tiber Park and put an end to it at once."

"Declan!" She put her hand on his knee to soothe him. "It is not anything as you imagine. You must understand that he is . . . he is a damaged man. He saw his innocent father hanged and his family destroyed, and he wants revenge, no matter how misguided it may be. I can hardly blame him for it."

"Most gentlemen who desire revenge do not exact it from innocent and unprotected women," Declan spat. "I will not allow him to treat you ill."

"I understand," Lily said, but her emotions were terribly jumbled: anger, humiliation, sorrow. And that bothersome bit of affection. "And yet . . . ," she said, choosing her words carefully, "am I not the one who essentially put his father on the gallows?"

"You cannot blame yourself!"

"Yes, but . . ." She twisted around in her seat to face

him fully. "It was I who gave the old earl precisely what he wanted—a body." She suddenly stood and began to pace before the settee. "And once that old man had his body, he could not wait to hang him! What I do not understand, what I shall *never* understand, is why my aunt did not stop it. She could have stopped it! She could have testified to where Mr. Scott was that evening, but she wouldn't even get out of the coach! She sent me into the trial all alone. I shall never understand why she let a man she supposedly loved hang for something he did not do!"

Declan's eyes widened. "Lily . . . did Keira not tell you, then?"

Lily's heart leapt; she stopped. "Tell me what?"

Declan came to his feet. "*Muirnín.*" He took her hands in his. "Your aunt did not come to her lover's defense because the earl had threatened her."

"With what?" Lily asked angrily. "Pray tell, what could he have possibly said to her that would keep her from sparing that man's *life*?"

"He threatened her with *you*."

Lily gaped at him. She did not understand him. How could the earl threaten Aunt Althea with her?

"Ach," Declan said, clearly distressed. "What I mean is, that he told her if she spoke out, he would put you in a London orphanage."

Lily gasped. She tried to step back, but Declan held her firmly. "She was forced to choose between you and Mr. Scott."

"No," Lily said, shaking her head. "How vile, how—How do you . . . who told you this?" she stammered angrily.

"A gentleman by the name of Captain Corbett. Do you recall him?"

Of course Lily recalled the captain. He was the man her aunt had dispatched to see Lily safely to Ireland. She remembered him as a jolly old soul who'd enjoyed chess and had taught her how to play the game.

"He knew your aunt quite well," Declan said. "They were old friends. And when he came for you, she told him of the threat. It's true, Lily. I tracked the man down to ask him that very question, to understand why Lady Ashwood had not testified on Mr. Scott's behalf. Captain Corbett told me what her ladyship had related to him all those years ago."

Lily suddenly felt ill. Her mind whirled with a host of fractured memories—the earl shouting at Aunt Althea that he wouldn't have Lily underfoot. Aunt Althea begging Lily to be quiet, to not upset the earl. Her aunt had saved Lily over her own lover. The weight of that grief, that guilt, began to sink Lily, and she sank down, almost to the floor, before Declan caught her with an arm around her waist and put her on the settee.

Lily was shaking. How could the earl have forced her aunt to make such a wretched choice? "But . . . the earl *adopted* me." Why would a man who did not want her adopt her?

"Aye, that he did," Declan agreed. "One can only guess why, but I'd wager there was something he stood to gain for it. Perhaps another concession from your aunt."

Lily sank back against the settee and stared up at the ceiling. It was an extraordinary discovery, and she was shocked and hurt—and surprised that the one person she wanted to share this astounding news with was Tobin.

SIXTEEN

❧❦❧

Word swept quickly through Hadley Green that Lord Donnelly had returned for his horses. By midafternoon the following day, a letter arrived at Ashwood inviting Declan and Lily to dine at Kitridge Lodge with the Darlingtons.

Mr. Fish, who was in the study with Lily when the invitation arrived, was beside himself with joy. "We could not have planned it better with Lady Horncastle's help," he said.

"Mr. Fish, do contain yourself. It is an invitation to dine, not an offer of matrimony."

"Perhaps you see it that way, madam, but it is the sort of opportunity I have been hoping for."

Mr. Fish put so much hope on the occasion that Lily felt a bit nervous. There seemed to be so much riding on this introduction. But Declan was quite at ease. He explained to her in the carriage on their way to Kitridge Lodge that he had known the duke for many years and considered him one of his closest friends.

Kitridge Lodge was as stark on the inside as it was on the outside, and unreasonably close, what with its thick stone walls and low ceilings. A fire blazed in the dining hall's hearth, which helped chase away the chill and the musty smell. The table had been set with an array of yellow daffodils Lily was amazed to see this time of year.

"From London," the dowager duchess said, noticing that Lily was studying the twin arrangements. "My daughter-in-law is quite fond of fresh flowers, and these daffodils grow in hothouses there."

"You say that as if it were a defect of character, Mamma," the duchess said cheerfully.

Lily had liked Lady Darlington instantly. She had greeted Lily at the door with one open arm, a baby in the other, and a warm smile. "Lady Ashwood! I've heard so much about you from Lord Donnelly!"

The duchess had insisted Lily hold her infant daughter, Allison, an angel with chubby cheeks and a tuft of honey blonde hair and pale blue eyes. Lily had felt a tugging deep inside of her; she wanted children. A lot of children.

The duchess had also insisted that Lily call her Kate. "I'm not really a duchess, you know," she'd confided with a smile. "More the usual sort of woman who fell into a bit of good luck."

Kate did not seem the usual sort of woman at all to Lily. She was uncommonly beautiful, with silvery blonde hair and blue eyes. It was obvious the Duke of Darlington—a tall, gray-eyed man—adored her. Lily envied the couple more than she wanted to admit to herself. They seemed very happy with one another, and very proud parents. And for one infinitesimal moment, she imagined a life with Tobin. The thought shocked her—it was imprudent and dangerous, and certainly not what she'd ever intended.

It was also absurd—to marry Tobin Scott was to give up Ashwood and her title, to give up society altogether.

She dismissed the notion instantly.

The duke's mother, the dowager duchess, was petite and gray, but possessing powerful opinions and a wide range of advice on any number of topics. "Well," the older woman said as they sat down to dine. "Your cousin created quite a stir in London with her tomfoolery."

Lily blinked.

"Mamma," the duke said, his voice full of warning.

But Declan laughed. "She creates quite a stir wherever she appears," he agreed. "I beg your pardon if you were offended, Lady Darlington."

"You know very well how I feel, Donnelly," the dowager said. "It is fortunate that I am quite fond of you, for I would not otherwise condone such shenanigans."

"For the love of heaven," the duke sighed, but Declan merely chuckled.

"Lady Ashwood, I knew your father many years ago,"

the dowager continued as she began to delicately consume the soup placed before them. "He was a mercurial sort, as I recall. Grayson, you were so young likely you do not recall this, but Ashwood very nearly shot Lord Alnwick on a hunt one autumn. Alnwick swore it was intentional, and Ashwood did not deny it."

Kate gasped with surprise, then laughed. "I suppose that is one way to dispose of your enemies, eh?"

The dowager lowered her tiaraed head and pointed a look at the younger duchess. "As I was saying," she continued when a smiling Kate had turned her attention to her soup. "He was a very volatile man, as was his sister. Awful woman, that one. I rather think that is why she never married, in truth. One cannot abide a woman who does not know her place."

Kate coughed; the duke patted her hand and smiled thinly in a manner that suggested he had done it many times before.

"You recall her, do you not, Lady Ashwood?" the dowager asked.

"No, madam," Lily said. "The earl was not my father, and—"

"Not your father!" the dowager said sternly, lowering her spoon.

"My lady aunt was his wife, and they adopted me after my parents passed."

The dowager put her spoon down and leaned across her soup bowl, peering closely at Lily. "You are not his blood kin?"

"I am not," Lily said apologetically.

"Then how in heaven have you come to inherit?"

"Madam!" the duke said sternly.

"She doesn't mind a friendly conversation, Grayson," his mother said, her gaze still on Lily.

"The entail of Ashwood is rather complicated," Declan offered. "The title and the lands were a gift of Henry VIII, and certain allowances were made. As she was his legal ward and the only surviving heir, she inherited."

The dowager blinked. "Well!" She picked up her spoon again. "Well, then you have done quite well for yourself, have you not, Lady Ashwood? An orphan! Whoever would have believed it?" She looked at Kate. "Here we have *two* titled orphans. Times have certainly changed since *my* day," she said with a shake of her head.

"And we are all eternally grateful that they have." The duke smiled warmly at Lily. "Please do forgive my mother. She considers herself to be the arbiter of all that is proper."

"At least I can rest easy that my second son shares my views," the dowager said with a sniff. "Are you acquainted with Lord Christopher, Lady Ashwood?"

"I have not had the pleasure, no."

"Regrettable. You would find him very interesting, as well as charming."

"Is he coming?" Kate asked.

"I think not," the duke said. "Although I cannot

imagine why he'd not want to be in close quarters with his family." He exchanged a wry grin with Declan.

Poor Mr. Fish, Lily thought. *He will be terribly disappointed.*

"I think you'd get on with Merrick, Lady Ashwood," Kate said.

"What *are* your prospects for marriage at present?" the dowager asked.

Lily almost choked.

The duke put his fork down and leveled a look at his mother.

"Her prospects are as good as anyone might expect out here in the midst of nothing, Lady Darlington," Declan said. "Perhaps you might be of some assistance in that regard."

Lily managed to kick him under the table, but the dowager duchess perked up. "I should be delighted!"

"Are you thinking of Merrick?" Kate asked her mother-in-law.

"Certainly not!" the dowager said instantly, but Kate smiled at Lily.

Lily very much desired to crawl under the table.

Fortunately, as the second course was served, the talk turned to hunting. The duke had been stalking a wild turkey for a few days. "I am determined to bag the blasted thing before we return to London."

"And when would that be?" Declan asked.

"A fortnight, I suspect."

"You'll stay for the ball, won't you?" Lily asked. All

heads swiveled in her direction. "The First Winter's Night Ball at Tiber Park," she clarified.

Kate and the duke exchanged a look, but the dowager groaned. "Not that again! I beg your pardon, Lady Ashwood, but we will most certainly *not* attend that ball, and I should hope that you wouldn't, either!"

Surprised, Lily looked to Declan, who was studying the roast beef on his plate.

"My dear, you *do* know that Count Eberlin's title was purchased in Denmark, do you not?"

"Yes," she said. "I have heard that."

"Well, that cannot be!" the dowager exclaimed. "He is a merchant, and moreover, he deals in the most vile of trades. His family cannot be recommended, nor does he have any proper connections in London. You are not yet married, madam, and you must be circumspect in who you associate with. That sort of association could have a negative impact for your happy future when you come to London to seek an offer."

It was not Lily's idea to "seek" an offer, but she rather imagined someone had given them the idea. Probably Declan, whom she would very much like to throttle at present. Her life was in enough turmoil without help from anyone else.

"What my mother means to say, Lady Ashwood, is that she does not care for Count Eberlin," the duke said with a smile. "I am quite certain she does not mean to insinuate you should follow her lead."

Lily looked from the duke to the dowager duchess, who was glaring at her son. "He's had a rather mean life, I grant you, but he has worked very hard to overcome—"

"He cannot overcome the circumstances of his birth or his family's reputation, Lady Ashwood, and he certainly cannot overcome the circumstances of his wealth or his title or his occupation."

Declan's hand touched hers beneath the table, warning her not to argue with the duchess. As wildly angry as Tobin had made her, Lily could not help but feel sorrow for him. How could a man who had worked so very hard to overcome the hardships of the past be so roundly condemned for it? It seemed as if the world refused to let him belong no matter what he did.

It all made Lily indignant and angry and terribly, terribly confused. The old woman was rigid in her thinking, but Lily understood the value of social connections, particularly in her precarious financial state. So she smiled and lifted her wineglass. "The weather has been rather impossible this autumn, has it not?" she asked, and silently fumed as the people seated around the table blithely discussed the weather.

SEVENTEEN

On a mild, sun-dappled morning, Tobin and his stable master rode to Kitridge Lodge to take possession of the horse he'd commissioned from the Earl of Donnelly earlier in the year. The broodmare, for which Tobin had paid a great amount of money, had been impregnated by a champion runner. The foal she carried would be trained to be the finest racehorse England had ever seen. It was a pity, then, that the Earl of Donnelly, whose reputation for training racehorses was unparalleled, would not be the one to train her, but Tobin had severed their agreement when he realized that Keira Hannigan was perpetuating a fraud.

If he hadn't done it then, he certainly would have when Donnelly kicked him out of Ashwood.

Or when he'd appeared at Tiber Park yesterday to inform Tobin that he was taking his horses to Ireland, and that the broodmare was ready to be moved. The Irishman had stood out on the drive, his legs braced apart, a dark expression on his face. Tobin had found his demeanor curious, given Donnelly's history in Hadley Green, which consisted basically of whoring and gambling and assisting Miss Hannigan to dupe everyone into believing she was Lily. Yet somehow the man gave off an air of superiority.

"Mr. Noakes will be happy to continue the care of the mare if you'd like," Donnelly had said, referring to the caretaker at Kitridge Lodge.

Tobin said nothing. He stood on the landing of his house, leaning against the stone wall, watching Donnelly. "Very well," he said, and turned to go inside, but Donnelly said, "Eberlin, a word."

Here it was then: the moment Donnelly would tell him to keep his distance from Lily. Perhaps he'd even call Tobin out, and frankly, Tobin would have welcomed the opportunity to do him bodily harm in that moment. "And what word would that be, my lord?" he'd asked calmly. "Do you mean to present yourself as the new king of England and order me off this island?"

Donnelly's expression had darkened even more as he'd walked up the steps to stand before Tobin. "I understand that you believe you've somehow been harmed by the Lady Ashwood. She refuses to tell me precisely what misery you have inflicted on her, but it is obvious that you've caused her distress. So hear this, sir: if you cause her harm, you will have me to deal with."

"You are quite determined to vex me, I think."

Undeterred, Donnelly moved closer. "I am a powerful man," he said evenly. "I could ruin you with a word."

"Then say it," Tobin snapped. "Say your bloody word, Donnelly. I have nothing to fear from you."

Donnelly smiled coldly. "Are you certain of that?"

"Take your leave," Tobin had snapped, and he'd turned and walked into his very grand house, his fist clenching. For once, it was not a spell that made him tense. This time, he kept his fist clenched to keep from hitting Donnelly square in the face.

Today, as Tobin and his stablemaster rode up the path to Kitridge Lodge—an old Norman castle that had been converted into a hunting lodge for the Darlington family—he saw a small carriage in the drive drawn by a single horse. Behind it was the larger Ashwood coach. And standing next to the coach were Lady Ashwood, Miss Taft, and Donnelly.

Tobin slowed his horse as he joined those gathered on the lawn. Lily was wearing a wide-brimmed bonnet, so he could see only the lower half of her face. Donnelly noticed him, of course, and leaned into Lily to say something before walking away.

"Good morning, ladies," Tobin said as he dismounted.

As usual, Lucy greeted him sunnily. "I am going to Ireland!" she announced grandly, as if this news was just this moment known to her.

"So you are," Tobin said. He reached into his saddlebag. "I have a gift for you, if Lady Ashwood will allow me."

"For me?" Lucy asked, clearly thrilled.

"For you," Tobin said, and held out a mink muff. "I understand it can be quite cold and damp on those Irish moors."

Lucy gasped with delight. "Thank you!" She touched her cheek to the muff. "It's so very soft! See what he has given me, Lady Aswhood!" She whirled around to Lily to show her. "May I accept it?"

"It is only a small token," Tobin said before she could refuse. "With winter coming, she will need it."

Lily stared at the muff, her bottom lip between her teeth. "That's a very thoughtful gift." She looked up at him. "Thank you."

Lucy stuffed her hands into it and whirled about to Tobin. "Thank you! I am to have my own carriage. See?" She pointed excitedly to the little carriage.

"Quite grand," Tobin said.

"And then I shall sail on a *boat,*" she continued. "Have you ever been on a boat?"

"Many times."

"May I put my muff in the carriage?" Lucy asked.

"All right. But do stay out of the way of the men," Lily said. She reached out to touch Lucy's head, but Lucy skipped away before she could reach her.

Lily lowered her hand and looked away from Tobin.

"Do you refuse to speak to me now?" he asked quietly.

"Should I not?" Lily said lightly, and wiped a gloved finger beneath her eye. "Have you done something untoward?"

Tobin frowned. He dipped his head a little to see under the brim of her hat, but Lily turned away again. He moved closer and dipped again. "Are those tears?"

"*Hush*," Lily whispered, and when Tobin touched her arm, she batted it away. "I don't want Lucy to see me. The poor girl feels responsible as it is, and I don't wish to upset her."

"Responsible?" Tobin said, confused. "For what?"

Lily sighed and cast her gaze to the heavens as if he tried her patience. "Does it matter?"

"I cannot begin to fathom what an eight- or nine-year-old girl might feel responsible for," Tobin said.

Lily swung around and pinned him with a look.

Baffled, Tobin looked her up and down. "What?"

"Can you not fathom even one thing?" she asked irritably. "For you seem to think that *I* should have felt some responsibility at that age."

"That is different," he said gruffly, but he felt stung, called out.

She clucked her tongue and turned away just as Lucy bounded into their midst again.

"Pappa said he is almost ready," she said. "He said I am to call him Pappa now and that it will take us a week to reach Ballynaheath if the weather does not turn." She glanced at Tobin. "That is where I shall live. It's a *castle* in *Ireland*."

"Yes," he said, smiling. "You have told me. At least four times now, if my count is accurate."

Donnelly appeared behind Lucy, his gaze cold. "If you have come for your horse, it is over there," he said, pointing away from them.

"I know where the stable is," Tobin said.

"Then if you will excuse us," Donnelly said, and put a protective arm around Lily's shoulder to lead her toward the carriage with Lucy skipping ahead of them.

Tobin did not walk on to the stables—he followed them.

Lucy was floating with excitement, and while Tobin kept a respectable distance, he watched as Lily sank down before Lucy. "You will do as Lord Donnelly asks you at all times, will you not, Lucy? And you will mind your manners as well?"

"Yes, I remember everything you told me," Lucy agreed, her head bobbing in agreement.

Lily grasped the girl's arms. "And promise you will write to me, Lucy. Lady Donnelly writes a letter a week, and you may send one along with hers so that I will have all your news."

"One letter every week," Lucy said solemnly.

Lily wrapped her arms around so tightly around Lucy that Tobin feared she was squeezing the breath from her. When the girl squirmed, Lily reluctantly let her go. "Godspeed, my darling," she said, and kissed her cheek.

"Farewell, countess!" Lucy said brightly.

Lucy was, Tobin realized, too young to understand Lily's loss, and too excited to notice her sadness.

Lily stood up. "Have a care for her," she told Donnelly.

"With my own life," Donnelly assured her, and hugged Lily. "Come home, lass," he said, and Tobin felt his heart quicken. "You need not stay here if you do not desire it, aye? You will always have a home in Ireland."

"Aye." She smiled sadly at Donnelly, but her smile brightened when she turned to Lucy. "Safe journey!"

"Good-bye, Count Eberlin! Good-bye, Lady Ashwood!" Lucy called as she bounded to the carriage. "Good-bye, Louis!" she said with a jaunty wave to the footman who sat next to the coachman.

"Good-bye, lass! Godspeed!" Louis called after her.

Donnelly swung up on one of the horses and looked down at Tobin. "We will return," he said. "All of us."

Tobin didn't know if Donnelly meant the king's army or Lily's family, but either hardly mattered to him. He shrugged.

Donnelly looked down at Lily and with a wink, he made a *tchk* sound that started the horses forward, the carriage following behind. Tobin moved to stand beside Lily as the carriage pulled away, and Lucy leaned out the window and waved furiously at them before disappearing inside once more.

Tobin glanced at Lily. As he suspected, tears were trickling down her face, and he felt another tiny leap of his heart.

The footman hopped off the Ashwood coach and opened the door. "My lady," he said. With her head down, the brim of her hat covering her eyes, Lily started for the coach. But as she walked past, Tobin reached out and touched his fingers to hers. She paused for a slender moment, and he felt her fingers brush against his. And with that, he felt a tiny little crack form in the black ooze inside him, and an even tinier bit of light shine through.

Tobin thought of what he should say, to ease her loss, to comfort her. But before he could think of the appropriate words, the door of the lodge was flung open and a beautiful woman stepped outside. "Lily, do come in for tea!" she called out. She glanced at Tobin, then at Lily again.

Lily hesitated.

Another man appeared at Tobin's side. "My lord, your horse is ready," he said.

"The tea is freshly brewed and Mrs. Noakes has made biscuits. Please come in, Lady Ashwood."

Lily seemed to hesitate before stepping forward, but she walked to the lodge without sparing him a glance. He watched her go inside with the woman, and the door close behind them.

Then he glanced around, and realized that everyone else had gone about their day, and he was utterly alone.

EIGHTEEN

Preparations for the First Winter's Night Ball kept the staff of Tiber Park in a state of chaotic activity for the next several days. Tobin had made it clear that work must be completed on the new courtyard, and that renovations to the common areas of the house must be finished as well. Dozens of men had been put to work, and the grounds were beginning to look immaculate and the house pristine.

To prepare the ballroom, Tobin had engaged the services of a gentleman from London who dressed theater stages for a living. Mr. Kissler had brought a crew of men and materials down from London to create a winter garden, a scene that would rival any decoration Carlton House had ever seen. Tobin had never seen the ballroom of Carlton House, or even knew what sort of decorations it had had, other than what he'd read in the *Morning Times*. But he'd heard of the Prince of Wales's penchant for scenery, and he was determined to have a ballroom every bit as grand as that at Carlton House.

Mr. Kissler completely transformed the ballroom. Soft white down covered the ceiling to look like clouds, and from those clouds hung dozens upon dozens of crystal stars that twinkled in the light from the three candelabras. Small pine trees had been arranged in huge clay pots, their limbs decorated with snow and crystal icicles. On the balcony, where the orchestra would sit, mountains had been made of wooden frames and cloth, which would hide the musicians but not impede their music. To Tobin's guests, it would seem as if the waltz was being played from the French Alps.

On the night of the ball, ice sculptures would grace either end of the ballroom, and a large circular fountain of libations would flow all night. A temporary dining room had been erected in the courtyard, where a full-course meal would be served at midnight. It would be one of the most splendid evenings the residents of Hadley Green had ever experienced.

Tobin was also preparing for the arrival of Charity and Catherine. Charity hadn't wanted to come, but he had implored her. He certainly understood her misgivings; she held no fond memories of Hadley Green either and, unlike him, she had no desire for revenge. Frankly, Tobin didn't know *what* she desired any longer. She kept her wishes to herself and said only that she wanted to be left alone with her daughter, rambling about his Mayfair town home and avoiding society.

Normally Tobin would do whatever his sister wished, but this time he needed her. He needed a familiar face, fearing what could happen if a spell descended on him. He would need his sister to help him unknot his body and his mind if they became taut.

"But what of Catherine?" Charity had asked when Tobin had told her he wanted her at Tiber Park.

"You cannot keep the child tucked away as if she were some precious Oriental flower," he'd said gently. "She needs society."

"She does not need Hadley Green society," Charity had sniffed.

Tobin had not been able to argue with her feelings, but he'd nevertheless prevailed, and Charity was due to arrive the following morning.

His sister's arrival would leave only one thing undone, Tobin thought that afternoon as he neared the end of his hedgerow. There was one thing that weighed heavily on his mind, and bloody hell if he hadn't been cursed with troubling thoughts—inexplicably *tender* thoughts—about Lily Boudine.

He could even point to the day he'd first had them. It was the day she'd come riding into the forest with that absurdly flintless gun, as if she were the sheriff. It was the moment she had been standing on the steps of Ashwood, gripping her riding crop as if her life had depended on it, determined to pick up the gauntlet.

He had greatly admired her pluck and cunning for doing precisely the opposite of what he'd expected.

The feeling he'd experienced that day had been nothing more than a noticeable tic—but it had rooted.

Tobin swung his ax and felt the resistance of the stubborn hedgerow reverberate through his body.

When she'd come to dine, he'd had every intention of seducing her. But he'd felt that abominable tic in him again when she'd left him standing there, reeling from the strength of her ethereal kiss and the uncomfortable knowledge that he wanted to see her again.

He'd had stronger, more tender thoughts of her when he'd seen her frolicking on the riverbank with Lucy, and he'd certainly felt something the day he'd found her at the cottage, where, in the haze of his formidable physical desire for a beautiful woman, he'd seen a glimpse of the girl Lily had once been, the incorrigible, spirited lass who had vexed him. He'd softened that day.

But when Tobin had gone to Ashwood, and had seen her in her sickbed, he'd felt the thing that frightened him the most. He'd felt concern. *Alarm.* She'd looked so small and forlorn, without anyone she loved to care for her. He'd almost felt the black mud in him begin to dry.

Such incomprehensible feelings were insupportable. He swung the ax again. Had this secret illness addled his brain? Had he not been beguiled by other beautiful women without developing such bothersome feelings? Yes, he had . . . but with Lily, there was a familiarity he'd not accounted for.

That familiarity and the bloody tender feelings had been eating away at him the day he'd gone to London with Bolge. He'd taken his sister to Bond Street to be measured for new gowns, and as he'd waited, he'd seen the blasted gold gown in the dress shop window. Like a green young lad with his first infatuation, he'd made an impetuous purchase, all because he'd remembered her swanning about in her aunt's gowns as a girl, acting the queen. She would tilt up her chin, and with her aunt's priceless ruby coronet on her head, she'd walk with her hand held out, as if she'd expected a knight to rush up and take it as he dropped to his knees and swore his fealty. "*Do* bring tea, young man," she'd say to him, and Tobin could remember rolling his eyes and turning his back to her so that he might finish the book he was reading.

Then, fifteen years later, he'd walked into a Bond Street dress shop and touched the shimmering gold brocade in the window, and he'd seen Lily, regal and beautiful, a winter queen in her own right, wearing that gown.

After she'd refused it and sent it back to him, he'd tossed it into the guest room, annoyed with himself for having succumbed to the creaky feelings of tenderness.

But then . . . then he'd felt a troublesome surge of tenderness again when he'd watched Lily say a tearful farewell to Lucy Taft. He hadn't wanted to empathize with her—God no, not after the way she and Donnelly had treated him at Ashwood. But he'd not been able to help himself. The expression on her face had been his undoing, and when she'd touched her fingers to his, he'd lost himself.

He wanted to see her in the gown. He wanted to touch her fingers once more, to feel her lips beneath his, taste her skin, smell her hair—

God, what was wrong with him?

Tobin chopped the last of the hedgerow and threw down his ax. He glanced at Mr. Greenhaven and said, "All done. Now find me another." And with that he stalked up to the house, wishing he could turn his flesh inside out and scratch the prickly sensation.

He took the stairs two at a time up to the first floor. He did not glance at the footman and the maid who stood to one side as he passed. He did not pause to ask someone to draw him a bath. He walked to the newly furnished suite of rooms he had designated for Charity and Catherine, and opened the wardrobe.

There was the gown, hanging alone.

Tobin looked down at his hand and remembered the feel of Lily's fingers touching his. When, exactly, had he lost sight of his reason for being here? When had his rage dissipated into the desire to be part of something more . . . uplifting? He still felt the rage, but its sharp edges had been dulled.

So it was not a great surprise to Tobin when he found himself on the road to Ashwood later that afternoon, the gown folded and attached to the rump of his horse. He rapped loudly at the door and stood with one foot on the threshold when Linford informed him that Lady Ashwood was behind closed doors with her estate agent.

"I'll wait," Tobin said and strode into the foyer before Linford could turn him away. He sat on one of two chairs, the bundle of the gown on his lap.

Linford looked pained by Tobin's obstinacy. "I cannot say how long she might be, my lord."

"That is quite all right." A moment passed before Linford, either too tired or too old to argue, lumbered away, leaving Tobin to sit in the foyer as if he were some youthful suitor who did not know these sorts of battles were won in the darkened stairwells at balls or behind the decorative greenery at supper parties. But he continued to sit, for he knew that if he stood, he likely would walk out the door and not come back. He would sink back into the blackness and allow it to cover his head.

He had no idea how much time had passed when he heard a door close and the sound of a man's footfall. He stood slowly, his bundle under one arm.

Mr. Fish appeared in the foyer with one of the footmen. He looked startled when he saw Tobin there and exchanged a look with the footman. He then glanced down the corridor from whence he'd just come before turning back to Tobin. "Is the countess expecting you?" he asked crisply.

Tobin resisted the urge to fidget with his neckcloth. "No."

Mr. Fish looked him up and down, obviously debating what his response should be. It was plain how determined the man was to despise him, so Tobin was not surprised when Mr. Fish strode across the foyer and glared up at Tobin. "You are a vile man," he said low. "You prey on an innocent and unprotected woman."

At any other time, in any other place, Tobin would have merely shrugged. But he'd now been accused twice in one week of distressing or otherwise preying on Lily, and he did not like the way the accusation made him feel. There it was again, that loathsome business of feelings!

"Step aside," he growled at Mr. Fish.

For a moment, it seemed as if the smaller man would not, but Mr. Fish was an intelligent man who probably weighed all the possible outcomes if he didn't, for he stepped back and pivoted about, striding to the door.

When he'd gone out, Tobin noticed Linford and the footman lurking near the corridor. "Well?"

"If you please, my lord," Linford said, gesturing to the corridor.

Tobin glanced at the footman, who likewise bore an accusatory expression, and followed Linford.

Lily rose from her desk when he entered the study. She was dressed in crimson, which had the effect of giving her a very healthy glow. "Tobin," she said flatly.

"Madam."

Her eyes flicked to the bundle he held. "What brings you to Ashwood today? There is no grain in our granary."

"Grain?" he uttered, momentarily confused. Then he remembered, and he could not help his smile.

Lily frowned and folded her arms across her. "You may find it amusing, but I assure you, we do not. A *free* granary!" Her gaze flicked to Linford. "That will be all, thank you." She glared at Tobin as the old butler went out, then swept around her desk, advancing on him, her eyes blazing with anger. "I don't understand you, in truth," she said. "On the one hand, you seem to want some sort of friendship. You were kind to Lucy, you loan people money who need it. You came to see after me when I was ill. But then you turn around and do things that are so cruel and ill-spirited."

His smile widened. "I grant you that I have done many cruel and ill-spirited things, but this was not one of them."

"Oh, for heaven's sake," she said and twirled away from him. "I may be easy prey, Tobin, but I am no fool."

"No," he agreed. "You are certainly no fool. However, I have not opened a free granary, nor do I have plans to do so. Even I cannot justify such expense."

Lily cast a suspicious gaze over her shoulder. "Don't lie to me—there is nothing I will not discover."

"I have not," he said. "But I said that I had. I've said any number of things in the last week, in the company of various servants, all so that I might discover the identity of your spy in my house. What is his name? Ah, yes. Ranulf. His sister Agatha is in your service."

Lily's lips parted with surprise.

Tobin moved closer still. "Tell me—how much do you pay Ranulf?"

Lily's hand fluttered to her throat. "I bade him do it. You must not punish him," she said quickly.

"Admirable of you to take the blame," he murmured, admiring her mouth. "Then I should exact my punishment from you?"

Her cheeks bloomed. "Please do not dismiss him, Tobin. He has two young children."

"I have no desire to dismiss Ranulf. He's too good a footman to be let go for that. And apparently a loyal one, too."

Lily's brows dipped into a dubious frown. "That's all you will say?"

"Not all. I warn you that if I find he is still spying after today, I will remove him and make certain he cannot find work in West Sussex."

Lily returned his gaze just as intently. "Fair warning."

Tobin smiled fondly and held out the bundle. "For you."

She glanced at it as if it were a snake. "What is it?"

He put it on the desk.

Lily continued to eye it warily as she untied the string. She moved the paper aside and her frown deepened. She carefully touched the gown, felt the satin trim. "Why did you bring it back?" she asked, her voice full of resignation. "I cannot wear it." She removed her hand from the garment and moved away.

Her pronouncement was met with a painful little twinge in Tobin's heart. "Why not?"

Lily snorted. "Is it not apparent, even to a man like you?"

A man like him . . . There it was, the painful twinge again. "Nothing is apparent to me."

"Really, Tobin," she said, as if she was exasperated. "How many ways can you humiliate me?"

The word confused him. How could she think a gift was designed to humiliate? "That was not my intent."

"Then what, pray tell, was your intent? To suggest to the world that I am a kept woman?"

"Pardon?" He suddenly felt hot. And dishonorable. He was so foolish. He should have understood how this gift might be perceived, how she would perceive it. But had he not spent his adult life keeping women at arm's length, treating them each as his *fille de joie* and lavishing them with gifts instead of affection? He cleared his throat; gripped his hand into a fist. "That was not my intent," he repeated roughly, and struggled to swallow. "I saw this gown in London and I thought it would look particularly lovely on you. That was my only thought, Lily. I did not think how it would . . . look," he said tightly.

Lily's cool gaze faded and she looked at him closely. "Tobin? What is wrong?"

He coughed and moved away, looking to the windows. "I am naturally displeased that you would construe this gift in that way, but perhaps I . . . I should have realized how it would be perceived." Her touch on his arm startled him. He flinched and tried to move away, but Lily was peering up at him.

"You look unwell. Would you like some water?"

"I am perfectly fine." Her eyes were filled with concern. He swallowed again and wished desperately that she would back away. "I regret the misunderstanding," he said and gestured lamely to the gown. "Do with it what you will, but I have no use for it." He stepped away from her and Lily's hand fell to her side.

"Thank you." But she was still staring at him curiously. "It's my fault as well," she said and looked down. "I thought I could play this game of yours." She fluttered her fingers. "This game of seduction and ruination. I thought I could win, but I have discovered that I haven't the stomach for it. I want more from my life than to be taken in by you, Tobin."

Tobin could feel a gulf opening in the mud inside him. He supposed he should have been offended, but what he really wanted to know was what she *did* want from life. He suddenly had a burning desire to know, but before he could force the words from his frozen throat, before he could lift his arm to reach for her, she'd turned back to her desk.

"I have news," she said lightly as she moved the gown to the corner of the desk and sifted through some papers. "I reviewed the Ashwood ledgers as you suggested, and I found mention of a man named Walter Minglecroft."

Tobin clenched and unclenched his fist, willing his body to return to its natural state. "Who is he?"

"I do not know," Lily said. She picked up a ledger and held it out to him. "But the earl paid him handsomely."

Tobin opened the ledger to the marked pages.

"Mr. Fish said he supposed that the earl had bought art or something like it from the gentleman."

Tobin looked at the entries. "That's because Mr. Fish is not the sort of man to frequent gaming hells. These look to me as if they could be gambling debts."

Lily sagged a little. "Of course." She looked defeated.

"I would think you would be pleased not to discover any evidence of wrongdoing," Tobin said as he closed the ledger and put it aside.

"I wish I had discovered the truth there, written in black and white. Something happened here, Tobin, and I feel helpless to know how to discover it. There are rumors that my aunt was murdered. Or that she drowned herself. And really, where is the earl?" Lily asked. "Earls do not simply disappear, do they?"

"Lily, this is not worth your distress—"

"It is worth every *bit* of my distress," she said sharply. "I may very well have set wheels in motion that destroyed the lives of so many!"

Tobin felt as if he'd managed to open Pandora's box

and now couldn't put all the ills back into it. "Please do not burden yourself so."

Lily sat on the chair at her desk. She reached into the pocket of her gown, withdrew a yellowed vellum, and handed it to him. "I found several letters like this one. It is from my aunt Lenore. She is the one who took me in when I was sent away from England."

Tobin opened the vellum and skimmed the salutations. *We have lost yet another governess,* the author had written.

> *The poor dear explained to my husband that while she was fond of the children, she found the twins quite unteachable. She was driven to that unkind characterization after they filled her boots with mud.*
>
> *Darling Al, I have thought quite hard about your last letter. It has left me at sixes and sevens, for I cannot bear knowing you are so astoundingly unhappy. It is terribly unfair that he should deny you simple pleasures while seeking his quite openly and without conscience. I have written Margaret and asked her to come to you straightaway, but she writes that her cough has returned . . .*

There was more about another sister, Tobin gathered, and a growing concern as to the state of that one's health. When he'd finished, he folded the letter and handed it to Lily.

She gave him an earnest look. "What does it mean?"

"What?"

"This," she said and opened the vellum, reading, "'*He would deny you simple pleasures while seeking his quite openly and without conscience.*' What precisely does that mean?"

Tobin looked at his hand again and imagined her fingers touching his. "I think you know very well what it means."

"I can speculate, but I do not truly understand it," she insisted.

"It means," Tobin said as he walked to the sideboard and helped himself to the decanter of whiskey and a glass, "that your aunt's husband likely had a mistress."

"But openly, and without conscience?" she asked, staring at the letter. "Do all men take a mistress without conscience? Is that the nature of marriage, that everyone must have an illicit affair?"

Tobin downed the whiskey. "Many men do, and many do not. I don't know why you fret so. It's hardly as if marriages among the Quality are love matches."

"How cynical," Lily said. "Does no one marry for love?" she asked plaintively. "Does no one desire to share a life and make a family? I cannot imagine a happier existence, yet I can count on one hand the marriages I know to be full of love and shared dreams and hopes. How many women live like my aunt must have lived, married to a selfish man who would take his pleasure openly and deny hers, without conscience?"

Tobin's father had been involved in an illicit affair with her aunt while his mother had remained at home with him and his siblings, waiting patiently for him to return from Ashwood. How many ways had his mother been made to suffer? Tobin felt a rumbling in the darkness. He stared into the amber liquid in his glass. "Is that what you want from life? Love and marriage?"

Lily drew a deep breath, then vaulted up from her seat and began to pace. "I have never wanted for anything more than a family I could call my own. I only vaguely remember my parents' passing, but I remember quite clearly the desire to *have* parents, to belong somewhere." She briefly closed her eyes. "I thought that I might have it here," she said, opening her eyes. "I did not want to come back, I did *not,* what with all that had happened here. But as I became accustomed to the idea that this was indeed my destiny, I allowed myself the fantasy that perhaps I might find my dream here. That perhaps I would meet a gentleman who would love me, and our children, and I would live in this peaceful setting until I died.

"But there has never been happiness here. There has been no history of love in this house." She pressed the back of her hand to her forehead as if it pained her. "I am a fool."

"Lily," Tobin said and touched her arm.

The touch seemed to ignite her; she suddenly whirled about and grabbed his hand. "Come."

"Wha—"

But Lily was moving, tugging at his arm. He scarcely managed to put the tot of whiskey aside as she pulled him out of the room.

In the corridor, she linked her arm in his and walked purposefully, her head down. They rounded a corner, went up his father's staircase, down the corridor, until Lily stopped before a door and opened it. She strode inside. When he didn't follow at once, she took his hand again, dragging him inside.

They were in the music room. Tobin recalled it now, for he had been here the day the pianoforte had been delivered. The countess had been beaming with delight, and she had taken Lily's hands and danced around in a circle as he and his father had stood to one side, watching. His father had been laughing, enjoying their delight, almost as if he were responsible for it.

Had his father been responsible for the countess's delight that day?

Lily let go his hand and went down on her knees beside the piano stool, moving to turn it over. Tobin caught it and turned it over for her.

"Look," she said.

He recoiled from it, feeling the swell of discomfort beginning to thicken in his throat.

But Lily tugged him down to one knee and pointed to the inscription: *You are the song that plays on in my heart; for A, my love, my life, my heart's only note. Yours for eternity, JS.*

"What of it?" He tried to stand, but she held him there.

"*That* is what I want, Tobin. I want a love like they must have had——"

"And destroy another's happiness in the bargain?" he asked sharply. "You put romance into their affair——"

"It *was* a romance."

"Lily, for God's sake. If that were true, if she truly loved him, would she not have stepped forward to keep my father from hanging?"

"She loved him, Tobin," Lily said softly. "But the earl gave her an impossible choice. He threatened to put me in a London orphanage if she spoke out." Lily told him everything she'd learned from Donnelly.

Tobin was appalled. He knew what London orphanages—essentially, workhouses—were like; Lily would not have survived it. He wondered if his father had known about the choice Lady Ashwood had been forced to make.

"Do you see?" Lily asked.

Tobin shook his head. "What I see, what I *know,* is that their love affair was carried out at the expense of my family and your happiness. Theirs was a selfish affair of the flesh that hurt many innocent people."

He pulled his hand free and stood up. He would not repaint history to suit her.

"They did hurt many people," Lily softly agreed, and gained her feet. "But you cannot look at this inscription, you cannot recall the many times we saw them together, and deny that they truly loved each other. Perhaps they were victims of circumstance—we will never know. I only know that I want that sort of love, one that runs so deep that I would face death rather than betray the one I love."

Tobin would never know what it was that struck him so violently. It seemed almost a waking dream, a snatch of imagery, a sensation unlike anything he'd ever felt. He caught Lily at the same moment she seemed to reach for him, his mouth finding hers, his tongue touching hers.

Tobin kissed her passionately as he tightened his embrace, crushing her to him as if he was afraid she would fly away if he let go. His desire exploded within him, enveloping them. It was as tormenting as it was pleasurable, as heart aching as it was heart-stopping. Tobin was jolted to his core; he could feel the mud in him drying and cracking, and great shafts of light shining through and warming him. Her body seemed to blend into his; she clung to his lips, her hands on his shoulders, her breasts against his chest.

The groan in Tobin's throat came from somewhere that seemed almost outside of him, a stifled cry of relief and of need. He nipped at her lips, sucking them, his tongue swirling around hers, his hunger and emotions clashing in a storm of desire.

Lily's response was as heated as his own. She eagerly met his kisses as her hands swept down his arms and up his chest; her fingers tangled in his hair, stroked his cheek, caressed his ear.

Tobin suddenly lifted her off her feet and moved her to a chair. He dipped down to the hollow of her throat.

"I shouldn't," she said breathlessly. "I should not . . ."

Tobin took her hand and pressed it against his chest, gazing into her eyes as his heart pounded wildly, hammering to be free. Lily's eyes widened—it must have felt as if his heart was about to burst—and Tobin forced himself to draw a breath. He brushed the back of his hand across her cheek. "You see what you do to me."

Lily's lips parted.

"Now see what I can do to you, lass." He caressed her neck. "Close your eyes," he whispered.

Lily closed her eyes and dropped her head back, giving in to her desire and to him. Her skin, warm and fragrant, seared his tongue. Her body, lithe and curving, scorched his hands. He felt white-hot inside, desire thrumming through his body, anticipation and longing shimmering throughout him.

He slid his hands down to her ankle, then his hand beneath the hem of her gown and on her calf. He moved up until he touched the bare flesh of her inner thigh. Lily's breath was warmly damp on his skin; her hands skated across his shoulders and his chest, insistent. As he turned his head her mouth met his, and she pressed against him, wanting what he wanted, and Tobin had never wanted like this. *Never.*

His kiss was not the least bit tender but one blistering with desire. He swept his tongue inside her mouth as he lifted his hand to her face and splayed his fingers along her jaw, tilting her head so that he could kiss her deeply. Lily made an alarmingly arousing noise that sounded almost like a soft growl. He pressed his body against hers, pushing in between her legs, pulling her closer into his body.

Lily wrapped her arms around his neck, pressing her breasts against him as she kissed him back with as much ferocity. This was extraordinary—he'd never felt the need for a woman battering down the doors of his defenses, clawing at his resolve in the way that this was happening to him. He'd never felt anything as urgent, as imperative, as the desire to have her.

He filled his hand with her breast, kissed her chin, her throat, and the enticing spill of her flesh above the bodice of her gown. He had a mad desire to put both hands on her gown and rip it open just to touch her flesh; it did not help that Lily pushed against his erection, rubbing against it.

He caressed her bosom, then slid his fingers into her cleavage, pushing deeper until he was able to free her breast from the low décolletage. He took the tip of her breast between his thumb and forefinger, rolling it, and Lily gasped. Her head fell back a moment, and then she looked at the door.

"Someone will come," she whispered.

His response was to topple her onto her back on the settee and move over her.

"Someone will see us," she said as she stroked his temple and his cheek.

Tobin was not the least deterred; he merely growled at her as he maneuvered her breast from her gown and took it into his mouth. With a gasp of pleasure, Lily arched into him. He nibbled at her peak, lashing across it with his tongue. "Dear *God*," she murmured, and another shot of desire rifled through Tobin.

He was so hard for her, his body straining. Her breath turned quick and shallow as he ravaged her breast, and when he began to stroke the bare flesh of her thigh, the soft mound of her sex, she gave a small cry of alarm.

"Be still," he whispered and kissed her eyes, her cheeks, and slipped his fingers into the slit of her drawers, and Lily's protest was lost. She closed her eyes, dug her fingers into his neck and chest, and allowed herself to sink into the pleasure he was giving her. Tobin could think of nothing but the feel of her body beneath his, the wetness of her sex, the hardness of his body. His fingers danced about the hardened core of her, then slid deep inside her and back again. His mouth moved over her cheek, her lips, her eyes, gliding so lightly that her skin simmered to the point she could scarcely endure even the whisper of his kiss. When he dipped his head to her exposed breast again, he felt as if he was sliding uncontrollably down a slope into something utterly explosive. When Lily drew her leg up beside him, he could smell her desire, could feel the heat in his hand. He kissed her as he fumbled with his trousers, freeing his erection. He slid the tip against her dampness, and Lily began to pant. She grabbed his neckcloth and pulled his head down to hers, kissing him passionately as he slowly, carefully, pushed himself into her body.

Desire and affection began to pound a beat through him, and Tobin was as appalled as he was inflamed by it. This was what he'd wanted: to have Lily and for all of Hadley Green to know it. But as he moved inside her, pressing up against her maidenhead, he realized this was something so profound, so deeply felt, that he would never ruin her. Quite the contrary—he would go to extraordinary lengths to protect her.

"Draw a breath," he whispered, and as Lily drew it, he pushed past her maidenhead. She made a small sound of distress and her body tensed, squeezing him as she absorbed the pain. He stroked her face, feathered it with kisses, and after a few moments Lily's discomfort began to ease. He moved slowly, gritting his teeth against the release building in him, savoring the feel of her body, warm and wet and tight around his.

Lily's hands stroked his back as she began to move with him. Tobin caressed her leg and watched the shades of pleasure move over her face as he moved inside her. When he thought she was ready, he put his hand between her legs once more and began to stroke her in time with his body. She flinched, then began to move more earnestly with him. Tobin did, too, watching her release come with a startled cry of elation that he caught with a kiss, just moments before his own release came pounding out of him like floodwaters.

When he had stopped moving in her, she pressed her lips to his neck, then his lips, and her hand fell limply across her breast.

Tobin was speechless. The mud had cracked, the light was shining in through the fissures, and he was blinded by it. He didn't know what to make of everything he was feeling for this woman, but it was so much more than anything he had ever imagined. He shifted, withdrawing from her, then removed his handkerchief and cleaned them both. When he had repaired his clothing, he helped her up, then helped her smooth her skirts and tuck her hair into its coif.

Lily looked up at him with those green eyes swimming with affection, and a slightly crooked smile. "This does not mean you have won."

Tobin smiled. There were things he wanted to say: *Come with me, don't leave me. Forgive me. It's done, we are done. I cannot have what I wanted from you, I want something far bigger than that.* But the words were lodged too deep inside him, so he said nothing. He picked up her hand and kissed it. "I must go."

She nodded. He kissed her cheek, then her mouth— a soft, lingering kiss—and turned away from her.

"Tobin?"

He paused and looked back at her. She stood with her hands clasped before her, her expression serene. There was a rosy blush in her cheeks he'd not seen since her illness, and she looked quite beautiful. Her lips parted, and it seemed as if she would speak. But then she shook her head and smiled sheepishly.

He walked out of the music room, away from Lily, away from the bench and the inscription. But he could not escape the warmth that was seeping in through the cracks in his black mud.

NINETEEN
❧❧❧

L ily supposed she ought to have regretted the loss of her virtue, but she did not. She did, however, feel a distant rumble of disappointment with herself for having fallen headlong without even a mewl of protest—in fact, she'd embraced her downfall, had craved it, had convinced herself that his touch was the salve her wounded soul needed. And it had happened so quickly. With Althea's letters in her pocket, and the inscription on the stool, the moment had attacked Lily, had cut down all her defenses, and she'd needed and wanted . . . *him*.

Did she imagine that Tobin had needed her, too? He'd seemed to be an entirely different man than the one who had come into this very salon some weeks ago and announced his intent to ruin her. He'd been persistent, wildly thrilling, and gentle all at once. Had he not felt the same as she? Lily had wanted to ask him, to say something, but she'd been at a loss as to what to say, exactly, and he had not offered any words . . .

Still, in the hours that had followed, Lily had allowed herself to imagine things, joyous, happy things. Such as love. And contentment. She'd allowed herself the fantasy that hers was an entirely different situation than Aunt Althea's had been. Hers was a union forged entirely by mutual desire. Lily believed that until the next afternoon, when Mr. Fish arrived.

"Pardon, madam," he said. "I am tardy, but I called on Mr. Grady. He has been ill you know, and I picked up the post."

"Is he still unwell?" Lily asked as Mr. Fish began to sort through the correspondence.

"Quite on the mend," Mr. Fish said absently as he looked through the correspondence.

Lily returned her gaze to the window, through which the day looked very gray.

"Well now, this cannot be good news," Mr. Fish muttered as he examined one piece of correspondence.

"What is it?" she asked.

"It has come from Tiber Park." He opened the letter and read the contents. "It is from Mr. Howell, the count's secretary," he said and glanced up at Lily. "It is extraordinary news."

Her pulse fluttered. "What news?"

"He writes that upon further reflection, Lord Eberlin has determined that the Tiber Park mill is not a profitable venture and that he'll not be operating it as such."

"What?" Lily said, as nausea began to spin in her belly.

But Mr. Fish suddenly smiled. "He has capitulated!" he exclaimed. "He has given in and he will not compete! That means, Lady Ashwood, that you have saved Ashwood!"

"Have I?" she asked unenthusiastically.

"Of course you have!" he said gleefully. "You were quite determined, were you not, and look at this—you have succeeded beyond our greatest hope, and you have emerged unscathed and with your estate intact. This," he said, shaking the letter at her, "is as good a surrender as any I have ever seen."

"On the contrary," Lily softly corrected him. "I have not emerged unscathed. I would say the battle has taken its toll."

"Well, I think you should reward yourself for a fight well fought. Perhaps a trip to London?"

"Reward myself?" Lily's head was beginning to ache. "I never knew you to be so fanciful, Mr. Fish."

"But you really should celebrate," he insisted.

Lily nodded, but all she could think was that she had given herself to Tobin, and he . . . he had stopped his assault on Ashwood. But where did that leave them? Was that all it had been to him? A bargain?

"Ashwood will thrive again, you'll see," Mr. Fish triumphantly continued. "God will not allow the advantage of wealth to undo what is good."

Lily didn't know if that was true or not.

Over the course of the next few days, her guilt and conflictions made her entirely too restless. She kept expecting to see Tobin riding up to Ashwood, but he did not come.

Why did he not come? After what had happened between them, had his heart not softened toward her, as hers had toward him? Could he engage in such an intimate act and remain unmoved?

When she wasn't feeling lost by all that had happened, she was brooding about her future. She chastised herself for moping over the man. It was an impossible situation, a far-fetched union. She could not risk her title and the loss of this estate. What would become of everyone then? Would she take the victory she had in hand and toss it out like feed to chickens? Of course not.

Lily decided Mr. Fish was right. She should accept Lady Darlington's offer to visit in London. She should move on from this extraordinary autumn, and from the battle she'd waged, and think of her future. She should be about the business of luring a titled man to her. It was the only feasible thing to do.

∞

On the evening of the First Winter's Night Ball, Lily dressed for the occasion in something of an emotional fog.

"I think this is the most beautiful ball gown I have ever seen, mu'um," Ann said, drawing Lily back to the moment. Seated at her vanity, Lily could see Ann puttering around behind her, preparing her clothing for the evening. "It came from Italy, did it?" Ann asked, holding up the gown for a better look.

"Not Italy," Lily said vaguely and smiled at Ann's reflection in the mirror. "I should dress." She rose from the vanity and removed her dressing gown. "Do you have a beau, Ann?" she asked as the maid held out the gown for her to step into.

Ann's response was a deep blush.

"I beg your pardon," Lily said laughingly. "I did not intend to pry."

Ann smiled sheepishly as Lily put her arms through the cap sleeves. "I do," she admitted. "But he's not offered, and I wouldn't want to speak. . . . You understand, mu'um."

"Of course." Lily put her hands on her waist as Ann began to button her in. "Has he kissed you?"

Ann's fingers stilled on Lily's back.

"And there I go again, prying into your personal affairs." Lily cast a smile over her shoulder. "I could use a bit of feminine nattering, really. And I promise to keep your confidence."

Ann looked down and resumed the buttoning of Lily's gown. "He has," she admitted shyly.

"How lovely," Lily murmured.

Ann finished buttoning her gown and turned back to the wardrobe for Lily's headdress. "Lord Eberlin seems rather . . . nice," Ann said awkwardly. "I thought it was kind of him to come and see you when you lay ill."

"We were acquainted as children," Lily said.

"As children!" Ann said, clearly surprised by the news.

"Yes." Lily gazed at her reflection in the full-length mirror. The gown was stunning. Exquisite. She couldn't imagine how much he'd spent on it. "He is quite different now," she added absently.

"He seems a bit lonely," Ann remarked.

"Really? What makes you say so?" Lily looked at Ann as she took the jewelry her maid handed her.

"Oh, I don't know that he is, mu'um," Ann said quickly. "I've only seen him here at Ashwood. But he has a look about him."

"What sort of look?"

"Sad," Ann said with a light shrug. "Seems to carry a weight on his shoulders."

"I think you are right," Lily said. "I think he carries a great weight." One far heavier than any she had ever carried or could conceive of carrying. Her skin tingled; she was suddenly impatient to see Tobin. She was impatient to see how she would feel with their encounter still fresh on her mind, on her skin, in her mouth. In her heart.

"Oh, mu'um," Ann said with a sigh. "You look like a princess."

Lily smiled. "Thank you." She donned a cloak and descended the stairs to the foyer. The Ashwood coach was waiting for her, as was Linford, holding her muff.

"Good evening, Lady Ashwood." He bowed and held her muff out to her.

"Thank you, Linford. You won't wait up for me, will you? I shall be quite late."

"No, my lady."

"Preston and Mr. Nettle have a picnic basket for the night?"

"Indeed they do, madam, as well as a flask of whiskey to warm them."

She smiled. "Goodnight, Linford."

"Goodnight, my lady," he said and slowly closed the door behind her.

∞

The line of coaches waiting to disgorge their passengers at Tiber Park reached into the road. In anticipation of the slow crawl, rush torches had been lit along the road, and through the coach window, Lily could see lights twinkling in the house and around the grounds. She could not imagine how many candles it must take to light a house as large and grand as Tiber Park.

As they drew closer, Lily could see people piling out of their carriages, shaking out gowns and making last-minute adjustments to neckcloths and headdresses. They came in pairs and threes and fours. Lily braced herself—she would be noticed, arriving alone. A few weeks ago, Lily supposed she might have been intimidated, but not tonight. She was conscious of society's expectations but not cowed by them. She had found her footing in an unlikely place, and it was in Tobin.

When her coach pulled to the door, a Tiber Park footman was there instantly to help her down. Lily stepped out and took a moment to arrange the cloak and the skirt of her gown. She said goodnight to Preston and put her hand on the arm the Tiber Park footman offered. They climbed the steps, and as they reached the doors, which were open to allow the steady stream of guests, she saw Tobin standing just inside.

He stood with his legs braced apart, his hand behind his back. He was wearing formal black tails and neckcloth and a black silk waistcoat embroidered with ivory. He looked tall and proud and impossibly handsome as he bent his head to hear the words of a guest. He smiled at whatever the woman said, his tea-brown eyes shining. But as the woman moved on, Tobin turned his head and his gaze landed on Lily.

Her blood rushed at the sight of him. She could see his swallow of surprise and the way his gaze drank her in, raking down to her toes and up again. She could feel the hunger behind his gaze. She smiled, truly happy to see him. But as she stepped inside, his expression shuttered. "Welcome, Lady Ashwood," he said, bowing his head.

Lily's gaze narrowed. He would assume this role, would he? The uncaring rake? "Lord Eberlin," she said, and curtsied. "How do you do?"

"Very well, thank you. I trust you are well?"

"*Very,*" she said pointedly.

His gaze flicked over her again. "May I introduce my sister?" he asked, and looked at the woman standing beside him.

It was funny that in the moment before Lily laid eyes on her, she would have said she could not recall Charity Scott's face. But in truth, she recognized Charity the moment she saw her. The little girl with the pale blonde hair had grown into a honey-haired, beautiful woman with pale amber eyes, as comely as her brother was handsome. And like Tobin, a hint of weariness rimmed her eyes.

There was another similarity to Tobin, as well—Miss Scott looked at her with the same expression of contempt Tobin had shown her at their first meeting after fifteen years. *Oh, no. You will not lay the blame of your father's behavior at my feet, too.*

"Charity." Lily put out her hand. Charity glanced at it but did not take it. "How long it has been. I am so very happy to see you well."

"Yes," Charity said as her gaze drifted over Lily. "It has been a veritable lifetime since last we met, *Lady* Ashwood." She made no effort to further engage Lily. In fact, Charity looked past Lily, to whoever was next. Lily had been dismissed.

"I hope that we might have an opportunity to speak later," Lily said, forcing Charity to look at her once more. She smiled. "I am certain we must have much to say to one another."

Waves of resentment seemed to roll off Charity. "I can't imagine what that might be."

Lily kept smiling. "It is good to see you well, Charity. I mean that quite sincerely." She glanced back at Tobin, but he was greeting the couple behind her, his expression inscrutable.

Her cheeks blazing with ignominy, Lily walked on with her head held high.

In line once again, she handed her cloak to a footman. She was hardly aware of anyone around her; she was aware only that her heart was racing with anger, indignation, and crushing disappointment. But she was smiling when she paused at the entrance to the ballroom for the butler to announce her.

"The Lady Ashwood," he called in a booming voice, and Lily glided into the room just as she and Keira had practiced when they were girls, when they'd pretended to be invited to grand balls exactly like this one. She nodded politely at acquaintances, kept her smile serene, and was grateful when Daria Babcock appeared at her side.

"Your ladyship, you are a star among some rather dull planets," Miss Babcock gushed as she admired Lily's gown.

"How kind of you," Lily said. "I am happy to see a friend among so many unfamiliar faces."

"Yet there is hardly anyone about, is there?" Miss Babcock asked with a wry smile.

Lily glanced around. Miss Babcock was right—the

room was not as crowded as one might have expected.

"They are all from Sussex," Miss Babcock said and linked her arm with Lily's. "No one of any importance has come down from town."

"No?" Lily said curiously, studying the crowd a bit closer.

"No one, on account of his title and occupation," Miss Babcock added sagely. "They do not wish to be associated with him."

How was it that Daria Babcock seemed to know the things she always seemed to know?

Miss Babcock was smiling prettily as she eyed the crowd shrewdly. "I heard a footman say there were not more than one hundred people in attendance this evening," she said idly. "Yet he invited three hundred."

Lily didn't know what to make of that news, but she found it disconcerting. Regardless of how she felt about Tobin, she was appalled by the strictures society placed on men like him. What did he have to do to be deemed acceptable?

"Well?" Miss Babcock said, playfully nudging Lily with her shoulder. "Did you make the acquaintance of the count's sister?"

"I did," Lily said, and could feel her cheeks warming.

"She's quite pretty," Miss Babcock said. "I've seen neither hide nor hair of her daughter," she added, as if she'd expected the girl to be paraded through the crowd so they all might have a look. "I find it unbearably sad that Miss Scott will never be accepted into proper society."

Lily tore her gaze away from the magnificent decorations and the crystal snowflakes overhead. "She is here at this ball, is she not? That would make her accepted to me."

"Well, of course she is *here*," Miss Babcock said, her fingers fluttering against her dangling earring. "We in Hadley Green have forgiven the Scotts their scandal, for they've done so well for themselves and they've been quite generous. But in *London*, well, that's entirely different." At Lily's continued silence, Miss Babcock shrugged. "There is the circumstance of her brother's title and occupation. And if that were not enough to warrant it, Miss Scott has a bastard child. It hardly speaks well of her."

That was precisely the sort of thinking that could drive Lily to madness. Society would condone illicit affairs as long as they were undertaken with discretion, but God forbid a woman should bear a child as a result of it. "Aren't the decorations magnificent?" she asked, changing the subject.

"Oh, indeed!" Miss Babcock said with great enthusiasm. "I understand that it will actually snow this evening—can you imagine it? At some point, it will fall on the dancers. Is that not divine?"

"Lady Ashwood! You have come!" Lily recognized Mrs. Morton's voice and turned to see her hurrying through the crowd, tugging Mr. Morton along behind her.

"Good evening, Mrs. Morton."

"I am so glad to see you," Mrs. Morton said as she dipped a quick curtsy. "I said to Mrs. Ogle that I was certain you would attend, for you do not seem the sort to be bothered much by propriety, but Mrs. Ogle was convinced that you would not attend without proper escort. And I was right." She smiled broadly, leaving Lily speechless. "Did you tell her the news, Daria?"

"What news?" Lily asked, fairly certain she would not like whatever the news was.

"Oh, but we were *thrilled* to see Mr. Robert Anders present this evening," Mrs. Morton said. "Have you made his acquaintance?"

Lest these women had forgotten, Lily had not made a lot of acquaintances, as everyone had treated her as if she'd had leprosy when she'd first arrived at Ashwood. "I have not."

"No? Then surely your cousin made favorable mention of him," Mrs. Morton said.

"Madam, you will do us all a great service if you will stop with your nattering before you say something we shall all regret." Mr. Morton muttered the words in a manner that suggested he'd said them so many times that he could say them and scarcely be aware that he had.

"My cousin did not mention him," Lily said pleasantly, but privately she wondered how many things Keira had not thought to tell her.

"Well!" Mrs. Morton squared her shoulders and her expectations. "I am pleased to tell you that he was *quite* taken with your cousin—that is, before the, ah . . . the event," she said carefully, referring to Keira's fraud. "It happily occurred to me that as he was taken with her, and that he has five thousand pounds a year, that he might very well be taken with you, as well!" She smiled brightly, as if this declaration was in no way ill mannered or even slightly humiliating. She actually seemed to think she was bestowing a kindness on Lily.

Mr. Morton looked appalled.

"At least he has come tonight," Miss Babcock said. "And of all of them here, he is the only one truly worthy of your consideration."

Lily hardly knew what to say to such blatant matchmaking. It seemed to be the only thing that interested these women.

"I thought Eberlin was worthy, in spite of what Lady Horncastle said," Mrs. Morton said with a roll of her eyes. "Think how lovely it would be to have them both here at Tiber Park! Alas, Eberlin is as good as gone to London."

"I have not heard he is to London," Miss Babcock said.

"Daria, you were standing just beside me when he

said he'd leave at Christmas with his sister and likely would not return for a year or more."

"But I thought he meant he'd not return again to London after that."

Lily's heart sank. Why would he leave now, after the breach between them had been bridged?

"Now then, Mr. Anders—"

"If you please, Mrs. Morton, I shall make his acquaintance another time," Lily said. "I really must find a bit of . . . punch." She hoped there was good Irish whiskey in this house. "If you will excuse me?" She turned away, wanting to make her escape, and almost collided with a gentleman whom she recognized as one of Tobin's friends. "Pardon me," she said and stepped to one side.

So did he, keeping himself directly before her. He smiled charmingly; his clear blue eyes sparkled with it. "Lady Ashwood," he said, bowing.

"Allow me!" Mr. Morton said, obviously pleased to have a useful role. "Lady Ashwood, may I present Captain MacKenzie of Scotland?"

"My lady," Captain MacKenzie said with a slight burr, and crossed one arm across his chest as he bowed low.

"Captain."

"Might I inquire, have you any space on your dance card for a sea captain?"

This was hardly a London assembly. "I do not have a dance card."

"Splendid! Then I might impose on you for this dance, aye?" he asked, and held out his arm to her.

Lily blinked.

"We best take our places, then. It's difficult to join a proper reel when the dance is in progress."

Lily was aware that the little group of acquaintances was staring intently at her, waiting to see if she accepted. Captain MacKenzie seemed amused, judging by the way his eyes shone. It was either him, or the Mortons. She assessed the lesser of two evils and put her hand on Captain McKenzie's arm. "Thank you."

He led her out to the dance floor, where they took their place with another couple for the Scottish reel. "I am right pleased that you accepted my invitation to engage in this dance," he said as the orchestra began to play. "For it is the only one I know how to do."

Lily smiled at that and curtsied, and on the proper beat, she slipped her arm into his and began the dance. He wheeled her about one way, then the other, and they went on that way without conversation, turning and moving about their little square. The last time she'd danced had been in Rome, many months ago. That seemed like another lifetime now.

When the song came to an end, Lily smiled and curtsied again. "Thank you, Captain."

"You are as lovely a dancer as you are a countess," he said, offering his arm and escorting her off the dance floor. "It's quite easy to see why my old friend is smitten with you."

Lily didn't know what to say to that.

"Eberlin," he said, mistaking her silence for ignorance. "Do you not know it, then? No, of course you donna know it. He's not the sort to proclaim his feelings with gifts or song, aye?" he said cheerfully. "But I do know it, lass, and in all the years I have known him, I've never seen him so beguiled."

Lily stopped walking. "What do you mean?"

McKenzie laughed. "I mean that he is smitten." He flashed his infectious grin once more.

"No," she said, shaking her head.

"Ah, lass, donna judge a man by his scowl. Aye, his is a rather fierce one, but he's no' as hard as he seems."

"Has he expressed his true feelings to you?"

"No' precisely. But I've known the lad for years now, and I've no' seen him chop down a hedgerow ere now."

The captain was confusing her. "Pardon?"

MacKenzie laughed. "You may trust when a man takes out a mile of hedgerow without benefit of wages or even a wee bit of help that he's either mad or he's smitten."

Was it true? And if it were, did it not complicate her jumbled feelings even more? She had wanted him to be smitten, had wanted him to want her . . . but at the same time, she realized that nothing could come of it. She had put herself into a deep morass.

Captain MacKenzie took her silence as doubt, apparently, for he said, "I saw the way he looked at you, and I took great notice in the change in him. I donna mean to belabor this, for I see it makes you uncomfortable. Yet I see he is befuddled by it, and how he convinces himself it is no' what he thinks—for he thinks himself above it. I tell you this because he has been me good and loyal friend, and I would like to see him happy for once in his bloody life." Captain MacKenzie bowed low. "Thank you kindly for the dance."

With that, he sauntered off.

Lily stood rooted to her spot as she watched him disappear into the crowd. She didn't know if there was even a bit of truth to it, or if it was one man's wishful thinking—but was it not what she'd set out to do? Had she not schemed for him to fall in love with her so that she could save Ashwood? But she'd never dreamed she would fall in love with *him*. She'd never thought she could possibly even care for him. But she did. Oh, God, she did. And now she didn't know what to do.

TWENTY

❧❧❧

"You seem weary," Charity said.

Tobin's sister was standing beside him, leaning up against a Grecian column. She was dressed in pale green muslin that went well with her complexion. She was lovely, even in her apathy. More than one male eye had turned in her direction. Yet Charity seemed oblivious. Or uncaring.

"I thought you'd be leaping with joy at having shown them all that we've survived," she said, her voice full of tedium.

He'd expected to feel satisfied by this ball, to feel as if he had gained what he'd sought for years. But no one had come. Oh, half of Hadley Green had come—the half who waited for an opportunity such as this to see how the *haut ton* lived. But the *haut ton* had shunned him. No one from London had come down, in spite of the three dozen invitations he'd had Howell deliver there. The Darlingtons, who were only a half mile away, had declined. Even Horncastle's mother had sent her regrets. The people he had wanted to see him would not look at him.

That left a tension in his veins, a thickening of his blood, a swelling in his throat.

"Why do you not dance?" Charity asked.

He shrugged. "What of you? You've got Horncastle practically on his knees begging you to dance. Why do you refuse him?"

Charity rolled her eyes. "He hardly seems whelped, much less capable of carrying out the figures required for a Scots reel."

"He is not the most polished of gentlemen, I agree. But I thought you'd be pleased with the change from London."

"It is different," she conceded. "I wonder why you are leaving this bucolic setting. You have been so determined to be here, and honestly, I thought I'd lost you to the country. I was surprised to hear you say that you'd likely leave by winter's end."

Tobin shrugged. He couldn't really say why he'd said that to the Mortons. It was as though the thought had entered his head at the same moment it had left his mouth. He'd not thought of when exactly he would return to London before this evening. But then he'd seen Lily, as beautiful as an angel, and he'd not been able to keep his gaze from her. He'd watched her laugh with a toad of a man, dance with MacKenzie, smile charmingly, and speak with animation as a few women had collectively admired her bracelet.

Tobin had not thought of leaving here until he'd felt the light begin to seep in through the fissures of his mud and he'd felt . . . afraid. And Tobin did not like to feel afraid. He'd never felt like this about another person. He'd never awakened in the middle of the night, desperate to be near her. So he did what he had always done when life was particularly difficult. *Rise up. Press on. Keep moving while you have a wind at your back.*

And then again, perhaps it wasn't Lily at all that had prompted him to say he was leaving. Perhaps it had been this ball. He'd expected his house to have been filled to the rafters, and it had not been. He'd expected to feel entirely himself in his own home, yet he had not. He had foolishly believed that here, in the private fortress he'd built, the spell could not come over him. Yet he could feel it creeping down his spine, spreading in his scalp, making his skin prickle with dreaded anticipation.

"Come, Tobin," Charity said, straightening. "You are the host of this lavish ball. You must dance."

He eyed the dance floor warily.

"I will not allow you to step on anyone's toes." She held out her hand.

Tobin reluctantly took it.

They danced a quadrille—or rather, Charity danced, and he moved woodenly about, trying to remember the figures and feeling entirely conspicuous. Dancing was not something that was taught in the galleys of merchant ships. He'd learned some basic steps out of necessity, and there had been a particularly enthusiastic partner in Malaga, Spain, who had taught him how seductive a dance could be. But he'd never excelled in it.

It didn't help that he could see Lily close by, dancing expertly with Lord Horncastle. With every turn he made, his gaze landed on her. She was smiling, clearly enjoying herself, and there was elegance in her step and the way she extended her arms. He'd seen women like her in London: the most sought-after, most attractive women in town. Women who married dukes and earls, who had beautiful children and privileged lives.

They did not give their virtue to men who traded arms and had purchased their titles.

When the dance came to its blessed end, Tobin offered to fetch Charity some punch, but she demurred, saying she would rather take the air. Tobin availed himself of a tot of whiskey, and then another, in an attempt to relax. He found himself standing beside Miss Babcock, and after she made several pointed observations of the dancers (so few!) and the music (so loud!), he felt compelled to ask her to dance. He suffered through another quadrille, but this time, it felt as if the dancers were crowding in around him, swirling too close.

Miss Babcock tried gamely to converse with him, but Tobin could not oblige her and keep his place in the figures. Especially since he kept seeking Lily on the dance floor.

His thoughts about her were confusing and unsettling. He'd come here to ruin her, but he wanted to wake up in the night and find her there, beside him. Yet judging by the evening's turnout, he could no longer pretend his purchased title would make him acceptable in the *haut ton*. He would never be more than the son of a thief, so there was no real future for them. Besides, how could he ever reconcile a future with a woman who had sent his father to the gallows? He had only to look at Charity to know it was impossible. The past he shared with Lily both drew them together and pushed them apart, and there it came again—another wave of fear over his feelings for her.

Tobin's competing thoughts had given him a blinding headache. He needed a hedgerow, something physical to do to ease the tension in his body, which was beginning to constrict so tightly that he couldn't draw a proper breath. He started for the terrace doors, thinking the brisk air would help him.

Unfortunately, before he could make his escape, Mrs. Morton and another woman he recognized as being from Hadley Green sailed through the crowd like advancing warships and accosted him.

"My lord!" Mrs. Morton said. "Do please tell Mrs. Langley that you are going to London. She refuses to believe me."

"This is most distressing news," Mrs. Langley said,

whose husband, Tobin realized, the only shoemaker in town, had relied on Tobin's loans these last two months. "You cannot mean to leave us!"

The women moved closer; Tobin's throat began to tighten.

"We've only just gotten you back. Look at all you've done since your return to Hadley Green!"

Others nearby began to turn toward them, to hear what the fuss was about.

"Madam, I have not—"

"Surely you find us agreeable," Mrs. Morton said laughingly, although she looked uncertain. "We certainly find *you* agreeable." People standing close by laughed.

The sound was like daggers into Tobin's head, almost buckling his knees. He blinked; he felt trapped, his back to the wall as the panic began to rise up in him like bile. He was desperate to find his voice, to quit this room, to find someplace he could at least draw air into his lungs.

"I do believe we've left him speechless," Mrs. Morton observed. "My dear sir, you are not aware how very much admired you are!"

He could see the door close by, that portal to privacy, yet he could not make his feet or his tongue move. His greatest fear was suddenly real—he would make a fool of himself before all of Hadley Green. He would crumble in a great heap and drown in their laughter. His lungs felt as if they were collapsing, and he gulped a breath—

The touch of fingers to his was so startling that every muscle tensed. He knew instantly that it was Lily, that she meant to help him. To *save* him.

"Ladies, you have discovered Eberlin's secret," she said in a stage whisper, and the soft lilt of her voice pierced the turmoil brewing inside him.

"His secret? But we have no secrets in Hadley Green, we are a community of friends, are we not?" Mrs. Morton asked laughingly.

"Please speak softly!" Lily said, laughing. "His sister is just there and you will ruin the surprise."

Mrs. Morton and Mrs. Langley exchanged baffled looks. "What surprise?" Mrs. Langley asked. "A surprise in London?"

"I cannot speak for his lordship," Lily said, smiling up at him, "but I will confirm that he has enlisted my help and I am sworn to secrecy. He must have Miss Scott believe he is returning to London. It's all part of his surprise."

"But . . . what is the surprise?" Mrs. Morton asked in a loud whisper.

Tobin tried to speak so that he would not appear as mortally wounded as he felt, but he could only cough.

Lily had Mrs. Morton by the elbow and was turning her away from him. "If he told us, it would no longer be a surprise, would it? You shall have to endure the wait until Miss Scott has had her surprise. Have I ever told you of the great surprise I received once from my uncle Hannigan? It was quite dramatic, really, and I was not the least expecting it."

As Lily moved the women away from him, Tobin began striding for the doors that led to the terrace. But when he caught sight of MacKenzie with Miss Babcock standing at the doors, he dared not pass them and face another moment in which he had no control. He turned about, looking for an escape before he began to disintegrate. His fists clenched, his breathing short and labored, he spotted a pocket door that led to a small retiring room just off the ballroom. He'd deemed it too small to accommodate the number of guests he'd expected tonight and had seen to it that a larger retiring room was available upstairs.

His head down, he quickly made his way there now, then stepped into the retiring room and quickly shut the door behind him. The room was dark, the only light filtering through the windows coming from the rushes in the courtyard. It was cold—good, he needed cold, something to sharpen his senses. He walked deeper into the room, braced his hands against the back of the settee, and leaned over it, squeezing his eyes tightly shut as he fought the demon in him, straining to push it out and find his breath.

His head was spinning, his skin clammy, his heart pounding. This debilitating madness was infuriating, and in a moment of frustration, he swiped his arm at the end table and sent a glass bowl crashing to the floor.

A spill of light startled him and he heard the sounds from the ballroom seeping into the room.

"*Tobin?*"

He blinked; it was Lily, framed in the doorway, and he suddenly could not breathe. He clawed at his neck-cloth and tried desperately to draw his breath, grabbing it in a shallow wheeze.

"Tobin!" Lily cried and pushed the door shut behind her as she rushed to his side. She put her hand on his shoulder and cupped his face with her hand. "Dear God, are you all right?" she begged him, her eyes searching his face.

He responded by fighting another paroxysm of breath. He tried to pull her hand from his face, but she refused to allow it and cupped his face with both hands. "Tell me what is wrong," she said. "Tell me so I may help you."

"*No.*"

Lily suddenly laid her head against his chest. "Oh, Tobin," she said sorrowfully. "I cannot imagine the nature of your discomfort, but my heart aches for you. I have seen you struggle against this illness with great distress, and I want so desperately to help you."

Tobin managed a breath. He had to find his footing or he would shatter into a thousand tiny bits. He was perspiring, he felt ill, and he wanted to crawl out of his skin. Lily stroked his brow, her cool touch soothing him. "It's all right," she said softly. "Everything is all right."

That quiet promise of hope seared him. His fists curled against his sides, he closed his eyes and bowed his head, his forehead touching hers. Her scent filled his nostrils. He did not try to speak. He could focus only on her touch, on the softness of her voice.

Everything will be all right. Everything will be all right. He tried to drink those words in, chanting them in his head over and over again until he felt the tightness begin to ease and he was able to breathe ... but his breathing was deep, and his hands, he realized, were on her body, his mouth on her skin, fragrant, soft skin. His lips were on her mouth, in her hair, his hands on her hips.

"Let me help you, Tobin," she whispered in the dark. "Whatever it is that ails you, let me help you."

His anxiety and fear were evaporating, and in their place was desire. The arousing thrill of her body was something Tobin felt powerless to resist. The desire made him feel like a whole man again, and he straddled her skirts with his legs, kissed her so ardently that she was bent backward at the waist until she put her hands between them and turned her head, drawing a breath.

"What are you *doing*?" she asked breathlessly.

"Kissing you," he muttered, and nipped at her lips.

"*Tobin,*" she said, as if he'd not been quite awake. "Let me help you. No matter what has happened, I will help you." She was speaking strangely, as if she was uncertain what to say. "If this is all there is between us, a physical attraction, then you may go to Perdition," she whispered. "But if there is more—and God help me, Tobin, there *is* more—then I want to help you."

He was not prepared for this. So many things whirled in his head, so many cautions. He knew only that he wanted her, every luscious inch of her body, every moment of her breath. "You don't know what you ask—"

"If there is any hope that you love me as I love you, Tobin, then let me help you."

Love! The word sent him into a tailspin. He could scarcely face his feelings, much less put a name to them. He'd spent years pushing away anything close to tenderness and burying it in the mud, and now she would speak to him of love? He closed his eyes. He tried to steady himself, to find his way back to that safe place of not feeling, of not caring. "You do not understand what you are asking me."

"I understand very well. Do you think me blind or unfeeling? Do you think I didn't see the change in you when we last met? You may pretend that your feelings do not exist, but I have *felt* them."

No, no, he could not have this. He could not have this. His chest began to constrict. "I . . . *esteem* you," he said.

Lily clucked and looked away.

"Lily . . . darling. You know who I am," he said hoarsely.

"I do," she said, folding her arms. "I know that you

have been gravely wounded. I know that you suffer a debilitating malady that you hopelessly try to mask. I know that you would like all to believe that you are a man hardened to the softer bits of this world, but I know that is not true."

"I am the son of a thief," he said sternly. "I trade armaments of war for my livelihood. I have lived a very mean life—and you would pretend that I was born to this manor? I suspect there are others in your life who would not be as quick to ignore these things. And neither would I."

"I do not *care*—"

"I *do* care," he said and put his hand on her shoulder, forcing her to look at him. "You deserve better."

"Do not presume to tell me what I deserve!" she said sharply and pushed his hand off her shoulder. "Do not presume that you suddenly know what is best for me, not after what we've been through, not after the dancing around this past of ours as we have done!"

"I do not want to ruin you," he pleaded, and turned away—from her, and from the fact that until recently, he had very much wanted to ruin her. He watched the light of the torches flickering against the panes of glass, wondering how this had happened, when he had gone from wanting to ruin her to wanting to protect her from harm?

"Am I to believe now you have had your way with me, that you plan to return to London because you have had your revenge?"

"That is not true," he said. He kept his gaze on the torchlights, and away from the green eyes that had haunted him every moment of chopping down that bloody hedgerow. "Things are much more complicated than that, and I think you know that they are."

"I cannot do this any longer," Lily said softly. "I cannot play this game."

He heard the rustle of her gown. She was leaving, and he felt a moment of panic.

But a tiny voice told him that this was the only solution. *Let her go.* Let her flee him and his illness and his past.

He heard her go out, and still he did not move. His fists clenched so tightly that his fingers ached. A ribbon of sweat slipped down the back of his neck. Tobin willed himself to be stronger and held it back. He could feel the mud deepening and swallowed down his revulsion to it. *Rise up. Press on.*

But for the first time in his life, he questioned what he was pressing on toward.

TWENTY-ONE
꙰

Lily's heart felt as if it were cracking and splintering as she wandered through the ballroom in a daze. As the evening wore on, she saw Tobin only once, when she somehow felt his presence and turned around. He was standing a few feet away, his gaze burning her up.

A few weeks ago, she would have expected to see a look of triumph, or cold satisfaction on his face. But tonight, Tobin's gaze was full of longing.

She turned away.

Lily had known that she'd fallen in love with him, but she did not understand what had possessed her to say it tonight. She imagined what Keira would say to her now: *Never tell a man you love him, goose!* She imagined the faces of her aunt and uncle if they believed she intended to—to what, *marry* the son of the man she herself had condemned to the gallows? A man who had purchased his title with the money he made selling arms? A man whose sister clearly loathed her, who had been shunned by the society to which she aspired?

Tobin was right. Lily's burning disappointment began to turn to anger at her own stupidity. She wandered about, oblivious to the people around her. But when the snow began to fall from the ceiling, she looked up—and saw Tobin watching her again.

She retreated to the ladies' retiring room.

Inside, she looked at herself in the mirror. She supposed she thought she might see something different in her expression, something wiser, some sign of worldly understanding. But she looked precisely the same as when she'd left Ashwood: young and foolish. Lily smoothed her gown and pinched her cheeks. When she thought she looked as best she might, given the circumstances and the lack of a smile, she started for the door, where she encountered the cool, almost porcelain face of Charity.

Charity's cool gaze ran over Lily. "Quite recovered, have you?"

"Excuse me?"

"What is that you want from him?" Charity asked pointedly.

Lily felt herself go cold.

"I cannot guess what you are about, Lady Ashwood, but if you think to harm my brother any more than you already have, you will have me to face. He has worked very hard to overcome the hell you banished my family to when you insisted you saw my father at Ashwood."

Lily's ire soared. "I find it remarkable that you and your brother lay blame for your father's sins on an eight-year-old girl," she said. "The fact is, Miss Scott, that your father put you in that hell quite all on his own. But by all means, blame me if that makes it easier to bear."

Something flashed in Charity's eyes. "He is toying with you," she said. "He makes a game of it. Don't fool yourself into believing differently."

Lily stepped around Charity before she did or said something untoward, and left the retiring room. Outside, she paused to press a hand to her churning stomach.

"Lady Ashwood, are you all right?"

Lily did her best to summon her composure before turning with a smile. "Miss Babcock. How are you enjoying the ball?"

"Very much indeed," she said, sidling up to Lily. "There are so few ladies in attendance that I've danced all night." Her eyes sparkled as she playfully tapped Lily with her fan. "But *you* are quite the admired one. The count has scarcely taken his eyes from you."

"You are mistaken—"

"I am not," Miss Babcock said gaily. "Mrs. Langley and I saw him watching you as one dance had concluded, and on my word, his gaze did not leave you for as much as a moment until he could see you no more."

That was it, then—Lily could no longer bear her sorrow. It was now an ache that sank painfully into her marrow. She had to leave. She had to be away from these people and the sight of Tobin and Charity.

"Supper is to be served soon," Miss Babcock said. "Will you join me?"

"In a moment," Lily said. But as soon as Miss Babcock had moved on, Lily walked to the foyer, where two footmen were on hand. "The Ashwood coach, please."

"Aye, madam," the young man said and darted out the door.

"My cloak," she said to the other footman.

He nodded and stepped into an anteroom. He returned with her cloak and held it open so that Lily could step into it. She felt it settle on her shoulders and fastened the clasp at her throat. As she moved away from the footman, she saw a movement from the corner of her eye.

Tobin was standing at the edge of the foyer, his expression pained. He moved slowly forward, his gaze moving over her as if he was seeing her for the last time. "You are leaving."

"There is nothing left for me here."

His gaze bored into hers. "I wish that you would stay."

Lily could scarcely look at him, and averted her gaze. "I do not see a reason to stay."

The footman who had gone to fetch her coach startled them both as he entered the foyer. "Your coach, madam."

"I will see you out," Tobin said. His hand closed

around her elbow, and Lily felt a jolt that snatched the air from her lungs.

When they reached the coach, Preston hopped down, opened the door, and lowered the step for her.

Lily looked at her coach. She had every intention of stepping inside, of never looking back . . . but she suddenly stepped back, away from the open coach door. She looked up at Tobin. "I do not . . . I do not know . . ." She was grasping at words, trying to explain the myriad emotions she was feeling. "I do not know what to do," she confessed in a whispered rush. "I do not know what to make of it all."

Tobin's throat bobbed on a hard swallow. He looked as if he wanted to speak, but his fists clenched and he swallowed as if he was swallowing down his words. "I understand. Perhaps better than you will ever know. Perhaps," he said, his voice rough, "this is for the best. Goodnight, Lily." He stepped back, his jaw clenched tightly shut.

There were no words to describe how Lily felt in that moment. She turned almost blindly to her coach. Tobin did not help her into it. He did not stand by and watch her go. He turned away and strode back into the foyer, disappearing into the bright light spilling out of it with his fist still clenched tightly at his side.

TWENTY-TWO

Tobin was aware of light coming from somewhere and the briny smell of the sea. He was reluctant to open his eyes; the slightest movement exacerbated the brutal pain just behind his eyes. His throat felt parched, his mouth tasted of dirt.

Someone nearby cleared their throat. Tobin opened his eyes and winced at the blinding light. In the next moment, a cold rush of water hit his face. With a choking sputter, he shot up so quickly that he almost heaved the contents of his belly. "What in blazes!" he said hoarsely.

"I would assure myself that you are indeed alive," MacKenzie's voice said.

Tobin wiped the water from his eyes and then blearily looked around him. As his eyes focused, he took in rough-hewn walls, a bare floor. He was lying on a bed that creaked and groaned with every movement. "Where am I?"

"Southampton," MacKenzie said and tossed a dry cloth to him. "The Spotted Owl Public House, to be precise. No' as grand as Tiber Park, mind you, but a room with a view."

Tobin wiped his face and squinted in the direction of MacKenzie's voice. His old friend was leaning casually against the recess of a cracked dormer window, one foot propped against the wall. The window was open, and the sounds of the sea and those who made their living from it began to filter into Tobin's consciousness. He could hear the calls of the fishmongers, and the dock-workers shouting back and forth as they handled cargo.

Tobin slowly moved his legs over the edge of the bed, cautious that any sudden movement could have an adverse effect on his stomach. "How have I come to be here?"

"Do you no' recall, then?" MacKenzie asked, a little too gleefully to suit Tobin. "It was too much of the inferior Irish whiskey and a determination to leave Tiber Park. That, and a horse willing to take you— bareback, naturally, until I made you stand still for the horse to be saddled. I came along to ensure you didna' harm yourself. As for this particular establishment? You examined them all, lad, and decided this one had the best lassies about."

"Lassies," Tobin said thickly.

"Aye. You were quite determined to find a pair who would appreciate your natural talents, as it were." MacKenzie chuckled.

Tobin buried his face in his hands. He had a vague recollection of two women in nothing but stockings, their hands and mouths on one another, and he . . . he *what*? "How long have I been here?" he asked, fearing the answer.

"Ach, donna fret, old friend. You've been here only two days."

Tobin lifted his head so quickly that an excruciating pain shot down his neck. "Two *days*?" he repeated as he rubbed his neck. "Where are Charity and Catherine?"

"Oh, tucked away at Tiber Park, I suspect." MacKenzie sat next to the bed, propped his ankle on his knee, and shoved his hands into the waist of his trousers as he leaned back. "But it wasna your sister's name you called out in your sleep," he added with a grin. "And it wasna your sister who kept you from enjoying the attentions of those two lassies. They were determined to make you forget your sorrows, and you'd no' have it." MacKenzie casually studied his cuticles. "Naturally, as your friend, I thought it me duty to stand in for you. No need to thank me."

Tobin groaned. He made himself stand and walk to the window. He had to brace himself against the frame, and when he saw the ships moored at the quays bobbing up and down on the incoming tide, he felt as if he was one movement away from tumbling head-long onto the cobbled street below.

He swallowed down a swell of nausea. Tobin was not a man to drink to excess; he did not like the aftereffects. But the drink had had the desired effect: he felt nothing. Just a bit of rumbling deep within and a desire to head for Tiber Park, to gather his sister and niece and return to London with them. Whatever he'd come to Hadley Green to accomplish, he'd done. It was over. *Finis.* As he struggled to find his balance, the blackness filled in again and covered the cracks of light.

"I am ready to leave," he said, pushing away from the window.

"No' as quick as that, lad," MacKenzie said. "I've ordered a bath and a meal for you. You willna want to return to Tiber Park looking as if you've been hanging from the highest mast."

As if on cue, there was a knock at the door, which MacKenzie was quick to open. "Well then, good afternoon." He smiled and stood aside as two young women with golden hair entered the room, carrying a hip bath between them.

∞

The afternoon after the First Winter's Night Ball, Lily went into the village, hoping that it would ease the restlessness that had kept her awake most of the night and had dogged her all morning.

She found herself at Mrs. Langley's Dress Shop. After exchanging a few pleasantries about the ball, she was studying the latest crop of gloves to arrive from London when Mrs. Shannon entered the shop with her young daughters.

Mrs. Shannon began to gossip with Mrs. Langley.

"How did you find the ball?" she asked. "Is Tiber Park as grand as they say?"

"More than one can imagine," Mrs. Langley agreed. "It snowed in the ballroom!"

The two girls turned wide eyes to Mrs. Langley, who nodded enthusiastically. "Imagine it, little white flakes of snow fluttering down on the dancers. It was all very whimsical and I'd wager as grand as any ball in London."

"I suppose it went all night," Mrs. Shannon said. "I've heard that London balls last until dawn."

"That was the most peculiar thing—Count Eberlin bade everyone leave when he left."

Lily's hand stilled on the kid gloves.

"Everyone had dined and the fourth set of dances had begun, when someone said that Lord Eberlin was in the stables, fetching a horse."

Lily turned around.

"Oh, Lady Ashwood! You were there, too."

"No, I returned early to Ashwood."

"As I said, it was all so peculiar," Mrs. Langley said. "He made quite a commotion fetching a horse." She glanced at Mrs. Shannon's daughters. "Mr. Langley said he'd fallen into his cups," she added softly.

"Alice, Allegra, go out onto the walk," Mrs. Shannon said and shooed her daughters out the door. When they were out, she eagerly turned to Mrs. Langley. "Do go on, Mrs. Langley. What then?"

Yes, what then? Lily wondered.

"Well, then he came into the drive, hardly able to sit his horse, really, and going round in circles as his friend tried to stop him. The count shouted that he was returning to London, and that we could all bloody well have Tiber Park, that he never meant to come back here, and he would not have come back had he not had his father's honor to avenge. Then he said some things about the innocent in God's eyes or some such nonsense, and demanded that we all bring our carriages round."

"No!" Mrs. Shannon exclaimed, looking as stunned as Lily felt.

"As I stand here," Mrs. Langley avowed. "We were all shocked, for he has always presented himself as a gentleman. Mr. Fuquay said that he has never heard him raise his voice or utter more than a few words. But my husband reminded me that Eberlin was a seaman, and that seamen are prone to drunkenness and vandalism."

"I beg your pardon," Lily said. "That seems unkind after he has invited you into his home."

Mrs. Langley merely shrugged. "Well he is a seaman and not Quality, is he? You did not see him, my lady. I was quite distressed by his inebriation."

"That is *quite* a tale!" Mrs. Shannon said, pressing her gloved hand to her lace-covered décolletage. "I tell you, when Eberlin returned to Hadley Green, and it came out that he was the son of Joseph Scott, I said to myself, the apple does not fall far from the tree, and if

I were among his set, I'd be rather cautious." She nodded, as if she had imparted some astounding insight.

Lily looked from one woman to the next. "I cannot believe what I am hearing. Your opinion of Lord Eberlin seems very low, yet the invitations to his ball and his very grand house were highly coveted. His generosity to proprietors and to the orphanage has been exalted by everyone in this village."

Mrs. Langley pinkened, but Mrs. Shannon did not look at all contrite.

"But you yourself saw his father riding away from Ashwood that night, madam. Everyone knows that," Mrs. Langley said.

Lily looked from one woman to the other. "Have a care, Mrs. Langley. Things are rarely what they seem. Good day, ladies." She walked out of the dress shop, feeling on the verge of exploding with frustration and guilt, knowing full well that the two women were now gossiping about her.

But was she really any different from them? She had fallen in love with Tobin but had let herself be persuaded that their affection could never evolve because she would never be allowed into society on his arm.

She stood beneath the shop front's awning, staring at the village green where Tobin's father had been hanged fifteen years ago. She wished she could turn back the clock, turn back the events of that night. She wished she'd been an obedient girl and had gone to bed. If she had, her aunt and her lover would have been safe. Tobin and his family would have lived here, in Hadley Green, and he likely would have—

"Lady Ashwood!" The sound of Lady Darlington's voice startled Lily; she whirled about.

Kate's warm smile faded. "Oh, dear. You seem distressed. May I assist you in some way?"

"No, I . . ." Lily drew a breath—an excuse was on the tip of her tongue, but instead, she said, "Yes. I cannot bear to hear a friend maligned. He's been unfairly treated, and I am the only one who might help him."

Kate did not seem surprised. "I understand completely. Perhaps a cup of tea might help?"

Lily shook her head. "I rather think nothing will help."

"I am a very good listener," Kate said.

Lily sighed. "Lady Darlington . . . *Kate* . . . it is a long and rather sordid tale, in truth."

"Then we shall have something in common, for I am no stranger to sordid tales. Perhaps it will require two cups of tea." She smiled at Lily. "Shall we?"

Lily had nothing to lose, and she could use a friend just now. "Thank you," she said.

TWENTY-THREE

❧❦❧

The only person at Tiber Park who did not look at Tobin as if he were the devil come directly out of the mouth of hell was Charity. She said nothing about his behavior the night of the ball—only that she and Catherine were ready to return to London.

"Then I shall escort you myself," he said over dinner the night of his return. He smiled at Catherine. "I have only a few matters I must see to before I leave here."

"Are you merely escorting?" Charity asked between dainty sips of soup. "Or are you decamping?"

It was an excellent question, and one he could not answer. In truth, Tobin was ashamed. He'd made a fool of himself at his ball. A man who was famously composed, no matter what the circumstance, he had lost his composure before everyone.

But at the time, it had seemed that his only choice had been to either drink or disintegrate in front of all those people, and he'd feared the spectacle of his dis-integration. Or worse. After Lily had left, he'd felt the spell come roaring at him like a wildfire. It was as if the walls were closing in, his guests piling on top of him, forcing the air from his lungs. Their laughter, the gay sounds of their voices, had agitated him, echoing in his head just as they had the morning his father had been hanged.

He'd begun drinking whiskey to calm himself, and since he was not a drinking man ... well, it had all gone to hell very quickly.

In London, Tobin had never felt the strange sensa-tion of strangling, as he had from the first day in Had-ley Green. He could not say why that was, but he knew instinctively that it was somehow tied into his father's death and the presence of Lily Boudine. So it was bet-ter for his health, and his increasingly fragile peace of mind, to leave here. Just walk away from it all and leave the past in the past.

Yet he could not leave without speaking to Lily. He could not leave without looking into her eyes once more. Nevertheless, while Charity grew increasingly restless, it took Tobin two days to pay his call at Ash-wood. His reluctance stemmed in part from the fact that he had no idea what to say. This was new territory for him—these feelings, these longings for a woman. She'd said she *loved* him. She loved him! *Him!*

He'd replayed those words over and over again in his mind, hearing her voice, seeing the softness in her eyes. At night, he heard her say those words and he imagined her there beside him, their bodies entwined, and the look of contentment on her face. *I love you, Tobin.*

He didn't know how he could leave that behind, but for her sake, he had to do it. He had a damaged body, a damaged past.

On Thursday afternoon, as Charity had her and Catherine's luggage taken down to the foyer in preparation for their departure, Tobin rode to Ashwood.

Linford met him at the door with a slightly crooked bow. "My lord."

"I have come to call on your mistress," Tobin said stiffly. "Shall I wait inside?"

"Lady Ashwood is not here at present."

"Not here?" he repeated. "Then where?"

"London."

Tobin was dumbstruck as he tried to absorb that news. Before he could find his voice, Mr. Fish strode into the foyer behind Linford, his face all smiles.

"Lord Eberlin, how do you do," he said crisply. "Won't you come in?"

Fish had never been happy to see him, and Tobin was immediately wary. He stepped inside and glanced at the staircase before focusing on Mr. Fish.

"I cannot tell you how pleased her ladyship was to receive your letter that you will not use your mill as you originally intended. It was the right thing to do," Fish continued. "I think there are enough profitable endeavors that our estates may flourish side by side."

Tobin had forgotten about that damn mill, had put it out of his mind. He'd instructed Mr. Howell to write the letter after Lily had been ill and Lucy had left, for Lily had seemed so distressed. That letter had been the first concession to the first little crack in his mud. Tobin shook his head and looked to the door. "May I inquire," he asked tightly, "where in London Lady Ashwood has gone?"

"She is the guest of Lord and Lady Darlington," Fish chuckled. "I think there is a move afoot to find a proper match for her ladyship."

The news felt like a kick in Tobin's gut. She had said as much, and now that he had sent her away from him, too afraid to face the truth of what he was feeling . . . He clenched his jaw. "I see."

"I should not be the least surprised if she receives an offer by the start of the new year," Mr. Fish blithely continued. "I am perhaps a bit prejudiced, but I believe there is no other as desirable as she, in looks and situation."

No. There was no other. And there she was at Darlington House, a bloody fortress housing a formidable family. Tobin could picture Lily seated prettily at some elegant table, laughing and conversing with men who held power and wealth. At a table where he would never be welcome. He could imagine Lily regaling them all with the tale of how she'd battled the arms trader with the purchased title and bested him at his own game. Smiling warmly, charming the titled men, reeling in her offers.

Tobin's chest tightened at the thought of her in the arms of anyone else. What in heaven had he expected? "Thank you," he said and went to the door.

"Is there a message, my lord?"

"No." He walked out, striding for his horse. He wanted to ride as far as he could from this house, from this village. From the impossible, absurd thought that he could *love* someone. That he could wake up to one woman all his life and bed her each night, and give her children and affection and receive her affection in return.

That was what had been lurking in him, was it not? The forbidden desire, the secret he had carried deep inside, beneath the muck and mire.

What an ass he was.

Tobin swung up on his horse and sent him galloping down the road. The cold wind stung his cheeks, his nose. That's what he wanted—he wanted to feel that cold seeping into him, freezing him, locking down all the impossible feelings that had begun to sprout in the cracks of his mud like so many blades of grass.

TWENTY-FOUR

W̲ith the Duke of Darlington's considerable help, Lily was able to find Walter Minglecroft. It took some doing, but at last the duke's secretary located the offices of Minglecroft and Gross in Southwark. "I am quite certain this is he," the young Mr. Patchett said. "However, I regret to tell you that he passed away a few years ago."

"Oh, no," Lily said, deflated.

"The good news," Mr. Patchett continued, "is that his partner is still in the offices. Might he be of some use?"

"Of course he shall be," Kate assured Lily. She had her baby, Lady Allison, on her knee and was bouncing the gurgling little girl.

"I cannot imagine what he might know of Ashwood," Lily said doubtfully. "It was so long ago."

"Yes, well, you have nothing to lose from speaking to him, do you?" Kate glanced over her shoulder at a tall footman with curly brown hair. "Benjamin, you will see Lady Ashwood to Mr. Minglecroft's office, will you?"

"Yes, madam," Benjamin said with a bow.

"You will return in time for supper, Lily? I understand Merrick will be joining us."

That would be the third time Lord Christopher had joined them this week, Lily thought wearily. "Of course."

Kate smiled like a cat in cream. "Wonderful! I shall look forward to your news."

She would look forward to her matchmaking, Lily thought, but she put that out of her mind as she went to gather her things.

∞

Mr. Gross was a rotund and gregarious man, seemingly anxious for company, who insisted on making tea for Lily. He moved a stack of ledgers from a chair and proceeded to dust the seat with vigor. "You should have summoned me, madam," he said happily as he stacked the ledgers precariously on a box of papers. "I should have been delighted to come to you."

"I wouldn't dream of putting you to the trouble," Lily said. She had a sneaking suspicion that if Mr. Gross were allowed into Darlington House, extracting him would have been a fairly significant proposition, perhaps requiring the help of at least a pair of footmen.

He settled in a chair across from her, his pudgy hands on his knees. "How may I be of service?"

"I am hoping to discover what Mr. Minglecroft's business was with Ashwood some fifteen years ago."

"Oh, that would be nigh impossible to say," Mr. Gross said instantly. "I fear our record keeping has not been as orderly as we might have hoped." He smiled.

Lily's heart sank. "Perhaps there might be some clue in Mr. Minglecroft's occupation at that time?"

"He was a trader, madam. Mostly cotton and coal, but he also dabbled in silver."

"I suspect that is my answer," she said. "I suppose he sold silver to the earl." She forced a smile. "Thank you for your time, Mr. Gross—"

"I cannot be certain that was the nature of his business with Lord Ashwood. However, Mr. Minglecroft's daughter might be of service. She lives here in London. I have her location just here," he said, hopping up and bending over a wooden box filled with papers. "I am *certain* it is just here."

"I don't want to put you to any trouble," Lily said again. She couldn't imagine that Minglecroft's daughter would know what her father's business had been with the old earl.

"Not the least bit of trouble!" Mr. Gross declared. "Poor old Minglecroft. He would have been thrilled beyond measure to receive such an illustrious guest as you." Mr. Gross continued to dig furiously through the box. "Aha! It is here, just where I knew it would be!" he cried triumphantly, yanking a paper from beneath a stack and waving it in the air. "Her name is Mrs.

Pruscilla Braintree. How I might have possibly forgotten her name is quite beyond me. Oh, but I had boxes and boxes of records and such ferried to her after her father's demise. I'll just jot down the directions, shall I?" he asked, picking up the quill and dipping it in ink.

Lily smiled and thanked him again as she tucked the vellum into her reticule. She guessed it would lead to nothing, but then again, she'd come this far.

∞

From the salon window of Tobin's Mayfair town home, he could just see the top of Darlington House. It had as many chimneys as Tiber Park. He knew that because he had counted them.

He stared at the chimney tops today through the mist of a light rain that had been falling for two days. He did not know the duke or any of his family. He did not have the requisite connections to accomplish an introduction. Tobin had his house in Mayfair; he had wealth that at times, to him, seemed immeasurable. But he did not have whatever it was the ton required to include him in their circle. He was an outcast, and he likely would always be an outcast.

Lily was in Darlington House. She might as well have been across the English Channel. Tobin could not see her, he could not call on her. He paced like a cat before that window, pausing at times to look at the tops of the chimneys again. For the first time since he'd made his fortune, he could not buy his way to what he wanted, and that enraged him.

"Uncle!"

Tobin turned from the window and chuckled as Catherine came bounding into the room. There was nothing like the little girl's smile to make him forget his troubles. He swept her up and held her tight until she began to squirm. "What are you about, sweetling?" he asked as he set her down and ran his hand over her crown.

"Mamma said I might come in and see you before I go up for my lessons. Look," she said and held out her hand. In her palm was a red rock. "I found it in the park yesterday. I've not seen a red one. Have you?"

"I have not," he lied and took the polished stone from her hand to examine it closely. "Agate, I think."

"Is it very valuable?" Catherine asked, going up on her toes to peer down at the rock in his palm.

"Extremely," Tobin said. "It is a precious jewel. The king's coffers are full of agate. Mind that you put it someplace safe."

Catherine stared wide-eyed at the rock as he handed it back to her.

"Really, Tobin, must you tell her such tall tales?"

Tobin winked at his sister as she strolled into the room. "I am sure I don't know what you mean."

"You know very well," Charity chastised him. "Catherine, my love, it is only a rock. I suspect the king would be quite at a loss to even name the sort of rock it is. Now go to Mrs. Honeycutt. She is waiting for you to begin your lessons." She kissed the top of her daughter's head.

"I think you are wrong, Mamma. It's very precious," Catherine said, giving her mother a withering look as she went out.

Charity frowned at Tobin. "She believes every ridiculous thing you say, you know."

Tobin smiled. "I see no harm in allowing her to believe she has found a treasure," he said. "There is tea, if you'd like." He gestured to the service Carlson had brought up, then turned back to the window.

"What are you looking at?" Charity asked, and joined him at the window. She looked out at the gray day. Her gaze swept up, then down. And then she turned and faced her brother. "You're thinking of her again, aren't you?"

"Her?"

"*Her*. Lily Boudine."

When Tobin didn't answer straightaway, Charity sighed and turned away from the window. "I am not blind, darling. It is very obvious to me that you are a different man than the one who left here so many weeks ago. And since that blasted ball, you've moped about as if you've been soundly beaten."

"Charity—"

"What I cannot understand is why *her*?" Charity said as she moved away. "She is the cause of all our unhappiness."

Tobin arched a brow in surprise. "Are you so unhappy?"

Charity made a sound of impatience and folded

her arms. "Of course not. I am perfectly happy being locked away in this grand house with my daughter. What would I need with companionship?"

"I am sorry—"

"That is precisely my point, Tobin," Charity said. "You have nothing for which you should apologize. You have tried in every way to give me back the life that she robbed from us when she accused Father of leaving Ashwood that night."

"No." Tobin shook his head. "No, Charity, I put those seeds in your head, but they are not true. Lily was younger than even Catherine is now. Think on that—Catherine is too young and innocent to invent such a tale. So was Lily."

Charity's eyes narrowed. "What are you saying? Has she convinced you that Father was at Ashwood that night? Dear God—"

"He never denied that he was, did he? Did Father ever once deny it, publicly or privately? He did not—because he *was* there."

"That is ridiculous! If he was there, why would he not say that he was?" she demanded. "Unless he stole the jewels. Is that what she has caused you to believe? Do you now believe our father was a *thief*?"

"Of course not," he said patiently. "But think—why would a man ride away in the night, in the rain, across a dark park instead of the road? We both know he was not guilty of the crime. So why, then? Because he was protecting someone."

Charity looked confused. "Protecting who? The thief?"

Tobin sighed. This was difficult for him—there was so much Charity did not understand. He moved to her side and put his arm around her shoulders. "A lover."

Charity gasped. She tried to twist out of Tobin's hold, but he would not let her go. "How *vile*, Tobin—"

"It is true, Charity. Father was involved in a love affair with Lady Ashwood. He would not confirm his whereabouts that evening because it would have destroyed her."

Charity angrily pushed him away. "That's madness! Even if it were true, he would not have given his *life* so that she would not suffer having her husband discover it! He would not have done that to us!"

"It was more complicated than that," Tobin said and took her hand. "Come and sit."

Charity resisted.

"Please," he said.

She reluctantly allowed him to pull her to the settee, where Tobin told her what he knew. That their father had fallen in love with Lady Ashwood. That there had been a heated affair. He told her about the piano stool, about the night the jewels went missing. He told her what it was that Lily saw, and how Lily had believed she was saving her beloved aunt and governess in repeating what she'd seen.

"Then why didn't the countess tell the earl?" Charity demanded angrily. "She would rather see her lover hang than admit her infidelity?"

"He threatened her. He told her he would put Lily in a London orphanage if she breathed a word. You know as well as I that an orphanage would have doomed a girl as young and sheltered as your Catherine is now."

Charity blanched. She sank back against the cushions. "But why?" she asked. "Why would the earl rob us of our father and put the rest of us in the poorhouse? How could anyone be so heartless?"

Tobin couldn't answer that for her. He'd wondered the same thing. In his travels, he'd run across cruel, empty men, slaves to pleasure who had lost their souls somewhere along the way. He wondered if the earl had been one of those men. "I suspect if we ever know what became of the jewels, we'd know the answer to that."

Tobin suddenly did not want to be that sort of man. He did not want to be a man without a soul, without love. He did not want to be bitter and cruel, yet he felt himself standing too close to the edge, teetering on the brink of that black, black hole.

He looked out the window again.

"I suppose that is one theory," Charity said and stood up. "Another is that Lily Boudine wanted to protect her aunt and her aunt's true lover, with no regard for us."

"Charity—"

Charity swung around, glaring at him. "I fear that you've bought into the fantasy she created because you love her. But you will never be accepted in her world, Tobin. She will toy with you, seduce you, but she will never have you. You will *never* be one of them." She swept out of the room.

Tobin stared at the door, her words ringing in his head. After a moment, he rang for Carlson. When Carlson appeared, Tobin said, "Have a carriage readied."

Tobin honestly didn't know who he was any longer, but he knew that he would not be that nebulous, bitter, empty man. Maybe Charity was right and Lily's world would never accept him.

But he had to at least try.

TWENTY-FIVE

The misty rain turned to snow late that afternoon, unusual at this time of year, if the servants' chatter in Darlington House was to be believed.

Lily didn't bother to look out the window to see it. Her mind was full of images of Ashwood and Tobin. The futility of her search for the jewels had begun to sink into her heart and the reality of her situation was becoming painfully clear. She could not repair the damage that had been done. She could not indulge in the fantasy of Tobin any longer. She had responsibilities to herself, her family, and to Ashwood.

Still, Lily felt lost. She could scarcely even think of a return to Ashwood after all that had happened. How odd, she thought absently, that she had come to consider Ashwood her home and wanted to belong there. In her determination to keep it from falling into Tobin's hands, she'd found a surprising affection for the house that held so many wretched memories. Once she'd swept out all the ghosts and goblins of her memory, she'd grown fond of it.

Until now, that was. Now that she realized she could never mitigate the tragedy of all that was lost there, she couldn't bear to return to it.

Lily had also indulged in a fantasy or two that involved Tobin and Ashwood in the past week. She could see the two of them there, puttering about the gardens, taking the long walk down to the lake beneath the boughs of the elms. Laughing—*laughing*? Lily couldn't help but smile at that image. Stoic, inscrutable Tobin laughing gaily at some silly thing.

But a future with Tobin would mean giving up all that she'd worked for at Ashwood and jeopardizing the futures of any children she had. Lily would, in essence, give up her right to belong to this society, to people like the Darlingtons—and belonging is all that she had ever really wanted.

Still, to imagine the children she and Tobin might have gave her a delicious little shiver. She could picture the little darlings: dark-haired like her, tall and sturdy like him. *Ah, Tobin.* Constantly in her thoughts. She'd wanted so desperately to find the jewels and free him from being forever branded the son of a thief. But it felt impossible—no one remembered things that had happened so long ago.

"Oh, they're throwing snowballs!" one of the maids said laughingly.

"There's scarcely enough snow for it," the other maid said. "Who is that?"

"Who?"

"The gent just there, standing at the gate."

"From town I suspect. There's always someone looking in like a wet dog, eh?" The pair laughed. Lily could hear one move from the window and about the sitting room where she was pretending to read.

"Ho there, he's coming in through the gate now."

"On my word, Bessie, do you intend to gape out the window all day?" the other chastised her, and they went out of the room.

When they'd gone out, Lily stood up and walked to the window to see the snow. Whoever they'd been chatting about had gone. She shrugged to herself and quit the sitting room—she was too scattered and restless to read.

She walked down the long corridor aimlessly, pausing occasionally to look at a painting or admire a piece of pottery. She heard raised voices downstairs but paid little heed to it. The servants often talked loudly across the wide foyer.

But a moment later, Bessie came huffing up the stairs. "Madam, there's a caller for you," she said breathlessly.

"For me?" Lily asked, surprised.

"It's a gent. The duchess said you should come at once."

Lily followed Bessie down the staircase. She'd gone

halfway when her heart stopped beating for a moment. Tobin was standing in the foyer, snow on his shoulders, his hat held so tightly in his hand that she could see the whites of his knuckles. He was fighting himself, standing stiffly. Lily's heart began to beat with a vengeance. He had come for her. She knew it. *He had come for her.*

Standing next to him was Kate, looking anxiously up at Lily.

Tobin showed no outward emotion as he lifted his gaze to hers. He stood very still, unmoving. Lily hurried down the stairs. When she reached them, Tobin's gaze seemed to melt over her.

"Lily," Kate said quietly, "Count Eberlin has come to call. The dowager duchess is in the salon. Shall I go attend her?"

There was urgency in Kate's voice. Lily knew very well that the dowager Lady Darlington would be beside herself to know that Tobin had come to her door. "Please," Lily said.

"Perhaps you might receive Lord Eberlin in the drawing room?" Kate suggested, gesturing to a door just off the foyer.

"I beg your pardon, have I called at an inconvenient time?" Tobin asked, his voice tight.

"Not at all!" Kate said quickly. "It is just that my mother-in-law is not . . . well. I should go see to her." She looked pleadingly at Lily as she hurried off.

"What are you doing here?" Lily whispered as Kate disappeared upstairs.

"I might ask the same of you," he said, his voice soft and low and sliding like a warm bit of honey down her spine.

A footman opened the door from outside. "Carriage in the drive," he called to another footman inside.

"As it happens," Lily said, craning her neck to see around Tobin to the door, "I had business in London. You?"

Tobin didn't respond. He swallowed.

"Are you all right?" she whispered and put her hand on his forearm. She felt him tense, his whole body quivering with it.

Outside, the coachman shouted out to the footmen; one of them picked up an umbrella and hurried outside. "Perhaps we should go into the drawing room," she said.

Tobin shook his head and swallowed again.

"Tobin, you really must say *something*—"

"I should like to invite you to dine," he said stiffly, just as the Duke of Darlington walked in behind him. The duke paused, his gaze first on Lily, then on Tobin's back.

Lily didn't know what to say. Dining alone at Tiber Park had been a questionable thing to do, but nevertheless, something she had done in relative privacy. In London, it was altogether different. As Kate had cautioned her, gossip traveled faster than light.

"You may bring your friends if you like," he added, as if reading her thoughts.

"Lady Ashwood?"

The deep voice of Lord Darlington seemed to reverberate in the marble foyer. She looked at Tobin, saw the craving in his eyes, the hard clench of his jaw. "My lord, may I introduce Lord Eberlin," she said.

Tobin's gaze held hers a moment before he turned his attention to the duke. The two men stood eye to eye; Tobin gave a curt nod. "Your Grace," he said.

"My lord." Darlington looked confused. He shifted his gaze to Lily again.

"His lordship has brought me news from Hadley Green," Lily said.

"Has he," the duke drawled skeptically.

"A private message," Tobin added, and Lily winced.

Lord Darlington's gaze narrowed slightly. "Then by all means, sir, give your message." He stepped around Tobin. "Lady Ashwood, you'll join us for tea, won't you?" he asked, deliberately excluding Tobin from that offer.

"Thank you," she said and watched him stride across the foyer, then jog up the stairs.

"I've missed you."

The words were spoken so low that Lily scarcely heard them. She looked at Tobin.

A corner of Tobin's mouth tipped up and his gaze swept over her as a footman went sailing past them. "I have missed you."

Her blood began to swell in her veins, and Lily couldn't help her smile.

"I was quite cross when I found you had gone from Ashwood." Emotion swam in his eyes—longing, esteem . . . only a few weeks ago, his eyes had seemed almost dead to her. . . .

Voices at the top of the stairs signaled that the Darlingtons were coming down for tea.

"I love you, Lily," he said.

Lily gasped.

"I know the circumstance is not ideal. I know you have come to make a match and you should, you should make a most advantageous match. I know that my past and my illness are not what anyone would want for you. But Lily, I love you."

Lily's heart began to beat wildly. "Tobin . . ."

"Grayson, who is that?" she heard the dowager duchess ask at the top of the stairs.

"You have to go," she said softly and turned away—but was stopped by the touch of Tobin's fingers as they tangled in hers. The world seemed to cease moving; Lily was immobilized, unable to move her feet. Nor could she look at Tobin, or the stairs for that matter, and the steady descent of the Darlington family. She could do nothing but stand in that grand foyer and feel Tobin's heat seeping into her through the tips of his fingers.

"I vow to love you, to cherish you. I will be your prince when you demand it, or sit on a rock and read if you prefer. I am yours, Lily, if you will have me."

There were so many things she wanted to say, so many things she couldn't think clearly.

"That is Lord Eberlin," she heard the duke say.

Tobin put his hat on his head. "Ask for a carriage tomorrow evening," he murmured. "Have it deliver you to Charing Cross. I'll meet you there at seven o'clock. Please come, Lily—there is too much left unsaid between us. Seven o'clock."

And then he was gone. His fingers left hers, and she could feel the cold, damp air as the door closed behind him. She made herself turn around and cast a smile up the stairs.

"Who was that?" the dowager duchess asked again as she reached the bottom of the stairs.

"A friend," Lily said lightly, avoiding anyone's gaze.

"Will you come for tea, Lady Ashwood?" the dowager asked.

"Ah . . . no, thank you," she said. "I am feeling a little tired, in truth. I should like to lie down before supper."

"My father always said that one should nap before supper," the dowager duchess said as she moved carefully past Lily. "Aids in the digestion."

Lily excused herself and went upstairs. Her heart was still racing; she thought of Tobin standing in that foyer, admitting that he loved her, the way his fist clenched, holding himself in check. She thought of how she loved him. She thought of all she stood to lose, of all the people at Ashwood who depended on her.

Lily had no idea how long she paced, but she was startled when the maid came to help her dress for supper. "Lady Darlington asked that I tell you Lord Christopher will be dining with the family this evening," the girl said.

Lily knew precisely what Kate was about, and at any other time in her life, she might have been thrilled. But today, the news was not particularly welcome.

At supper, the dowager duchess lectured Lord Christopher—Merrick, as he'd invited Lily to call him—on various political issues, as he served in the House of Lords. Over a meal of lamb stew, the duchess lectured beneath the tiara she wore, with two large diamonds that twinkled in the candlelight.

For his part, Merrick was relaxed in his seat, occasionally teasing his mother, and smiling at Lily from time to time as he promised his mother to do better with his votes. Merrick was as handsome as his brother and quite charming in a very quiet way.

"You should be thinking of your future, Merrick," the dowager said. "You should be concentrating on nuptials. Not politics."

Merrick winked at Lily. "Then perhaps Lady Ashwood will save me and agree to the happy state of matrimony."

Lily's breathing suddenly constricted.

"How can you jest about something so important!" the duchess huffed, and Kate stifled a smile behind a bit of lamb.

"Before you give him your answer, Lady Ashwood," the duke interjected, "it is my duty to warn you that Merrick is notoriously liberal in his views."

Merrick laughed.

"We are attending the opera tomorrow evening," Kate said brightly. "Why don't you come along, Lily and Merrick?"

"Only if Lady Ashwood promises she will join me," Merrick said.

"I . . . thank you. Thank you kindly for the invitation, but regrettably, I have a prior engagement tomorrow evening."

"I am desolated," Merrick said mournfully. "Will you abandon me to the clutches of the grandes dames of society with their unmarried daughters? Please say you will cancel your engagement and protect me from them."

"So dramatic," the dowager sighed.

"Lady Ashwood, will you leave me alone and defenseless?" Merrick asked playfully.

"Really, Merrick!" the dowager complained. "If you intend to court her, do it properly! Now what is this I hear about reforms?"

Merrick chuckled and happily turned the conversation to the latest political news.

Lily scarcely heard any of it; her thoughts were on the handsome man sitting across from her. The charming man with the title that could save Ashwood and restore it to the crown jewel it once had been.

∞

The next morning, Kate found Lily in the small salon. She entered the room with a bright smile, her green eyes sparkling, and after exchanging pleasantries, she said, "I hope Merrick didn't offend you last evening. All of the Christopher men believe themselves to be extraordinarily charming." She laughed as she sat beside Lily on the settee.

"He didn't offend me in the least," Lily said.

"I think," Kate said, "that he rather esteems you." She beamed. "Honestly, Lily? I was a bit surprised. I had high hopes, naturally, but Merrick has never shown any particular interest in anyone that I am aware. But he spoke to me last night and said that he found you quite intriguing and inquired into your character."

Heat began to creep up Lily's neck.

"He would be an excellent match," Kate said. "He is quite wealthy in his own right, and he is a viscount."

"Ah." Lily couldn't seem to think. "He is . . . I am at Ashwood, not London—"

"But Ashwood is so close," Kate said quickly. "One can reach it in a day."

She had clearly given this a lot of thought. "Well." Lily rubbed her palms on her lap. "That is . . . it's very interesting."

Kate smiled curiously at her. "I thought you would be pleased. You know that Merrick is quite sought after in London, and one could not ask for a better match."

"No, none better," Lily agreed. She felt as if she might explode at any moment. "It's just . . ."

"Never fear," Kate said and reached for Lily's hand,

squeezing it fondly. "I will make certain that you are well acquainted. I am confident you will find him the most agreeable, kindest, most thoughtful man."

Lily smiled.

Kate squeezed her hand again. "I am certain you realize that to disregard the attentions of a member of the Duke of Darlington's family for someone else could be catastrophic for you. And I would not like to see that happen to you, for I am very much aware of what it is like to be on the outside looking in." She gave Lily a meaningful look. "You know how these things are done."

"Yes," Lily said slowly.

"And really, I think this the perfect solution to all your troubles!"

Lily sorely regretted telling all of her troubles to Kate. "You may be right," she said, folding her arms.

"Then you will attend the opera with us tonight?" Kate asked. "I will consider it a personal favor."

She made it impossible! A swell of great disappointment rode through Lily, but she nodded. "Then naturally, I shall."

"Thank you!" Kate said, smiling brightly. "I will be so very thrilled when I've made two of my favorite people happy. I will leave you now," she said and went out.

Lily stared at the floor. Kate was right, of course. She would never find a more advantageous match. The Darlington family could restore Ashwood ten times over, and she could provide them with heirs. She had stumbled into a prodigious match, and yet . . .

She could not imagine life with Merrick, not when she loved Tobin. But couldn't she come to love Merrick? For if she gambled on Tobin, she stood to lose so much.

She stood to lose everything.

TWENTY-SIX

Predictably, but aggravating nonetheless, Charity did not want to accompany Mr. Howell, Tobin's secretary, and his wife, to the opera. "The opera?" she scoffed. "I have no interest in the opera."

Charity was so rarely in society that Tobin thought she might welcome the diversion. "The Howells would like you to join them," he said stiffly. Could she not see that he needed her to go? Could she not guess why? Could she not, just once, give into his wish?

"Your disgraced sister and your secretary and his timid wife. It's laughable."

"It's not open for debate," he said sternly, drawing a look of surprise from her. Tobin gripped his hands together. "I understand your unhappiness," he said. "God help me, I understand it better than anyone. I have spent my adult life trying to make it up to you. But in this one thing, I cannot accommodate you, Charity."

Her face fell. Tears filled her eyes. "Do you think to marry her?" she asked, her voice almost a whisper.

A flutter of panic winged through Tobin's body. "If she will have me," he admitted.

Charity shook her head as tears fell down her cheeks. "Oh, Tobin, please, not that. Not her."

"I would that I could have directed my heart to a more suitable prospect—"

"But why?" Charity cried. "What does she possess that you cannot live without? You have everything you could possibly need! What will I—"

There was something in Charity's words that registered somewhere deep inside Tobin. He suddenly understood that it was not that he'd fallen in love with Lily that had his sister so distraught, but that he had fallen in love at all. He was all she and Catherine had, and she feared what would become of her.

He swiftly crossed the room to her. Charity stumbled backward, trying to escape him, but Tobin caught her and held her tightly. He felt the sobs rack her frame, felt the tension began to drain from her body. "I will never leave you, Charity," he said. "Never."

"She won't want us," Charity said mournfully into his coat. "She will think Catherine is too loud, or that I am too present—"

"Not Lily," he soothed her.

"How can you be sure?"

"I *know* her. And I am sure."

He didn't truly feel as certain as he sounded. There

were so many unanswered questions, so many things he'd not considered. The only thing he knew was that he was wildly in love with Lily. He could not deny it; he could not push it down into the mud, for it kept sprouting up. So many little hopeful sprigs—if he pulled up one, two more followed.

Charity carelessly wiped the tears from beneath her eyes and tried to smile. "I pray that you are right," she said sadly and touched his cheek. She walked to the door and paused, glancing back at him over her shoulder. "What time shall I expect the Howells?"

He smiled. "Thank you. Seven o'clock." He watched his sister walk out of the salon, then cast his gaze out the window to the Darlington House chimney tops. He didn't know if Lily would come tonight. He'd not allowed himself to contemplate that possibility, for fear of the pain.

Pain. How curious, he thought, that he could feel it at all.

If Lily did come, he would make certain that she never left again.

Rise up.

Press on.

For once, he knew what he was pressing toward.

∞

Lily dressed in the gold gown Tobin had given her. It was the most beautiful thing she had ever worn, and with the modest tiara with a large pearl at the center that the dowager duchess had lent her, she looked regal.

She looked like a countess, a woman born and bred for this post in life. No one who looked at her would suspect that her heart was breaking, but Lily could see the regret in her eyes, piled up like so much snow.

"The family is awaiting you downstairs, mu'um," her maid announced.

Lily nodded. She picked up her gloves and walked out of that grand suite of rooms, with its soaring ceilings and velvet curtains and thick Aubusson carpets.

From the top of the staircase, she could see the Darlingtons gathered below. The dowager was wearing a dusty pink gown with a tiara much like the one Lily wore. Kate was stunningly beautiful in emerald green. Lord Darlington and Merrick were turned out in formal tails. As Lily started down the stairs, the duke and his brother turned to look at her, and she could feel their admiring glances. She smiled as Merrick walked forward and bowed before holding out his hand to her.

"If I may, Lady Ashwood, you are stunning."

"Thank you," she said, blushing a little. Just behind him, Kate was smiling approvingly.

"We'll take two carriages tonight so that we don't crush the ladies' gowns," the duke said. "Merrick, would you be so kind as to escort Lady Ashwood?"

So the matchmaking had begun in earnest, Lily thought. She looked at her escort. He was a handsome man; any woman would be thrilled to be the object of his attention.

They proceeded out to the waiting carriages, where

a team of four footmen handed them into their conveyances. As their carriage started forward, Merrick smiled admiringly at Lily. "Thank you for coming tonight," he said. "I had rather feared you wouldn't."

Lily smiled. "I can dine with friends at Ashwood any time, but I can hear the opera only in London."

"Quite true. Are you a fan of the opera?"

"Yes, of course," she said, hoping she sounded convincing. She really didn't care for it. She'd been forced to attend three in Italy, and after the first act of each performance, she'd had more than her fill of it. But she supposed that the *haut ton* thought opera essential.

"You must have a better ear for it than me," Merrick said. "I find it rather tedious."

Lily wanted to groan. She should have told the truth, but she felt so uncertain about everything. "Then why do you go?" she asked curiously.

Merrick smiled and leaned slightly forward. "Madam . . . is it not obvious?"

Lily smiled; the compliment and obvious interest in her gave her a shiver of delight.

"I hope I am not too forward," Merrick said as the coach turned a corner.

With a coy smile, Lily looked out the window. They were coming to the end of the Strand and would be passing by Charing Cross in a moment.

"I have rarely met a woman as intriguing as you are," Merrick said. "There is something so pure about you."

"You are very kind," Lily said absently. She spotted Tobin instantly. He was standing by the statue of King Charles, with his legs braced apart, that fist forever clenched against the tension that raged inside him, and Lily's heart leapt at the sight. He was watching the first Darlington carriage roll by, and she could see his hand unclench and clench again.

"Stop," she said softly.

"Beg your pardon?"

"Stop!" She couldn't turn her back on Tobin, not now—not after what they'd shared and overcome. They were both outsiders—they both needed someone, and someplace to belong. They belonged together. "*Stop the coach!*"

Merrick banged on the ceiling at the same moment Tobin turned his head and saw her coach. "What is the matter?" Merrick asked, alarmed. "Are you unwell?"

Tobin strode forward, his gaze locked on her coach as it stopped with a jerk. Lily fumbled with the door latch. "I beg you forgive me, my lord, but I cannot attend the opera with you, for I have—I have given my heart to someone else." She flung open the door just as Tobin reached her. Lily had no idea how she managed to get out—she sort of tumbled out, but Tobin was there to catch her in his arms.

"Lady Ashwood!" Merrick cried with alarm. "What are you doing?"

"What I should have done days ago," she said breathlessly. "You must go, my lord. They will be waiting."

Merrick looked as stunned as he was angry. He gestured to the coachman who had jumped off the back to shut the door, then he knocked the ceiling to signal the driver, and the coach rolled away.

Lily looked at Tobin. His expression was swimming in relief and adoration. "I thought you wouldn't come," he said roughly and gathered her up in an embrace. "I thought you wouldn't come."

Cradled against his chest, Lily smiled. This was where she belonged. "Come," she said. "We've caused enough scandal for one evening. Shall we go?"

With his arm around her waist, he directed her to a coach that was waiting at the curb.

∞

Tobin's Mayfair home was as grand as Tiber Park. Clearly no expense had been spared, from the fine Belgian carpets, to the silken draperies and wall coverings.

Tobin guided her down a wide hallway to a pair of highly polished oak doors. Inside, a fire was blazing in an enormous hearth.

Tobin strode across the room to a sideboard and poured two glasses of whiskey. He handed Lily one.

"I do not—"

"Drink," he commanded. "It's been rather a dramatic half hour."

She closed her eyes and tossed the drink down her throat, wincing at the burn. A moment later, warmth began to spread through her. She opened her eyes; Tobin was watching her, drinking her in, his eyes shining. "You wore the gown, and it's as stunning as I knew it would be. A perfect vision."

She smiled.

"I thought you wouldn't come," he said again.

"Nor did I," she confessed quietly.

Tobin swallowed. "I would not have blamed you if you hadn't. But I am very glad that you are here."

"I came to London to make a match," she admitted. "It seemed the thing to do after the ball."

Tobin clenched his jaw and glanced down, nodding.

"And I came because I wanted to find the jewels. But why did you come?"

He sighed and pushed a hand through his hair. "I intended to escape, but something extraordinary happened to me. I tried to deny that it had, but in the end, I could deny it no longer. Frankly, I didn't care to deny it any longer."

A swell of emotion filled Lily. She knew what he meant, for something extraordinary had happened to her, too.

"I had no intention of acting on it," he confessed. "I thought I would put you behind me. I am not a man who is accustomed to having anyone inhabit this," he said, tapping his chest. "Yet somehow, you found the door and walked in as if you had possessed it all along."

She smiled as her own heart filled with joy. "I feared losing everything," she said. "My title, my estate. My place in society. But when I saw you standing there, waiting for me, I realized that there are really very few things in life worth having."

The hard planes of Tobin's face softened, as if the tension holding them taut had disappeared. "What are those things?"

"Love," she said without hesitation. "I do love you, Tobin. Much more than I would have ever dreamed was possible. And belonging. I thought I had found the place I belonged in my title and the inheritance of Ashwood. But those are only things. I realized that where I belong is with you. That's the sort of belonging I have been seeking all my life."

She never did finish her speech. Tobin suddenly grabbed her in his arms, kissing her fiercely. "I love you, Lily. I never thought myself capable of it, but my poor heart is laboring with the heaviness of it. You are the light in me, you are the green in the mud—"

"*Mud*?"

"And I belong with you. God in heaven, I belong with you. I have been a fool to have taken so long to accept it. But now that I have you, I will not let you go."

It was almost as if a dam within Tobin had burst. His emotions, his desire, his need for her, were flowing out of him, raining down on Lily in his kisses and in the strokes of his hands.

He cupped her face in his hands and gazed at her. "You are extraordinarily beautiful," he murmured. "In all ways." He kissed her, then grabbed her hand in his and started striding for the door.

"What? Wait!" Lily cried. "Where are we going?"

He said nothing but marched her down the hall, past his footmen, past Carlson, then up his curving staircase and to the end of the corridor, where a chambermaid with her arms full of linens scampered out of their way. He opened a door and ushered Lily inside, then closed it and locked it.

"Tobin!" Lily said breathlessly. "This is a bedchamber!"

"It is," he agreed. "And this is where I shall make you my wife—in spirit, that is, until we have put ourselves before a minister."

Lily laughed. "So you *do* intend to make an honorable woman of me?"

He reached for her. "I cannot guarantee anything we do in here will be particularly honorable . . . but I promise not to tell. And I will promise you this—I will always love you, Lily Boudine."

"And I love you, Tobin Scott."

His hands began to move on her. Lily was consumed by the moment before he'd even begun to show her what it meant to make love. His lips seemed to glide over her skin. His touch was light and reverent, but so intense that she almost felt as if she'd been floating in his arms. When she sighed with pleasure, Tobin responded with a molten kiss. She could feel desire spiraling down her body, pooling in her breasts and groin.

Lily didn't realize they were moving until she felt the bed at the back of her legs. Tobin stood back a moment to admire her. He gave his head a funny shake and drew a very deep breath. "Each time that I see you, you look even more beautiful than before." He wrapped his arms around her and slowly began to undo the row of buttons on her gown. Lily leaned into the circle of his arms; Tobin stroked her cheek, then pushed the gown from her shoulders. It fell to her waist. He reverently touched her shoulder with his hand. "I think I must have died and received my heavenly reward," he said and slipped his finger under the strap of her chemise.

Lily's smile deepened. She felt more desirable than she ever had in her life as she pushed her chemise off her shoulders and pushed it down with her gown, until all her clothing slid down her body.

"God help me," Tobin said and pulled her into his embrace, kissed her eyes, her cheeks, her ears. And then he laid her on the bed and watched her eyes as he discarded his coat and waistcoat. He came over her, putting himself between her legs, and kissed the hollow of her throat. "I will insist that you lie there, looking beautiful," he said, "while I make love to you."

He traced a path from her neck to her breast with his tongue. He took each breast in his mouth, lavishing them with attention, then continued his slow path down her belly, to her abdomen. Lily gasped; he grabbed her hands and held them against her legs, and moved again, to her sex, tantalizing her beyond her bearing.

She wanted him, she needed him as sustenance, and sank deeper and deeper into the depths of the pleasure he was giving her until she was completely submerged in it, suspended weightlessly in it. His tongue began to lash her, swirling in and around her sex. She could scarcely bear the pleasure and gasped for her breath, writhed on his bed, desperate that it not end, but just as desperate that it end. And when the end came in a blaze of hot white, Lily cried out with the force of it, her body falling away from her consciousness, her heart filling and growing, expanding in her chest.

A moment later, Tobin moved over her, releasing his breath in one agonizingly long sigh. He brushed the back of his hand against his mouth and then began to undo his trousers.

Lily untied his neckcloth and unwound it, tossing it aside, and then pulled his shirt over his head, tossing that aside, as well. "You cannot imagine what you do to me," he said. "I could perish from the desire for you."

"Show me," she whispered, and arched into him.

Tobin needed no more encouragement than that. He lowered himself to her and drew a rigid nipple into his mouth. Lily closed her eyes, adrift once more on the sea of erotic sensation. He gathered her in his arms and pulled her into his chest, pressing her body against his as he buried his face in her neck.

Lily's skin felt on fire, and the stroke of his fingers

ignited her. He pushed her leg aside, stroked her wetness, then shifted and pushed the tip of his erection against her.

For only a moment—she was startled when he rolled onto his back and pulled her on top of him. Guiding her with his hands on her waist, he pulled her around to straddle his lap. She could feel his erection in her folds, and she instinctively moved across it, tantalizing herself.

"How radiant you are." He stroked her face, then moved her again, lifting her up so that he could slide into her. It was exquisite. The sensation was raw; she closed her eyes as her head lolled helplessly to her shoulder. He slid in and out of her sheath, while his thumb began a gentle, swirling assault over and around the nub of her arousal. Lily braced herself against his shoulders, her fingers digging into his flesh to anchor herself as her body moved on his.

Tobin kept his gaze on her face as he stroked her cheeks, her lips. "I love you," he muttered.

That sent her over the edge. Her climax erupted without warning, rippling through her body once more. Tobin was caught in her wake; she heard his guttural sound of pleasure, felt his release in her with a powerful thrust.

The experience was as emotional as it was physical—the joining of their bodies in such perfect harmony, the feel of his body so deeply imbedded in hers.

Tobin put his arms around her and pulled her down

to his chest. He rolled them onto their sides, their legs still wrapped around each other, her forehead pressed against his chest. His ragged breath was warm on her neck, his heartbeat staccato against her chest.

Lily rolled onto her back and glanced up at the gold canopy above his bed. She spread her hand out to the side of her and felt something silky. She picked it up—it was a rose petal.

Lily sat up and looked around them. There were rose petals scattered across the bed, some crushed, some untouched. She looked around the room; by the light of the hearth, she counted six candelabras with fresh candles in them. He'd planned this, had made his suite inviting for her, hoping that she would come to him, and yet believing she would not. It was as heart aching as it was touching.

Tobin pulled her down beside him and kissed her once more. "What are you thinking?"

"That I am in love."

He grinned. "We should marry as soon as possible, given our behavior."

She laughed at that. "As soon as we return to Hadley Green." She traced a finger along his jaw.

"I assume that will be on the morrow."

She shook her head. "I've a bit of business to finish before I can return."

Tobin frowned and touched the tip of her nose. "Not the jewels."

"Yes, the jewels. I have one stone left to turn, and

I've come all this way. It might come to naught, but I cannot leave without inquiring." She told him about her visit to Minglecroft's offices, and about his daughter, Pruscilla Braintree.

"Lily, love—let it go," Tobin urged her and laced her fingers with his. "What's done is done. It is fifteen years too late."

"It is never too late," she said stubbornly. "I'll never stop looking until I have found them."

"Bloody stubborn lass," he said and kissed her. "I suppose this is what I am to expect? A lot of stomping about and doing as you please?"

Lily laughed. "You may count on it, my lord." She kissed him back, pushing away all other thoughts but the suddenly overwhelming realization that she loved this man beyond measure.

TWENTY-SEVEN

T obin wanted to send for Lily's things at Darlington House and have them delivered to Ashwood.
They had done something rather scandalous, and he
wanted to avoid any unpleasantness for her.

But Lily would not agree. "I owe them my thanks,"
she insisted.

So at half past nine the next morning, Lily and
Tobin were shown into the salon, where the dowager
duchess and the duchess of Darlington received them.

The meeting did not begin well. The dowager duchess obviously knew about Lily's leaping from Merrick's
coach. "Scandalous," she said. "And you, sir, inviting
her to scandal! Lady Ashwood, you will be quite fortunate if no one hears of it. But if they do, you mark
my words; you will be ostracized! Do you agree, Lady
Darlington?"

"It is true," Kate said thoughtfully. "But then again,
one cannot deny the power of true love."

"For heaven's sake," the dowager snapped. "I should think you, of all people, would know how painful such actions can be for an entire family."

"I know," Kate said with a slight shrug. "But if the family hadn't suffered a bit of scandal, we'd not be such dear friends, would we? Nor would Allison come to greet you at tea every day."

"Don't make excuses," the dowager said. "I am trying to impart to Lady Ashwood that to go off with this . . . man," she said, gesturing at Tobin, "will earn her nothing but a cut from all of society."

Kate looked at Lily. "Do you know that what she says is likely true?"

"I do," Lily said.

Kate smiled. "Then follow your heart, Lily."

"Lady Darlington, I will thank you not to speak!" the dowager said angrily.

But Lily smiled gratefully at Kate. "I cannot thank you enough for your hospitality, Kate. You have been most kind. Good day."

"You are throwing everything away, Lady Ashwood!" the dowager warned her.

Lily smiled and looked up at Tobin. "Shall we?" With that, she walked out of the salon, her head held high.

Tobin had never loved anyone as much as he loved Lily in that moment.

As their carriage pulled away from Darlington House, Lily burst out laughing. "We've gone round the bend!" she said gaily. "You realize that, don't you? We've flouted every social convention there is."

Tobin chuckled. "I hardly care. Do you?"

"It hardly matters if I do, for I am ruined in London. What do we do now?"

"We call on Mrs. Braintree, then collect my sister and my niece and return to Tiber Park."

∞

The Braintree home was on a busy pedestrian thoroughfare with narrow sidewalks. The streets were not tended as tidily as those in Mayfair, and in places, the mud looked ankle deep. Tobin lifted Lily out of the carriage and placed her on the sidewalk, then instructed his driver to wait.

"I cannot imagine how you found the street," Lily said, peering up at the row of identical town houses. "How do we find the right one?"

"We ask." Tobin looked around and spotted a boy who was lugging a pail. "You there, lad!" he called. "Where might we find the Braintrees?"

"Eleven, milord," the boy said, and caught the coin Tobin tossed to him.

"But the houses are not numbered," Lily pointed out.

"Then we count," he said, and together, they counted to the eleventh door.

A very old woman with a cap placed crookedly on her head answered their rap on the door. "Braintree!" she said, as if offended by the name. "Course not! Braintree is over there!" she said, waving her hand down the street.

"Would you happen to know which—"

The old woman shut the door before Tobin could finish his question. It startled him so much that he didn't quite know what to say.

Lily burst into laughter.

He looked at her laughing, her eyes sparkling, her smile so infectious. Tobin laughed, too, the sound bubbling up from inside him. It made him feel alive in a way he'd not felt in a lifetime.

They tried again, this time counting from the opposite end of the street, and knocked on the eleventh door. A middle-aged woman with tight curls and a plain gray gown buttoned up to her throat answered the door. She looked at them both suspiciously, as if she expected bad news.

"Mrs. Braintree?" Tobin asked.

"Yes. Who are you?"

"Please forgive us for calling unannounced. I am Lord Eberlin, and this is Lady Ashwood."

"Ashwood!" Mrs. Braintree said, eying Lily. "Why, I thought they'd all passed on."

"Not all of them," Lily said, smiling. "If you please, we've been looking for some information regarding Ashwood for some time now, and we wondered if perhaps you might help us?"

"Me! What do I know of Ashwood?" she said. Her hand fluttered nervously to her throat.

"Your father knew Ashwood, did he not?"

"That has nothing to do with me," she said defensively. A pair of boys suddenly appeared at her side, staring at Lily and Tobin curiously. "My father has been gone some six years now."

"Is it possible that you have information you aren't even aware you possess?" Tobin suggested.

"I've naught to do with the Ashwood estate," she insisted. "I've not even seen it."

Tobin could see Lily's disappointment, but he'd dealt with tougher characters than Mrs. Braintree. "Madam, if you would indulge us?" Tobin asked and withdrew a pair of coins. "We are prepared that you might not have the information we seek, but we really must ask." He held the coins out to her. The two boys gasped and looked up at her. "It's a pair of *crowns*, Mamma."

Mrs. Braintree eyed the coins. "Well," she said with a shrug. "If it's just a question or two." She took the coins from Tobin's hand and stepped back. "If you please," she said.

She showed them into a small parlor cluttered with china vases and figurines. There were some wooden toys scattered about the floor, and a man's pair of shoes. Mrs. Braintree's needlework was on the settee where she'd left it, and she made no move to put it away. The house smelled faintly of fish and paraffin candles. It was well lived in, and it occurred to Tobin that he would be a lucky man indeed if he might one day sit in his favorite chair like the one here with the lump on its left side, and look around at the figurines he and Lily had collected in a life spent together.

"I've always wondered about Ashwood," Mrs. Braintree said. "My father described a very grand estate."

"It is," Lily said, nodding. "We've been trying to reconstruct some of the business in the years your father was associated with it. In reviewing the books, we noted that the late earl paid Mr. Minglecroft various sums over a period of a few years. Unfortunately, the amounts were not labeled, and we wondered what they might have been for?"

Mrs. Braintree shrugged. "I cannot say," she said. "Pappa traded silver and cotton."

Lily sighed softly. "Yes. Mr. Gross told us as much."

"Perhaps we might look at it another way," Tobin said. "Did your father deal in anything other than cotton and silver?"

"Not that I would know."

Lily glanced up at Tobin, her eyes full of disappointment.

"But he did perform particular tasks from time to time," Mrs. Braintree added.

Lily's eyes widened. "What tasks?"

"He'd go and pick up this or that, or deliver important things to important people. That sort of thing."

"And he did that for Lord Ashwood?"

"Oh, that I do not know," she said.

"Maybe it's in the box, Mamma," one of the boys said.

Mrs. Braintree looked at her son.

"The one that come from Southwark," the boy reminded her.

"Oh, yes. Mr. Gross did send some things after Grandpappa passed. Go and fetch the box, William."

Both boys raced out of the room. Mrs. Braintree smiled thinly. The three of them remained standing awkwardly, waiting. It seemed to Tobin that the children were gone the entire afternoon before they returned with a box that was neatly labeled Minglecroft.

"Now, what did Mr. Gross think we would do with all of this!" Mrs. Braintree said. "Put it down, William," she said to her son.

The boy set it on the floor in the middle of the room.

"May I?" Tobin asked.

"Suit yourself, my lord. You won't find nothing but a lot of papers and whatnot."

Tobin lifted the lid off the ledger. He and Lily peered down at the contents. It was only ledgers and papers, and bills of sales for things such as linens and silver. Tobin studied the pages, while Lily dug a little deeper.

While he was reading one of the bills of sale, Lily said, "Tobin."

He looked up; she was holding a small portrait of a

golden-haired woman. Tobin shook his head—he had no idea who she was.

But then Lily pointed to the woman's throat, and Tobin's heart stumbled. The woman was wearing a large ruby necklace. So large that one could assume the jewel had once belonged to a king who had given it as a gift to a woman he'd admired.

"That's Mrs. Tolly," Mrs. Braintree said.

"Who is she?" Lily asked.

Mrs. Braintree colored and looked down at her sons. "One might say a friend . . . if you take my meaning."

Lily blinked, but Tobin understood Mrs. Braintree's meaning quite well.

"Does she still live?" Tobin asked.

"No. When she died, Pappa had to collect her things."

"Oh, no," Lily murmured and looked at the portrait, turning it over, then back to the painting once more.

"I believe her son still lives, however," Mrs. Braintree added.

"That is welcome news," Tobin said. "And the boy's father?"

Mrs. Braintree drew herself up. "Don't believe the boy had a father." She glanced at her children, who were occupied with a top, or something that passed for one, that they'd found in the box.

"Do you suppose that if the boy had had a father, he might have been an earl?" Tobin asked carefully.

Mrs. Braintree's color deepened. "Might have been. You may assume what you like, my lord. I mean to say only that Mrs. Tolly had a son."

Lily gaped at Mrs. Braintree, then at Tobin. "He had a son," she repeated softly. "A son."

Which meant, Tobin assumed, that there was another, more legitimate claim to Ashwood. "Where is this son now?" Tobin asked.

"I've not the slightest idea, my lord," Mrs. Braintree said. "If the answer is not in that box, I cannot help you."

"Thank you, Mrs. Braintree," Lily said. She returned the portrait to the box.

"You may keep it if you like. I've no use for it."

"Are you certain?" Lily asked, retrieving it.

"Of course. You may have the whole box if you like. It's nothing but kindling to me."

"You've been very helpful," Tobin said, picking up the box. "We won't take any more of your time."

In the coach with the box, Lily held the portrait in her hands. "We must find her, you know."

"We haven't even a name, love," Tobin said. "There is nothing in this box but old ledgers. It will take us days to sort through it all."

"We have a name," Lily said with a smile. "She was Lisette Elizabeth Tolly." She grinned at him and turned the portrait over. At the bottom, her name had been written. "That's the necklace, Tobin. I remember it clearly. This is exactly what we need to find her!"

"Yes, well . . . I think we have a few other things that demand more immediate attention," he said, taking her hand.

She grinned and leaned across the carriage to kiss him. "I agree. I'll have Mr. Fish begin to look while we take care of other things."

"Then put that aside and come here," Tobin said, and pulled her across the carriage to him.

TWENTY-EIGHT

I t took only a week before gossip began to filter into
Hadley Green that something untoward had happened in London between Lady Ashwood and Count
Eberlin. The assumption among members of The
Society was that it must have been unspeakably scandalous, for the vicar had been called to Ashwood to
perform a wedding, at which only the count's sister
and niece had been in attendance. It was said that the
Duke of Darlington himself had secured their dispen-
sation to marry without posting the banns.

"Lord Eberlin has *wed*?" Miss Babcock wailed to
her mother when she heard the news.

"Lady Ashwood has married *him*?" Mrs. Ogle
sniffed to Mrs. Morton. "She could have brought a *real*
title here. Hasn't she a certain responsibility to us all?
That seems rather selfish to me."

Lily and Tobin were blissfully unconcerned about

the gossip. They were quite happy to settle in to their new lives as husband and wife and the journey of rediscovering the children they had once been. They did, however, finally venture into the village a fortnight after their hasty marriage to sign the parish marriage register. When they entered the small common hall where Tobin's father had been tried and where fifteen years later Tobin had been given one hundred of Ashwood's acres, he felt the tightening of his chest. He tried desperately to push it down, and coughed. Lily did not say a word but wrapped her fingers tightly around his, as if to say, *"Hold on to me."* It was comforting to Tobin in a way nothing else was, and while the spell did not disappear entirely, it was much less severe than it had been in the past.

Everything seemed better than before with Lily.

Mr. Fish was perhaps the most perplexed by their marriage. "I thought he was our foe," he said, clearly confused.

"He was. But not really." Lily laughed; it was impossible to explain. "And there is more," she said. She showed him and Linford the portrait of Mrs. Tolly and pointed to the necklace.

"There's the countess's necklace," Linford said, squinting at the painting. "Is that the countess, then? Don't recall that she looked quite like that."

Lily explained to Mr. Fish and Linford that there was likely another, more legitimate heir to Ashwood.

"Impossible," Mr. Fish said.

"Quite possible, actually. We must find him, of course."

Mr. Fish gaped at her. "Madam, I advise you leave well enough alone. Do you understand what it would mean if another heir were to be found?"

"I do." She smiled serenely. "It means that I would no longer be the countess. I will be simply Mrs. Scott. Or Lady Eberlin." She paused and frowned thoughtfully. "At least I think I will be Lady Eberlin. I am not entirely certain how one assumes a purchased title." She laughed and shrugged. "Nevertheless, we shall keep Ashwood in the best of shape until we find the true heir. You will find him, won't you, Mr. Fish? And the jewels! We must find the jewels as well, if he has a hope of turning Ashwood about."

Mr. Fish sighed. He thought back to the two ladies he had served and wondered if a man would make his job easier in any way. It would certainly make it less interesting. "I will endeavor to do my best."

In the meantime, Tobin decided to give up his trade in arms, believing it was not the best of occupations when one had a family. He began working out the terms for passing his trade to MacKenzie and Bolge.

Lily and Tobin made their home at Tiber Park. It seemed only right, seeing as how she likely had no claim to Ashwood. And since Tiber Park was so large, Lily found a way to bridge the chasm between her and Charity: she appealed to Charity's far superior house management skills. Charity was resistant at first, but after a few days of seeing maids running here and there without planned purpose, she sighed and looked at her sister-in-law. "Did they teach you nothing in Ireland?"

"They taught me to ride," Lily cheerfully boasted.

Charity rolled her eyes and put out her hand for the household account books that Lily was perusing. "Let's have a look," she said.

It was a fragile peace, but one that would be strengthened over time.

Lily's life seemed perfect to her. She was as happy as she'd ever been in her life. Only one thing seemed missing, and that was Lucy. She expressed that to Tobin in passing.

Late one Sunday afternoon, when Charity and Catherine had gone to London, Lily and Tobin lay naked in their bed, watching the fire in the hearth.

"Are you happy?" Tobin asked and kissed her shoulder.

Surprised, Lily paused. "Happy?" She thought of all she'd lost: her title. Her estate. Her good name and reputation. But she looked at all she'd gained: a husband whom she loved more with each passing day and who loved her. A sister, reluctant as Charity was to be one. A sense of belonging. Lily and Tobin would form their own society, filled with laughter and, hopefully, lots of children. An army of them if Lily had her way.

"Yes. I am happy," Lily said and kissed his chest. "Happier than I thought was possible."

He smiled at her and kissed her hand. "I have a surprise for you."

She laughed. "You have given me more jewelry than I can possibly wear."

"It's not jewelry. And it requires you ride."

"But . . . it's almost dark," Lily said, looking out the window.

"Are you afraid? I'll keep you safe. Come, then." He playfully pushed her toward the edge of the bed.

Lily reached for her dressing gown. "What sort of surprise must one ride to?"

"You will see."

A half hour later, the pair rode down to the river road and turned up toward the idle Tiber Park mill. The winter sun was just beginning to slide down the horizon in shades of orange and pink. It was strange, Lily thought, how their destinies had been forever linked on a cold and rainy summer night fifteen years ago, and had come full circle to this, a crisp, cool winter evening with stars beginning to twinkle over their heads.

Tobin guided his horse to the mill road and Lily followed. As they neared the mill, she could see light in the windows.

"The mill is operating?" she asked. "But I thought . . ." She was distracted by the sight of an enormous red bow on the mill's wheel. "What is that?" she exclaimed.

"My surprise for you." He jumped down from his horse and came around to lift her down. "You were so determined to have your mill at Ashwood that I thought I would give you one of your own here, as well."

Lily looked at the mill. Candles were blazing in the windows. "Tobin . . . I don't want a mill. I don't *need* a mill."

He smiled enigmatically. "You will want this one." He took her hand and led her forward. As they neared the door, it opened and light spilled out.

Mr. Hollis stepped out. "There you are, my lord, all at the ready."

"Thank you. You may go home to your family now."

Mr. Hollis touched the brim of his hat and nodded at Lily before walking on.

"I cannot imagine what you are about," Lily said, but Tobin only smiled. He held the door open for her.

Lily stepped inside and looked around. She had to remind herself to breathe. The mill had been turned into a playhouse. There were structures to climb and a pair of swings that hung in the middle of the space. There were tables built into the walls at a height for children. There were easels and balls and rocking horses.

"It is for our children," Tobin said. "Granted, we haven't any as yet, but I believe Sister Rosens might also find it a pleasurable destination for her orphans."

Lily whirled around and gaped at him. "Tobin Scott!"

Tobin blinked. "Why do you look at me thus? Is it not to your liking?"

"Not to my liking?" She half leapt, half ran into his arms, throwing hers around his neck and smothering him with kisses. "Thank you, thank you. I could never ask for a better surprise. I love you!"

Tobin laughed. "I love you," he said, nuzzling her neck. "I want to make you happy, Lily."

"You've made me very happy." She leaned back and grinned at him.

Tobin gathered his wife in his arms and swung her around. He kissed her deeply, then said, "Want to swing?"

Lily didn't need to swing. She was already soaring.

EPILOGUE

A deluge was pouring from the sky on the afternoon that Mr. Fish found the Carey estate. It was, as the crofter had said, off the main road . . . *far* off the main road. So far off that Mr. Fish struggled to navigate his little phaeton down the muddy lane.

At the gates of the estate, a gateman appeared, peering at Mr. Fish curiously as rain ran in rivulets off his hat. "Mr. Tolly? If he ain't at the main house, then he's at the dowager's house. That's where he stays. Bear right at the elm."

Mr. Fish glanced at the lane. He could not risk getting his carriage stuck, so he pulled aside and decided to walk. He stuffed the papers beneath his coat, adjusted his hat against the rain, and struck out, his Wellingtons splashing through puddles with each step.

The main house, which he could see through yet another gate set in ivy-covered stone walls, was as large as Tiber Park, but considerably older. It was a type of house that one often saw in England, obviously in the family for centuries, with bits and pieces added on through the years. There was money here, obviously.

At the elm, Mr. Fish bore right. He expected to see a small cottage, something suitable for a doddering old woman. But the dowager house was no cottage. It was at least as large as Kitridge Lodge.

He could see light flickering in the ground-floor windows as he approached the house. He tried to knock the mud off his boots but was unsuccessful. He scraped the bottoms as best he could and walked up the steps, lifted the brass knocker, and knocked.

A maid answered the door. "Aye, sir?"

"Mr. Harrison Tolly, if you please."

A man appeared behind the maid. "Thank you, Rue," he said, and filled in the space the girl left. He was tall, with dark brown hair and eyes the color of a stormy sky. "Yes?" he said, looking, Mr. Fish thought, as if he was in something of a hurry.

"Mr. Harrison Tolly?"

"Yes," he said, frowning. "Who are you? What is this about?"

"I am Mr. Theodore Fish, sir," Fish said, bowing slightly. "I may have some rather stunning news for you."

Mr. Tolly sighed, as if he'd heard stunning news all day and was weary of it. "And what would that be, Mr. Fish?"

"Are you familiar with the name Ashwood?"

The man's demeanor changed. He stilled, staring at Mr. Fish as if he was seeing a ghost.

"I take it that the name is familiar to you," Mr. Fish said.

Mr. Tolly's eyes narrowed. "Who *are* you? And what the devil is this about?"

"If I may come in, sir? It is all quite convoluted and requires more than a cursory explanation."

Mr. Tolly glanced quickly over his shoulder, then at Mr. Fish, his gaze taking him in from head to toe. "Yes. Come, come," he said reluctantly, gesturing for Mr. Fish to come inside to share his convoluted news.

Turn the page
for a special look at
the exciting conclusion to
the Hadley Green trilogy

The Seduction of Lady X

by *New York Times* bestselling author

Julia London

Coming soon from Pocket Star Books

T he hallway at Everdon Court that led to the Marquis of Carey's private study was as long and as daunting as the choir aisle at Westminster Abbey, and with every step, Alexa sniffed a little louder and tried to suppress her sobs a little harder.

It felt as if the two of them were slowly proceeding toward the gallows, one leaden step at a time. "Buck up, Alexa," Olivia muttered as they passed a pair of footmen and pulled her younger sister closer into her side. "There is nothing to be done for it. You must face up to what you've done."

"Yes, I know I must," Alexa said weakly. "But I do not understand why you cannot tell him for me."

Olivia sighed. Alexa knew very well why. Olivia had waited as long as she might before Alexa's thickening waistline would draw attention, but she could wait no longer. If her husband discovered Alexa's condition before Olivia told him, she and Alexa would both suffer for it.

She could guess what sort of suffering Edward would inflict on them, and on that rain-soaked afternoon, Olivia thought it entirely possible that she dreaded telling him even more than Alexa did.

After what seemed an interminable walk, they reached the polished oak doors to the study. As Olivia lifted her hand to rap, Alexa sagged against her. "I am so weary," she uttered. "I do not feel well."

"Stand up," Olivia said and jostled Alexa, forcing her to stand, then rapped on the door.

One of the twin-paneled doors swung open immediately, and behind it, a footman bowed. "Is my husband within, Charles?" Olivia asked.

Before Charles could respond, she heard her husband's voice. "Come."

Olivia looked at Alexa and entered, half pulling, half leading her sister with her. But as she crossed the threshold, she discovered her husband was not alone. Mr. Tolly was present as well.

Mr. Tolly smiled warmly as they entered, inclining his head in greeting. "Lady Carey. Miss Hastings. How do you do?"

"Ah . . ." Olivia tried to think of an appropriate response, given that they did not fare well at all.

"Yes? What is it?" her husband asked curtly without lifting his head from the papers on his desk.

Olivia shifted her gaze to Edward. "Alexa . . . and I . . . have something we must tell you," she said. "May we have a moment?"

"Go on," Edward said impatiently, "and be quick about it. As you can see, we are presently engaged."

Olivia's gaze flew to Mr. Tolly, whose smile made his gray eyes seem to dance. He bowed as he started to make his leave.

"Where are you off to, Tolly?" his lordship said. "You may stay."

"Edward . . . it is personal," Olivia said quickly. For Alexa's sake, she did not want Mr. Tolly to be present.

"Mr. Tolly has heard more personal and private details about this family than even I. He will stay." Edward lifted his head and looked at Olivia. "What is it?"

Mr. Tolly slowly stepped back, his expression suddenly stoic.

Olivia was thankful Mr. Tolly remained. He was the one person who could reason with Edward. Where others were quickly dismissed, Edward valued Mr. Tolly's opinion. And once, on a particularly awful day, when Edward had lifted his hand to strike Olivia for some perceived slight, Mr. Tolly had been there to catch his arm and prevent him from striking her.

Shocked, Edward had bellowed, "You think to lay a hand on me? I will have your position!"

Mr. Tolly had calmly returned Edward's gaze, as if the effort of stopping him required no strength at all. "Then have it. If you believe that my position here is more important to me than my code of conduct, you are mistaken. I will not stand by and allow any man to strike a woman."

Olivia had expected his instant dismissal, even a

brawl. But amazingly, Edward had gathered himself. And he'd never tried to strike Olivia again.

He preferred to strike her with words.

He'd not always been so cruel to her. Indifferent, perhaps, but not particularly cruel in the beginning. Yet as the years had slipped by and Olivia had not conceived a child, Edward's regard for her had dwindled to nothing. The cruelty had begun three years ago, when Olivia had believed herself, at long last, to be pregnant. Edward had been so very happy. He'd pampered her, showered her with gifts . . . but after two months, her courses began to flow again, and Edward's cruelty flowed right along with it.

"Why do you keep me waiting, Olivia?" Edward asked curtly, bringing her back to the mission at hand. "I told you I had work to do."

Alexa shuddered; Olivia put her arm around her sister's shoulders and began the little speech she'd privately rehearsed: Alexa had gone to Spain. Alexa had behaved poorly, for which she was terribly sorry. Alexa was with child. From the corner of her eye, she saw Mr. Tolly flinch, and wondered if it was revulsion at what Alexa had done or recognition that this would not go well for anyone.

Olivia's speech was followed by pure silence. There was not a breath, not a creak, as Edward turned his cold gaze to Alexa, who stood shaking before him.

Edward's gaze flicked to her abdomen, then to her face. "Is this true?"

"Yes, my lord," Alexa admitted, her voice scarcely more than a whisper.

"Who has done this?" he asked, his voice so soft and dangerously low that a shiver shot down Olivia's spine. When Alexa did not answer straightaway, Edward smiled a little and said, "You may trust me, Alexa."

No, Alexa, you cannot trust him! Never trust him!

Alexa lowered her gaze to the floor and shook her head. "I will not say."

Olivia glanced at Mr. Tolly. He held her gaze a slender moment and she thought—or perhaps hoped—that she saw a flicker of reassurance in his eyes. He was always so calm, so hopeful! Olivia wanted to lean on him now, to put her head on his broad shoulder, to feel his arms, strong and protective around her, keeping her safe from Edward.

"You will not say?" Edward asked, rising from his seat.

"I will not," Alexa repeated.

Edward made a sound of surprise. "But my dear, you must surely realize that if you refuse to tell me who has put this by-blow in you, I can only surmise that he is unsuitable in every imaginable way. Or . . . that you are a whore."

Alexa choked back a sob.

"Edward, please," Olivia pleaded.

Her husband shifted his hard gaze to her. "Please what?" he asked, the venom dripping from his cold smile.

"Please leave her be," Olivia implored him. "She knows her mistake, and the good Lord knows she will pay for it in many ways for the rest if her life. You need not punish her further."

"I see," Edward said casually as came around to the front of his desk. "You suddenly believe yourself in a position to tell me what I need not do. Shall I tell you what I find interesting?" he asked as he sat on the edge of the desk.

'No," Olivia said quickly.

"I find it interesting that while you are as barren as a Scottish moor, your sister is a whore who will conceive a by-blow apparently with any man who lifts her skirts."

Olivia's face flamed. The conflict between her and her husband was no secret, but it was humiliating nonetheless.

"There is only one," Alexa foolishly tried, but Edward quickly turned on her.

"Only one, eh?" He chuckled as if that was somehow amusing, and gestured to Alexa's belly. "The only difference between the two of you is that one of you is only half a woman. One of you led me to believe she could give me heirs and cannot. Or will not."

He shifted that hard gaze to Olivia, and Alexa burst into tears. Behind Edward, Mr. Tolly turned to look out the window, his hands on his hips. Olivia could see the tension in his jaw, as if he were fighting to keep from speaking.

"The question we have before us is what to do with this one," Edward mused, his gaze raking over Alexa. "With your mother buried, there is no one who will stand up for you, is there?" he asked her. "Certainly not your scofflaw uncle Barstow. You are entirely at my mercy as your benefactor and provider. And yet, I am the second cousin to the king. The Carey name means quite a lot in this country. Do you mean to defile my good name? A name from which you derive social benefit from mere association?"

"No, my lord," Alexa said softly.

"Then why would you allow some man to defile *you*? Did you think of your sister, who bears my name? Did you think of anything but your own base desires?"

She bowed her head and wisely did not answer.

"What shall I do, Alexa?" he continued coolly. "I dare say your sister connived her way into this marriage and there is precious little I may do about that. Yet I cannot keep the blight of your judgment from bringing scandal to my family's name, and therefore, the king's name, can I, Alexa? I still hold at least some degree of influence over this family, do I not? Or is there someone else to whom you may turn for assistance in this . . . unpleasant matter?"

Alexa paled. "No," she said, her voice almost a whisper. "I am at your mercy, my lord." She regarded Edward uneasily as she dabbed at her tears with her handkerchief.

Olivia's scalp tingled with foreboding. "Perhaps if we take a moment—"

Edward's gaze turned even harder. "Thank you, madam, but I do not need your assistance in determining what is to be done with the whore. If there is no one to marry her, than I shall send her to St. Brendan's convent in Ireland with a generous endowment. The sisters may determine what is to be done with the child."

"*What?*" Olivia felt the blood drain from her face.

Mr. Tolly turned from the window, his brow furrowed with a deep frown.

"What do you mean, what is to be done with it?" Alexa asked, stricken.

Edward shrugged. "It is a bastard child. It will be better off raised by an Irish crofter than seeking acceptance in our society. If you think that I intend to put you up and allow you to raise some by-blow at Everdon Court for all to see and at the end of my purse strings—"

"You will not take my child from me!" Alexa exclaimed.

"And you will not presume to tell me what I will or will not do," Edward said tightly.

The tone of his voice was bitterly cold, and Olivia knew from experience it would go from bad to worse. She stepped in front of Alexa to save her, to keep her from saying anything more. "My lord, perhaps you might consider an alternative?"

"By all means," he said grandly, flourishing his hand at her. "Amuse me with your suitable alternative, for the Lord knows I am in want of amusement after this news."

"Olivia, I cannot give my baby to anyone!" Alexa said tearfully behind her. "I won't!"

Olivia willed Alexa to be silent. "My lord, my father's young cousin lives in a small manor in Wales and has four young children. It is quite remote and there is very little society. Perhaps Alexa might go there, and when the child is born, my cousin will take her in."

She heard Alexa gulp down another sob.

Edward's brows lifted. "That is your idea? Send her to this agrarian cousin?"

He was the cat now, toying with the mouse. Olivia never won these rounds, but she never stopped trying. "To remove her from your sight, husband," she said. "My cousin is my father's blood—I know she will not speak of this to anyone," she added desperately, but Edward chuckled as if Olivia was speaking nonsense.

He stood up from his perch on his desk and put his fingers under Olivia's chin, forcing her to tilt her head back so that she was looking into his cold dark eyes. "Dearest Olivia," he said, sighing a bit. "Do you honestly believe I would trust anyone in your family? Was it not your family who deceived me into believing that you were the best match for me?" He lowered his head and touched his lips to hers, sending a shudder of revulsion through her. "We both know that you were the worst choice for me."

She wanted to claw the smirk from his face. But she was aware of Mr. Tolly in the room, of Alexa whimpering behind her. "I am aware of how much you despise me, Edward," she said softly. "But do not punish Alexa for it. She's done nothing to you."

"She will go to St. Brendan's Convent on the morrow, and there she will remain. Or she may go to hell."

"No!" Alexa sobbed, and collapsed to the floor. Olivia whirled around and knelt beside her sister, trying to help her to her feet, but Alexa was inconsolable. "Stand up, stand *up*," she urged her. "Do not let him defeat you," she whispered.

"I shall marry her," Mr. Tolly said clearly.

Olivia's heart lurched in her chest and her gaze flew up. Mr. Tolly had appeared at Alexa's side and he exchanged a look with Olivia as he leaned down and took Alexa by the arm. He hauled her to her feet, forcing her to stand. Olivia stumbled to hers, gaping at him. He was mad—*mad!*—to offer such a thing, but Mr. Tolly had firm grip of Alexa and was looking at Edward, his eyes slightly narrowed, the muscles in his jaw clenched.

Edward laughed. "*You* will marry her Tolly? Come now, I thought better of you! You cannot demean yourself to marry her—she is ruined," he said, as if explaining whey Mr. Tolly should prefer whiskey to gin. "I understand that perhaps you have some sentiment for the child, as you yourself are a bastard. But you've pulled yourself up to the top of the trees, Tolly. This one will merely drag you down to the bottom again."

"*No*, Mr. Tolly," Olivia said quickly, her heart pounding. "It is a truly noble offer, but—"

"Noble," Edward snorted. "It is half-witted."

"I won't marry him!" Alexa wailed. "I will not! You cannot force me to it!"

"Miss Hastings!" Mr. Tolly said, and put his hand under Alexa's chin and forced her to look up at him. "Please listen to me," he said, his voice softer. "For now, we shall say we are to be married, and we will seek to devise a plan that protects you and the Carey family from scandal." Alexa started to shake her head, but he dipped down a little and looked her in the eye. "Be strong now, lass," he said kindly. "Now is the time you must think of the child you carry and be strong."

Alexa's hand fluttered to her abdomen. She seemed to consider what he said as she sniffed back her tears. She conceded by sagging helplessly against him, looking as if the slightest touch would cause her to collapse into pieces.

"Tolly, you astound me," Edward said almost cheerfully. "I do believe there is little you won't do to protect the good Carey name. One might think you were one of us. But in this case, I think you are a fool. Alexa Hastings will do as well in an Irish convent as she will do as a wife to you."

Mr. Tolly looked as grave as Olivia had ever seen him. "If you will permit me, my lord, I shall address this unfortunate complication so that you may turn your attention to more pressing issues."

Edward eyed Mr. Tolly skeptically for a long moment, but Mr. Tolly steadily held his gaze, not the least intimidated. Edward finally shrugged and turned away. "Do as you wish. But keep her out of my sight. I don't care to be reminded that I have a slut wandering about Everdon Court. Take her down to the dowager house until you find a place to put her."

As if she were a broken piece of furniture.

Mr. Tolly wheeled Alexa about, moving her briskly to the door.

Olivia tried to follow, but Edward stopped her with a hand to her arm. "Lady Carey," he said sternly. Olivia closed her eyes for a moment before she turned back to him. "I did not give you leave." He settled back against the desk, his arms casually folded over his middle. "Go on with you now, Tolly," he said dismissively. "Take her from my sight."

Olivia glanced over her shoulder at Alexa, but it was Mr. Tolly's gaze that met hers, and she thought that she saw a flash of anger in his eyes.

The door shut behind Mr. Tolly and Alexa, leaving her alone with Edward.

Edward gazed at Olivia for a long moment, his eyes wandering over the peach-colored gown she wore, lingering on her décolletage in a manner that made her skin crawl. "How is it," he said at last, "that your sister may spread her legs to God knows whom in Spain and conceive, and yet you cannot?"

The question did not surprise Olivia, but it nonetheless snatched her breath as it always did. He spoke to her as if there were some defect in her; yet he never considered that he could be the reason they had yet to produce a child.

"I asked you a question, madam."

"I cannot say."

"It seems to me if one sister is fertile, the next would be as well."

Olivia swallowed. "I do not think it necessarily follows. We are all individuals, no two alike."

"Perhaps," he said. "And then again, perhaps it is because you take some elixir to abort my seed. Brock said some old crone called on you recently."

Confused, Olivia thought back to her recent callers and remembered Mrs. Gates, who had come on behalf of the charity they had begun for the poor. She was elderly, with a shock of gray hair that seemed as unruly as her wards. "If you are referring to Mrs. Gates, she is a patron of the parish workhouse," Olivia said.

"She is a crone."

Olivia struggled to keep her voice even. "She did not bring me an elixir. I want a child every bit as much as you do. You must know that I would never indulge in such tactics; I cannot bear to even hear you speak of it."

Edward laughed and shoved away from the desk, coming toward her. "Do you indeed want a child, Olivia? For I do not see any evidence that you do. One might ask if you desire a child, then why on earth have you not born one? Either you are incapable, in which case your mother lied to me. Or you deceive me every day," he said as he casually studied her face. "I tend to think the latter. I tend to think you want to vex me in any way you might."

Anger began to bubble in her. "That is not true," she said. "I never wanted anything other than to be a wife and mother."

"Liar," he said. "You are surrounded by riches and staff, yet you never bring me joy, Olivia. You burden me with the troubles of your orphaned sister and expect me to somehow make them go away, as if by magic. You tricked me into marrying you, and the one thing I have asked of you, the *one* thing I have required for all the generosity I have bestowed on you, is to give me an heir. That is all I ask—an heir. And yet, you do not conceive. And when you do, you abort them."

Olivia gasped; her knees quaked with the force of that remark. "How dare you say such a vile thing," she said roughly. "Dr. Egan said that I have done no harm to my body. I am an obedient wife—"

"*Obedient?*" Edward said, surprised. He grinned. "Is that what you would call your performance in our marital bed? Obedient?"

"I cannot call it anything else," she said, her eyes narrowing.

Edward's nostrils flared. He clenched his jaw and walked to the sideboard, where he poured whiskey for himself.

Olivia's belly churned with nerves, and she tried to focus on a painting above the mantel. It was of an ancestor sitting on a rock, staring at the artist while his dog gazed up at him. Olivia felt like that dog. She had to be ever vigilant, to watch everything Edward did.

"I don't find you the least bit obedient." Edward tossed back the whiskey. "I think you plot to remove my seed from your body." He poured more.

The trepidation was making Olivia nauseous, but she was determined to hold her ground with him. "How can that be? You make me lie there, and watch me so that I don't move. How could I possibly remove it?"

"Women have a bevy of tricks at their disposal," he said and turned back to her. His gaze began to wander her body as he moved closer. "Perhaps I have gone about this the wrong way," he added thoughtfully. "Perhaps I am not seeking my marital rights as determinedly as I ought." His gaze lingered on her bosom, and Olivia resisted the urge to cover her breasts with her arms. "Perhaps I have not been as forceful as is required."

Alarm shot through her. "What do you mean?"

"I mean, *wife*," he snarled, "that perhaps I have been

too gentle in my desires. Perhaps you would make a more *obedient* wife if I were a more insistent husband."

Alarm quickly turned to fear and Olivia looked to the door, gauging her chance at escape.

Edward startled her with a caress of her cheek, and then a hand to her shoulder and neck. "If your sister can get a child in her, there must be some way to put one in you." He pressed his thumb lightly into the hollow of her throat. "If it is your desire that I do not turn your sister out, as I have every right to do, then you will find a way to give me an heir, Olivia. Do not think to defy me. Who will take you and your sister once I am done with you? *Who?* Your cousin in Wales with four mouths to feed? Your mother's brother, who languishes at King's Bench? The entire country will turn against you. No one will touch you and risk the wrath of Carey. Think on that when you take your elixirs and herbs," he said quietly, then released her with a shove backward. "Now go. I have work to do."

Olivia caught herself on the arm of a chair. She watched Edward walk to the sideboard and pour more whiskey, then quickly left the room.